# True Love

Jude Deveraux

LARGE PRINT PRESS
*A part of Gale, Cengage Learning*

Farmington Hills, Mich • San Francisco • New York • Waterville, Maine
Meriden, Conn • Mason, Ohio • Chicago

GALE
CENGAGE Learning


The Nantucket Brides Series.
Large Print Press, a part of Gale, Cengage Learning.



*True Love* is a work of fiction. Names, characters, places, and incidents are the products of the author's imagination or are used fictitiously. Any resemblance to actual events, locales, or persons, living or dead, is entirely coincidental.

The text of this Large Print edition is unabridged.
Other aspects of the book may vary from the original edition.
Set in 16 pt. Plantin.

**LIBRARY OF CONGRESS CATALOGING-IN-PUBLICATION DATA**

Deveraux, Jude.
True love / by Jude Deveraux. — Large print edition.
pages ; cm. — (The Nantucket brides series) (Thorndike Press large print core)
ISBN-13: 978-1-4104-5843-8 (hardcover)
ISBN-10: 1-4104-5843-1 (hardcover)
1. Large type books. I. Title.
PS3554.E9273T78 2013b
813'.54—dc23
2013014695

ISBN 13: 978-1-59413-787-7 (pbk. : alk. paper)
ISBN 10: 1-59413-787-0 (pbk. : alk. paper)

Published in 2014 by arrangement with The Ballantine Publishing Group, a division of Random House, LLC.

Printed in the United States of America
2 3 4 5 6 18 17 16 15 14

# TO SEA FOREVER

# PROLOGUE

## JARED MONTGOMERY KINGSLEY

*NANTUCKET*

"She's coming on Friday," Jared said in answer to his grandfather Caleb's question, "so I'm leaving before then — and I think it'll be better if I stay away the whole time she's here. I'll get someone to pick her up at the ferry. Wes owes me for drawing the plans for his garage, so he can do it." Jared ran his hand over his face. "If someone doesn't meet her, she'll probably wander down an alley and never be seen again. Some ghostly figure might carry her off."

"You always did have too much imagination," Caleb said. "But perhaps in this instance you could imagine less and try for some kindness. Or has that become an outmoded commodity in your generation?"

"Kindness?" Jared said, suppressing his anger. "This woman is going to take over my house for an entire year and force me out. *My* house. And why? Because as a kid she could see a ghost. That's it. My house is being confiscated because now, as an adult, she might possibly be able to see someone other people can't." His tone conveyed his disgust at the whole arrangement.

"It's a little more complicated than that, and you know it," his grandfather said calmly.

"Oh, right. I can't very well forget all the secrets, now can I? First of all, there's the girl's mother, Victoria, who is hiding twenty years of visits to this island from her own daughter. And of course there's the Great Kingsley Mystery that needs to be solved. It's the two-hundred-year-old unanswered question that has plagued our family since —"

"Two hundred and two."

"What?"

"For two hundred and two years it's been unsolved."

"Right." Sighing, Jared sat down on one of the old chairs in the house his family had owned since it was built in 1805. "A mystery that no one has been able to solve for two hundred and two years, but for some unfathomable reason this outsider is supposed to be able to figure it all out."

Caleb stood with his hands clasped behind his back and looked out the window. It was early in the summer season, yet traffic was already increasing. Soon the cars would be bumper to bumper even on their quiet lane. "Perhaps the mystery hasn't been solved because no one has truly looked into it. No one has really tried to find . . . her."

Jared closed his eyes for a moment. After his great-aunt Addy died it had taken months to sort out the ridiculous will she'd left. The will said that a young woman, Alixandra Madsen, who hadn't been in the house since she was four years old, was to live in it for one year. During that time she was to try to solve the family mystery — if she wanted to, that is. Aunt Addy's will clearly stated that if she didn't want to do any searching, she didn't have to. Instead, she could spend her time sailing or whale watching or doing any of the thousands of things that Nantucketers came up with to occupy the god-awful number of tourists who invaded their island every summer.

If that was the only secret involved, Jared could have handled it, but concealing a lifetime of people and events was too much to ask of him. He knew it would make him crazy to try to keep this young woman from discovering that her mother, Victoria Madsen, had spent a month each summer at his aunt Addy's house in order to research her bestselling historical novels. Jared took a breath. Maybe he should change tack. "I don't see why an off-islander was given this job. You can't throw a harpoon without hitting someone whose family has been here for centuries. If one of them was given the job of researching, this girl wouldn't need to come here. The researchers could solve the mystery, and the secrets Victoria insists on keeping would be safe."

His grandfather's look stopped his words. There wasn't anything that hadn't already been said.

"You've made your point," Jared said. "One year and that's all, then this girl leaves here and everything goes back to normal. I will get my family home and my life back."

"Except maybe by then we'll know what happened to Valentina," Caleb said softly.

It was annoying to Jared that he was so angry and the old man was so calm. But he knew how to even out the playing field. "So tell me again why dear Aunt Addy didn't look for your precious Valentina."

His grandfather's handsome face immediately changed to stormy. Like at sea. His shoulders went even farther back, his chest out. "Cowardice!" he bellowed, a sound that had frightened shiploads of men. But Jared had been hearing it all his life and was unperturbed. "Pure cowardice! Adelaide was afraid of what would happen if she *did* find out the truth."

"Meaning that her beloved ghost might disappear and leave her all alone in this big old house," Jared said, grimacing. "And besides, people thought she was a spinster lady with money inherited from Kingsley Soap. The soap money was long gone, but you and Aunt Addy and Victoria figured out a way to keep a roof over this house, didn't you? That it involved airing our ancestors' dirty laundry to the world seems to have bothered only me."

His grandfather looked back out the window. "You are worse than your father. You have no respect for your elders. And you must know that I advised Adelaide in the matter of the will."

"Of course you did," Jared said. "And everything was done without consulting me."

"We knew you would say no, so why should we have asked?"

When Jared failed to answer, his grandfather turned to look at him. "What are you smiling about?"

"You're hoping this girl will fall in love with the romance of the Kingsley ghost, aren't you? That's your plan."

"Of course not! She knows about that world thing, that . . . What's it called?"

"Why ask me? I'm not consulted about anything."

"Spiders . . . No, that's not it. Web. That's it. She knows about the Web and can look on there."

"For your information I also know about the Web, the Internet, and I can assure you that the Valentina Montgomery you're looking for isn't on there."

"It was all a very long time ago."

Jared got up from the chair and walked to the window to stand by his grandfather and look out at the tourists who were already beginning to arrive. They were as different from Nantucketers as dolphins from whales. However, it was amusing to watch them stumble across the cobblestones in their high-heeled shoes.

"How is this girl going to find what we can't?" Jared asked, his voice calm.

"I don't know. It's just something that I can feel."

Jared knew from long experience that his grandfather was lying, or leaving out information. There was a great deal more about why Alix Madsen was being given possession of Kingsley House for one whole year, but Caleb wasn't telling. And Jared knew that he'd never hear the full story until Caleb was ready to tell it.

But Jared wasn't giving up. Not yet. "There are things about her that you don't know."

"Then you must tell me all."

"I talked to her father last week, and he said his daughter is in a bad way right now."

"And why is that?"

"She was engaged to be married, or something, but they recently broke it off."

"Then she will enjoy being here," his grandfather said. "Her mother has always loved this island."

"Is that the mother she doesn't know was here every year?!" Jared was having difficulty getting his anger under control. He waved his hand. "Forget that. This girl just broke up with her boyfriend or her fiancé — one of them, I don't know. You know what that means, don't you? She'll be all weepy and miserable and stuffing herself with chocolate, then she'll see . . ."

"A ghost."

"Yes," Jared said. "A tall, handsome, never-aging ghost who is so very sympathetic, so courteous, so charming, and she'll fall in love with him."

"Do you think so?"

"This isn't a joke," Jared said. "She'd be a woman from yet another generation to give up her real life for an empty one."

His grandfather frowned. "Adelaide never wanted to get married, and her life was far from empty."

"If you call four tea parties a week fulfilling, then no, her life wasn't empty at all."

Caleb looked at his grandson with a face full of fury.

"All right," Jared said as he threw his hands up in the air. "So I'm off base about Aunt Addy. You know how much I loved her. This whole island did and it wouldn't be half what it is today if it weren't for my dear aunt's hard work." He took a breath. "It's just that this girl is different. She's not from our family. She's not used to ghosts and family mysteries and two-hundred-and-two-year-old legends. She's not even used to creaky old houses or islands where you can buy a thousand-dollar jacket but no store carries cotton underwear."

"She'll learn." His grandfather turned to him with a smile. "Why don't *you* teach her?"

A look of dread went across Jared's face. "You know what she is and what she would want from me. You know that she's training to be . . . to be an . . ."

"Get it out, boy!" his grandfather yelled. "What is she training for?"

"To be an architect."

His grandfather knew this but he didn't understand Jared's dislike of the subject. "Isn't that what *you* are?"

"Yes," Jared said. "That's exactly what I am. But I have an office. I have — I am —"

"Oh," Caleb said. "I see. You're the master and she's the cabin boy. She'll want to learn from you."

"Not that you have any reason to know this, but there's a recession going on right now. A collapse in the housing market. One of the jobs hardest hit has been the architect's. No one is hiring. It makes recent graduates desperate and aggressive. They're sharks feeding on one another."

"So give her an apprenticeship," his grandfather snapped. "After all, you owe her parents for your entire life."

"Yes, I do, and that's another reason why I can't stay. How can I hide all these secrets from her? How do I keep what Victoria did while she was here on this island from her own daughter?" Jared asked, his voice showing his frustration. "Do you realize what a position my aunt's idiot will has put me in? Not only am I supposed to guard the secrets of people I owe my life to, but my firm is in New York and this girl is a student of architecture. It is an impossible situation!"

Caleb ignored the first part of that rant. "Why should her studies bother you?"

Jared grimaced. "She'll want me to teach her, to look at her drawings, to analyze and critique them. She'll want to hear about my contacts, my . . . my everything."

"Sounds to me like a fine thing."

"It isn't!" Jared said. "I don't want to be the bait that gets fed on. And I like to *do,* not teach."

"So what glorious deeds do you plan to *do*" — he emphasized the word — "while she's here? Will it involve any of those floozies you parade past the windows?"

Jared gave a sigh of exasperation. "Just because girls today wear fewer clothes doesn't mean they have low morals. We've been over this a thousand times."

"Are you referring to last night? How were that one's morals? Where did you meet her?"

Jared rolled his eyes. "Captain Jonas's." It was a bar near the wharf and it wasn't known for its decorum.

"I daren't ask what ship *he* captained. But who are the parents of this young woman? Where did she grow up? What is her name?"

"I have no idea," Jared said. "Betty or Becky, I don't remember. She left on the ferry this morning, but she might be back later this summer."

"You are thirty-six years old with no wife, no children. Is the Kingsley line going to die out with you?"

Jared couldn't help mumbling, "Better that than an architecture student to deal with."

Although Jared was taller, his grandfather managed to look down his nose at his grandson. "I don't believe you need to worry about her attraction to you. If your sainted mother were alive, even she wouldn't recognize you as you are now."

Jared stood where he was by the window and ran his hand over his beard. His grandfather had told him this would be Aunt Addy's last year alive, so he'd rearranged his architectural firm to spend the final months with her on the island. He'd moved into the guesthouse and spent as much time as he could with Aunt Addy. And she was an understanding woman. She'd always warned him when she was going to have a tea party so he could go out on his boat. She never mentioned the women who occasionally came home with him. And most of all, she pretended that she had no idea why he was there.

In their last weeks together they'd shared a lot. Aunt Addy had told him stories about her life, and as the days passed she began to mention Caleb. At first she explained who he was. "He's your fifth great-grandfather," she said.

"I've had five of them?" he teased.

She was serious. "No. Caleb is your great-great-great-great-great-grandfather."

"And he's still alive?" Jared had asked, playing dumb as he refilled her glass with rum. All the Kingsley women had a remarkable capacity for rum. "Sailors' blood in them," his grandfather said.

Jared saw the way his aunt got slower every day. "She's getting closer to me," his grandfather had said to Jared, and Caleb began to stay with her every night. They had lived together for many years. "The longest of any of them," Caleb said and there were tears in those eyes that never aged. Caleb Kingsley was thirty-three when he died, and over two hundred years later he still looked thirty-three.

But for all that Jared had shared with his aunt, he never came close to telling her that he too could see, talk, and argue with his grandfather. All the Kingsley men had been able to, but they didn't tell the women in their lives. "Let them think Caleb belongs to them," his father told Jared when he was a boy. "Besides, it emasculates a man for it to be known that he spends his evenings with a dead man. It's better to let the women worry that you're having a flirtation." Jared wasn't sure of that philosophy, but he'd maintained the code of silence. All seven of the Jared Montgomery Kingsleys could see Caleb's ghost, and most of the daughters and a few of the younger sons could. Jared thought the truth was that Caleb could let people see him or not, but the old man would never clarify the matter.

To say it was odd that this young woman, this Alix Madsen, could see the Kingsley ghost was a great understatement.

His grandfather Caleb was frowning at him now. "You need to go to a barber and remove that beard from off your face, and your hair is much too long."

Jared turned to look in a mirror. Caleb had chosen the mirror in China on that last disastrous voyage so long ago. Jared saw that he did indeed look bad. Since his aunt's death, he'd hardly been off his boat. He'd not shaved or cut his hair for months. There were gray streaks in his beard and strands of gray in his hair, which now reached down the back of his neck. "I don't look like my New York self, do I?" Jared said thoughtfully. If in the next year he couldn't stay away from his beloved island, it would be better if he was unrecognizable.

"I do not care for what you're thinking," Caleb said.

Jared turned back to smile at his grandfather. "I'd think you'd be proud of me. Unlike you, I'm not trying to make some innocent girl fall in love with me." That was another statement guaranteed to take the smile off his grandfather's face.

The explosion was instant. "I have *never* made a woman —"

"I know, I know," Jared said, taking pity on the handsome ghost. "Your motives are pure and clean. You're waiting for the return — or the reincarnation, whatever — of the woman you love, your precious Valentina. And you've always been faithful to her. I've heard it all before. Heard it all my life. You'll know her when you see her, then you two will go off into the sunset together. Which means that either she dies or you come back to life."

Caleb was used to his grandson's disrespect and general insolence. He'd never say it, but this particular grandson was the one most like himself when he was alive. He kept the frown on his face. "I need to know what happened to Valentina," he stated simply. What he didn't add was that he now knew there was a time limit. He had until the twenty-third of June, just weeks away, to find out what had happened to the woman he loved so much that even death couldn't separate them. If he didn't put it all back together, he didn't think that any of them — all the people who had been involved so long ago — would find the happiness they deserved. All he had to do was make his stubborn, never-listens-to-anyone grandson *believe.*

# Chapter One

Alix continued weeping as Izzy handed her one chocolate after another. So far it had been two doughnuts, one of those flat bars of sixty percent cocoa, a whole Toblerone, and a Kit Kat. If this kept on Alix was going to start in on chocolate chip cookies, which meant Izzy would join her and would probably gain ten pounds and not fit into her wedding dress. Wasn't that above and beyond the call of friendship?

They were on the fast ferry that went from Hyannis to Nantucket, sitting at one of the tables by the snack bar. All sorts of delicious, fattening things were within their reach.

Alix had done well in the past few weeks as she and Izzy finished their last semester of architecture school. They'd turned in their final projects, and as always, Alix had been praised by the teacher to the point of embarrassment.

It was that night that Alix's boyfriend had broken up with her. Dropped her flat. Eric said he had a different plan for his life.

After the disastrous date, Alix went straight to Izzy's apartment. When the knock came, Izzy and her fiancé, Glenn, had been snuggled on the couch with a big bowl of popcorn. She wasn't in the least surprised when Alix told her what happened — she'd even prepared for it by having two quarts of chocolate caramel ice cream in the freezer.

Glenn kissed Alix on the forehead. "Eric is a stupid man," he'd said before heading off to bed.

Izzy thought she'd be in for a whole night of misery, but an hour later Alix was asleep on their couch. In the morning, she was quiet. "I guess I better go pack," she said. "Now there's no reason for me not to go." She was referring to spending a year on the island of Nantucket. A few years before, right after Izzy had met Glenn — and she'd immediately known she was going to marry him — the girls had made a pact. After their last semester of school, they would take a year off before going job seeking. Izzy wanted time to just be a wife and to think about what she wanted to do with her life.

Alix had always known that she wanted to prepare a portfolio of designs that she'd present to a possible employer. Since most students went directly from school to a job, all they had to show was the work they'd done for assignments, all heavily influenced by the likes and dislikes of a teacher. Alix wanted to show her own work, all of it original.

When Alix was told of the year in Nantucket, she had been reluctant. Going somewhere she knew no one was too much. And then there was Eric. Could their relationship stand so much separation? Alix began to come up with excuses for why she couldn't go, starting with Izzy needing her for the wedding.

But Izzy had said that this was a once in a lifetime chance and Alix *had* to take it. "You *have* to do this!"

"I don't know," Alix said. "Your wedding . . . Eric . . ." She shrugged.

Izzy glared at her. "Alix, it's as though your fairy godmother waved her magic wand and gave you just what you need at exactly the right time. You *must* do this!"

"Think my fairy godmother has green eyes?" Alix had asked and the two of them had dissolved into laughter. Alix's mother, Victoria, had emerald eyes. Of course she'd been behind obtaining this year of work and study for her precious daughter.

What made them sure Alix's mother was behind the hiatus was that she'd been the one to tell Alix about the strange provision in Adelaide Kingsley's will. Izzy had always been in awe of Victoria. Even if she weren't internationally famous for all those wonderful, exciting books she wrote, she'd still be magnificent. For one thing, she was gorgeous. She had thick auburn hair, a figure like a Spanish soap star's, and a personality that commanded a room. Victoria wasn't loud, wasn't really flamboyant, but when she entered a room everyone took notice. A hush fell over people as they stopped talking and turned to look. It was as though they felt Victoria's presence as much as saw her.

The first time Izzy met Victoria, she wondered how Alix would react to her mother getting all the attention, but Alix was used to it. To her, that was how her mother was and she accepted it.

Of course it helped that whenever Victoria spotted her daughter entering a room, she stopped charming the people who'd gathered around her and went straight to Alix. They would link arms and turn away to some quiet corner, just the two of them.

When Alix had first been told about the contents of the will of some woman she didn't remember, she'd said no. Yes, Alix had always planned to take a year off, but not on some isolated island.

The real problem was that she hadn't told her mother she had a boyfriend whom she was thinking about marrying. If Eric asked, that is.

"I don't understand," Izzy said. "I thought

you and your mom told each other everything."

"No," Alix said. "I said that I find out everything about her. I am very selective about what I tell her."

"And Eric is a secret?"

"I do my best to keep my love life with any man away from my mother. If she knew about Eric, she'd be here interrogating him. He'd probably run away in terror."

Izzy had to look away so Alix wouldn't see her frown. She'd never liked Eric and she wished Victoria would do whatever it took to get rid of him.

After Alix had finished her designs for the last school year and made her model, she'd "helped" Eric with his. The truth was that she'd almost done his whole project for him.

After the breakup and Alix's decision to go to Nantucket, she'd been very adult about it. "I'll also have time to study." To become a licensed architect, one had to take a series of truly horrific exams. "I'll do well on the tests and make my parents proud," Alix vowed.

Izzy thought that Alix's parents couldn't be more proud of her than they already were, but she didn't say so. When Alix finally said she was going, it was her depressed, fatalistic tone that made Izzy decide that she would travel with her friend and stay in Nantucket until Alix got settled. She wanted to be there when Alix finally broke down.

It happened when they stepped onto the ferry to Nantucket. Until then there'd been so much to do to get ready for the trip that Alix hadn't had time to brood about Eric. Her mother had covered all expenses, even shipping their luggage to the island, so the two young women would only have to deal with overnight bags. And they'd left days earlier than the original plan because Izzy was afraid Alix would see Eric again.

Alix had seemed to be doing well until the ferry pulled away from the dock. When she looked at Izzy, there were tears running down her cheeks. "I don't understand what I did wrong."

Since Izzy had known this was coming, she had a big Toblerone bar in her bag. "What you did wrong was to be born smarter and more talented than Eric. You intimidated the hell out of him."

"I didn't," Alix said as Izzy opened the chocolate and they took a seat at a table. It was still early in the season so the big boat wasn't packed with people. "I was always very nice to him."

"Yeah," Izzy said. "You were. That's because you didn't want to hurt his teeny tiny ego."

"Come on," Alix said, chewing. "He and I had some great times. He —"

"He used you!" Izzy'd had to stand back and watch Eric cuddle up to Alix while she practically did his work for him. All the other males in their classes were intimidated by her. Her father was a successful architect, her mother a celebrated writer, and, worse, Alix's designs won every competition, every prize, and were praised by the entire school. "And what did you expect from him when you were always in the top five in your class? I thought Professor Weaver was going to kiss your feet when he saw your last project."

"He just appreciates designs that can actually be *built.*"

"Well, duh. That thing Eric designed before you started helping him couldn't have been put together by the crew that built the Sydney Opera House."

Alix gave a small smile. "It was rather like a spaceship, wasn't it?"

"I expected it to go into orbit at any second."

Alix seemed to be recovering but then her eyes turned sad again. "But did you see his date at the farewell party? She was barely twenty, if that."

"Go ahead and say it," Izzy said. "She was dumb. Really stupid. But that's what Eric needs for his fragile ego. To make him go up, others have to come down."

"I don't know if you're a therapist or a guru."

"Neither. I'm a woman and I see things. You're going to be a great architect and the only way you're going to find love is with a man who is in a completely different field." She was speaking of her own fiancé, who sold cars. He didn't know Pei from Corbusier from Montgomery's latest organic masterpiece.

"Or I could find an architect who is so good he isn't intimidated by me," Alix said.

"Frank Lloyd Wright is dead."

Alix gave another small smile and Izzy was encouraged to change the subject. "Didn't you tell me there was a man living in the guesthouse of where you're going to be staying?"

Alix sniffed as she bit into a chocolate muffin Izzy had bought for her. "The lawyer said that Miss Kingsley's nephew is staying there and that he can answer any questions I have. Or if the house needs repair he can do it. He's called Mr. Kingsley."

"Oh." Izzy's voice showed her disappointment. "If Adelaide Kingsley was ninety-something when she died, that means her nephew is at least sixty. Maybe he'll give you a ride on his electric scooter."

"Don't make me laugh."

"I'm trying to. Is it working?"

"Yes," Alix said, "it is." She looked toward the snack bar. "Do they have any chocolate chip cookies?"

Groaning, Izzy silently cursed Eric the ex-boyfriend. As she went to the counter she muttered, "If I gain weight, I'm going to put hair gel in all his glue. His models will fall apart." She was smiling as she took four big plastic-wrapped cookies out of a basket and paid for them.

By the time the ferry docked, Alix had stopped crying, but she still looked like a martyr about to be led to a stake.

Izzy, full of cookies and hot chocolate — she couldn't let Alix eat alone — had never been to Nantucket and she was looking forward to seeing the place. With their big leather bags (gifts from Victoria) over their shoulders, they stepped onto a long, wide wooden wharf. Little shops that looked like they used to be fishermen's shacks were filled with shirts with tasteful logos of Nantucket on them. She would have liked to stop to buy her fiancé some caps and sweatshirts but Alix was plowing on, chin up, eyes straight ahead, looking at nothing, just walking.

Izzy saw some kids come around a corner, ice cream cones in their hands. Maybe if she could get Alix settled with a cone, she could do some shopping.

"This way!" Izzy called and Alix followed her. There was a little ice cream place on the edge of the wharf and Izzy sent Alix inside. "Butter pecan for me," Izzy said.

Numbly, Alix nodded and went inside.

Izzy took out her cell phone and called her fiancé. "Not good," she said in answer to his question. "And I don't know when I'll be back. The way she is now, she'll climb into bed and never get out. I know," she said. "I miss you too. Uh-oh. Here she comes. Oh, no! She's bought herself a cone with three scoops of chocolate on it. At the rate she's going she won't need the ferry to get back. She'll float. I think —"

Izzy broke off because a man walked between her and Alix. He was tall, a little over six feet, broad shouldered. He had a rough, graying beard and a tangle of hair that reached almost to his shoulders. He walked with long strides, and his jeans and denim shirt showed his toned body. He glanced at Izzy, seemed to dismiss her, then looked at Alix, who was walking toward her friend, her hands filled with two ice cream cones. He looked Alix up and down, seemed to hesitate for a moment, as though he were going to speak to her, but then he walked on and disappeared around the corner.

Izzy stood there staring after the man, her eyes wide, her mouth open. Her phone was still to her ear and Glenn was talking but she wasn't hearing him.

When Alix reached her, Izzy said in a whisper, "Did you see him?"

"Who?" Alix held out Izzy's cone to her.

"Him."

"Him who?" Alix asked with no real interest.

"HIM!!"

From Izzy's phone came Glenn's shout, "Isabella!"

"Oh, sorry," she said into the cell. "I just saw him. Here on Nantucket. I have to go." She clicked off the phone, took her cone from Alix, and dropped it into a nearby trash bin.

"Hey!" Alix said. "I could have eaten that."

"You didn't see him?"

"I didn't see anyone," Alix said as she bit into her ice cream. "Who did you see?"

"Montgomery."

Alix paused, her lips on the piled-high ice cream. Big chocolate chunks stuck out the sides.

"I saw Jared Montgomery walk right past here."

Alix pulled her mouth away from the ice cream. "*The* Jared Montgomery? The architect? Designed the Windom building in New York?"

"Who else would I mean? And he looked at you. He almost stopped to speak to you."

"No," Alix said, eyes wide. "He couldn't. He didn't."

"He *did*!" Izzy said. "But you —"

Alix dropped her triple cone in the bin, wiped her mouth, and grabbed Izzy's arm. "Where did he go?"

"There. Around the corner."

"And you let him get away?!" Alix dropped her friend's arm and hurried forward, with Izzy close behind. They arrived just in time to see the bearded man standing on a beautiful white boat, with a cabin below. He was smiling up at some girl on the dock who had on indecently short shorts. That it was a cool day didn't seem to make any difference to her. He smiled at her, a grin of such warmth that Alix thought it rivaled the sun. He took the bag the girl handed down to him, then sped off alone, leaving dual waves of water behind him.

Alix fell against the weathered shingles of a building. "It *was* him."

Izzy leaned back beside her, both of them staring at the boat that was quickly disappearing in the distance. "His office is in New York. So why do you think he's here? Vacationing? Building something divine?"

Alix was still staring out to sea. "It really *was* him. Remember when we heard him speak at that hotel?"

"Like it was yesterday," Izzy said. "When he smiled at that girl just now, I was sure it was him. I'd recognize those eyes anywhere."

"And that bottom lip," Alix murmured. "I wrote a poem about it."

"You're kidding. I never saw any poem."

"That's because I didn't show it to you. It's the only poem I've ever written."

They stood there in silence, not sure what to do or say. Jared Montgomery was their hero, a man whose designs were legendary in the architectural world. To them he was the

Beatles, all the vampires, and Justin Bieber rolled into one.

Izzy was the first to recover. To her left was a young man tying up his old boat. She stepped over to him. "Do you know the man who just left in that white boat?"

"Sure. He's my cousin."

"Reeeaaallly?" Izzy asked, sounding as though that was the most interesting thing she'd ever heard in her life. "What's his name?"

Alix had come to stand beside her friend and they were looking at the man with their breaths held.

"Jared Kingsley."

"Kingsley?" Alix asked, puzzled, then her face fell. "He isn't Jared Montgomery?"

The man laughed. He was not bad-looking, but his clothes looked like they hadn't been washed in a while. "Oh. It's like that, is it?" He was obviously teasing them. "He's Kingsley here but he's Montgomery in America."

"America?" Izzy asked. "What does that mean?"

"There." The man pointed across the water. "In America. Where you just came from."

Both Izzy and Alix smiled at the idea that the island of Nantucket was a separate country.

Izzy wanted to make absolutely sure he was the man they thought he was. "Do you know what he does for a living?"

"He draws house plans. He drew a garage for me and it's a nice one. I rent out the apartment over it in the summer. You girls need a place to stay?"

It took the two young women a moment to digest the idea that one of the greatest architects in history had been reduced to "he draws house plans."

Alix spoke first. "No, thanks. I'm —" She broke off because she didn't want to tell this stranger her business.

He smiled as though he knew what they were thinking. "If you girls are interested in him, you'd better get in line. And you'll have to put it off because ol' Jared's going to be out for at least three days."

"Thanks," Izzy said.

"If you change your mind, I'm Wes. Just think of the direction of the beautiful Nantucket sunset and that's me."

Izzy and Alix went back around the building to the ice cream shop. They were both starry-eyed. Stunned.

"Jared Montgomery is also Jared Kingsley," Alix finally managed to say.

It dawned on Izzy what was in her friend's mind. "And you're staying in Kingsley House."

"For a year."

"Do you think he's the Mr. Kingsley who lives there *with* you?" Izzy's eyes were so wide they were circles. "That he's the man who's supposed to help you if you have any problems with the house?"

"No. I mean, I don't think so. I couldn't imagine such a thing."

"But you hope so!" Izzy put her fingers to her temples. "I foresee plumbing disasters by the dozen. You'll forget and turn on the water and douse him. He'll have to remove his clothing and you'll be wet too, then you'll look at each other and tear your clothes off and —"

Alix was laughing. "I won't be *that* blatant but I could see . . . maybe dropping a packet of my latest designs that just happen to land faceup and right at his feet."

"That's good," Izzy said. "The fabulous sex can come later. First let him see what you can do in the way of architecture, then you sit back and let him take over and be the man. That's a good plan."

Alix was dreamy-eyed. "He'll tell me that he's never seen such innovative and well-thought-out designs in his life. He'll say that I have a talent like he's never seen before and he wants me with him every moment so he can teach me everything he knows. An entire year with my own private tutor. A year of learning and —"

"That's it!" Izzy said.

"What is?"

"This whole will thing," Izzy said. "Your mother said that this old woman who you never even met —"

"Mom says she and I spent a summer with her when I was four. And I guess they stayed in touch."

"Okay, she's a woman you don't remember meeting, but she left you her house for a year. Victoria said it was because you wanted the break before you got a job. I've always thought the whole thing was fishy, because the old woman —"

"Miss Kingsley."

"Right. Miss Kingsley didn't know when she was going to die. For all she knew she could have lived to be a hundred and you'd be running your own company by then."

"Maybe," Alix said, "but only if I pass my tests." It was an inside joke among architecture students that they spent longer in school than doctors, and at the end was a series of agonizing tests. But when they got out there were no jobs. "I don't get your point."

"I think Miss Kingsley, and probably your mother too, wanted you to meet the unmarried architect nephew, Jared Montgomery. Or in this case, Kingsley."

"But if she'd lived to be a hundred, by that time he could have half a dozen kids."

"Why let facts ruin a good story?"

"You're right," Alix said. "Miss Kingsley wanted me to meet her nephew, so she — with my mother's encouragement — put me in the house next to him. Of course he lives and works in New York and is probably only here two or three weeks a year, but what does that matter to a whopping good story?"

"Are you saying you don't think your mother had an ulterior motive for getting you into this old house?"

Alix knew her mother far too well to say no to that. The truth was that Alix didn't care why or how this had been arranged. All that mattered was that she was being given this unbelievable opportunity. And was it actually possible that Jared Montgomery would be living right next door to her? In a guesthouse on the same property? "I will pick his brain clean," she said. "I'm going to learn everything he knows, from design down to the drains. Remind me to send my mother roses. Come on, let's go to the house."

"No more ice cream?" Izzy asked.

"Are you kidding? Let's walk fast and work up a sweat. Why did you let me eat all that chocolate?"

"Of all the ungrateful —" Izzy began but Alix's laugh cut her off. "Very funny. Pardon me for not laughing. We have three days before he returns so we have a lot of work to do."

"And I hear the shopping on Nantucket is good," Alix said.

"Oh, no you don't," Izzy said. "I'll do the shopping. You need to work. This is going to be the presentation of your life."

"I do have a few ideas in my head," Alix said, and Izzy laughed, as Alix always had an abundance of design ideas.

As they started walking, the first thing they noticed, now that the specter of what-Eric-did-to-Alix was no longer hanging over them, was the incredibly beautiful view of downtown Nantucket. The street was cobblestones, difficult to walk or drive on, but so very beautiful. The sidewalk was wide and laid with bricks. Over the centuries the trees and the settling of the earth had made them undulate and flow in an artistic way.

But what stood out the most for Alix were the buildings. One after another, each was exquisite. Perfect in design and execution.

"I think I'm going to faint," Alix said as she stood in one spot and stared down the street at the town's beauty.

"Yeah, it's even better than the pictures I saw."

"It's . . . I don't know, but I think it's heaven. And . . ."

Izzy was looking at her friend in curiosity. They'd met each other on the first day of architecture school and they'd both been trim, pretty young women, but there the similarities stopped. Izzy's ambition was to live in a small town and have an office where she did remodeling work. Her primary goal in life was a husband and children.

But Alix had inherited from her father a

deep love of building. Her paternal grandfather had been a contractor and his son had spent his summers building houses. In the winter her father had worked in a shop and made cabinets. He'd earned his degree in architecture before Alix was born, and later it had been natural to him to begin teaching at the university level.

Her parents had divorced when Alix was a child and, as a result, she had grown up in two worlds. One was with her father, which involved everything about building, from her father's design to hammering in the studs to choosing paint colors for the interior. And he loved teaching his daughter what he knew. She could read blueprints by the time she was in first grade.

The other half of her life revolved around her mother's writing. Part of the year Alix and her mother lived quietly, just the two of them, while Victoria wrote novels that the whole world enjoyed. Every August her mother went away to a cabin in Colorado to isolate herself so she could plot that year's novel. Her wildly popular books took a seafaring family down through the ages. When each book was finished, there were cocktail parties, extravagant dinners, and vacations. Alix's life with her mother was a wonderful mix of quiet work and great excitement.

Alix had loved it all! She liked sitting on

the tailgate of a pickup with her father's crew and eating sandwiches, and she liked wearing a designer dress and laughing with the top publishing people in the world.

"They're all the same," Alix always said. "They all work for a living. Whether their tools are claw hammers or six-syllable words, they're all workers."

Between her two very successful parents, Alix had come out talented and ambitious. She had her father's love of building and her mother's belief that the top was the only place to be.

Izzy looked at Alix, her friend's eyes glazed as she studied Nantucket, and Izzy almost felt sorry for Jared Montgomery. When Alix wanted to know something, she was insatiable.

"I've seen this before," Alix said.

"Maybe you remember the place from when you were four."

"Not likely, but . . ." Alix was looking around her. Across the road was a beautiful white wooden building with dark green window-frames across its front. On one side was painted a map that showed the distance from Nantucket to other parts of the world. Hong Kong was 10,453 miles away.

" 'We are the center of everything,' " Alix quoted. "That's what I hear someone saying when I look at that map. 'Nantucket is the epicenter of the earth.' I must have heard that when I was four. I had never heard that word before, but in a funny way, I knew what it meant. Does that make sense?"

"Actually, it does," Izzy said, smiling. It looked like she *was* going to be able to leave soon. She could tell by Alix's tone that her friend remembered more about Nantucket than she thought she did. And even better, she was beginning to feel like Nantucket was home. If Victoria and the late Miss Kingsley had planned all this so Alix could meet the famous Jared Montgomery, it seemed to be working.

"Let's go in here," Izzy said. "We need to celebrate." It was Murray's Beverage store and inside were rows of wine, beer, and liquor. Izzy felt that they needed something cold and fizzy so she headed to the refrigerator against the back wall.

But Alix went to the old-fashioned wooden counter and looked at the shelves behind it. "I want rum," she said to the woman behind the counter.

"Rum?" Izzy asked. "I didn't know you liked that."

"Me neither. I think I've had one rum and Coke in my life. But here on Nantucket I want rum."

"It is a local tradition," the woman said. "Which one do you want?"

"That one." Alix pointed to a bottle of seven-year-old Flor de Caña.

"No rotgut for you," Izzy said as she put a bottle of champagne on the counter.

Alix pulled her cell out of her bag and checked past emails. Her mother had given her directions to Kingsley House but in her upset over Eric, Alix hadn't printed out a map. But then her mother's directions were rather cryptic — which wasn't uncommon. Her mother thought and wrote like a novelist, and she liked mystery.

Alix looked at the woman behind the counter. "I'm staying at a house here on Nantucket and my mother said it's walking distance from the ferry. It's number twenty-three Kingsley Lane and she said" — Alix checked her phone — "the lane turns beside West Brick. I don't know what that means. How do I find West Brick Road?"

The woman, very used to tourists, smiled. "I bet it says *the* West Brick."

"It does, actually," Alix said. "I thought it was a typo."

"You must mean Addy's house," the woman said.

"Yes. Did you know her?"

"Everyone did, and we all miss her a lot. So you're the one who's going to live there for a year?"

Alix was a bit shocked that the woman knew that. "Yes," she said hesitantly.

"Good for you! And don't let Jared bully you. He may be my cousin but I can still tell you to stand up to him."

Alix could only blink at her. To her mind, Jared Montgomery slash Kingsley was a person to be revered, a god in the world of architecture where Alix lived and worked. But no one on Nantucket seemed in awe of him.

Izzy stepped forward. "We already met a man who says he's . . . uh, Mr. Kingsley's cousin. Are there many more?"

The woman smiled again. "A lot of us are descended from the men and women who first settled on this island, and we're related one way or another." She went to the register and rang up their purchases. "At the bank, go left. That's Main Street. Up the road on the right are three brick houses that are just alike. Kingsley Lane turns to the right beside the last of the three brick houses."

"The West Brick," Alix said.

"You got it."

They paid, said thanks, and left the store.

"Now all we have to do is find the bank," Izzy said.

But Alix had gone back into her trance of looking at the town. Across the road was a building that stopped Alix in her tracks. A two-story center flanked by one-story additions with low, slanted roofs. A half-moon window above, a louvered octagon above that.

"I hate to interrupt your moment here but at this rate it's going to be night before we get there."

Reluctantly, Alix began to walk again, still studying each building they passed and admiring its perfection. When they came to what looked to be a movie set for a nineteenth-century drugstore Alix got excited. "I remember this place! I know it." She opened the old-fashioned screen door and rushed inside, Izzy right behind her. To their left was a well-used counter, complete with stools in front and a mirror behind.

Alix put down her packages and sat on a stool. "I want a grilled cheese sandwich and a vanilla frap," she said decisively to the young woman behind the counter.

Izzy took the stool next to her. "How can you be hungry, and what's a frap?"

"Milk, ice cream." Alix shrugged. "I don't know. It's what I always ordered and I need it now."

"Ordered when you were four?" Izzy asked, smiling, pleased that her friend was remembering things.

A "frap" turned out to be an Americanized term for frappé — a milk shake. Izzy ordered the same and got tuna sandwiches to go.

"She bought things here," Alix said as she ate her sandwich, which was served on a thin paper plate. "In the back."

Izzy couldn't resist a look around the store. At first glance it seemed to be a rather simple place, but a closer examination showed that the merchandise was very high-end. The skin products were the kind you found on Madison Avenue in New York.

"I bet your mother loved this store," Izzy said when they were back outside on the sidewalk.

Alix looked at her friend. "What an interesting thought. If my mother did arrange all this about the will, when did she do it? She told me we spent a summer here when I was four. That's when she and Dad split up, but she's never mentioned Nantucket since then. When was she here? How did she know this Miss Adelaide Kingsley?"

"What I want to know," Izzy said, "is who is 'she'?"

"What are you talking about?"

"In the drugstore you said, '*She* bought things here.' Did you mean your mother?"

"I guess so," Alix said. "But I don't think so. Right now it's like I'm sinking down into another time. I have no conscious memories of this island but with every step I take I see something familiar. That store . . ." She was looking at Murray's Toggery with its gray and white painted wood and the full glass front. "I know that children's wear is upstairs and she . . . someone, that is, bought me a pink cardigan there."

"If it was your mother, surely you'd remember *her.* Victoria is rather distinctive."

Alix laughed. "Are you referring to her red hair and green eyes and a figure that causes car wrecks? I'm glad I look more like my father. Where do you think the bank is?"

Izzy was smiling at her friend. To hear Alix tell it, a person would think she was a plain little sparrow when compared to her mother, but far from it. While Alix didn't stand out in a crowd as her mother did, she was extraordinarily pretty. She was taller than her mother and slender, with reddish blond hair that was naturally streaked. She wore it long with wispy bangs swept to one side and fat curls at the end. Whereas Izzy had to work to get curls in her dark hair, Alix's were natural. She had blue-green eyes and a small mouth with full lips. "Like a doll's," Victoria had said at lunch one time, and her daughter had turned red at the compliment.

Alix's modesty about her looks, her background, and even her talent was something Izzy had always admired about her friend.

Alix drew her breath in and came to a halt. "Look at that." She was pointing to a tall, majestic-looking building at the end of the street. It was on a raised foundation, with a steep curved staircase leading up to the front door, which was set under a curved roof portico. The elegant building seemed to look over the town, a grand empress watching her subjects.

"A knockout," Izzy said, but she was more interested in finding Kingsley House.

"No. Look at the top."

Raised letters said THE PACIFIC NATIONAL BANK.

Izzy had to laugh. “Doesn’t look like my bank. What about you?”

“Nothing here looks like anything anywhere else,” Alix said. “If that’s the bank, we need to take that road on the left.”

They crossed the cobblestones on the brick walkway and headed up Main, past Fair Street. It was a road of houses, and each place was a historian’s dream nestled under graciously weathered old shingles. There were very few of the usual gaudy Victorians that so many small American towns treasured as historic homes. Nantucket had been formed by Quakers, people who believed in plainness in their clothes, their attitudes, and especially in their houses. As a result, the homes weren’t covered in unnecessary ornament. To Alix’s trained eye, every roof, door, and window was a work of art.

“Think you can stand looking at this town for a whole year?” Izzy asked, laughing at Alix’s expression.

When they reached the three brick houses Alix looked like she might go into an old-fashioned swoon. Big, tall, impeccably maintained, the three houses were indeed impressive.

Alix seemed to be glued to the sidewalk as she looked up at the buildings, but Izzy moved past her.

Next to the last house a narrow lane opened up, the entry to it almost hidden by trees. A little white sign said KINGSLEY LANE.

"Come on," Izzy called and Alix followed.

There was a narrow sidewalk on the right and silently the two of them started down it, looking at the house numbers.

"They're named," Izzy said in surprise. "The houses have names on them."

"Quarterboards," Alix said.

"Is that a word you just made up?"

"No. It's — I don't know how I know the word but that's what those wooden plaques are called."

"FIELD OF ROSES," Izzy said, looking at a house set close to the road.

"BEYOND TIME," Alix read on another house on the right. There was a driveway beside it but a gate blocked their view into the garden behind. In fact, there was a parking place beside each house they passed. Some were so narrow the cars nearly scraped the sides, but it did get the vehicles off the street.

"Look, that's a B&B. SEA HAVEN INN."

"And that . . ." Izzy said, looking across the road, "is number twenty-three. It's called TO SEA FOREVER."

Before them was a large, stunningly beautiful white house. Since the simplicity of it gave it a timeless feeling, the house could be new or hundreds of years old. There were five windows above, four below, each flanked by dark shutters, with a wide white door in the center. The roof was topped with a railed walkway.

"This is it?" Alix whispered from behind Izzy. "Where I'm to live for a whole year?"

"I think so," Izzy said. "It's the right number."

"Remind me to send my mother orchids."

Alix fumbled in her big Fendi bag in search of the keys her mother had sent. She found them and made it to the door, but her hands were shaking so much she couldn't get the key into the lock.

Izzy took the key and unlocked the door. They walked into a big hallway with a staircase going up on the left. To the right was a living room, to the left a dining room.

"I think . . ." Izzy began.

"That we just traveled even further back into time," Alix finished for her. She hadn't given much thought to how such an old house would be furnished, but she'd assumed it would be rather formal, done by some decorator's idea of how the house should look. But this house had been occupied by the same family for centuries. Everything was a mixture of old and new — and new meant no later than about the 1930s.

The hallway had a tall secretary desk and a trunk inlaid with what looked to be ivory. In the corner was a big Chinese porcelain umbrella stand painted with branches of cherry blossoms.

They peeked into the living room to see furniture upholstered in striped silk, the arms showing wear. The rug was a pink Aubusson with walking patterns worn into it. There were tables, ornaments, and portraits of distinguished-looking people.

The two young women looked at each other and started laughing.

"It's a museum!" Izzy said.

"A *living* museum."

"And it's *yours,*" Izzy said.

In the next second they started running from one room to another, exploring and yelling comments.

There was a small room behind the living area, which held a television.

"What do you think of that TV?" Alix asked. "Circa 1964?"

"Send that one to the Smithsonian and get your mom to buy you a flat screen."

"Top of my list."

All the way to the back was a large, light, airy room with bookshelves on two walls. Two chintz-covered couches flanked a huge fireplace; a wing chair and a club completed the picture.

"This is where she lived," Alix whispered. "Tea was served to the ladies in the more formal front parlor. But *family* stayed in here."

"You want to stop that?" Izzy said. "It was

fun at first but now you're beginning to creep me out."

"Just memories," Alix said. "I wonder why Mom never brought me back here?"

"Miss Kingsley's gorgeous nephew probably had the hots for your gorgeous mother. That would have been awkward."

"If I was four, then that nephew was just a teenager."

"My point exactly," Izzy said. "Race you upstairs!"

Izzy beat her, but that was because Alix slowed down to look at the framed cutout silhouettes hung on the wall. There was one of a lady wearing a big hat with feathers in it. "I remember you," she whispered so Izzy couldn't hear. "You look like my mother."

"I found him!" Izzy yelled over the railing. "And I'm going to get into bed with him."

There was no need to ask who "he" was.

Alix ran up the stairs and looked for Izzy in the bedroom on her left. It was a pretty room, all chintz and gauzy muslin — but no Izzy.

Across the hall was a truly beautiful room, quite large, and done all in blue, from a pale creamy shade to deep and dark. In the middle was a four-poster bed with damask hangings. To the left was a big fireplace and beside it was a portrait, but she couldn't see all of the picture for the draperies on the bed.

"Here," Izzy said as she crawled to the end of the bed. "Get in and look at his royal highness, Jared Montgomery. Or Kingsley, as he's known here in the country of Nantucket."

Alix climbed onto the bed, which was rather high off the floor, and looked where Izzy was pointing. There on the wall to the right of the fireplace was a life-sized portrait of what looked to be Jared Montgomery. Maybe the man was a few inches shorter and he was dressed like some sea captain in a period drama, but it was him — or more precisely, his ancestor. The face was clean shaven, the way Jared Montgomery's had been when she and Izzy had seen him years ago at one of his rare lectures. The hair was shorter and curled a bit by his ears. The strong jaw and those eyes that seemed to look through a person were there.

Alix turned onto her back and flung her arms out. "Dibs."

"Only because you live here," Izzy said as she put her hands behind her head and looked up. The underside of the big canopy had pale blue silk pleated into a sunburst pattern with a rose in the middle. "Do you think Miss Kingsley lay here when she was in her nineties and drooled over that man's picture?"

"Wouldn't you?"

"If I wasn't about to get married . . ." Izzy began but didn't finish because she knew it wasn't true. She wouldn't trade Glenn for any man, famous or not.

Izzy rolled off the bed and went to do more exploring, but Alix turned over to look at the portrait. The man in the picture intrigued her. When she was four had she snuggled on this bed and looked at that portrait while Aunt Addy — as she was beginning to call her in her mind — read her a story? Had she made up her own stories about him? Or did Aunt Addy tell her about this man?

Whatever happened back then, Alix could almost imagine him moving about, almost hear him talking. And his laugh! Loud and deep, a roar, really. Like the sea.

There was a little plaque at the bottom of the picture and she got off the bed to look at it. CAPTAIN CALEB JARED KINGSLEY 1776 TO 1809, it said. Only thirty-three years old when he died.

She straightened to look up at his face. Yes, it looked like the man she'd seen years ago and again today on the wharf, but something else about the picture stirred a memory deep within her. It was there but she couldn't quite get hold of it.

"I found your mother's room," Izzy shouted down the hall.

Alix turned to leave but then stopped and looked back at the portrait. "You were a beautiful man, Caleb Kingsley," she said, then on impulse, she kissed her fingertips and put them on his lips.

For a second, less than a second, she

thought she felt breath on her cheek, then a touch. Very soft, very quick, then gone.

"Come on!" Izzy said from the doorway. "You have a whole year to lust after that man and the one in the guesthouse. Come see the room your mother's done."

Alix thought about saying that maybe the man in the picture had kissed her, but she didn't. She took her hand from her cheek and went to the door. "How can my mother have a room here? And how do you know for *sure* it's hers?" she asked, following Izzy down the hall, past the stairs, to another bedroom.

But the instant Alix saw it, she knew her mother had decorated it. It was done in shades of green, ranging from a dark forest color to a pale yellowish shade. One of her mother's vanities was her green eyes; she often dressed to match them and nearly always chose colors for her house to complement her eyes.

The bed was covered in a dark green silk with tiny honeybees woven into it. The pillows, a full dozen of them, were subtly monogrammed with her distinctive, intertwined VM.

"Think it's hers?" Izzy asked sarcastically.

"Could be," Alix said. "Or maybe Miss Kingsley was a great fan of Mom's books."

"Could I . . . ? You know . . . tonight?"

Alix had teased Izzy that she was her mom's

biggest fan, and with every book, one of the first copies off the presses was given to Izzy. "Sure. Just as long as you also don't sleep in the nude." Alix left to explore the other rooms.

"What?" Izzy asked, following her. "Your mother sleeps naked?"

"Shouldn't have said that," Alix muttered as she looked in the fourth bedroom. It was pretty but didn't look as though anything new had been put in it for about fifty years. "It wasn't me who told you," Alix said.

Izzy crossed her heart and made a motion of zipping her lips and throwing away the key.

"It's just one of my mother's many peccadillos. Extremely expensive sheets and her bare skin together. A true love match."

"Wow," Izzy said. "Your mother . . ."

"Yeah, I know." Alix opened a narrow door at the back of the house and entered what had obviously once been the maid's quarters. A sitting room, two bedrooms, and a bath.

As clearly as though she were seeing a movie, she knew that she and her mother had stayed in these rooms. She looked in the doorway to her right and saw a pretty little room done in pink and green, and she knew that as a child she had chosen the fabric for that bedspread and those curtains. On the floor was a needlepoint rug with a mermaid swimming about in coral. She'd always loved mermaids. Was that rug the source of her fascination with them?

A white desk had a bowl of shells that Alix knew she had collected off the beach. And she also knew that the hand she'd been holding while walking through the sand had been old. Certainly not her mother's hand.

When she heard Izzy in the sitting room, Alix left the little bedroom and closed the door.

"Anything interesting?" Izzy asked.

"Nothing," Alix said, knowing she was lying. She looked in the other bedroom. It was larger but impersonal; everything was of the most utilitarian nature. The bath was all white, with a pedestal sink and a big enameled tub. She could remember how cold the tub could be and how she'd had to stand on a box to reach the sink.

"You okay?" Izzy asked.

"Great. In awe, I guess. Shall we open the bottles and toast the Kingsley family?"

"Now you're talking."

# Chapter Two

An hour later they were sitting on the floor of the little TV room eating tuna sandwiches and a pizza they'd found in the freezer.

"Wonder what the grocery stores on Nantucket are like?" Izzy asked. They'd found some beautiful crystal glasses and she was using one. "Maybe Ben Franklin drank out of it," she said, knowing his mother was from Nantucket.

As for Alix, the only thing she wanted to drink was rum.

On their first survey of the house they'd missed the kitchen. They found it hidden away at the back of the house, behind the dining room. Compared to the kitchen, the rest of the house was downright modern. Nearly everything was exactly as it had been in about 1936. The stove was green and white enamel with a lid over the burners. The big sink had drainboards on both sides and all the cabinets were metal. The fridge was new but quite small, as it had to fit into a space that had been made for a thirties-era refrigerator. On the far wall under the window was a seat and a little table with a well-worn top of wood that she'd be willing to bet was once decking on a ship. Alix knew that she used to sit there and color while someone made her a sandwich. Again she had a vision of an older woman. If that was Aunt Addy, the owner of the house, where was her mother? And if they were guests of Aunt Addy, why had they stayed in the maid's quarters? None of it made any sense.

"Doesn't this make you itch to tear it out?" Izzy asked as she looked around the kitchen. "I think there should be granite countertops and maple cabinets. And I'd take down that wall into the dining room."

"No!" Alix said with too much force, then calmed herself. "I'd leave it just as it is."

"I think this place is taking you over," Izzy said, then exclaimed over finding a frozen pizza. "We'll feast tonight! Think this thing works?" She was referring to the oven in the old range.

To the amazement of both of them, Alix knew how to ignite the pilot light in the oven, knew that the knobs were quirky and just how to jiggle each one.

Izzy stood back, watching her, but refused to comment.

Alix was looking around the kitchen and again she had the idea that she knew something but couldn't remember what it was. When she saw the doorknob of a pirate's head next to the fridge, she said, "Ah-ha!" and gave a pull.

Izzy went to see what she'd found.

"This cabinet was always locked and I was fascinated by it. I even tried to steal the key but I couldn't find it." She had a vague memory of a man with a deep voice telling her that she couldn't have the key, but Alix didn't tell Izzy that.

For a moment the two women stood there staring in disbelief. The cabinet held bottles of booze and mixers. What was unusual was that nearly all the bottles were rum: dark, light, gold, white, and at least a dozen flavored varieties. In the middle of the cabinet was a marble-topped surface, and below it was a single-drawer refrigerator full of fresh citrus fruits. The kitchen may not have been modernized in nearly a century, but the bar was straight out of a decorating magazine.

"We can see where Miss Kingsley set her priorities," Izzy said.

Alix wondered if the reason she'd associated rum with Nantucket was from having seen people drinking it in this room. Whatever the logic behind the cabinet, there were drink recipes taped to the back of the doors and she wanted to experiment. "How about a Zombie?" she asked Izzy. "It takes three kinds of rum. Or maybe a Planter's Punch?"

"No, thanks," Izzy said. "I'll stick to champagne."

It didn't take them long to get their food and drinks into the TV room. For tonight the other rooms were too big, too intimidating for them to use.

"You have three days," Izzy said and they both knew what she meant. "He" would return in three days. "I wonder if today is one of the three? Which means that you only have two left. I'll have to do a lot of shopping quickly."

"The luggage should be here tomorrow and I have plenty of clothes."

"I saw what you packed. All you have are sweats and jeans."

"Which is what I'll need," Alix said. "I plan to work while I'm here. I thought about asking my dad if he knows anyone who summers here and if I can get a job. It would have to be under his license, and his approval, but maybe it could work out."

"I'm not talking about your father," Izzy said.

Alix took a deep drink of her Planter's Punch. Usually she got drunk easily but she was on her second rum drink and wasn't even feeling a buzz. "I want to *learn* from Jared Montgomery. If I show up in shorts and a halter or some designer concoction, he's going to look at me like he did at that girl today."

"So where's the problem with *that*?" Izzy asked.

"I don't think he took her seriously as an intelligent being, do you?"

Izzy sipped her champagne. "You and work! Don't you ever think of anything else?"

"And what's wrong with that?"

"What's wrong with you thinking only about work?" Izzy was incredulous. "Jared Montgomery is over six feet of muscle! He walks into a room and every female in there goes limp. Her forehead lights up with a sign that says TAKE ME. PLEASE. There's never been a woman who has turned him down, but you . . . All you can think about is his *mind.* I didn't know he had one. Alixandra, you're getting old."

Alix took another long drink, then set her glass on the rug. "You think so? You think I don't see him as a *man*? Stay here and I'll show you something."

She ran up the stairs to get her laptop and turned it on so that by the time she got back down to Izzy the screen was on. She had to go through about eight levels of files before the document she'd always hidden came up.

*Jared's Lower Lip*

Soft and succulent, luscious and firm
Beguiling, enticing, calling to me
A Siren's song, Pied Piper's flute
I dream of it asleep, awake

To touch it, caress it, kiss it
The tip of my tongue, breaths mingling
To draw it in, to caress it
To feel it against my own
Ah, Jared's lower lip.

Izzy read it three times before she looked up. "You *do* think of him as a man. Wow! Do you ever!"

"It was a few years ago — after we'd heard him speak, and you and I'd spent hours talking about him. Remember how he built his final project for school? No drawings or model for him. He *built* it with hammer and nails. My dad says that it should be mandatory that one year of architecture school be spent doing construction. He said —" She broke off because Izzy had stood up.

"Come on. Let's go."

"Go where?"

"We're going to look inside his guesthouse."

"We can't do that," Alix said as she stood up.

"I saw you looking out the windows, just as I was, and you saw the place in the back. Two stories, big window in front."

"We can't —"

"This may be our only chance. He's away on his fishing boat and you know that we came early. He doesn't know we're here."

"What does that mean?"

"I don't know," Izzy said. "But maybe when he knows a fanatical architecture student is here in this house he'll put bars on his windows and doors."

Alix hadn't thought of that. "I'll be subtle. I'll tell him how much I admire his work and —"

"And his lower lip? Did you ever consider that he might have a girlfriend? Just because he isn't married — or wasn't the last time either of us searched the Internet — and because he was alone on a fishing boat doesn't mean he's celibate. Do you think *she* is going to let you in the house?"

Alix knew that what Izzy was suggesting was wrong, but on the other hand maybe he had drawings here. Maybe this was her one and only chance to have a private viewing of a Montgomery design before the world saw it.

Izzy could see that Alix was wavering and she half pushed, half pulled her out the side door and down the garden path to the guesthouse. It was tall and had heavy curtains over the windows; it looked almost forbidding.

Izzy took a breath and tried the front door. Locked.

"We can't do this," Alix said as she turned back toward the house.

But Izzy caught her arm and led her around the side.

"Maybe we can see his bedroom," she whispered. "Or his closet. Or his —"

"*How* old are you?"

"Right now I feel about fourteen."

Alix took a step back. "I really don't think we should —" Suddenly, she halted, her eyes wide.

"What is it?" Izzy gasped. "Please tell me you aren't seeing a ghost. I read that Nantucket is one of the most haunted places in the world."

"It's a light," Alix whispered.

"He left a light on?" Izzy stepped back to look up and she saw what looked to be a desk lamp, the kind that would reach across a drafting table. "You're right. Do you think he has a home studio? *Now* do you think we should go in?"

Alix was already at the window and trying to raise it. It slid up easily. "Andersen Thermopane, twelve over twelve," she mumbled as she gave a jump and hoisted herself inside, leaving Izzy to get in by herself.

Once she was inside, Alix quickly glanced around. There was a dim light on in the kitchen so she could see a living room and dining area. All one room. It looked to be a nice place, but she wanted to see where that light was. She hurried up the stairs, opened the door on the right, and saw a room with windows on three sides. She knew the light would be beautiful during the day. There was an old rug on the hardwood floor and under the windows was an antique drafting table, probably from the Edwardian era. Beside it was a little cabinet, the top covered with drawing supplies. In a day of computer drafting systems, it was wonderful to see actual drawings with pencil, pen, and ink. She touched his mechanical pencils, all of them lined up by lead, from hard to soft. There was an erasing shield, brushes, and a T-square. There was no drafting machine anywhere.

To the right was a wall covered by his drawings. They were for the construction of small structures, not houses, and each one was exquisite in both concept and execution. There were two sheds, a guesthouse, a children's play set. Three garage plans were next to sketches for garden structures. Nearly every bit of empty wall space had been covered with his drawings and draftings.

"They're beautiful, wonderful. Magnificent," she whispered.

She stepped back to the doorway to take it all in. The room felt like a shrine or a sanctuary. "I bet he never invites anyone in here," she said aloud.

What surprised her was how much she and this man thought alike. She deeply believed that beauty could and should be found in the smallest object. Whether it was a soap dish or a mansion, to give it beauty was of utmost importance.

"Wow!" Izzy said from behind her. "It's like . . ."

"Something on a ship?"

"Yeah, it's very much like a movie set for a captain's cabin."

Alix was trying to take in every inch of the room. There were old things everywhere. A piece of antique china with "Kingsley" written on it. Taking up one corner was a carved wooden ship's figurehead of a mermaid, weathered as though she had sailed through many oceans.

"Didn't their family used to have whaling ships?" Izzy asked.

"Mostly the China trade." Even as she said it, Alix had no idea how she knew that. "I didn't read of any whalers in the family," she added to cover herself. She walked around, touching things, memorizing them. If she had a home office it would look exactly like this. "Isn't it wonderful?"

"Frankly, no," Izzy said. "I want everything computerized. Deliver me from pen and ink. This place isn't my style." Outside, a car door slammed and they looked at each other in panic. "We better get out of here."

Reluctantly, Alix started to follow her friend down the stairs but turned back for one last look. On the floor had fallen a freehand sketch of a little garden pavilion. It was octagonal with a roof like an upside-down tulip. Without thinking about what she was doing, she picked it up, stuck it in the waistband of her trousers, and hurried down the stairs.

# Chapter Three

Alix leaned back in the chair and looked at the paper model she'd made of the chapel she'd designed. It hadn't been easy to construct since all she'd had was card stock and tape. It was late afternoon and she was in the big room at the back of the old house, the one where she felt warmth and happiness. She knew without being told that when she was a child she'd spent a lot of time in this room. She remembered building little houses that had towers and turrets. At first she'd used old wooden blocks, and had piled up objects she found in drawers and on shelves. Then came Legos, her favorite childhood toy. There had been a great box full of them and in the bottom were little boats that she built sheds for.

While she'd played, there was music playing, soft and light, but no TV. Most important, there was a woman always nearby. Alix could almost see her smiling and approving. And sometimes there were other people. A young man who always looked worried. And a tall boy who smelled like the sea. There were smiling ladies who ate little cakes with yellow rosebuds on them. She could remember the taste of the petit fours and the itchiness of her new dress.

Over the big fireplace was a portrait of a lady. MISS ADELAIDE KINGSLEY, the label said. From her hair and clothes it looked to have been painted in the 1930s. She was pretty in a sedate, respectable-looking way, but there was a twinkle in her eye. The woman Alix was remembering more clearly by the hour was much older than in the portrait, but Alix well knew that sparkle in her eye. It seemed to say that she knew and saw things that others didn't, but she wasn't telling what. Except that she had shared her knowledge with Alix. She couldn't remember exactly what Aunt Addy had told her, but Alix still felt the love that had been there — and the shared secrets.

Alix had wanted to spend the day with Izzy exploring the old house and walking around Nantucket. After all, her friend would leave soon. And Alix feared that once she was back on the mainland, Izzy would delve so deeply into planning her wedding that she and Alix wouldn't have much contact. Toward the end of the summer, Alix would be Izzy's maid of honor and Izzy would be married — and that would be the end of their girl friendship. Alix tried not to think how Izzy's impending marriage would separate them.

It had been an excellent plan to spend the day together, but it didn't happen. Alix awoke early with her mind fully on the possibility of showing her work to the Great Jared Montgomery. If he liked what he saw, maybe she could get an interview for a job at his firm. At the very least she'd show him what an eager-to-learn student she could be.

She lay in Aunt Addy's bed in the early morning, her arms behind her head, looking up at the silk rose. Even if she didn't get a job with him, to be his student — even if it was just for a few weeks — would be the highlight of her architectural studies. She could definitely put it on her résumé. And more important, she'd learn masses from him.

She wanted to design something to impress him. A house? How could she do that in just a couple of days? She was good at freehand sketching so maybe she could do some façades. But then she'd need to see the land. Everyone knew that Montgomery believed in buildings coming from the land, from the environment. He did *not* believe in mock Tudors in Dallas.

"What can I draw to impress him?" she whispered aloud.

As Alix lay there thinking and coming up with nothing, a small framed picture fell off the table against the far wall. Surprisingly, the disturbance in the still room didn't startle her, but it did make her sit upright.

She got out of bed, her old T-shirt and threadbare sweatpants drafty in the cool morning. While she didn't understand why, she knew the picture that had fallen was important. Picking it up, she saw a photo from the 1940s of two young women laughing. They wore pretty summer dresses and looked happy.

It had been a nice thought that the picture held some significance, but she couldn't see what that was. She put the photo back on the table and headed for the bathroom, but then she stopped, turned back, and picked up the picture again. In the background, in the far distance, was a small church. Maybe not even a church but a chapel, like those private family ones she'd seen when she and her father had visited England.

For a moment Alix envisioned Jared Montgomery's home office and his designs for garden sculptures and gazebos, for arbors and a little garden shed.

"Small," she whispered. "He'd like to see something small and exquisite." She looked over at the big portrait of the Kingsley ancestor, Captain Caleb, and had an almost irresistible urge to say thank you.

Shaking her head at her nonsense, she went to the bathroom and tied back her hair. When she came out, she pulled her big red notebook from her new bag, and got back into bed.

Maybe it was the nearness of Izzy's wedding, or maybe it was the search for something small that Montgomery had not designed, or perhaps the idea came from the fallen photo. Whatever the cause, Alix started sketching chapels. She rarely forgot a building, and she drew what she remembered.

Every August since her parents had split up, her mother went to Colorado, and Alix would stay with her father. If his work schedule allowed him to travel, they went where they could study the local architecture. They'd been to the southwestern U.S. to look at pueblos, to California for mission style, to Washington State to see Victorians. When Alix got older, they went to Spain to see Gaudi's work, and of course they visited the Taj Mahal.

Alix used everything she could remember and sketched as fast as she could. When the pages filled, she tore them off and tossed them onto the bed.

When the bedroom door opened she looked up to see Izzy, fully dressed as though she meant to go out.

"Somehow, I knew you weren't sleeping." Izzy moved drawings to sit down on the bed and picked up some sketches. "A church?"

"A chapel. Small and private."

Izzy looked at one drawing after another in

silence, while Alix held her breath. As a fellow student of architecture, she greatly valued her friend's opinion.

"These are gorgeous," Izzy said. "Really beautiful."

"I'm getting there," Alix said. "But I keep trying to incorporate everything in one design. Bell towers, magnificent doors, half-round staircases. Everything! I need to decide what I can and cannot use."

Izzy smiled. "You'll figure it out. I just wanted to tell you that I'm going out shopping."

Alix threw back the covers. "I'll get dressed. It won't take me but minutes."

Izzy stood up. "Nope. You're not allowed to go. This is your big chance and I want you to take it. Stay here and design something that will astound Montgomery. By the way, there's food downstairs."

"How did you find a grocery open this early?"

"For your information, it's eleven A.M. and the whole beautiful town of Nantucket is just outside. I've been out and come back and now I'm ready to go do some serious clothes shopping. You can*not* meet the Lord High Emperor Montgomery wearing *that.*" She gave Alix's old sweats a disparaging look.

Alix knew her friend well. "You know, on second thought, I think I'll go with you. I need some new sandals."

Izzy stepped back to the door. "Oh, no you don't. I'll be back for dinner and I want to see what you've done." She hurried out of the room, shutting the door behind her.

"I'll do my best to make you happy," Alix called out. She knew that Izzy wanted to go by herself. She loved shopping for clothes, and if Alix was in the mood, so did she. But not today. Besides, the two young women were similar enough in size that Izzy could buy whatever Alix needed and charge it all to Victoria.

At noon, Alix's growling stomach finally made her get dressed and leave the bedroom in search of breakfast. Izzy had bought bagels and tuna salad, fruit, and bags of spinach. All healthy and filling.

Alix made herself a sandwich, but then she went back upstairs to get her drawings so she could look at them as she ate. To her horror she saw that she had only two blank sheets of paper left.

Surely, she thought, if her mother had stayed here more than once she would have paper somewhere, probably in the green bedroom. Feeling a bit like she was snooping, Alix went down the hall to the room Izzy was using.

Alix again wondered when her mother had stayed on Nantucket. And why would she keep her visits a secret? Alix remembered saying that she found out everything her mother did, but it looked like that wasn't true. But then, to be fair, since Alix had left home to go to college she'd had her own life and had kept things, such as boyfriends, from her mother. It looked as though her mother kept secrets of her own. But why? Was there a man involved?

There were two big armoires in the bedroom, both old and beautiful. One had a few bags in it that Izzy must have purchased that morning, and the other was locked. Alix looked around for a moment to see if a key was nearby but didn't see one. On impulse, she returned to her room for her handbag, retrieving the ring of keys her mother had sent. Alix hadn't been told what the individual keys were for, but then Victoria never explained much. She'd always thought her daughter was intelligent enough to figure out everything on her own.

One of the smaller keys fit the lock. Alix opened the double doors to find an entire office inside. There was a printer and drawers full of paper and supplies. Shelves held what Alix recognized as old manuscripts. There were some photos taped on the back of the door. One of them was of Victoria with her arm around a small older woman who Alix knew was Adelaide Kingsley. The date on the photo was 1998, when Alix was twelve years old.

Alix couldn't stop the wave of hurt that ran

through her. It was becoming apparent that her mother had spent a lot of time here on Nantucket in this house. But she'd never told her daughter a thing about it. Of course she'd done it in August, Alix thought. That month had always been sacrosanct to Victoria. She claimed she went to Colorado to her cabin, where she said the solitude helped her to plot her latest book. But obviously, she'd not gone there *every* year.

Alix stared inside the cabinet. It made sense that her mother would go to Nantucket, as all her books were set in a seafaring community. But why had she kept it a secret?

Alix's impulse was to call her mother and ask questions. But Victoria was on a twenty-city book publicity tour right now, and being the smiling, laughing author the world thought they knew. Alix wasn't going to interrupt that. She could wait to find out, and knowing her mother, it would no doubt be an entertaining story.

Alix got the paper she needed, some office supplies, even found an old package of matte photo paper, and hauled everything downstairs to the big family room. She knew that one of the little tables opened and inside were TV trays. She got one out and set down her sandwich. She spread her drawings on the floor, sat on the couch to eat, and looked at them.

At first everything seemed to be a great

hodgepodge of styles and designs. Too much! she thought. None of this would fit into the quiet elegance of Nantucket.

She finished her lunch, moved the table out of the way, and kept staring, but saw nothing to salvage. She was just starting to get frustrated when one of her papers rustled in the breeze. That all the windows and doors were closed didn't register.

"Thanks," she said before thinking, then shook her head. Thanks for what? To whom?

She picked up the paper that had moved. There in the corner was a tiny sketch she'd done so quickly that she hardly remembered it. It was a combination of Spanish mission and Nantucket Quaker. Plain to the point of severity, but at the same time it was beautiful in its simplicity.

"You think he'll like this?" she said aloud, then started to correct herself, but who cared? She was alone, so she could talk out loud if she wanted to.

She put the drawing on the tray table and looked at it again. "This window needs to be changed. A bit taller. And the bell tower needs to be shorter. No! The roof should be taller."

She grabbed more paper and redrew the design. Then she drew it three more times. When she had a sketch she liked, she picked up the architectural scale she'd brought with her and started a scale drawing.

At three P.M. she made herself another sandwich, got a ginger ale out of the fridge, and went back to the family room. The floor was covered with papers and nearest to her were the new sketches.

"I like it," she said, stepping around the drawings and looking down at them.

She finished her sandwich and drink, then picked up the photo paper, scissors, and tape dispenser. Making a model this way wouldn't be easy but if it could be done, she'd somehow manage it.

When she heard the door open it was nearly six P.M. Izzy was home! For a moment it ran through Alix that her friend would leave soon and she'd be alone — not a happy prospect.

Alix ran to the door and was greeted by Izzy with what looked to be a dozen giant shopping bags embossed with store names. "I take it the shopping on Nantucket is good?" Alix asked.

"Heavenly, divine," Izzy said. She dropped the bags and rubbed her fingers where the handles had made grooves in them.

Alix shut the door behind her. "Come on and I'll make you a drink."

"Not rum," Izzy said as she followed Alix into the kitchen. "And there's food in one of those bags. Scallops and salad and some dessert with raspberries and chocolate."

"Sounds great," Alix said. "Why don't we take it all outside? I think it's warm enough to eat out there."

"You want to keep watch on his house, don't you?"

Alix smiled. "No. I want to soften you up so you'll be gentle in your critique of what I did today."

"Is it still a church or have you made it into a cathedral? I can see flying buttresses of unfinished cedar. Will the windows be stained glass of some brawny sea captain?"

Alix started to defend herself and explain, but instead she went into the family room, got the model, brought it back, and set it on the kitchen table.

Izzy had retrieved the plastic containers from the bags and she'd put them down on the counter. For several moments she just stood there and stared at the little white model. It was so simple with its slanted roof and bell tower, but the proportions were perfect.

"It's . . ." Izzy whispered. "It's . . ."

Alix waited but Izzy said nothing else. "It's what?"

Izzy sat down on the built-in seat behind the table. "It's the best thing you've ever done," she whispered, then looked up at Alix.

"Really?" Alix asked. "You're not just saying that?"

"Truthfully," Izzy said. "It's the epitome of all you've worked for. It's truly beautiful."

Alix couldn't help doing a few dance steps

of triumph around the kitchen, then she began pulling dishes out of the cabinets and putting food on them. "I was really fighting it. I thought I was never going to come up with new and original, and old and traditional, at the same time. I went against the well-known Montgomery creed of following the land, but I did think of it as being built on Nantucket so that —" She broke off because when she looked back at Izzy, her friend was crying — just sitting at the table, tears rolling down her face, her eyes focused on the model of the chapel.

Alix went over and hugged her. "We'll see each other," she said. "I'll only be here for a year, then I'll be back. You and Glenn will —"

Izzy pulled away, sniffing. "It's not that. I know you'll be back."

"Oh. Is it Glenn? Do you miss him?" Alix got up and opened a drawer to pull out a box of tissues and handed one to her friend.

"Do you know where everything in this house is?"

Alix knew Izzy needed time to recover and Alix was going to give it to her — then she was going to find out what the problem was. Her best friend was deeply upset over something, but Alix had no idea what it was. Her intuition told her that whatever the problem was, Izzy had been holding it in because of Alix's recent emotional drama.

Alix turned away to let her friend have time to recover her dignity. Using an old blender that looked to be from the fifties, she made a tall drink for Izzy. For herself, she made a rum and Coke, with lots of lime juice added. Alix pulled a serving tray from inside a cabinet, knowing just where to find it, filled it, then took it all outside. It was almost too cool for sitting outdoors, but Alix knew that Izzy loved gardens.

She treated her friend gently as she settled her in a heavy teak deck chair and handed her a drink. Alix wasn't going to push her friend but just waited for her to speak.

"Glenn called and I have to leave in the morning," Izzy said.

"He wants you back?"

"Yes, of course, but . . ."

Alix waited in silence. Izzy and she had been friends since the first day of architecture school. By the end of that week it was clear that Alix was more talented, that she had a shot at doing something that the world would notice, but Izzy had never been jealous.

On the other hand, everyone had liked Izzy so much that she was invited everywhere. When she'd become engaged in their third year, Alix had only felt joy. They were two different people yet they suited each other well.

"If it's not Glenn and it's not me, what is it?" Alix asked softly.

Izzy looked around the garden. The only time she'd seen it was last night when she and Alix had made their wild dash to break into Montgomery's guesthouse. At the time it had been wonderful to think only of Alix's problems, to feed her chocolate, to see her delight at the old house, to laugh over the portrait of a handsome sea captain. For a few hours Izzy had been able to put aside her own problems.

"This garden is beautiful," Izzy said. "When it flowers, it's going to be magnificent. I wonder who takes care of it?"

"Montgomery," Alix said quickly. "Isabella, I want to know what's going on. Why is Glenn demanding that you leave so soon? I was hoping that you and I could see some of Nantucket together."

"Me too," Izzy said, "but . . ."

Alix picked up the pitcher and refilled Izzy's glass. "But what?"

Izzy took a deep drink. "It's my wedding."

"I thought all of that was settled. We bought you the most beautiful dress ever made."

"Yes, and I thank you and your mother for that." Izzy and Alix smiled at each other in memory.

Glenn, not surprisingly, had proposed over dinner one Friday night. The next morning Izzy was at the door of Alix's little apartment looking stunned and not knowing what to do.

After admiring the engagement ring, Alix took over. "I know a great place for breakfast, then we can go window-shopping. You're going to need an entire trousseau."

It was an old-fashioned word and concept, Izzy had said while doing her best to look as though she was too sophisticated to care about such silly things. But Alix wasn't fooled. She knew her friend loved the whole idea of a romantic wedding.

In the end, they bought Izzy's wedding dress that day. They hadn't meant to. Alix had been the one to persuade her friend to go to a tiny, exclusive shop on a side street across town.

"We should go to one of those gigantic places and try on fifty dresses and drive the salespeople crazy," Izzy said.

"That's a great idea," Alix said, "and I look forward to it, but Mom told me that when I get married I'm to buy my dress at Mrs. Searle's shop."

Izzy looked hard at her friend. "Which just happens to be near here?"

"So it does," Alix said, smiling.

The third dress Izzy tried on brought tears to both their eyes. They knew it was the one.

The dress had a plain silk satin top with a round, low neck and wide straps. The full skirt was whisper-thin tulle over a satin skirt embellished with tiny crystals in a flower pattern.

"I could never afford this," Izzy said as she looked for a price tag that wasn't there.

"It'll be a gift from my mother," Alix said. "To her number one fan."

"I can't take this."

"Okay," Alix said, "she'll give you a toaster instead."

"I shouldn't," Izzy said, but she did. Later she thought that at that moment she'd been the happiest person on earth. What she'd not told Alix was how, later, her wedding plans had all fallen apart. When others began to get involved, Izzy had tried her best to be firm about what she wanted for her wedding, but her future mother-in-law said, "I can see that you're going to be one of those bridezillas like they have on TV. We aren't being filmed, are we?"

Izzy looked across at Alix. "I don't want to be a bridezilla."

"You mean one of those spoiled prima donnas who makes everyone's lives hell?"

Izzy nodded.

"That's as far from you as could be. Izzy, who put this idea in your head?" Alix filled her friend's glass again.

"Glenn and I just want a quiet wedding. Small. Maybe a barbecue. The dress from your mother is the only extravagance I want. It's so beautiful and . . ." Again, tears started flowing.

"It's a mother, isn't it?" Alix said. "If there's

one thing I know about, it's mothers. Well-meaning, but they can eat you for breakfast."

Nodding, Izzy took a deep drink and held up two fingers.

"I take it that means *two* mothers?"

Again Izzy nodded.

Alix poured herself another rum and Coke. "Tell me everything."

It all tumbled out. Alix knew that Izzy was the only girl in her family, but she hadn't known that Izzy's parents had eloped. "My mother used to play with bride paper dolls, but then she got pregnant with my brother, and she and my dad ran off together."

"So now she wants you to have the wedding she didn't have," Alix said.

Izzy grimaced. "But she isn't even the only problem."

Alix knew that Glenn was an only child and that his parents had money, but that's all. "What's his mother like?"

Izzy clenched her teeth. "She's an avalanche of granite blocks that destroys anyone who stands between her and whatever she wants. And what she wants now is for me to have a lavish wedding that will impress all her friends. She has a guest list of over four hundred people. Glenn knows only six of them and I've never met any of them."

"Izzy, this is serious, and why haven't you told me about any of this?" Alix asked.

"It just happened, then you and Eric . . ."

Alix put up her hand. "And I was wallowing in my own misery and didn't see what you were going through. Listen, tomorrow I'm going back with you to help straighten this out."

"No," Izzy said, "you can't do that. I feel in my heart that all this was arranged so you could meet Montgomery and show him your work. I can't imagine what your mother had to do to get you this house for a year. You can't throw something like this away just for some wedding."

As Alix finished her drink, she looked around at the beautiful garden. It was growing cooler and they'd have to go inside soon. "Why do you have to leave in the morning?"

"Glenn's mother has arrived, and she wants to show me some bridesmaids' dresses. Glenn said they have ruffles all over them and that she's brought in two cousins who are to be in the wedding."

"Flower girls?" There was hope in Alix's voice.

"I wish. They're thirty-eight and thirty-nine, and mean. And everyone hates my date of the twenty-fifth of August."

Absently, Alix handed Izzy a plate of food. For a while they ate in silence. Alix was thinking of all the times she'd had to be strong to keep her mother from steamrolling over her. "So," Alix said, "I can't leave here and you can't stay."

"That's about it," Izzy said. The drinks had given her the ability to smile. "You should have seen Glenn's mother's face when I told her I'd already bought my wedding dress. She turned a lovely shade of purple. I wanted to hold a fabric sample up to her cheek and see if I could match it."

Alix gave a laugh. "Did you tell her my mother paid for the gown?"

"Oh, yes," Izzy said, then filled her mouth with food.

"What did she say?"

"That she thought Victoria Madsen's books had no literary merit and should never have been published."

"Reads them avidly, does she?"

"Oh, yes!" Izzy said, laughing. "I told Glenn what she said and he said her eReader is nothing but Victoria's novels."

The two women laughed.

"This is probably cruel of me, but I'd like to see them together," Izzy said.

"My mother and your mother-in-law?" Alix asked.

"And my mother too! She controls with tears. She looked at my beautiful wedding gown and cried because she didn't get to help me pick it out. She cried when I said I wanted to be married outside under a rose arbor. She said it would break her heart if I didn't get married in some church she went to as a child. I've never even seen it! And she cried when she told me she was disappointed that I hadn't chosen our next-door neighbor's daughter to be my maid of honor. I couldn't stand her as a girl, much less as a woman."

"Tears and tyranny," Alix said.

"The same difference as far as I'm concerned. Tomorrow I'm facing the war of the bridesmaids. I have to tell three women that they can't be in my wedding because I don't *like* them. Then Glenn's mother will —"

She broke off because Alix got up and started pacing around the garden. Toward the back was a pergola and Alix stopped to look at it.

"I think these are — Ow! Yes, they're climbing roses." She'd pricked her finger on a thorn. "Izzy," she said firmly, "you're going to have your wedding here in this garden."

"I can't do that," Izzy said.

"Why not? It's *your* wedding."

"The two mothers would make my life a living hell."

"So we'll make sure *my* mother is here," Alix added, devilment in her eyes.

Izzy's eyes widened. "If there's anyone . . ."

"Who could stand up to your two mothers, mine can." Alix smiled.

Izzy looked across the fading light to Alix. "Do you think this could work?"

"Why wouldn't it? You just have to be firm and tell them what you're going to do."

"I would have to leave Glenn and move

here to plan this thing."

"No," Alix said. "You need to spend time with him. Besides, if you divide, they'll conquer. Tell Glenn he has to back you up on this or there won't be a wedding."

"But I can't do that!"

"Okay, then split yourself down the middle and figure out how to please both mothers and let Glenn hide out with his cars."

Izzy couldn't help laughing. "Sometimes you sound just like your mother."

"And here I thought you were my friend."

Izzy closed her eyes for a moment. "I think I'm like my mother because I may start crying right now. Alix, you are the best friend anyone ever had."

"No better than you," she said softly. "I couldn't have survived Eric if you hadn't been there."

"Ha! It was the sight of Jared Montgomery's lower lip that brought you out of the doldrums. Hey! I have an idea. Since you can write so well, how about helping me with my vows?"

"We'll get Mom to do it. Of course she'll want a contract, a due date, money on signing, and a copyright, but they'll be killer vows."

The two young women looked at each other and went into a fit of uncontrollable laughter.

Upstairs, standing by an open window, Caleb Kingsley looked down at them. He was smiling. You could spend two hundred years making plans and you could die again when they fell through, but sometimes you saw and heard things that gave you hope.

He was glad to see the two young women together again. Sisters in one life; friends in this one.

Maybe, just maybe, this time he would get to hold Valentina for real. Forever.

That night Alix called her father, Ken. Before she punched the buttons, as always, she reminded herself that it was better if she didn't mention her mother. It wasn't that the two of them hadn't learned how to get along over the years, but give them any ammo and the questions started — with Alix caught in the middle.

"Hi, baby," her dad said on answering. "Did you get to Nantucket okay?"

"You'll never in your life guess who's staying in the guesthouse."

"Who?" Ken asked.

"Jared Montgomery."

"That guy who's an architect?"

"Very funny," Alix said. "I know you teach about him in your classes, so you know that he's a genius."

"He's made some respectable buildings. I like that he knows something about construction."

"I know that's your mantra. Dad?"

"Yes?"

"I designed a chapel."

"You mean a church?" Ken asked. "What for?"

"I'll tell you but only if you promise not to get straitlaced with me."

"What does that mean?"

"Dad?" Alix said, warning in her voice.

"All right. No lectures. What did you do?"

For the next ten minutes Alix told her father about breaking into Montgomery's home studio and seeing his designs, his private sketches. "They were beautiful, so perfect."

"So you designed something small to impress him," Ken said. She could hear the disapproval in his voice.

"Yes, I did," she said firmly. "I don't know how long he'll be here, but I hope I can show him some of my work."

"I'm sure he'll be impressed," Ken said.

"I doubt that, but at least maybe I can get him to *look* at it."

"I am quite *sure* that he'll do that," Ken said emphatically. "Where is he now?"

"On his boat. Izzy and I saw him sail away. He's a beautiful man."

"Alix," Ken said sternly, "from what I know of this Montgomery guy, he's a tough player. I don't think —"

"Relax, Dad. I just want to be his student. He's much too old for me." Alix rolled her eyes. She knew from experience that when it came to men her father thought none of them were good enough for her. She changed the subject. "So how are you and . . . you know . . . doing?"

Instantly, her father went from hot to cold, but Alix wasn't worried. Her dad was a softie.

"Are you referring to the woman I've been living with for these last four years?"

"Sorry," Alix said. "I'm being rude. Celeste is very nice. She dresses beautifully and she —"

"You can stop looking for good to say about her. Those clothes nearly bankrupted me. But it doesn't matter now because she moved out."

"Oh, Dad, I'm sorry. I know you liked her."

"No, I don't think I did," he said thoughtfully.

Alix gave a sigh of relief. "Thank heaven! Now I can tell you that I never actually liked her."

"Really? I never would have guessed. You were so good at keeping your opinions to yourself."

"I am sorry, Dad," she said and this time she meant it. "Really, I am."

"Oh, well, bad taste in the opposite sex runs in our family."

"That's not true. I mean it is for you and Mom, but Eric was . . ." Alix grimaced. "Actually, he was awful. Izzy said I only liked him because he gave me the opportunity to do two designs instead of one."

Ken laughed. "I've always liked Izzy! And she knows my daughter well."

"I'm going to miss her. She's leaving in the morning." Alix thought it was better not to tell him yet about moving the wedding to Nantucket. He might think she was taking on too much. "That blasted fiancé of hers wants her to be with *him.*"

"Inconsiderate devil!"

"That's just what I said."

"Look, Alix, it's late and we both need to sleep. When's Montgomery getting back?"

"I have no idea. I stayed in and worked while Izzy spent the day buying me new clothes." She didn't tell him that Izzy said the clothes were to impress Montgomery.

"And sending the bills to your mother, I hope."

"Of course. Those two and Mom's AmEx are the very best of friends. A holy trinity."

Ken chuckled. "I miss you already. So get some sleep and call me after you meet Montgomery. I want to hear every word of what happens."

"Love ya," she said.

"Love ya back," he replied.

# Chapter Four

"I've decided to leave tomorrow," Jared said to his grandfather Caleb. It was early evening and they were in the kitchen of Kingsley House. Jared had just returned from his fishing trip and hadn't yet showered and changed. "I'm going to clean these fish, take them out to Dilys in the morning, then leave the island."

"Wasn't your original plan to stay for the summer? Didn't you have some work to do here?"

"Yeah, but I can do it in New York." Jared pulled the fish out of a bucket and tossed them onto the drainboard.

"It was about some house, wasn't it?"

"I have a commission to design a house to be built in L.A. for some movie stars. That the marriage won't last two years is none of my business. I thought I told you about this."

"I remember you said that in New York you had so many responsibilities outside of designing that you could no longer think. You said you wanted to spend a year on Nantucket. . . . What was that saying you had? Something about roots."

"You know I said that I wanted to get back to my roots."

"I believe the word was 'needed.' You *needed* to find where you belong. Is that right or have I contracted some illness that distorts my mind?"

"You're too old for any disease." Jared was dirty and tired and hungry and angry. Yes, he'd planned to stay on Nantucket for the whole summer, but then his aunt had left his house to . . . to *her.*

"So you're running away," Caleb said. He was standing by the kitchen table and glaring at his grandson. "Abandoning young Alix."

"I think of it as a sort of protection. You, better than anyone, know what my life's been like. Does she deserve *that*? Besides, it would be better if she never found out who I am off the island. As a student, she probably thinks I'm a hero. I'm not even close."

"So now we hear the *truth,*" Caleb said softly.

"What did you think? That I was afraid she'd ask me for my autograph? I wouldn't mind that." He gave a half smile. "Preferably on some body part. But not this girl." He got up to start cleaning the fish, but changed his mind. Instead, he went to the tall cabinet by the refrigerator and poured himself a rum and Coke. "What happened to all the limes that were in here?"

"I ate them." Caleb was glaring at his grandson.

"Never a straight answer from you." Jared drank deeply, poured himself another one, then sat down at the table and looked around at the kitchen.

"Thinking of tearing it out and putting in granite countertops?" Caleb asked.

Jared nearly choked on his drink. "Where did you hear that piece of blasphemy?"

"Just something someone said. Maple cabinets and granite countertops."

"Stop cursing!" Jared said. "You're turning my stomach. This kitchen is perfect just as it is."

"I remember when it was put in," Caleb said.

"The Fifth, wasn't it?"

"The Fourth," Caleb said, referring to the number on the end of the names of the eldest sons. His son with Valentina, back in 1807, had been named Jared for Caleb's middle name, Montgomery because it was her last name, and Kingsley for Caleb's family. Even after all these years, what she'd had to do to get that last name for their son still sickened him. Since that time Caleb had made sure that Valentina's choice of name had been honored, with each succeeding eldest son being named Jared Montgomery Kingsley. This one, the most obstinate of the lot, was the Seventh.

"I'm sure you know who did what." Jared was still looking around the old kitchen.

"Are you trying to memorize the place?" Caleb asked.

"Considering all the things I'm not supposed to tell Victoria's daughter, I think it's better that I don't come back. At least not while . . ."

"While Alix is here?" It was easy to hear the disapproval in Caleb's voice.

"Don't start on me again!" Jared said. "I'm not a teacher and have never wanted to be."

"Didn't you have teachers?" Caleb asked.

"And so does she!" Jared groaned. "Look, I've spent the last few days thinking this through. I can't live up to what these students expect of me. They expect me to be a fount of wisdom, which I'm not. Tomorrow I'll ask Dilys to introduce this girl to Lexie and Toby. The three of them can be friends. They can have lunch together and go shopping. They'll be fine."

"So Dilys will mother her and Lexie will befriend her. And you'll run away and hide."

For a moment Jared's face turned red at the accusation, but then he smiled. "That's me. Yellow-bellied coward. Terrified of a girl with a T-square. But then, she probably doesn't even know what one is. I'm sure she's up on the latest CAD system, the latest everything that is modern and high tech. She probably has some kit that has a dozen roofs, twenty doors, and sixteen styles of windows. They're little punch-out shapes and she puts them all together to form buildings."

Caleb's anger showed in his eyes. "I'm sure she's just like that. I think you're right and you should run away and never even meet her." With that he disappeared.

Jared knew he'd angered his grandfather, but that was nothing new. He'd been doing that since he was twelve years old.

He knew he should get up and start cleaning the fish, but he sat at the table and looked across the room at the old stove. He could imagine some student of architecture coming up with a design for a sleek new kitchen. An eight-burner Wolf with three ovens. Tear out the wall and put in a Sub-Zero fridge. Take out the sink with its porcelain backsplash and long drainboards and put in some stainless monstrosity.

No, he couldn't bear having to explain to some architecture student why that shouldn't be done. He couldn't —

"Hello."

Jared turned to see a pretty young woman standing in the doorway. She was wearing jeans and a plaid shirt, her long hair pulled back off her face. She had big, greenish eyes with thick black lashes, and a truly gorgeous mouth.

"I thought I heard voices," she said, "but I assumed it was someone in the street and didn't pay any attention. But then a picture fell off a wall and some dirt fell down in the fireplace and that made me look up and —" She broke off to take a breath. Be cool, she told herself. This is *him.* This is . . . She couldn't think of anything else to call him, but *Him.* Capital H.

He was looking at her as though she were a ghost, as though she weren't quite real.

Alix had to work not to gush about how much she loved his designs, admired what he'd done in the architectural world, to ask what was he working on now, did he have any words of wisdom for her, and could she please, please, please show him the chapel she'd designed?

She suppressed all that even though her heart was pounding. "I'm Alix Madsen, and I'm staying here for . . . for a while. But I guess you know that. Are you Mr. Kingsley? I was told that you would take care of the house if it needs repairs." She thought it would be better to let him introduce himself.

He liked her curvy little body. "Yeah, I can fix things."

Alix searched for something else to say. He was still sitting at the table, his long legs stretched out in front of him. He had on the same clothes he'd been wearing when she'd seen him get on the boat days before. They were dirty and she could smell the fish on him. But even with his scraggly beard and long hair he was still formidably good-looking. Maybe right now he was a bit intimidating in the way he was scowling at her, but then maybe he hadn't expected her to be there. She couldn't help glancing at his lower lip. It was exactly as she remembered, had dreamed about, written about.

When she made herself look away, she saw a pile of striped bass on the drainboard. "You've been fishing," she said.

"I was just going to clean them. This sink is bigger than mine in the guesthouse, but I wouldn't have come in if I'd known anyone was here."

"My friend Izzy and I came earlier than we'd planned, and she left this morning," she said. The intensity of his gaze was making her so nervous that she needed to be busy. As she walked across the kitchen she could feel his eyes on her. Without thinking, she opened the third drawer down and got out a steel mesh glove and an old knife with a long, thin, flexible blade. "You mind if I help?"

"Knock yourself out." He was surprised that she knew where the glove and knife were kept. "I take it you've been through the house thoroughly."

She took a fish head in her gloved left hand and cut down to the backbone. "Not really. I'm an architecture student and I've mostly been working since I got here." She paused to give him time to say something, preferably to tell her who he was. But he was silent. "Anyway, I didn't see all of the house."

"But you saw the kitchen."

"Yes." She didn't know where he was going with this. She clamped her hand on the side of the fish and cut from the head down to the tail.

Jared got up and went to stand next to the drainboard as she flipped the fish over to cut the other side. He watched as she pulled the fillet away, leaving the skin attached at the tail. A few more quick slices and the fish was done, perfectly filleted.

He leaned back against the sink. "Who taught you to do that?"

"My father. He loves to go fishing, so we went."

"Was he any good?"

"Excellent." As she spoke she picked up another bass off the counter.

"Would you like a drink?"

"That would be nice," she said. Inside, she was jumping up and down. Jared Montgomery is making *me* a drink. Can I put this on my résumé?

"I'm afraid I don't know how to make appletinis."

At his condescending tone, the elation left her. She was glad she had her back to him, as she couldn't help the frown that ran across her face at his put-down. “That’s okay. Since I got to Nantucket all I’ve wanted to drink is rum. I like it with Coke and lots of lime.”

It was Jared’s turn to frown. It’s what he drank, when he wasn’t sipping rum straight, and it’s what his aunt Addy liked the most. Rum was what all the Kingsleys, male and female, drank.

“So what do you do?” Alix asked, and held her breath. How would he describe himself and what he did?

“I build things,” he said.

“Oh?” Her voice went up an octave. She lowered it. “Design and build?”

“Naw. I’m not fancy. I just run around in my pickup and build what I can.”

Alix paused in slicing the fish. It looked like he didn’t plan to tell her who he was. But did he have to flat-out lie? Did he actually think that a student of architecture wouldn’t know who he was? Wouldn’t recognize him? Could he be that naive? On the other hand, maybe he was just being modest. “Do you work here on Nantucket?” she asked.

“Sometimes. But I have a company off-island.”

“Do you?” She’d been in the lobby of the building in New York where his office was. Security wouldn’t let her get on the elevator, but she’d run her fingers over his name on the directory.

“Yes, and I need to get back to work, so

I'm leaving the island tomorrow morning. I probably won't be back while . . ."

"While I'm here?"

He gave a quick nod.

"I see," Alix said, and she was very much afraid that she did understand. She'd been told that "Mr. Kingsley" would be on the island all summer, but it looked like he'd decided to stay away. Why? Did he really have a job that needed to be done? Or was he leaving because he didn't want to be near a student? But maybe he didn't want to brag. Perhaps if she encouraged him he'd open up. "My father's an architect and he's done a lot of construction," she said. "What are you working on now?" She heard him pop the top on a can of Coke.

"Nothing important."

"Who designed what you're building?"

"Nobody anyone's ever heard of."

"Since I'm involved in architecture, I may know of him."

"They probably got the plan out of a magazine," he said. "Here's your drink. Want me to finish the fish?"

"Sure," she said. As she removed the glove and passed it to him, she took the drink he held out and met his eyes. What a liar, she thought.

What a beauty, he thought.

She went over to the table, sat down, and watched while he filleted the fish. Odd, she thought, that he cut it *exactly* the way her father had taught her to do it. Not a single stroke was different. There was a long, awkward pause. Maybe it would help if she directed him toward the small structures she'd seen hanging in his studio. "Nantucket is beautiful," she said.

"It is."

"Too bad you're not staying. I'd love to see more of the houses on the island. Actually, I like any buildings. Well, with the exception of concrete block structures, and a few others. Anyway, I saw what I think were two garden sheds on Main Street that took my breath away. White, octagonal, green domed roofs, linked by a garden seat. Quite extraordinary."

Jared said nothing. He wasn't about to get rooked into being a tour guide. She'd find out his profession soon enough, then she'd turn into a human question machine and drive him crazy. "How's your drink? Too strong?"

"I was wondering if you'd put any rum in it."

"That's —" Surprise made him stop talking.

"That's what?"

"It's just that that's what my aunt used to say."

"Oh," Alix said. "I'm sorry. I didn't know that. Reminders of her must be painful." She hesitated. "She was a nice woman."

"You remember her?"

Alix was startled at his question and wasn't sure what to reply. "I was here when I was four. Do you remember a lot from when you were that young?"

A happy family, he thought. Father alive; mother alive. There were no clouds in their lives back then. "I remember this house," he said, "and I remember Aunt Addy being in it."

There was a softness in his eyes that made her want to tell him the truth. "Did she sit in the family room and make something with her hands?"

For the first time he didn't look as though he'd just eaten something sour. "She did embroidery, and there are framed pieces around the house."

"And in the front parlor she had ladies to tea. I remember little cakes with yellow icing roses."

"Yes," Jared said, smiling. "She loved yellow roses."

"You must miss her a lot," Alix said softly.

"I do. I spent the last three months of her life with her. She was a grand lady." For a moment he looked at Alix. "You know how to fillet fish, but do you know how to cook them?"

"I'm no chef but I do know how to fry bass. And I can make hush puppies."

"With beer or milk?"

"Beer."

"And cayenne pepper in the batter?"

"Of course."

"There isn't much food in this kitchen, but I have onions and cornmeal in the guesthouse."

Alix realized that he was asking her to dinner. "Why don't you go get them and I'll . . ." She shrugged.

"That sounds good."

The instant he was out the door, Alix ran up the stairs to her bedroom. Her suitcases had arrived but she hadn't unpacked them. And the bags of clothes Izzy had bought for her were on the floor. But it would be too much to change clothes. Too obvious, too eager.

She ran to the bathroom to put on a little mascara and a blot of lipstick. Why was her face so shiny?! She used the pretty compact her mother had given her and toned down her skin.

She got back to the kitchen just as he opened the door. Their eyes met, but Alix turned away, her heart seeming to flutter. Too soon, she told herself. Too soon after Eric, too soon after meeting this illustrious man, too soon for everything.

He had a paper bag full of exactly what she needed to make hush puppies the way her father had taught her. It was interesting that he had the ingredients in his kitchen. Self-rising cornmeal and self-rising flour weren't usually to be found in a bachelor's kitchen.

Without thinking what she was doing, she reached up and pulled a big porcelain bowl out of the cabinet, then took a wooden spoon from a drawer.

"For someone who doesn't remember when she was four, you do seem to know where things are."

"I do," she said. "Izzy said it was creepy so I've kept quiet."

"I'm not easily creeped out," he said as he handed her an egg.

"Are you sure? What about horror movies? Or ghost stories?"

"Horror movies, especially ones with chain saws, turn me into a whimpering jellyfish, but ghost stories make me laugh."

Alix was pouring oil into a deep saucepan. "Laugh? Don't you believe in ghosts?"

"I believe in real ones, not the chain-rattling kind. So tell me what you do remember. Places? Things? People?" He was watching her intently as she mixed the batter.

"Some of all of it, I guess. I remember this kitchen well. I think I used to sit —" She put the bowl down and went to the table with its built-in seat. Beneath it was a drawer and she opened it. Inside was a thick tablet of drawing paper and an old cigar box that she knew was full of crayons. He peered over her shoulder as she lifted the cover of the pad.

The drawings Alix had done as a child were still there — and each one was of a building. Houses, barns, windmills, a rose arbor, a potting shed.

"It looks like I haven't changed," she said and turned to look at him. But he had walked away, and his back was to her. Again he was making sure she knew that he wanted nothing to do with her as a lowly student of architecture.

Part of her wanted to say that she knew who he was, but the bigger part didn't want to give him the satisfaction of knowing that she knew. If he wanted to think he was anonymous, so be it. She went back to the stove.

"Do you remember any people?" he asked, not looking at her as he put fish in a hot skillet. They were standing quite close together, not touching, but she could feel the warmth of him.

"Mainly just the older woman, who I assume was Miss Kingsley," Alix said. "And the longer I'm here, the more I seem to remember about her. She and I walked on a beach and I collected shells. Is it possible that I called her Aunt Addy?"

"Probably. It's what all the younger relatives called her. I did. Was anyone else with you? Not on the beach, but here in the house."

Alix held her hand above the pot of oil to see if it was hot enough before she began to drop in globs of batter. "Sometimes I . . ."

"Sometimes you what?"

"I remember hearing a man laugh. A very deep laugh and I liked it."

"That's all?"

"Sorry, Mr. Kingsley, but that is all I remember." She glanced up at him, her eyes asking him to invite her to use his first name, but he didn't respond. "What about you?"

"No," he said, then seemed to come out of his trance. "My laugh is high pitched, breaks glass, not deep at all."

She smiled at his self-deprecation. "I meant, who do you remember? Did you grow up on Nantucket?"

"Yes, but not in this house."

"Who gets it after my year is up?"

"Me," he said. "It nearly always goes to the eldest Kingsley son."

"Then I'm taking away your inheritance."

"Postponing it. Are these done?"

"Yes," Alix said as she took the hush puppies out and drained them on paper towels.

"What china do you want to use?"

"The wildflowers," she said without thinking, then looked at him in surprise. "Before I came here I told Izzy I didn't remember anything about being here. But it seems that I even remember the china patterns."

He was reaching up to a top cabinet and pulling down dishes that Alix knew she'd always liked.

"Maybe something bad happened later that made you forget."

"Possibly. I know my parents were separating then, so that could have traumatized me as a child. My dad and I have always been close. He and I have traveled all around the world to see the most magnificent buildings. Have you ever seen — ?"

"There's salad in the bag if you want some."

Alix had to turn away to hide a flush of anger that she knew was showing on her face. She wanted to say, "Okay, I get it. You're a famous architect and I'm a nobody student. You don't have to rub it in." She went to the liquor cabinet and busied herself with making a drink from one of the rum recipes taped on the back of the door. She didn't bother asking him what he liked.

Jared put the dishes and the hush puppies on the table, dumped salad in a bowl, and put out a bottle of dressing. Then he sat down and watched Alix at the liquor cabinet as she made some fruity drink. He liked her. He liked that she'd pitched in and cleaned the fish. Liked her ease at whipping up the batter for the bread. He liked the way she drank the rum. No giggles, no flirtiness. Just straightforward and good company.

Most of all, he liked how attracted he was to her. He hadn't expected that. He remembered her as an intense little girl sitting on the rug in the family room and piling up things his ancestors had brought home from their voyages around the world.

Back then he'd been unaware of how valuable the objects were. To him they were just things he'd seen all his life. Jared still remembered all those years ago how Dr. Huntley, the young man who'd recently been made the head of the NHS, the Nantucket Historical Society, had nearly passed out the first time he'd visited Aunt Addy and seen little Alix sitting on the floor.

"That child is playing with . . ." He'd had to sit down to get his breath. "That candlestick is early nineteenth century."

"Perhaps earlier," Aunt Addy had said calmly. "The Kingsley family lived on Nantucket long before this house was built and I'm sure they used candles."

The director was still pale. "She shouldn't be allowed to play with those things. She —"

Aunt Addy had just smiled at him.

"Where did you live?" Alix asked as she set two drinks on the table.

"What? Oh. Sorry, I was miles away. My mother and I lived in Madaket, on the water."

"I don't mean to be nosy, but why didn't you grow up in Kingsley House?"

Jared gave a little chuckle. "When Aunt Addy was a girl she found the man she was to marry in a compromising situation, knickers down, knees up, that sort of thing. My dad told me that she used her father's sympathy to get him to change his will to leave the house to her instead of to his son. Everyone thought that he would eventually come to his senses and change it back, but there was an accident and he died young, so Aunt Addy got the house instead of her brother."

"Was the family angry about that?"

"No. They were relieved. Her brother probably would have sold the place. He wasn't good with money and didn't care about the house. He would have let the roof cave in." What Jared wasn't telling her was that Caleb had worked with Addy to make it all happen. It was because of the two of them that Kingsley House had stayed in the family all these years.

"But now the house is to come back to a son who is very good with roofs."

"I like to think so," Jared said, smiling.

Alix could see the pride in his eyes and she thought about what he must have felt when he was told that his ownership was to be postponed for a whole year. "Is where you grew up a town?"

"Not like you mean. Madaket is more of a place than an actual town. But there's a restaurant there and of course there's the mall."

"A mall? What stores does it have?"

He smiled. "It's commonly referred to as a dump, but we have a big take-it-or-leave-it area and . . ." He shrugged. "It's Nantucket."

They ate in silence for a while and Alix began to think of the reality of being alone in a place where she knew no one. "What are the wedding facilities like on the island?"

He paused with a fork on the way to his mouth. "You're getting married?"

"No. My friend is, and . . ." She trailed off, her face red with embarrassment.

"What's wrong?"

"I told her she could have the wedding in the garden here. I shouldn't have done that. I don't own this house, you do. It was presumptuous of me."

Jared bit into another hush puppy. "These are good." He found he rather enjoyed the way she was looking at him in question, waiting for his answer. "You have my permission to have the wedding here. This house could use some music and laughter."

Alix smiled at him so warmly that he leaned his head toward her, almost as though he expected a kiss in thanks. But she turned away.

Jared pulled back. "I'll get Jose and his guys to clean the place up for you."

"They're the gardeners? I was worried that I'd have to mow and rake and everything else. Not that I couldn't do it, but I don't think I'd be good at it. I want to spend this summer working." She waited for him to be polite and ask what she'd be working on, but he said nothing.

Suddenly, Alix had had enough. It was clear that he didn't think the two of them shared a love of land and buildings. To him, she wasn't even worthy of telling the truth about his profession.

She knew he was physically attracted to her — a woman always knew that — but as sexy as he was, she wasn't interested. She didn't want to be just another one of the Great Jared Montgomery's conquests. Bottom lip or not, she liked a man as a whole. Not just a piece of him.

She stood up. "I'm sorry to leave you with cleanup detail, but I'm very tired and I want to go to bed. If I don't see you again, thank you for dinner, Mr. Kingsley." She said his name pointedly.

He stood up, looking as though he meant to shake her hand or kiss her cheek, but Alix turned away and left the room.

For a moment Jared stood there staring after her. He knew he couldn't be right, but it was almost as though he'd made her angry. How? By asking her about his aunt? That didn't make any sense.

He sat back down and picked up the pineapple and rum drink she'd made. It wasn't to his taste, but it reminded him of his great-aunt. As he poured himself a shot of very old rum to sip, he expected his grandfather to appear in the room and bawl him out, but there was only silence. It was just like the old man not to warn him that Alix Madsen was in the house, that she'd arrived early — and that she'd been "working." Designing some fanciful structure that a person would need a magic wand to be able to build?

As he leaned back in the chair with the drink, he ate the rest of the hush puppies. They were the best he'd ever had.

He knew it was thoroughly stupid of him to be attracted to his aunt Addy's beloved Alix. When she'd first been here, she was four and he was fourteen. She was a cute little girl who liked to sit on the family room floor and build things. After the NHS president had nearly come unglued to see the child piling up valuable scrimshaw, antique tea caddies from China, and netsuke from Japan, Jared had gone home and rummaged through the attic until he found his old box of Legos. His mother had insisted on running them through the dishwasher. He remembered how pleased she'd been that he was doing such a kind thing for a little girl. But back then, Jared hadn't exactly been a model son. His father, the sixth Jared, had died just two years before and he was still very angry about it. His mother had made him personally take the Legos to Alix.

The little girl had never seen the building blocks and had no idea what they were, so Jared got down on the rug and showed her how to use them. She'd been so pleased that when he was leaving, she threw her arms around his neck. Aunt Addy, sitting on the couch and watching her beloved Alix, said, "Jared, someday you're going to make an excellent father."

His grandfather Caleb, hovering in the background, snorted and said, "But he'll make a bad husband." Back then his grandfather didn't have much faith that Jared would do anything but spend his life in jail. As Jared had learned to do, he didn't react to his grandfather's comments when his aunt was near.

But Alix, who'd heard it all, looked up at Jared with serious eyes and said, "I would marry you." That had made Jared jump up, his face red, and Caleb had given his great bellow of a laugh.

Later, Jared saw the intricate Lego structure Alix had made, and he was impressed. Caleb said that Jared had never made anything that good when he was four years old. Alix gave him a bunch of flowers from Aunt Addy's garden to thank him for his gift. That night Jared went out with his buddies, got drunk, and ended up spending the night in jail — which wasn't unusual for him back then. He never saw little Alix again, as soon afterward her mother's first novel was accepted for publication. Victoria had immediately taken her daughter away, and never brought her back to Nantucket.

Jared's thoughts returned to the present. He thought it was definitely better that he leave the island. He'd tell Dilys about Alix, she'd introduce her to his cousin Lexie and her roommate, Toby, and within a week Alix would be deep in the Nantucket summer social whirl. And Jared would be back in New York creating . . . he didn't know what. And right now he was between girlfriends so he'd . . . Damn! He kept envisioning Alix's eyes, her mouth, her body.

This wasn't good. Alix Madsen was a young, innocent girl and he couldn't touch her. Yes, he'd better leave as soon as possible.

# Chapter Five

Alix was in bed, trying to keep her mind on a murder mystery she'd found in a table drawer, but the words seemed to blur. All she could think about was Jared Montgomery — or was his name Kingsley? Everything about him seemed to be a lie, up to and including his name.

Why did he have to lie like that? As she went over every word of their conversation, she saw how he'd eluded her many hints. If he didn't want to answer her questions, he could have said no. He could have —

Her cell phone rang and cut off her thoughts. It was her father. Why, oh why, had she told him that Montgomery was staying in the guesthouse?

She took a breath and tried to smile. "Dad!" she said cheerfully. "How are you?"

"What's wrong?"

"Wrong? Nothing is wrong. Why would you ask that?"

"Because I've known you all your life so I

know your false cheerfulness. What happened?"

"Nothing bad. It's just Izzy and her wedding. Both her mother and mother-in-law are making her miserable, so I told her I'd put on the wedding here. But how can I do that? What do I know about weddings?"

"You love a challenge and you'll figure it out. What's really bothering you?"

"That's it," she said. "I think making a wedding for someone else is impossible and I'm thinking about leaving Nantucket and returning home. I'm Izzy's maid of honor, so I need to help her choose cakes and flowers and everything else. Or maybe I'll stay with you for a while. Would that be all right?"

Ken took a moment before answering. "It's Montgomery, isn't it? Did he show up?"

Alix felt quick tears come to her eyes, but she wasn't going to let her father know. "He did," she said, "and we had dinner together. He cleans bass just like you do."

"What did he say when you told him you were a fan of his?"

"Nothing."

"Alix, he must have said something, so what was it?"

"He didn't say anything because I didn't tell him. He pretended he wasn't who he is."

"I want to hear every word of this. Don't leave out anything."

Alix told him as succinctly as she could

manage. "Maybe I would have been a pest to him or whatever he thought I'd be — if that's the reason he didn't tell me who he is — but to just sit there and tell one lie after another was . . . was . . ."

"Despicable," Ken said, and she could hear the anger in his voice.

"It's okay, Dad. He's a big shot and I can see why he wouldn't want to announce to a student that he's *the* Jared Montgomery. He was probably worried that I'd kiss his ring or do some groupie thing. And to be fair, I would have. Anyway, it doesn't matter. He's leaving in the morning and he won't be back while I'm here."

"Are you saying that you'll be alone in that big house for an entire year?" Ken asked. "You know no one on that island and you've promised to put on a wedding for your friend. How are you going to do that?"

"Dad, you're supposed to cheer me up, not make me feel worse."

"I'm being a realist."

"Me too," Alix said, "and that's why I think I should return to the mainland. Besides, this house belongs to Mr. Kingsley and he wants it back, if for no other reason than for the big sink."

"Who's Mr. Kingsley?"

"Jared Montgomery."

"He told you to call him Mr. Kingsley?" Ken was aghast.

"No, Dad. That's what the lawyer called him. But I called him that and he didn't correct me."

"That upstart!" Ken said with his teeth clenched. "Look, honey, I have something I have to do. Promise me that you won't leave the island before I talk to you again."

"All right," she said, "but what are you planning to do? You aren't thinking of calling his office, are you?"

"Not his office, no."

"Dad, please, you're going to make me sorry I told you. Jared Montgomery is a very important person. When it comes to architecture, he's in the stratosphere. It's understandable if he doesn't want to deal with a nothing, nobody student. He —"

"Alixandra, it may be a cliché to say this, but you have more talent in your little finger than that man has in his whole body."

"You're sweet but that's not true. When he was my age, he —"

"It's a wonder he *lived* to be your age. All right, Alix, how about this? I'll give him twenty-four hours to come to his senses. If he's the same this time tomorrow and your feelings are still being hurt, then I'll come and get you. And furthermore, I'll help you and Izzy with the wedding. Is that a deal?"

Alix thought about telling her father that she was a grown woman and could take care of herself, but she knew it wouldn't do any good. "That sounds like a bet you don't want to lose," she said, trying to sound cheerful. She had no hope that Jared Montgomery was going to change anything about himself.

"Good! I'll call you this time tomorrow. Love ya."

"And I love you back," Alix said, and hung up. She was tempted to call Izzy and tell her there was going to be a change in the wedding venue, but she didn't.

Jared was bent over his drawing board, working on what had to be his fiftieth sketch for the house in California, when his cell rang. Since so few people had his private number, he always answered it.

Right away he recognized the *very* angry voice of Kenneth Madsen.

"When I met you, you were a fourteen-year-old juvenile delinquent. You'd been in and out of the local jail so many times they knew your breakfast order by heart. Your poor dear mother was on six medications because you were driving her insane. Am I right? Am I saying anything wrong?"

"No, you have it right," Jared said.

"And who straightened you out? Who dragged you out of bed in the mornings and put you into a truck and made you work?"

"You did," Jared said meekly.

"Who searched under your bad-boy act and found your talent as a designer?"

"You did."

"Who paid for your goddamn schooling?"

"You and Victoria did."

"Right! Alix's father *and* her mother," Ken said. "Yet you made our daughter cry?! Is that how you repay us?"

"I don't know what I did to make her cry," Jared said honestly.

"You don't know?" Ken took a breath. "Do you think my daughter is stupid? Is that what you think?"

"No, sir, I never thought that."

"She knows who you are. She saw you on the day she arrived and she recognized you right away. Heaven help me, but you're some sort of hero to her."

"Oh, Lord," Jared said. "I didn't know. I thought . . ."

"Thought what?!" Ken half yelled, then calmed somewhat. "Look, Jared, I understand that she's just a student and that someone like you might see her as a pest, but I'll be damned if you're going to treat her like one."

"I didn't mean to," Jared said.

Ken took a couple of breaths. "My daughter only agreed to go to Nantucket so she could spend the time there assembling a portfolio of designs. Right now it's hard for me to stomach the idea, but she wants to apply for a job at *your* firm. But tonight you —" He had to pause for a moment. "So help me, Jared Montgomery Kingsley the bloody

Seventh, if you ever again make my daughter cry I'll make you regret it. You understand me?"

"Yes, sir."

"And if you *do* spend any time with my daughter I don't want your usual shenanigans you pull with women. This is my daughter and I want her treated with respect. You get what I mean?"

"Yes, sir, I do."

"Do you think you can be *nice* to a girl *and* leave her clothes on? Is that possible with you?"

"I'll try," Jared said.

"Do more than try, *do* it!" Ken clicked off the phone.

Jared just stood there, feeling like he had when he was a teenager and Ken, the man who'd been a second father to him, had bawled him out. Again. Just like old times.

Jared went downstairs, started to reach for the rum, but knew that wouldn't calm him down. He found a bottle of tequila, and had two shots before he allowed himself to think about what had happened tonight.

He went into the living room and sat down and his mind went back to when he was, as Ken had said, a fourteen-year-old juvenile delinquent.

As Aunt Addy and Ken later told Jared, Kenneth Madsen had come to the island to find his wife — who he thought would be living in abject poverty and therefore glad to see him — to let her know that he'd think about taking her back. He might even forgive her for her one-night stand with his business partner, followed by her flight to Nantucket with their small daughter, Alix. Eventually.

The truth was that he missed her and his daughter so much he could hardly function.

But what he found on Nantucket wasn't what he'd expected. His wife had written a novel, it had been accepted for publication, and she was planning to divorce him.

She was fabulously happy; he was fabulously depressed.

After Victoria took little Alix and left the island, Addy suggested that Ken stay in the guesthouse until he recovered from his melancholia. After he'd been there a couple of months and showed no signs of going back to his architecture business or even of coming back to life, she said he could renovate an old house owned by the Kingsley family.

"But I can't afford to pay *you,*" she said. "I can just afford materials."

"That's all right," Ken said, "my former business partner is footing my bills. He owes me big time."

Addy waited for him to continue but Ken didn't say any more about why his partner owed him. "You can hire workmen on the island, but you'll have to pay them. On the other hand, my nephew Jared is young and inexperienced, but he'll work for free. But then it doesn't matter because I don't think you can handle him." She looked Ken up and down in a way that said he wasn't man enough to deal with the boy.

Ken'd had enough of being treated like less than a man. He said he'd take on the kid.

From the first meeting, Ken and Jared were a match. Ken's life was a mess, but then so was Jared's. A big, angry teenager and an elegant, angry young architect were a perfect pair. Ken's attitude was that if Jared didn't behave he was out of a job. Since the job was a free remodel of the falling-down old house he and his mother were living in, Jared felt he had to stay with it. Besides, Ken listened to what Jared had to say about how he thought the house should be changed.

Jared knew nothing about construction, and at first he'd worked every day with a hang-over. At fourteen he was on his way to being an alcoholic. To his mind at that time, drinking was okay because most of the kids he ran with did drugs. Jared's teenage mind thought that if he stayed away from drugs he could drink all he wanted to.

But being hungover on a construction site was bad. He'd ended up with smashed thumbs and one accident after another until he'd finally learned to say no to going out at night with his buddies. It hadn't been easy as they told him what they thought of him.

"Selling out to the other side," they'd said.

Ken had helped, even though his "help" hadn't been gentle. He didn't put up with any nonsense, never felt sorry for Jared's circumstances, and made him work no matter what.

One day after the boys had skidded off in their cars, their catcalls that Jared was a wimp still hanging in the air, Ken said, "You might make a man after all. Who would have guessed?"

Gradually, Jared began to want to prove himself. Ken stayed on the island full time for nearly three years and the two of them worked construction constantly. One time Jared saw Ken crying and he'd stepped away, not wanting to embarrass him. Later he found out that the divorce papers had come that day. "It was all my fault," Ken said over his sixth beer. "I was the one to ruin it all. I thought I was of a higher class than pretty little Victoria Winetky and she knew it."

That night Jared had to throw a drunken Ken over his shoulder, put him in his pickup, drive him back to the guesthouse, and put him in bed. The next day neither of them acknowledged what had happened and they never spoke of it.

Eventually, Ken recovered enough that he wanted to go back to architecture — and by then he'd discovered that he liked teaching. But by that time he and Jared were like father and son and the thought of separation hurt. "I can't stay here," Ken said. "Victoria won't allow Alix to return to Nantucket. That book of hers sold millions and she says she has an image to uphold. Between you and me, I think Victoria doesn't want Addy to take over Alix." He looked at Jared. "If I want to be part of my daughter's future, I have to go back to the mainland and set up a life there. I'll come back when I can."

Jared worked to conceal his pain. A few years before he'd met Ken, his father had gone out on his boat one day and never returned. It was days before they found him. He'd had a heart attack in his sleep. Jared had loved his father to the point of worship and losing him had brought out the worst in the boy. He'd always been a big kid, nearly six feet when his father died, and Jared started drinking just months later. Fistfights, racing cars, vandalism — you name it, he'd done it. His mother, trying to deal with her own grief, had no control over him.

Then Ken, also angry at the world, had stepped in and taken over.

When Jared said goodbye to Ken, he thought that would be the end. Nantucketers were used to summer visitors. They came and went and you never saw them again.

But Ken had returned often. He was the one who got Jared into college, then into architecture school. And when Jared made his mark by building his final project, it had been Ken who left his office and his classroom, strapped on a tool belt, and helped Jared build it.

Yes, Jared owed Ken, and he owed Victoria because she was part of his life too. And now he owed their daughter.

He stood there for a moment and all he knew for sure was that he wanted to talk to his grandfather.

Jared was sitting in the family room of Kingsley House. He hadn't turned on any lights, but he didn't need to. He knew that if he sat there long enough, his grandfather would show up.

When he did, Jared didn't even look up. "I messed up. Really big. Ken is angry at me, and when Victoria hears what happened she's going to tear me apart, piece by piece. I doubt if I'll live through it. Our friendship certainly won't survive it." He looked toward the window at his grandfather. "If you'd only told me she was here, I could have escaped."

"Young Alix has always been a considerate person," Caleb said.

When Caleb started to say more, Jared cut him off. "If you're about to tell me some of that reincarnation mumbo-jumbo, don't do it. I don't want to hear."

"I never try to put knowledge into that hard head of yours. You only believe what you can see and touch. Turn on the light and look inside that far cabinet."

Jared hesitated, almost afraid of what he'd see. Reluctantly, he got up, switched on the light, and opened the cabinet. What he saw wasn't what he'd expected. Inside was a model of what looked to be a little chapel, complete with bell tower.

Right away he could see the influence of his own work on the design, but he also saw that of Ken Madsen. But most important, it was a new and fresh design, Alix's own voice, unique to her.

"Lost your tongue?" Caleb asked.

"Pretty much."

"She made it to show you. But you —"

"You don't have to rub it in. What made her choose this to work on?"

"I made sure she saw an old photo."

Jared nodded. "The one of Aunt Addy and Grandma Bethina laughing together?"

"Yes, that one."

He picked up the little model and held it on the flat of his hand, turning it around to study it. "This is better than I would have done." He put it back in the cabinet, then took out her freehand sketches and went through the pages. "She's good. Three of these are buildable."

"She and her friend broke into your house."

"They what?" Jared was still looking at the drawings.

"What is that heretical thing you say about heroes and Our Father?"

Jared had to think for a moment to understand that one. His grandfather often mixed up old and new slang. "Hero worship."

"That's it. Alix used to feel that way about you, but after tonight I don't think she does."

"That's exactly what I didn't want to happen," Jared said. "Some kid looking at me with big puppy-dog eyes, thinking I hung the moon. That's impossible to live up to."

"And there you were, lusting after Ken's daughter."

"I did no such thing!" Jared said angrily, but then he grinned. "Well, maybe I did. She's a beauty — and built. I'm only human."

"You like that her father taught her what you showed him about fish."

"Which my dad taught me."

"And *I* taught all of you," Caleb said, and the two men smiled at each other.

"So now what do I do?" Jared asked.

"Apologize to her."

"And she's going to forgive me? I just say I'm sorry and that's it?" Jared hesitated. "I know. I could give her a job at my office in New York. She could —"

"You could help her with the wedding."

"Oh, no! I don't know anything about that. If she wants to stay here I'll get the office to send her some work and I'll . . . I'll buy her a drafting table. Or a CAD system. Maybe she could use the guesthouse as an office. I'll go back to New York and . . ." He broke off at the look on his grandfather's face and sighed. "What are you plotting against me?"

"She's here alone. She knows no one on this island."

"I said I'd get Dilys to —"

"Young Alix is planning on leaving for good," Caleb said.

"Ken and Victoria want her here." Jared took a breath. If he was the reason she left, everyone would be angry at him. "When is she planning to leave?"

"I heard her father — the man who made you what you are, I might add — ask her to give him twenty-four hours to change things. Did he mention that time allotment to you?"

"No, he didn't. At least I don't think he did, but then he yelled a lot. It was hard to keep up with every word."

"Good man. Protective of his child. It looks like Kenneth's leaving it up to you to figure out something to do to make her stay. If she weren't his daughter, what would you do to keep her here?"

"Go upstairs and get in bed with her."

Caleb grimaced. "In this case, that's not an option."

"When it comes to women, I'm better in bed than out of it," Jared said in a matter-of-fact way.

"There must be something you know how

to give to women outside of bed."

"You're talking about your old-fashioned ideas of courting, aren't you? And when have I had *time* for that? I've worked seven days a week since I was a teenager. I only stopped to be with Aunt Addy. As for gifts, my assistant took care of that, usually from Tiffany's. Maybe —"

"No jewelry."

Jared stood there in silence, thinking, but he came up with nothing.

"How did a descendant of mine get so smart yet so dumb?" Caleb asked in disbelief.

"Maybe we better not talk about stupid acts of the Kingsley men. Tell me again what happened to your ship that was so horrible that you aren't allowed to leave this earth?"

Caleb glowered, then shook his head and smiled. "All right, we're equally befuddled when it comes to women. However, I'm trying to teach you what I've learned in my lifetime."

"Which spans a few years."

"More than a few of them. How about flowers?" Caleb asked.

"Okay, so tomorrow morning I go buy her a bunch of flowers. That's easy."

"In my experience, 'easy' doesn't win a woman. They like men to climb mountains for them."

"Right. And get the single, rare blossom on the top. Of course nowadays we know doing that will wipe out an entire species."

Caleb grimaced. "And you wonder why women don't hang around you."

"For your information —"

"I know," Caleb said, "you leave them, they don't leave you. I think she should wake up to find flowers."

"Where would I get them? It's too early in the season to pick them in the garden. Think I should break into a florist shop?" He was trying to add some humor to the whole thing, but Caleb wasn't smiling.

"It wouldn't be the first time you'd done something like that," Caleb said.

"No, but it's been a while."

"If only we knew someone who grew flowers even when it's cold outside."

Jared blinked at Caleb as understanding came to him. "No," he said, then stood up. "No, no, no. I won't do it."

"But —"

"I'm not going to. Lexie will give me hell and I don't want to hear it. I've had enough of being yelled at today." Jared left the room and went to the back door in the kitchen.

Caleb put himself in front of the door.

"No," Jared said again and reached through his long-deceased grandfather to turn the knob, then went outside.

Jared got all the way to the guesthouse before he stopped. He mumbled curse words as he stood there, knowing that his grandfather was watching, and worse, knowing that he was *right.* As Jared went toward the gate, he raised his hand in a very old gesture.

Caleb chuckled. He'd known his grandson would do the right thing. He just had to be pushed hard — something Caleb was good at doing.

Jared's cousin Lexie lived just a few houses away and he hoped that at this hour she'd be asleep so he could use that as an excuse not to bother her. Last summer he'd restored an old greenhouse on the property. For years it had been buried under several feet of vines and briars and poison ivy. He'd tried to talk her into letting him bring in a dozer and level it all. "Then I'll buy you a brand-new Lord and Burnham greenhouse," he'd said.

But neither Lexie or her roommate, Toby, would have any of it.

"You've been away from Nantucket too long," Lexie said. "We were recycling and reusing before it became fashionable."

"My whole house is reused and recycled," he'd snapped, not liking being accused of having off-islander tendencies.

In the end, the two women won because Jared had made the mistake of asking Toby what she wanted to do. Toby was tall, slim, blond, with a dreamy look in her blue eyes. Ethereal, fragile. There was an otherworldly air about her that could turn grown men into mush.

"I rather like the idea of an older greenhouse," she'd said as she smiled up at Jared.

"Then I'll do it," he said.

Lexie had thrown up her hands. "I ask and you argue. Toby asks and you give in instantly."

"What can I say, little cousin?" Jared said. "Toby is magic."

"Whatever," Lexie said. "If it gets you to do the work and pay for it, that's all that matters."

Toby worked in the best florist shop on the island, while Lexie was a PA to a man she described as a "helpless idiot." When he wasn't on Nantucket and demanding her attention, Lexie planned to help Toby raise flowers that they could sell to shops around town.

Jared had sent a text message to Jose Partida, who owned Clean Cut Landscaping, and he hadn't blinked an eye at the daunting job of cleaning up the poisonous tangle.

When the debris was cleared away they saw that there wasn't much left of the old greenhouse, but Lexie expected her cousin to put the pieces back together.

"This thing is rotten," Jared said. "A new one —"

"I want *you* to do it," Lexie said. "I want you to be a Kingsley — if you can remember how — and put it back together yourself. Or have you become too much of an off-islander to put on a tool belt?"

For a moment Jared thought about strangling his cousin, and he pondered ignoring her challenge, but he didn't. Instead, he'd called New York and postponed what he was doing for a rich client. He went to the drawing board in the guesthouse and spent three days designing a garden for flowers and berries.

As Lexie had requested, Jared put on a tool belt and worked with contractor Twig Perkins's men to put the old greenhouse back into working order. They also installed raised beds, made a compost area, and added a seating place for clients.

When it was all done, Toby stood on tiptoe and kissed his cheek. "Thank you," she said.

After Toby left, Lexie said, "If you're so enraptured with her, why don't you ask her out?"

"Toby? That would be like dating an angel."

"I get it. And you're too much of a devil."

"At last someone truly understands me. I get any thanks from *you*?" He tapped his finger on his cheek.

"That's not the side Toby kissed," Lexie said as she planted one on him.

"I'm never going to wash the cheek *she* touched ever again."

Lexie groaned. "Come on and help us fill the pots full of dirt."

Jared held up his hands. "These were made

for holding tall glasses of beer. You girls are on your own from now on."

That had been over a year ago, and since then the two roommates had been able to supplement their income with the flowers they grew.

Jared tapped on their front door lightly. All the lights were out so he doubted if they would hear him. He'd have to wait until morning to get the flowers — which meant that he wouldn't get told off by Lexie. He didn't know why he let his grandfather goad him into doing things he didn't want to. Ever since he was a kid —

The door opened and there stood Toby, her long blond hair in a fat braid down her back, wearing a white robe with little pink flowers on it. He was relieved it wasn't his opinionated cousin. "I screwed up with Ken's daughter and I need flowers."

Toby just nodded and stepped outside. "Let's go around the house so we don't wake Lexie."

"Plymouth on island?" Jared asked. Roger Plymouth was Lexie's boss and when he was on the island she was worked nearly to death. According to her he couldn't tie his shoelaces by himself. He lived in a mansion out on Polpis Road, arrived and left on his own plane, and none of Lexie's friends or family had ever seen him. They teased her that he didn't actually exist.

"Yes, he's here," Toby said, "and she's exhausted. He calls her night and day. He wants her to move into his guesthouse but she won't do it. So what did you do to mess things up with Ken's daughter?"

"Lied to her," Jared said. "I told her I was a building contractor, but it turns out she knew what I do for a living. She's an architecture student and she's good."

"Since she's Ken's daughter, that's no surprise. But wouldn't she have found out about you anyway?"

"Yes, but I meant to be gone by the time she arrived. She came early and walked into the kitchen and caught me off guard. I thought we had a nice time. We ate dinner together. If I'd admitted my profession, it would have turned into work. Or at least that's my excuse."

"It's not a bad one. I've heard worse." They were at the back greenhouse door and Jared held it open while she entered first. She turned on some soft lights that were hidden at the top of the glass wall. Before them was a long expanse of flowers and greenery, and flats full of seedlings, all of it in perfect condition.

"Looks good," Jared said.

"Yes, it does, but then we had a superlative architect design it for us."

"I don't think that's the word Alix would use about me right now. Her dad said I'd made her want to leave the island."

"Was he *very* angry at you?" Toby picked up a trug and removed cutters from a jar of alcohol and started down the aisle.

"Furious. If I'd been there he would have shot me. After he ran a truck over me. I think I made her cry."

"Oh, Jared, I'm so sorry. For both of you. You must take her some roses and of course we'll cut some daffodils." She opened a big wooden door against the back wall and revealed a refrigerator full of cut flowers.

"When did you get the fridge?"

"For my birthday. My father asked what I wanted and this was it."

"Is your mother still angry at you for staying on the island?"

Toby gave a little smile. "Oh, yes. She barely speaks to me."

At that, she and Jared exchanged looks. Toby's mother was a harridan and her not talking was no punishment.

"Any advice on getting Alix to forgive me?"

"Spend some time together and let her get to know you," Toby said.

"I'm going to see Dilys tomorrow."

"Perfect. Take Alix with you."

"And I want her to meet you and Lexie."

"I'd be honored," Toby said and looked up at him, her hands full of little pink roses. "You like her, don't you?"

He followed her outside and watched as

she used the light from the greenhouse to cut daffodil blooms. "She's just a kid. I was drinking and driving when she was just four years old."

"We girls have a habit of growing up."

"And you do it very well," Jared said, smiling at her.

She handed him the basket of flowers. "Put some outside her door. Do you know how to make pancakes?"

"I know how to drive to Downyflake."

"Good enough." Toby walked back to the greenhouse, checked the thermometer, and turned out the lights.

"How's your love life?" Jared asked. "Weren't you dating . . . Who was that?"

"The eldest Jenkins boy, and 'boy' is the key word."

"I used to date a cousin of his. She was —" He didn't finish that thought.

"Not someone you'd take home to meet the family?"

"Toby, you're a born diplomat. Can't Lexie fix you up with someone?"

"I'm fine," Toby said. "Really, I am."

"Waiting for Prince Charming?"

"Aren't all women? And you're waiting for Cinderella."

"Actually," Jared said slowly, "I'm rather hoping to find the Evil Queen. I think she'd be much more fun."

They laughed together.

# Chapter Six

When Alix awoke, her first thought was to wonder if Montgomery-Kingsley had left the island yet. Has he gone back to his pickup and his project that's being constructed from a plan in a magazine? she thought. She couldn't help feeling a resurgence of anger at his lies.

She got out of bed and glanced at the tall portrait of Captain Caleb, but she didn't really see it. No feathery kisses this morning.

She went into the bathroom to shower and wash her hair. Now what do I do? she wondered as she lathered. Being lied to by HRH Montgomery shouldn't make any difference to being on Nantucket. Before she came, she hadn't even known he was on the island. And never in her life had she thought that she'd meet the man in person. Of course she'd planned to apply for a job in his firm, but so had most of the other students.

She got out of the shower, blow-dried her hair, pulled it back, put on a touch of makeup, then went back to the bedroom to get dressed. The clothes Izzy had bought for her were still in their bags in a corner of the room. She emptied one from Zero Main onto the end of the bed, opened the tissue paper, and couldn't help smiling. The clothes were simple, and of the most exquisite fabrics she'd ever seen. How very Nantucket, she thought. Just like the houses. There were two shirts, a knit top, a scarf, black linen trousers, and a box containing some turquoise earrings.

"Might as well go out and see this island," she said aloud and glanced at the big portrait. "What do you think, Captain? The blue shirt or the peach one?"

Alix wasn't surprised when the collar on the blue shirt moved. It had been folded so it made sense that it would go back into place. But Alix preferred to think that the Captain had done it. "Thanks," she said. Just thinking that she wasn't alone in the big house made her feel better. That her housemate had died over two hundred years ago wasn't something she was going to think about.

When she was fully dressed, she took a breath and opened the door. The first thing she saw was a daffodil on the floor. Under it was a large white envelope.

Her first thought was that her dad had sent it to her. Second thought was that maybe Eric had found her.

Opening it, she saw the distinctive lettering that came from years and years of drafting.

Please accept my apology for the misunderstanding. Jared Montgomery Kingsley VII

Alix stared at the note. The seventh! Who had a name that was the seventh one?

But of course, his name wasn't the issue. Last night he had flat-out lied to her about what he did for a living. He'd known she was coming and that she was a student of architecture, so he'd done everything to keep from talking to her about what they both loved.

There were more flowers on the stairs and she picked them up one by one, and by the time she got to the bottom, she was smiling. She took them into the kitchen, knew where the vases were kept, and filled one with water. The cheerful daffodils looked lovely on the kitchen table.

She glanced out the back window at the guesthouse but all the lights were off. He's still sleeping, she thought, and went into the family room.

He was sitting in one of the big chairs, his long legs stretched out, holding a newspaper open in front of him. For a moment she stared at his profile and couldn't help the little flutter that happened to her heart. Forget that he was brilliant at his career; as a man he was a gorgeous specimen.

When he turned and saw her, there was a flash of light in his eyes, as though he saw her as a woman. But then he changed and he looked at her as . . . well, as her father did.

Should have worn the peach shirt, she thought.

"Good morning," he said. "Sleep well?"

"All right," she answered.

He folded the newspaper, put it on a table, and picked up a bouquet of little pink roses. "These are for you."

She stepped forward to take them, but when her hand came near to touching his, he jerked back. She turned away to hide her frown. "I'll get a vase and put these in it." Okay, she thought. Last night he'd made it clear that there was to be no talking about architecture, and now it seemed there was to be no touching.

"I'm sorry about lying to you about my job," he said from behind her. He'd followed her into the kitchen. "I just thought . . ."

"That I'd try to make you into my teacher?" She almost smiled at the way he'd called what he did a "job."

"Actually, yes." He gave a little half smile.

Alix did her best to not look at his lower lip and the way it curved across his teeth. She turned her back on him so he wouldn't see what she was sure was in her eyes.

"How about if I take you to Downyflake for

breakfast?"

There was something in the way he said it that put her off. It was as if he thought he *had* to apologize, *had* to take her out. Did he think that because she was living in *his* house that they had to spend time together — even if he didn't want to?

She looked back at him and gave a big smile. That the smile didn't reach her eyes wasn't her fault. "Actually, I have some schoolwork to do, so I think I'll stay here. There are some bagels in the fridge."

"I ate them," he said, and there was annoyance in his tone.

I bet he's not used to women refusing anything from him, Alix thought. "I'll go out and get some more."

"You can't live on bagels." There was the beginning of a frown on his face.

Alix couldn't help it as her smile started to become genuine. "I bet Nantucket sells food besides bagels. I could probably even find a restaurant in the downtown area."

"Downyflake has doughnuts. Made fresh every morning."

"Oh," Alix said, as that did sound good.

"How much of the island have you seen?" he asked. "From the ferry to here? That's just a small part of it."

Alix just stood there looking at him. Something about what he was saying wasn't ringing true. What had made him change? Last night he'd refused to tell anything about himself, and he'd said he was leaving the island. Today he was handing her flowers and apologies. Why? "I'll rent a car and —"

Jared rolled his eyes skyward. "I'm sorry I lied. All right? Nantucket is my home. The place where I get away from people asking me how I come up with my ideas, or what I plan for the future. And students are the worst! I had one of them ask me if I had any words of wisdom for him. Wisdom? What am I? Some Old Testament prophet? And female students —" He broke off and took a breath. "I apologize. Last night you caught me off guard. I had a horrible vision of having to answer questions and . . . and other things."

Alix stood there blinking at him. He'd just said everything she'd planned to do, up to and including the "other things." While she'd been making the model of the chapel she'd imagined how he'd tell her it was great, then they'd . . . Well, she'd finally get to taste that lower lip of his.

Of course she couldn't tell him any of that. "I need time away from work too," she said, and knew that now she was doing the lying. She'd planned to double her workload while she was on Nantucket.

"So how about if we go to breakfast and make plans for your stay here? I'll show you where the grocery is and Marine Home and some other essential places."

"Okay," she said. "And I promise to ask you no questions about architecture."

"Ask me anything you want," he said.

His words didn't fit his tone. He sounded like he was saying she could hit him with a baseball bat whenever she wanted to. "All right," she said seriously, "if you could pass on one bit of wisdom to a student, what would it be?"

"I . . ." he said, struggling with an answer.

"I was kidding," Alix said. "It was a joke."

He was looking at her as though he couldn't make her out. He opened the back door. "Mind if we go in my pickup?"

"I've spent half my life in one," Alix said, but he didn't answer.

His truck was old and red, and there was a cooler and a big toolbox in the back. The inside of the cab had sand and dirt in it, but no trash. The seats were worn but in good condition.

He backed out onto Kingsley Lane and headed down the way she and Izzy had walked in. The narrow street was quiet.

At the end, just before he turned onto Main, he nodded toward a house on the right. "My cousin Lexie lives there with her roommate, Toby, and they raise flowers to sell."

"Is that where you got the daffodils and roses?"

"Yes," he said, smiling. "Toby cut them for me."

"Did he ask why you wanted them?"

"She. Toby's real name is . . . I don't remember what it is, but she's always been called Toby. She's only twenty-two and she's always spent summers here with her parents, but a couple of summers ago, when they left, she stayed."

She was looking at him as he drove, his scraggly beard and hair making him look older than the thirty-six she knew he was. "You sound like you're in love with her."

Jared smiled. "Everyone is in love with Toby. She's very sweet."

Alix looked out the window at the beautiful procession of houses on Main. The cobblestones were jolting the car so much that she had to hold on to the door handle. In spite of the beauty around her, she couldn't help feeling deflated. Since the moment she first saw Jared Montgomery standing in his boat and smiling at some girl in shorts that were much too short, she'd been on a high. She'd assumed she was going to learn from him, work with him. And that night as she'd reread her poem, she'd even thought of having an affair with him. It would be something to tell her grandchildren. Those thoughts had driven her so that she forgot about her boyfriend dumping her and about her fear of spending a year alone where she knew no one.

But, gradually, everything she'd imagined had dropped down through the cracks. No talking of architecture to this illustrious man. And certainly no hanky-panky with him. He seemed to be attracted to her, but jumped away when her hand almost touched his. He probably had an unbreakable rule against students, but now he was melting into the seat at the mention of some very young girl named Toby — whom everyone loved.

"Are you always this quiet?" he asked. Before them was the glorious town of Nantucket, one divine building beside another. He halted at a stop sign and turned right. They went past a pretty little bookstore, then a magnificent church. It was a street full of houses, each one fascinating.

"It's like going into the past," she said. "I can see why you come here to escape. I think maybe my mother visited here, and maybe rather often."

Jared looked at her quickly. Victoria had been coming to Nantucket every August since he was a kid. She was beautiful and fun and he'd loved every minute he spent with her. But he was well aware that her daughter didn't know that she came to the island. "This is my place of privacy," Victoria had often said. Caleb said, "This is where she steals her plots." On the first day of every August, Aunt Addy handed Victoria one of the journals that had been written by the

Kingsley women over the centuries. For the rest of the month, Victoria would spend the mornings reading the antiquated handwriting and making an outline for her next novel. She skipped the boring bits about how many quarts of pickles the women put up, and went right to the drama and excitement.

Victoria had never wanted anyone to know that she — as Caleb said — "stole" her plots, so she kept her visits to Nantucket a secret from her friends, her publishing house, and especially her daughter. But the secret was relative, as everyone on the island knew about it. For eleven months of the year, Kingsley House hosted Addy's committee meetings and good works, but in August — while Alix stayed with her father — the house rang with music and dancing and laughter.

Jared came back to the present. "Here's a bakery," he said to Alix at the next stop sign, "and they do wedding cakes."

"And Toby does flowers," Alix said. "I'm going to talk to my friend Izzy, but I don't think I'm going to stay. It's just that . . ."

He waited for her to finish, but she didn't. Great! he thought. If she doesn't stay, everyone will be angry at *me.* His grandfather was convinced that Alix held some key to finding out what had happened to his precious, long lost Valentina. Ken wanted his daughter to assemble a portfolio of work. And Victoria was the worst. She called frequently and though she never came out and said so, he knew she wanted to see Aunt Addy's own personal journals, which were hidden somewhere in the house.

Besides them, Lexie would give Jared hell for scaring Alix off, and even Toby would probably be sad. And no doubt every relative on the island would say that Jared had run her off because he wanted his house back.

Any way he looked at it, Alix leaving before the year was up was bad.

Alix was looking out the windshield as they went down the streets and around two English-style roundabouts, one of which was called a rotary. Wherever they went, she was amazed by the courtesy of the drivers. Jared motioned to any vehicle that was stuck on a side street to go ahead of him and all the drivers waved back their thanks. He stopped for all pedestrians, who also raised their hands in gratitude. Cars, people, bicycles, road-crossing critters, were all given spaces and all actions were acknowledged with courtesy and thanks.

They pulled into the parking lot of a pretty little building with a big doughnut above the door. DOWNYFLAKE was painted on it.

"Why's it called that?"

"I have no idea," Jared said. "You can ask Sue."

He opened the door for her and they entered a homey-looking restaurant that Alix immediately liked. And she had her first glimpse of what it meant to have grown up on an island. Jared knew *everyone.* He said hello to the staff and to nearly every table full of people.

"Sit anywhere," a pretty woman with a menu said.

"Thanks, Sue," Jared answered and went left to a booth by the windows. He stopped to exchange greetings and comments about deer and boats and fish with a group of men sitting at a large round table, then took his place across from Alix.

"Sorry about that. I've been away for days and I needed to catch up. Hi, Sharon," he said to a cute, tall, slim waitress.

"You get back last night?" she asked.

She had a lovely Irish accent and she handed Alix a menu as she poured coffee for him. Alix nodded yes for the coffee. When she left, Alix looked at the menu. "What's good?"

"Everything."

"I think I'll have the blueberry pancakes and a couple of doughnuts."

He turned, nodded to Sharon, and when she returned, Alix gave her order. Jared said nothing.

"You aren't ordering?" Alix asked when the waitress left.

"I always get the same thing and they just bring it."

"I can't imagine living somewhere that a restaurant knows your order."

He glanced out the window for a moment. "When I'm in New York, sometimes I get so homesick I think I'm going to evaporate."

"What do you do then?"

"If at all possible I get on a plane and come home. Aunt Addy was always here and always up to something, and my —" He stopped talking. He'd been about to mention his grandfather — which was unusual, as that had been an unbroken taboo all his life.

But it was as though Alix read his mind. "Izzy said that Nantucket was one of the most haunted places on earth. Have you seen any ghosts? Or maybe Kingsley House is haunted."

"Why do you ask?"

Alix was aware that he'd avoided answering her questions. "Odd things keep happening. Pictures falling off tables, fireplace soot coming down in a lump, that sort of thing. This morning I was trying to decide between a blue shirt and a peach one and the collar of the blue one moved."

Jared knew his grandfather liked blue the best. "It's a drafty old house. Have you heard the floors creak?"

He was still avoiding her questions. "No, but I think a man kissed me on the cheek."

Jared didn't smile. "Were you frightened?"

"Not at all. It was rather nice." She started

to say more but an older couple came by and wanted to say hello and how very sorry they were to hear of Addy's passing. Alix drank her coffee and watched him as he smiled and talked. With his messy, graying beard and his long hair, he looked tired. She'd followed his career enough to know that he was a hard worker. Sometimes it seemed that everyone in the U.S. who could afford it wanted a house designed by Jared Montgomery. There were at least four books about his work, and many others that contained photos. His work seemed to be featured in half the magazines on the stands. She'd often wondered if he ever slept.

It was odd to think of him as a person with a life, friends, and family. That he had a talent that was off the charts was just something that happened. He was supposed to stay on the island but he'd said he was leaving, and she had an idea that it was to get away from her and all the things she'd planned to ask him.

When the people left, he turned back to his coffee.

"Thank you for the flowers," she said. "That was very thoughtful of you."

"I shouldn't have lied."

"No, you should have. If you hadn't, I would have bombarded you with questions. You don't have to leave Nantucket. I promise I won't bother you." She'd said this earlier, but this time there was no resentment in her voice. "I won't ask questions about designing, or about where you get your ideas. I won't even ask how you came up with the Klondike building. Not while we're on Nantucket. Here, you'll be Kingsley to me, not the great and famous Jared Montgomery. But . . ." She smiled at him. "Off-island, all bets are off. Is that a deal?"

Jared gave her a weak smile, and he wasn't sure what to reply. This morning he'd gone into the house early to have another look at the model of the chapel that she'd made. His business partner, Tim, had sent him yet another email saying he needed the design for the California house *now*! The movie couple wanted a Jared Montgomery design — not one from someone else in the firm, but from Jared personally.

This morning Jared had the idea of persuading the movie stars to build something designed by Alixandra Madsen. He'd tell them of her father, who'd taught Jared everything he knew. He'd lay it on thick about how she was up and coming and they'd be the first to have one of her designs. And a private chapel secreted away on their big estate would be just the thing.

And giving Alix a commission would partially pay back Ken for all he'd done for Jared. "Pass it on."

"What did you say?"

He didn't realize he'd spoken aloud. "I was thinking about what a generous deal you're offering. When I was a student I was insatiable for knowledge." In between carousing, he thought. Away from home, all those long-legged college girls . . . Half of his designs had been done three hours before he had to present them.

He smiled at her. What he had to do now was to get Alix to show him her model so he could act surprised at the sight of it. He didn't want her to think he'd been snooping — or that someone who didn't exist had shown him her plan.

Their breakfast orders were put before them, scrambled eggs with spinach, bacon, and cheese, a toasted cranberry muffin on the side for him. Alix had pancakes rich with blueberries and a couple of chocolate-covered doughnuts.

As Jared started to eat, he thought that he needed to get her away from her thoughts of leaving. She needed a reason to stay on the island. "Did you know that weddings are a big business on Nantucket? Multimillion. I don't know much about it, but I'm sure it wouldn't be too difficult to make a wedding for your friend here."

"And your girlfriend Toby could help?"

Jared smiled so broadly that the hairs on the back of Alix's neck stood up. That lip of his! She looked away.

"Toby's not my girlfriend. She's out of my league. I'm much too . . ." He ran his hand over his beard as he searched for the right word. Earthy? Salty? Too male?

"Too old?" Alix asked.

Jared looked at her. "Old?"

"You said she was a kid. Twenty, wasn't it?"

"She just turned twenty-two. Her father gave her a refrigerator for her birthday."

"Oh!" Alix said. "Did he wrap it?"

This time Jared realized she was joking. "Knowing her dad, he probably filled it with hundred dollar bills — all of which Toby returned. She's determined to support herself."

"By raising flowers?"

"That and working in a florist shop. She can advise you about wedding flowers."

Alix wasn't sure if she greatly admired this young woman or hated her for making people fall in love with her.

"And of course, there's always Valentina. You can find out about her."

"What does she do for weddings? Cakes? Photography?" Alix wondered how many girlfriends he had on the island.

He was looking at her so intensely she felt like she'd been put under a microscope. "You weren't told about Valentina?"

"It seems that I wasn't told about a lot of things. My mother visits Nantucket and from the quantity of supplies in the cabinet in the green bedroom she's been here many times. And then there's *you.* It's hard for me to believe that it's an accident that I, a student of architecture, was put into a house owned by an American Living Legend."

"A what?" He looked horrified.

"An American —"

"I heard you, but that's absurd."

She took her time chewing as she looked at him. "Is it my imagination that every time I ask you a direct question, such as about my mother or ghosts or even why I'm here, you change the subject?"

Jared almost choked as he held his laughter in. If no one had told him she was Victoria's daughter, in that instant, he would have known. "Isn't your mother that famous writer?"

"If you grew up on Nantucket and later ran home every chance you got, and my mother stayed here often enough to turn a room in your house into the Emerald City, then you *must* have met her."

Jared picked up his coffee cup to hide his smile.

It was Alix's turn to look at him with the intensity of a kestrel falcon homing in on its prey. "I know my mother arranged this year in Kingsley House, so what's she after?"

"Mind if I have one of your doughnuts?"

"Help yourself. The big question is why you're trying to give me so much to do that I don't leave the island."

"Hey, Jared, old man," a male voice called.

"Saved!" Jared said under his breath.

"Ha! You're not safe by any means."

A young man who looked vaguely familiar came to the table. "I see you found him," he said to Alix. "You don't remember me, do you?"

Wes, where the sun sets, she remembered, but said, "North by northwest, isn't that your name?"

He laughed. "How wonderful to be remembered by a beautiful woman. You and this old man aren't a couple, are you?"

Alix was still smiling and out of the corner of her eye she could see Jared frowning. "Mr. Kingsley and me? No way."

"Great," Wes said. "How about going to the Daffodil Festival with me this weekend? We'll ride in my dad's old car for the parade, then later we can go to 'Sconset for a tailgate picnic."

"What do I bring?"

"Just your pretty self. My mom and sister will do the cooking."

"Keep it in the family, I guess," she said, remembering that Wes had said he was a cousin to the Kingsley family.

"Doing that would include half the island. I'm going out on my boat today. Want to go with me?"

"I'd —"

"She and I are going to see Dilys," Jared said, his voice firm. "And we have some things to do around town."

Alix kept her eyes on Wes. "And Mr. Kingsley and I have a lot of things to talk about."

"On second thought," Jared said. "Maybe she could go with you."

Alix turned and gave Jared a warm smile. "You're my host and I think we should get to know each other, don't you?"

"I came here for breakfast, so maybe I could join you two," Wes said. "And I haven't seen Dilys in weeks."

"We're finished." Jared stood up and put money on the table. Downyflake didn't take credit cards.

"See you Saturday," Alix said to Wes as she left, Jared right behind her.

They got into his truck and he had the job of maneuvering out of the close parking lot, which he did with ease.

"So why does my mother want *me* here?" Alix asked as soon as they were on the road.

"I have no idea," he said.

She heard the honesty in his voice.

"Look, this whole thing is a shock to me," he said. "My aunt Addy died and I was told that she'd left our family's house — which should have gone to me — to Victoria's daughter for a year. I will admit that I was quite angry when I was told." He looked at her to see how she'd take that.

"I don't blame you. I would be too. Why did my mother come here?"

"For inspiration?" he asked, trying to sound innocent. "Aren't her books set in a seaside town?"

"You haven't read them?"

"No." He didn't say that he hadn't because he knew they were based on his ancestors. Who wanted to read that his great-great-grandmother had affairs? Or that a distant cousin probably murdered his brother-in-law?

"Why didn't she tell me she came here? Every August she sent me to stay with Dad. Mom said she went to her cabin in the Colorado mountains to think and plot her novels."

She spent that month reading my family's journals, one by one, Jared thought but didn't say.

"How often did she come here instead of going to Colorado?"

"She's come here every August since I was fourteen."

Alix opened her month to speak, then closed it. Did this mean the whole cabin-in-Colorado was a myth? "Why did she lie to me all these years?"

Jared wished none of this had started; it wasn't his business to tell any of it. "Maybe you were too close to my aunt," he said softly. Both his grandfather and his mother had told him how Aunt Addy went to her bed for weeks after Alix was taken from her that first summer. She'd been through the deaths of most of her family, but she'd always been strong. She'd been the one to give comfort to the grieving.

But that summer had been different. After Ken had found his wife and his business partner in a compromising situation, his orderly, easy life had turned upside down. In the ensuing turmoil, Victoria had taken four-year-old Alix and run away to give him time to calm down. She ended up on the island of Nantucket, broke and with no discernible skills. She took a job as a housekeeper-cook for Miss Adelaide Kingsley. Even though Victoria couldn't so much as turn on the old stove, and she refused to clean anything, Addy put up with her because she and little Alix became inseparable. It was after Victoria found the journals and began to rewrite the first story that Addy began to hope that Victoria and Alix would stay.

It might have happened except for Victoria's insistence on secrecy. When she took little four-year-old Alix off the island, it had nearly killed Addy. And only Jared could see how it had affected his grandfather. His mother, not a Kingsley, couldn't see Caleb, but Jared could. Even the death of Jared's father had not upset his grandfather so much.

"Why would she take her away?" Caleb had whispered to Jared. "Alix belongs here. She always has."

Jared couldn't get his grandfather to say any more, but by that time Alix's father was there and Jared's life changed dramatically.

"I think that could be true," Alix said in reply to his comment. "My mother does have a bit of a problem with jealousy."

"What about you?"

"Yes, she's always been jealous of anyone who got close to me. In high school I could hardly have a boy over or she'd —"

"No, I mean, do you have a problem with jealousy?"

"A month ago I would have said no, but recently my boyfriend, Eric, dumped me and took up with someone else. I wanted to shoot him."

"Not her?"

"She was too dumb to know what was going on."

Jared laughed, and Alix couldn't help smiling.

"It's too soon to laugh about!" she said. "On the way here on the ferry I was crying and eating lots of chocolate."

"Were you?" Jared asked. "Is that a usual female remedy for being thrown over?" He put as much innocence in his voice as he could muster.

"In my case, it was."

"That was just a few days ago. What brought you out of it?"

"I saw —" She broke off. She'd come close to saying "I saw your lower lip." Instead, she looked out the window of the truck. They were in a rural area now, the houses farther apart, but still sided in that unfinished gray cedar that made a person aware that it was Nantucket.

"I thought maybe you did some work that took your mind off your problems," he said.

She thought of the chapel model hidden away in the cabinet downstairs. With the way the man sauntered in and out of the house at will, she knew she needed to move the model and the papers so he didn't accidentally see them. "Nothing important," she said. "So tell me who Dilys is."

# Chapter Seven

They turned down a little road that was close to the water, and pulled into a driveway beside a house that Alix could have picked out as having been designed by Jared Montgomery. Tall windows peeped out of the roof, doors were recessed, and there were angles that no one expected. The trademarks of his designs were all there.

He sat in the truck, watching her, as though waiting for her to say something, but she didn't. She was determined to keep to her bargain. Here on Nantucket he was Kingsley, not Montgomery.

A short, gray-haired woman, sixtyish, came around the house. She had skin that had spent a lot of time exposed to sun and salt water, but her eyes were exactly like Jared's. And like Captain Caleb's, Alix thought.

Jared practically jumped out of the truck and ran to his cousin, picked her up, and twirled her around.

"My goodness, Jared, what a greeting. I just

saw you a few days ago."

"Don't mention Ken," he said. "You never met him. Victoria is fine, but Ken no."

Dilys looked around him at Alix, whom she'd already heard a lot about. Lexie had called with an extraordinary story about Jared showing up at night asking for flowers. "I'm not to mention her own father?" Dilys asked as Jared set her down.

"You never heard of him. I'll tell you why later."

Dilys nodded as she pulled away to go to Alix. "Welcome to Nantucket. Won't you come in? I have tea made."

Jared was at the truck getting the cooler out of the back. "She'd rather have rum."

"I would not!" Alix said, afraid Dilys would think she had a drinking problem.

"Don't let her innocent look fool you. She packs away the rum like a Kingsley sailor."

As he took the cooler into the house, Alix stood there with a red face. "I really don't drink very much. I —"

Dilys laughed. "He gave you a compliment. Come inside and look around. I hear you're a student of architecture."

"Yes," she said and went inside — then drew in her breath. The inside of the house was glorious. There were huge windows that looked out on the sea, a tall cathedral ceiling, a splendidly equipped galley kitchen, a built-in banquette. Old meets new. It was part beach house, part modern convenience — and all of it was pure Jared Montgomery. But Alix knew that this house had never been photographed and put in a book.

As she turned in a circle to look at all of it, she glimpsed Jared's face as he unpacked the cooler. Smug, she thought. He knew just what she was thinking — and he was waiting for her praise.

"I can see that the architect Jared Montgomery did this," Alix said rather loudly. "It's early, but it's his. The windows, the way this room flows into the other — they give it away. It's his work; I'd recognize it anywhere." She looked at him. "Mr. Kingsley, do you and Dilys mind if I look at the rest of the house?"

"Please do," he said, and Alix walked down a hallway.

Dilys's eyes were wide. "Doesn't she know that *you* are Montgomery?"

"She does," Jared said, smiling.

"Oh." Dilys didn't understand. "Why does she call you Mr. Kingsley?"

"I think that's what the lawyer called me, so she keeps doing it."

"Have you told her to call you Jared?"

"Naw." He smiled. "I kind of like it. It's a sign of respect."

"Or age," Dilys said.

"What is it about my age that everyone's harping on today?"

"I don't know. Do you think it could be

your ZZ Top beard and hair?"

Jared paused, fish package in his hand, and blinked at her.

"Shall I call Trish and make you an appointment?" Dilys asked. "Three today okay?"

Jared nodded.

"You fit in here so well it's difficult to imagine that you've ever lived anywhere else," Alix said. "Did you want to leave the island?"

Jared was on his back, stretched out on the grass, while Alix was sitting up, and they were both staring at the water. Behind them was his house. He'd given her a tour of his childhood home, telling her how it had been when he was a kid, dark and dank, little more than a fisherman's cottage. "But I fixed it," he said, looking at her. "It was the first house I ever worked on."

She'd wanted to comment on the brilliance of his remodel, but she was afraid she'd start gushing so she kept quiet. He told her the house had been remodeled when he was fourteen, and seemed to think that was significant, but Alix didn't know why.

After the tour Dilys had shoved them out, saying she needed to make lunch and that Jared should show Alix his old neighborhood.

They'd walked for over an hour and, just as in the restaurant, Jared knew everyone. Alix had been introduced to all the people they encountered by her first name, and she'd been invited on boating trips, to come by for scallops, and to visit gardens.

Two older couples asked Jared to look at something that wasn't working in their houses and he promised that he would. No one even came close to treating him as though he were anything but the grown-up version of a boy who used to live down the road.

They were back now, and again Dilys had sent them outside. Jared took his time in responding to her question. "After my father died I was angry, furious," he said, "and I had a lot of energy pent up inside me. I wanted to beat the world at its own game. To do that I had to leave the island, first to study and get my degree, then to go to work."

"Did you work hard in school and get rid of the energy that way? Wait. Sorry. I'm not supposed to ask that."

He ignored the last part. "Actually, I didn't really. School was rather easy for me."

Alix groaned. "I have just decided that I hate you."

"Come on, school couldn't be too difficult for you. You're Victoria's daughter."

"It's been more my father's perseverance that I inherited that got me through than my mother's . . . What should I call it?"

"Charisma?" Jared asked. "Charm? Joie de vivre?"

"All of that. Her job is so easy for her. She

goes away for a month every year and —" She looked at him. "But I guess you know that better than I do. Anyway, she goes away and plots her novels, then returns home and writes them. She has a daily quota of pages and she never falters from her original plot. I change my mind fifty times before I decide what I want to do."

"Do you change your mind or do you look at what you've drawn, see what's wrong with it, then fix it?"

"That's exactly what I do!" she said, smiling.

"To be able to see the flaws in your own work is a gift."

"I guess it is. I'd never thought of it that way. I know that Eric thought every design he made was perfect."

"The fiancé, Eric?"

"Don't elevate him. He was merely a boyfriend. Now an ex." For a moment they looked at each other and Alix wanted to ask him if all his girlfriends were exes, but he looked away and the moment was lost.

"What are you working on now?" he asked.

She thought of her little chapel, but it was insignificant compared to the magnificent structures he'd designed. "Nothing important. I need to study for the coming tests and plan my final project."

"Are you going to build it?" he asked, eyes twinkling.

She laughed. "That trick was done by someone else."

"It could bear repeating, couldn't it?"

"I don't think so. I —" She broke off because Dilys called them in to lunch.

Minutes later they were sitting at the table in the beautiful house eating fried fish and coleslaw and homemade pickled beach plums. Dilys and Jared were on one side, Alix across from them.

"Alix makes great hush puppies," Jared said.

"Did your mother teach you how?" Dilys asked.

"My mother —" Alix began, then saw the laughter in Dilys's eyes. "I can see that you know her well. By the time I was six I could dial every restaurant in our area that delivered."

"Victoria may have faults, but it's a party wherever she is," Dilys said. "What we loved was that your mother could get Addy to leave the house."

"I didn't know she was a recluse," Alix said. "I remember tea parties and lots of guests."

"Oh, yes, Addy invited people to her home, but she didn't go out very often."

"She was agoraphobic?" Alix asked.

Dilys leaned forward as though in conspiracy. "My grandmother used to say that Addy had a ghost lover."

"Anyone want more slaw?" Jared asked. "There's plenty left."

Both women ignored him.

"It had to have been Captain Caleb," Alix said. "My memory is that Aunt Addy — as she told me to call her — and I used to lie in her bed and look at his portrait and she'd tell me mermaid stories. I thought it was all madly romantic."

"You remember that?" Dilys asked. "But you were only four."

"She knows where everything in the house is," Jared said.

Dilys smiled. "That's because she used to search through the drawers and cabinets to find things to use for her buildings. If you hadn't given her those Legos she might have started pulling the bricks out of the walls."

Alix looked at Jared in question, then memory lit her face. "You're the tall boy who smelled like the sea."

Dilys laughed. "That's Jared. He always smelled like fish and sawdust. I don't think he took a bath until he was sixteen and started liking girls."

Alix was still staring at him. "You showed me how to use the blocks, and we sat on the floor and built . . . What was it?"

"It was a crude replica of this house. My mother kept saying it needed work and I was thinking about how a room could be added." Later, he'd sketched his ideas; Ken had seen them, and had used Jared's drawings for the remodel. That Jared couldn't now tell Alix that she, as a four-year-old builder, had inspired him in the beginning of his career greatly annoyed him.

Alix was trying to take all of it in. She had been given Lego building lessons by a boy who would grow up to be one of the world's greatest architects. Her face must have told what she was thinking because Jared looked away. She could see that he was frowning. He certainly didn't want to be seen as a celebrity!

Alix didn't want to say anything that would deepen that frown. She looked back at Dilys. "So Captain Caleb was Aunt Addy's ghost lover?"

Dilys nodded. "That's what my grandmother said. My mother told her she was being ridiculous, but truth or not, I loved the stories. And so did Lexie."

"Lexie? I've heard of her but not met her."

"Lexie and her mother moved in with me after Lex's father died. When Jared left for college, he very kindly let us move into this house." For a moment she looked at Jared with such love and gratitude that it was almost embarrassing.

Hiding his face so they couldn't see his expression, Jared stood up and started collecting dirty dishes. Alix moved to help, but Dilys's look said that Jared would do it.

"How do you have an affair with a ghost?" Alix asked. "I mean, wouldn't there be some physical limitations?"

"I've always wondered about that too," Dilys said. "In fact . . ." After a glance at Jared, who had his back to them, she leaned toward Alix. "I asked my grandmother that very thing."

"And what did she say?"

"That one time Addy said she loved the man so much that she kept him a prisoner."

Alix leaned back in her chair. "What an odd thing to say. I wonder how she could have done that."

"Actually, I asked her that once and she said that she didn't do any searching for the key that would unlock his cell door."

"That sounds cryptic. What do you think she meant by —" Alix began but Jared cut her off.

"Do you two think you could stop gossiping for a while?" he asked. "I have an appointment at three."

"The Kingsley men do *not* believe in ghosts," Dilys said. "They pride themselves on being sane and sensible, and ghosts don't fit into that image. So, dear," Dilys said, "if you see a ghost in Kingsley House *you* will have to be the one to tell me all about it."

"Dilys," Alix said slowly, "if I see Captain Caleb, ghost or not, I'm keeping him for myself."

The two women laughed so hard that Jared went back into the kitchen.

After lunch Jared went to his truck to get

some tools to make a repair. When they were alone, Dilys told Alix she had a boat and that in a week or so Jared would get it out of storage and put it in the water for her.

"He seems to do a lot for people on the island," Alix said.

"He has responsibilities. He's the oldest son of an old Nantucket family. The name carries duties with it."

"Not a modern concept," Alix said.

"There's a lot about us Nantucketers that isn't modern."

"I'm beginning to see that," Alix said. She wanted to give Jared and Dilys time alone, so she went outside to walk along the dock that protruded into the sea.

When Jared came back to the house, Dilys noted the way he looked around for Alix, then seemed to relax when he saw her outside on the long dock. Minutes later, he was on his back on the floor, his upper half inside a cabinet as he repaired Dilys's leaky faucet.

"I've never seen you so comfortable with any woman before," Dilys said.

"I owe Ken. Hand me that wrench." He took it. "Unfortunately, her parents have kept Nantucket a secret from her."

"What do you mean?"

"Neither of them told her that they visit here."

"But Victoria comes every year."

"Alix knows that now, but Victoria told her

daughter that she goes to some cabin in Colorado."

"Why would she do that?"

"I don't know," Jared said. "Try the water now."

Dilys turned on the faucet and it worked perfectly.

Jared got out from inside the cabinet. "Ken told me that Victoria didn't want anyone to know her books were actually set on Nantucket and based on the Kingsley family."

"Everyone on the island knows that."

"And we keep what's ours to ourselves. She doesn't want the outside world to know."

"So what's Ken's excuse for not telling Alix that he visits often?" Dilys asked.

"He was forbidden by Victoria. She said that if Alix knew her parents visited Nantucket, then she'd want to come here too."

Dilys had trouble understanding that idea, but then she nodded. "It has to do with Addy, doesn't it?"

"Maybe. I know that Victoria didn't want her daughter visiting Aunt Addy. They got too close when Alix was here and Victoria didn't like it."

Dilys shook her head in memory. "I remember how depressed Addy was after Victoria took Alix away. I really thought we were going to lose Addy. Actually, I thought the whole business was cruel of Victoria. And it hurt Alix too. How that child cried!"

"Alix seems to have turned out all right. I don't think she consciously remembers much, but she knows more than she thinks she does. She moves around the kitchen like she's spent her life in it."

"Don't tell me she can work that horrible old green stove."

"That stove is great! And Alix turns those knobs without even thinking about it."

Dilys pulled back to look at him. "What's that strange sound I hear in your voice?"

"It's respect, and it's what I have for Ken and Victoria's daughter."

"Don't give me that, Jared Kingsley. I've known you all your life. You see something different in her."

Jared hesitated for a moment. "She designed a chapel," he said softly.

"And?"

"And it's good."

" 'Good'? On a scale of one to ten?"

"Eleven."

"Well, well, well," Dilys said. "Brains, beauty, and talent. Seems like she's a complete package."

"It's too soon to tell."

"Jared, honey, my advice is that you don't take too long to make up your mind. Brains, beauty, and talent tend to get snatched up on Nantucket. We're wise people."

Jared washed his hands in the sink. "Wes asked her to go to the Daffy Festival with him on Saturday."

"Your cousin Wes Drayton? The good-looking, unmarried young man who has a thriving business in repairing boats? *That* Wes?"

"That's the one." Jared didn't smile at her description. "I can't fool around with Ken and Victoria's daughter. If we got serious and it didn't work out . . . How would I live that down? I owe my entire life to her parents. You should have heard Ken bawling me out because . . ." He waved his hand. "It doesn't matter now. Here she comes. Just keep it light, will you? She's a nice kid."

"So are you," Dilys said, but Jared was already at the door and smiling at Alix.

# Chapter Eight

"I like Dilys," Alix said. They were in his old red truck and heading back toward town, passing beautiful landscapes of marshes and ponds. It was early in the season yet, so some of the shrubs were still leafless. "What are the white flowers?"

"It's the shadbush. 'The shadbush blooms when shad are running,' " he quoted.

"I guess that means you'll be heading off in your boat soon."

"I have some things to do here on the island." He didn't say what because he knew that he had to get Alix settled enough that she wouldn't jump on a ferry the second he disappeared. He reminded himself that he needed to hook her up with Lexie and Toby.

Alix glanced out the window. Did "some things" mean he was working on a design for some fabulous building?

"Dilys is nice," Jared said. "You wouldn't happen to need some computer supplies, would you?"

"There's enough in my mother's cabinet to last me. Why?"

"Because if I drive home to drop you off I'm going to be late for my appointment. I could call Trish and change the time, I guess."

"Oh," Alix said. "Are you two going out?"

"No, Tricia is a hairdresser and Dilys told me I had to get this off my face." He ran his hand through his beard.

"You're going to shave? And get a haircut?"

He was glancing at her as he drove. "You don't think I should?"

She liked him with the beard but to say that seemed too personal. "I just don't want to mix you up with Montgomery, that's all. The hair seems to suit a Kingsley who deals with the sea and lives on an island."

"All right," he said, smiling. "I'll get the beard trimmed, not shaved, and not get my hair cut short. Is that better?"

His tone made her frown. Why was he trying so hard to please her? "Who told you I knew about your . . . your job?"

"You were angry at me," he said. "And you kept dropping heavy-handed hints about my work. Sorry I didn't pick up on them until later."

"But you went out to get me flowers," Alix said, softening. "That was very nice of you."

He turned left off the wide road and into the parking area of some little shops. One was Hair Concern, another was a computer store. “I don’t know how long this will take. If you want to go home I’ll run in and tell Trish that I can’t make it right now. Or you could visit the other shops.”

Alix got out of the truck. “I’ll go in with you and you can introduce me. I’ll need a hairdresser while I’m here.”

“I thought you were leaving tomorrow,” he said as he walked around the truck.

“So were you. Changed your mind?”

“Now that I know you aren’t going to ask me for my wisdom, maybe I will stay.”

“If I meet Jared Montgomery that’s the first thing I’m going to ask him, but Mr. Kingsley just seems to go fishing and . . .” She looked up at him. “What else do you do?”

“I don’t know. It’s been years since I had any time off. All winter I went back and forth to New York and even now I have one project that my partner is on my case to do.” They had stepped up onto a little porch and Jared was holding the door open for her.

Alix had to clamp her teeth down on the sides of her tongue to keep from asking what project he needed to work on. But a deal was a deal and she wasn’t going to break it.

The salon was large and well lit. Jared introduced Alix to Tricia, who was small, trim, and quite pretty.

“I don’t want him shaved,” Alix said, then turned red. “Sorry for being so bossy.”

“I’m not allowed to anyway,” Trish said and

explained that she didn't have a barber's license so she couldn't shave Jared. For a few minutes the two women discussed what to do with his mess of hair and beard while he sat in the chair in silence. When they had it settled, Alix sat down in the empty chair in the next booth.

It turned out that Trish seemed to have read every novel published in the last ten years. She and Alix kept up a steady stream of conversation while Trish trimmed, washed, and cut Jared's hair. If he so much as said a word, neither woman noticed.

When Trish finished, the two women stood side by side to inspect her work.

Jared looked at least ten years younger, and the beard and long hair suited him very well. His whiskers were perfectly trimmed around his strong jawline and his hair reached down the back of his neck. There were gray patches in his beard and hair, but on him they looked good.

Alix wouldn't have thought it was possible, but he looked even better now than he did a couple of years ago when she and Izzy heard him speak. Alix couldn't help looking over his head in the mirror at his lower lip.

"Is it all right?" Jared asked, looking at Alix in the mirror.

"Yes," she said and turned away.

At the register, Jared paid, they said goodbye, then left.

"Grocery?" Jared asked.

She opened the truck door. "I'm beginning to feel guilty taking up your time. Maybe you could take me to a car rental agency and I could get a vehicle."

"If you're going to be here for a whole year maybe we should buy you a used car. I have a friend who has a VW for sale."

"I think I'll wait on buying a car. When Mom gets here she'll probably do something. What does she drive when she's here?"

"Nothing," Jared said. "She walks to town to eat. There's a grocery a few blocks down and she gets fruit there. She and Aunt Addy went out to lunch often, but then most of the time your mother was here, she worked."

"Oh, yes. Plotting her novels," Alix said.

Reading my family's journals and making notes, Jared thought. One year Victoria sneaked in a portable copy machine. She'd used it only in the privacy of her bedroom, but his grandfather, Caleb, told Aunt Addy about it and there'd been a huge fight. Victoria had accused Addy of spying on her.

When Jared was told of it, he'd laid into his grandfather for doing the spying. "Do you sneak around and watch her dress and undress?!" Jared had meant his words to be a put-down, but Caleb had grinned and said, "Oh, yes. But only for Victoria," then he'd disappeared.

It didn't matter how Addy knew, Victoria

was told to get rid of the copier or leave. Reluctantly, she handed it over to Addy. Last time Jared looked, it was still in a cabinet in the second parlor.

"Yes, plotting," Jared said at last. "Would you like to go to the grocery or not?"

"I could use a few things."

He pulled into a parking lot that she recognized. Across the road was Downyflake with its big doughnut on the front. It was the first time she hadn't felt lost.

"Know where you are?" he asked.

"Vaguely."

He reached behind the bench seat, pulled out a big flannel shirt, and handed it to her.

"What's this for?"

"You'll see."

The Stop and Shop grocery was the coldest one she'd ever been in and she quickly put on the shirt, which engulfed her.

"You're beginning to look like a Nantucketer," he said, grinning.

"Why do I feel like I've just been given a huge compliment? Right after being called a rum-drinking Kingsley sailor, that is."

Jared laughed. "Speaking of which, there's a liquor store next door. Think we should visit? Get a case of dark rum for you, maybe?"

"If I remember correctly, you drank as much as I did."

"But, alas, neither of us got drunk." He walked ahead to pick up a couple of bags of baby lettuce.

Alix held on to the cart, watching him. He'd just said his first almost flirty thing to her. Just minutes before she'd had to stop herself from drooling when she saw him in the mirror, but he'd continued to look at her the same way her father did.

"So tell me about this date I'm having on Saturday," Alix said. They were at the coffee and tea shelves and he was reading the packages.

"Not much to tell. There are millions of daffodils on the island. There's some story about a lawn mower nearly wiping them out, but they're still here. There's a parade of antique cars and a picnic out in 'Sconset." He put two bags of coffee in the cart.

"I take it you don't participate."

"I did when I was a kid. My parents took me to it every year. My mom used to cover me in daffodils, then she'd put me in the back of an old pickup with my cousins. But when I got older I was too cool for any of that."

He was leaning on the cart handle and watching Alix put things in. They stopped at the big glass counter that held an assortment of meats and salads. Jared greeted everyone who worked behind it by name.

"What do you want to get?" she asked without thinking, then said, "Sorry. It's not like we'll be sharing a lot of meals."

"Chicken salad," he said, "and get me some

of the ham for sandwiches. We forgot tomatoes. I'll go back and get them. Oh! And get me some of that smoked turkey." Turning, he went back to the produce section.

Alix couldn't help smiling. It looked like she wouldn't be eating every meal alone after all.

The rest of the grocery shopping was fun, but by the time they got to the frozen foods, Alix's teeth were chattering. Jared put his hands on her upper arms and rubbed briskly. "If you're going to live here, you need to toughen up."

They headed to the checkout, but Alix stopped at the magazines. She got a *Nantucket Today* and hesitated over an issue of a remodeling magazine. Jared picked it up and put it in the cart.

"Later, you can tell me everything they've done wrong," she said, smiling.

"Didn't you learn anything at school? You tell me."

They were unloading the cart onto the checkout belt.

"Right. I'm going to tell an American Living —" His look cut her off. "What does a Kingsley sailor know about remodeling?"

He gave her a smile of such sweetness that Alix's knees began to give way.

"You learn quickly, don't you?"

"I do when it's in my own best interest. Did you get any eggs?" she asked.

"No. They're straight down that aisle, and be sure to open the carton to see if any are broken," he said.

Alix stood up from the cart and looked at him.

With a sigh, he hurried down the aisle to get the eggs.

When Alix finished unloading, the young woman at the checkout said, "Are you and Jared a couple?"

For a moment Alix was speechless. Did everyone on this island know everyone else? "No," she said at last. "We just met yesterday."

The woman raised her eyebrows. "You two argue like you're married."

Alix started to say something but Jared returned with the eggs.

"Did you get any Greek yogurt?" he asked. "I can't stand those little cartons with all the sugar in the bottom."

Alix, very aware of the woman watching, held up the Greek yogurt.

"Good," he said, smiling. "That's just the kind I like." Ken had introduced it to him.

She glanced at the checkout girl, who again raised her brows. Jared held out his key ring with the Stop and Shop card on it, then paid.

Outside was warmer than inside and they hurried to the truck. Alix handed him bags and he put them in the back. When they were inside the truck he took one look at her and turned on the heater. "How are you going to survive winter here in a drafty old house?"

"I'm going to get a fat boyfriend," she said.

When Jared didn't reply she looked at him. He was pulling out of the parking lot and saying nothing. It looked like boyfriends were another subject she wasn't supposed to mention. But the truth was that if she didn't get a man to distract her, she was going to make a fool of herself over Jared Montgomery slash Kingsley.

"How about if we go home, put the groceries away, then walk around town for a while?" he asked.

"And maybe you'll see someone you know."

He looked at her quickly and saw she was joking. "We all know each other now but that won't last long."

"What do you mean?"

"Theeeey're commming."

She couldn't help laughing. He sounded like an announcer on a horror movie trailer. "Who is coming?"

He turned down a street that looked too narrow to have even one-way traffic, but another truck was coming right at them. Neither Jared nor the other driver seemed to think anything about passing one another in such a narrow space and of course they lifted their hands in greeting.

"You'll find out," he said, which wasn't really an answer.

When they were back at the house they carried in the groceries and quickly put them away. Alix knew where everything went in the lower cabinets, and that made them laugh. Twice she ducked under his arm to get to the fridge. All in all, they worked well together.

Twenty minutes later they were back outside and walking through the streets of Nantucket. She followed Jared as they went down one gorgeous street after another, stopping now and then to comment on a door or some other extraordinary feature of a house.

After a while he stopped in front of a small house and for a moment Alix didn't know why he'd halted. But then she looked over his shoulder and her eyes widened. "You did that, didn't you? I mean, Jared Montgomery remodeled that house."

"He did," Jared said, his eyes twinkling. "And I happen to know that he was just fifteen years old when he designed it. Of course this is nothing compared to his later work, but it is his."

"Are you kidding?" Alix said. "I knew it was his. Look at the way that door is set into the wall. That's pure Montgomery."

Jared lost his smile. "Are you saying that he hasn't changed in his whole career?"

"I think he has very wisely stuck to what works."

After a moment's hesitation, Jared laughed. "Very diplomatic of you."

"I know I shouldn't ask, but how did he get to design a building when he was just fifteen?"

"He worked with a master builder who let him . . . let *me* design it." His voice grew softer as he remembered that time and they began to walk again. "I drew my ideas with a stick in the dirt, so he taught me rudimentary drafting. He showed me how to use a triangle and a T-square, and my first drafting table was an old door on sawhorses, with —"

"With triangular pieces of plywood to put it on a slant," Alix said.

"It's like you've seen it."

"My dad made me one like that. But he used the bottom half of a Dutch door."

"How old were you?" Jared asked.

"Eight." She gave a little laugh.

"What's funny?"

"I was just thinking about the Legos. I guess I left the ones you gave me behind, because later I was in a store with my dad and I saw boxes of them. I still remember how I went crazy and started crying. I was never a tantrum-throwing kind of kid, but I don't think I've ever before or since wanted anything as much as I wanted those. Dad seemed to understand because he filled a cart with sets of them."

Jared was grinning. "Did you use them?"

"Constantly! But my mother hated them because the little pieces were all over the house. She used to say, 'Kenneth, my child is going to grow up to be a writer. She doesn't need those annoying little blocks.' "

"What did your father say to that?"

She lowered her voice. "He said, 'She's already an architect. I don't think she can be what both of us are.' "

"It looks like he was right," Jared said.

"He was. While I was growing up, Mom tried to get me to make up stories but they just weren't there. If I heard a story I could write it, that was easy for me, but I couldn't do what my mother does and come up with fantastic plots."

"You can write but not plot?" He sounded amused by something that used to plague Alix when she was growing up.

"That's about it, but then whoever heard of things in real life like what happened in my mother's books? Murder, secret rooms hiding criminals, forbidden love, scheming and plotting to get some old house, and —" When she looked at him, she saw that he was staring at her in shock. "Why are you looking at me like that?"

"I'm horrified by what people read. Now you're the one looking strange."

"I'm still adjusting to the fact that my mother spent every August here and not in Colorado."

He didn't think she had told him everything on her mind, so he waited for her to continue.

"I just thought of something," she said.

"Your family is old, and your house is old."

"Please tell me you aren't thinking that *my* family is the prototype for a bunch of murderers."

She barely heard him. The idea that her mother had based all of her books on the Kingsley family was becoming stronger and stronger. Was it possible that her mother's outrageous novels were *true*?

Jared had an idea of what Alix was thinking and he didn't like it. He truly believed that a person's family history should be kept private. He put his hands on her shoulders and turned her around to face a house. "This is Montgomery at sixteen."

Alix just stood there blinking. One of her mother's books was about a soap recipe that had become the basis for the whole family's wealth. "Kingsley Soap," Alix whispered, her eyes wide. It was a real product and the wrapper said it had been around for centuries. It wasn't a big seller today, but bars of it were still in every grocery in the country. Her dad's mother used to swear by it.

"You're right," Jared said loudly. "This couldn't be a Montgomery design. The windows aren't right and he would never make dormers like those monstrosities." He started walking down the street.

"He would make them just like that," Alix said as she tried to pull her mind away from the soap.

Jared stopped walking and turned to look at her.

"The Danwell house," she said. "It has dormers exactly like that."

Smiling, Jared started walking again.

Alix ran to catch up with him, tripping once over the uneven sidewalk. He turned down an alleyway that didn't look wide enough to get a motor scooter down, but there were cars parked on both sides. He was walking fast, his long legs eating up the distance.

Alix nearly had to run to keep up with him.

Abruptly, he stopped at a house that was close to the road, reached into his pocket to withdraw his keys, and unlocked a door. Alix followed him inside.

"I think the electricity is on," he said as he felt along the wall and flipped a switch.

They were in a downstairs kitchen, an old brick wall to the right. Through the doorway she could see what was probably a dining room with a big fireplace on the far wall.

Jared was glad to see that finally the faraway look had left Alix's eyes. The house seemed to have overridden her thoughts about his family and her mother's novels and how they were connected.

"This house is quite old," Alix said, her voice low and full of the reverence such a house deserved. She looked into the far room, saw the huge fireplace, then looked back at the old kitchen. There was an old Tappan range, a scarred and chipped sink. The cabinets had been made by someone who had never heard of a mortise and tenon joint.

"Maple cabinets and granite?" Jared asked.

"I'm not sure I'd go that far, but I'd —" She broke off as she remembered who she was talking to. "Whose house is this?"

"My cousin's. He wants me to do a design for a remodel, he'll do the work, then sell the house. Want to see the upstairs?"

She nodded and they went up the steep, narrow stairs to see a rabbit warren of rooms. The house had been added onto in a very haphazard way. Some of the rooms were beautiful, but others had been cut apart by ugly Sheetrock partitions.

Jared sat down on an old couch that was propped up in the back by phone books and waited while Alix wandered from room to room. He saw her looking up at the top of the walls and knew she was figuring out what was old and original, and what had been thrown up in the sixties in an attempt to make as many bedrooms as possible.

He let her have about twenty minutes, then the growling of his stomach made him stand up. "You ready to go or should I go home and get you a measuring tape?"

"Like you don't already have the whole floor plan on paper," Alix said.

Jared gave a one-sided grin. "Maybe I do. I'm starving. Let's get something to eat."

"We have lots of groceries and we could —"

"Takes too long. Let's go to The Brotherhood." He led her outside by another door and into what looked to be a horribly overgrown garden.

"Are you going to do the landscaping?"

"Not me," he said as he began walking, Alix close behind him. "I thought I'd try to sweet-talk Toby into doing it. Keep it in the family."

"Oh? I didn't realize she was related to you." Alix couldn't help feeling an itty bitty bit of joy at hearing that the Toby whom everyone loved was off limits to him. She was glad her feelings weren't in her voice.

But Jared did hear it. "She's related through my heart, not by blood," he said as he put his hand on his chest and gave a deep sigh.

"You idiot!" Then she realized what she'd said — and who she'd said it to.

Jared laughed. "Only about Toby." He opened the door to the restaurant for her.

Shaking her head, Alix went in ahead of him and entered an old-fashioned pub sort of place, only she knew the walls and fireplace were real. "Nice," she said.

They were escorted to a booth in the back, with Jared saying hello to people as they walked through the restaurant.

"You couldn't sneak around and have an affair on this island, could you?"

"A few people have found ways," he said as

he looked at the menu, "but they're usually found out."

The waiter came and they gave their orders, and Alix thought about what he'd said. "I bet Aunt Addy heard all the gossip. Even if she rarely left the house, she had people over often and they'd tell her what was going on. Maybe my mother heard about —"

Jared put a paper napkin and a pen in front of Alix. "So what would you do with that house?"

"You're trying to distract me, aren't you?"

"I just thought your own future would interest you more than your mother's past. I guess I was wrong." He reached out to take the napkin away.

Alix put her hand over it and began to sketch the layout of the house. "When I was a kid my dad used to take me to visit houses, then when we got home he'd have me draw the floor plan."

Jared wanted to say that her father had done the same thing to him, but he didn't. When Alix found out the truth, he really hoped she wouldn't be angry at *him* for not telling her that her father also spent a lot of time on Nantucket.

The restaurant was dark and he looked at the top of her head as she drew. Dilys had said he was "comfortable" with Alix and it was true. Maybe it was because they'd both been taught by her father, or maybe it was because they were interested in the same thing. Whatever it was, he enjoyed being with her.

But it wasn't easy to suppress his physical desire for her. He liked the way she moved, liked to watch her lips when she spoke. He kept having fantasies of touching her — and it wasn't easy to keep his hands off her. In the grocery when she'd been so cold he'd wanted to put his arms around her. But all he'd done was put his hands on her arms and rub. On the street he'd turned her toward the house. They were tiny touches, and he shouldn't have done them as they just made him want her more.

"Is this right?" she asked as she pushed the napkin toward him.

He barely glanced at the drawing, but then he'd been doing this since he was a teenager. "This wall isn't right. It should be over here."

"No, you're wrong," she said. "The fireplace is there." She drew it.

"Your scale is off. Wall here, fireplace there." He didn't draw it, just ran his fingertip where the lines should be.

"Absolutely not. You are —" She broke off, yet again thinking of who he was. "Sorry. I'm sure you know better than I do."

"What is that disgusting thing you called me?"

She had to think what he meant. "An American Living Legend?"

"That's it. That makes me sound like a pre-Revolution artifact." He held out his hand. "I'm warm. Flesh and blood. I *can* make mistakes."

Alix put her hand on his and his fingers closed over her hand. For a moment her eyes locked with his and sparks seemed to fly through her body.

They broke contact when the waiter brought their sandwiches.

"So how would you remodel it?" Jared asked as soon as they were alone again.

Alix looked down at the sketch and forced herself to put her mind back on it. "It depends on what the owner wants."

"He left it up to me," Jared said. "It's for resale."

"Carte blanche. What an intriguing idea. My dad said the hardest part of being an architect was dealing with the clients. Think Montgomery had any problems in that area?"

"I think he told them that if they wanted a Montgomery design they had to do it his way or get out."

"That's a road to starvation."

"It was a better economy back then, and he had enough anger in him to pull it off."

Alix looked across the table at him. The restaurant was dark, very atmospheric, and his eyes had a look that she couldn't read. She could imagine that his anger, talent, and looks were a lethal combination.

Jared was having a difficult time remaining still when Alix looked at him like that. If she were any other woman he would have said, "Let's get out of here," then taken her home and to bed. But this was Ken's daughter.

"You don't have any ideas for the remodel?" He sounded as though he was disappointed in her.

Alix looked down at the drawing and tried to control her frown. She felt almost like she'd just had a man tell her no, that she'd made a pass at him and he'd turned her down. She told herself to get a grip. For all she knew he had a serious girlfriend, maybe even a fiancée.

But still . . . he could have *pretended* he was interested.

"If I were Montgomery," she said firmly, "I'd change this door and widen these dormers. Inside I'd remove this wall and this one, and in the kitchen I'd put the sink over here." She made marks as fast as she talked, and when she finished she looked up at him.

Jared was staring at her with wide eyes. It was *exactly* the way he'd planned the remodel, even down to the sink position.

It took him a moment to recover. "How would *you* do it?"

"Softer," she said. "Less invasive. Leave the kitchen alone except to put an island here. Take out the downstairs wall, and upstairs, take out the frame walls here and here."

"And the exterior?"

"Leave it alone but add a room here. Dig down so it doesn't block the upper windows, then put windows all along the south side. Door and stairs up into the garden here."

She halted. The drawing was barely readable with all the marks on it. "That's what I would do."

Jared could only stare at her. If he'd fallen into a rut so deep that a student could predict what he was going to do, that was bad. But then this student was what he once was — and her design was better than his.

It ran through his mind that he should leave the island immediately, get away from this upstart girl who thought she was better than the famous Jared Montgomery.

In the next second, he leaned back in his chair and smiled.

Alix had seen the emotions pass across his face and for a moment she thought he was going to walk out of the restaurant and she'd never see him again.

"It's yours," he said, still smiling at her.

"What is?"

"The house. It's yours to redesign." He'd told his cousin he'd do the work for free but he wasn't going to tell her that. "I'll make sure you get credit for it and you can put it on your résumé." He leaned toward her, his face serious. "Which I truly and sincerely hope that you'll submit to *my* company when you apply for a job. It will have my personal endorsement on it and since I own the place, I'm quite sure that you'll be employed by me."

Alix just sat there blinking at him, not quite able to comprehend what he'd just said.

"If you start crying and embarrass me, I'll take back my offer."

"I won't," she said as she blinked faster.

Jared signaled to the waiter to come over and ordered two chocolate desserts and two rum and Cokes. "With double lime," he added.

"Drunk and fat," Alix murmured and started to pick up the napkin to wipe her eyes.

"You might need that later," he said and handed her a clean one that he took off an empty table. He put the napkin with the jumbled drawing in his shirt pocket.

Leaning back in the booth, he watched Alix as she ate all her chocolate dessert and half of his. With his encouragement, she chattered about her childhood and what it had been like to grow up around two extraordinarily talented parents.

While she talked, he thought that maybe his designs had become predictable, that he had become a sort of trademark. Alix, new to the world of architecture, brought with her an energy that he hadn't felt in a long time.

"You ready to go home?" he asked. "I have an overwhelming desire to look at some house plans I made over the winter. I think I need to change them. They're too much like what I've already done. I don't have a CAD system here, but maybe together we could —"

"Yes," Alix said.

"You didn't let me finish."

"I don't need a CAD or a computer. You had me at the word 'together.' " She stood up. "You ready to leave?"

"I think I should pay the tab first, all right?" He was smiling.

Reluctantly, she nodded.

# Chapter Nine

Jared wasn't sure what woke him, but the first thing he saw was his grandfather hovering over him. Sunlight was flooding the room and going through his grandfather's body. When Jared was little and his aunt was out of the room, he would run through his grandfather, then laugh hysterically. His mother, who couldn't see Caleb, thought it was funny that when they visited Aunt Addy her son would run back and forth across the room and laugh so hard at something imaginary.

Jared's father, who could see Caleb, smiled indulgently. As a child, he'd done exactly the same thing.

When Caleb disappeared, Jared saw Alix sprawled across the other couch and sound asleep. An empty plate and glass were on the rug; piles of papers and great rolls of blueprints were scattered everywhere. It looked like they'd again fallen asleep while working. But then they'd been at it for four days and nights and had slept only twice.

Jared sat up on the couch, running his hands over his face, and looked back at her. He knew from experience that she slept hard. The first time she'd fallen asleep on the couch he'd played the gentleman and tried to get her upstairs.

It didn't happen. He'd tried nudging her, but she'd just murmured and kept sleeping. Even when he put his hands on her shoulders and pulled her upright, she didn't wake up. He had an idea that if he picked her up she'd snuggle against him like a child. Since he was as tired as she was, he was afraid that if he carried her up to bed he'd climb in with her.

In the end he'd kissed her forehead and let her sleep on the couch. He thought he'd go to the guesthouse, shower, then sleep in his own bed. Instead, he glanced at one of the plans on the floor and realized it had an error on it. He sat back down on the couch, meaning to fix it, but the next thing he knew Alix was standing over him, holding the plan, and saying, "This wall is wrong. It should be four inches to the south."

It had taken him a moment to wake up but when he did, he said, "I agree."

That had been two days ago and they hadn't slept since. They had just worked.

Jared looked back at Alix, smiling at her sleeping. Last night — or rather, early this morning — when she'd fallen asleep, this time, he'd kissed her on the mouth. A sweet kiss, one of friendship more than passion. She'd kissed him back a bit then smiled in her sleep.

Jared had looked up to see his grandfather wearing a look that said, You're pathetic, then he'd disappeared.

The second time around, Jared never even considered sleeping anywhere but on the couch facing Alix.

A movement caught his eye and he looked up to see his grandfather reappear by the doorway. He looked like he was going to say something, but in the next second Lexie stepped through the man.

"Jared!" she said loudly. "Where have you been? No one's heard from you since you went out to see Dilys. Toby's been so worried that she sent me over here to see about — Oh! Is that — ?" She was looking at Alix asleep on the couch.

Jared crossed the floor in two strides, took his cousin's arm, and led her out of the room and into the kitchen.

"Was that Alix on the other couch? Are you two a couple now? Already?"

"No," Jared said. "At least not in the way you mean. And lower your voice. She needs her sleep."

"What have you two been doing besides drinking rum?" There was an empty bottle on the counter and a half full one beside it. Lexie held up her hand. "Don't tell me.

You've been working."

"Right," Jared said. "She is worse than I am."

"Couldn't be," Lexie said, then took pity on him because he looked tired. "At least she and Dilys got you to cut that mass of hair you had. Sit down and I'll make you some breakfast. Toby sent over some jam she made. Will Alix get up soon?" She filled the coffee-maker.

Jared sat down at the banquette, rubbing his eyes to get the sleep out of them. "She'll wake up when she does."

"What does that mean?"

"That before she's ready, an anchor falling on her feet wouldn't wake her."

Lexie had her back to him as she got things out of the fridge so he couldn't see her smile. She was a very pretty young woman with the dark hair and eyes of all the Kingsleys, and the jawline was unmistakable. Her father had been an off-islander with blond hair and blue eyes, and his coloring had tempered the Kingsley darkness so that in the sun, lighter streaks could be seen in Lexie's hair. And Dilys always said that Lexie's eyes were lighter than the Kingsley blue that was so dark it was almost black.

"And you know this how?" Lexie asked as she put a carton of eggs on the counter.

Jared wasn't about to answer that question. "How is Dilys?"

"Full of talk about you and Alix. Is it true that you make her call you Mr. Kingsley?"

Jared laughed. "It started that way but that was back when she was in awe of me. Now it's just Kingsley, as in 'Kingsley, you don't know what you're talking about.' "

"I thought architecture students thought you were some god to be worshipped." Lexie's tone told how absurd she thought that was.

"Not this one." Jared was smiling. "At least not anymore, even though I *was* right about the wall in my cousin's house."

Lexie paused in breaking eggs to look at him. "You *listened* to her? From what I've seen, when it comes to buildings, it's your way or get out."

"Except with Ken," Jared said.

"And that extends to his daughter? Dilys thinks that man can perform miracles. She used to tell me what you were like before Ken showed up. I was just a kid but —"

"You're the same age as Alix. Dilys used to bring you over here to Aunt Addy's to play with her."

"I didn't know that. She didn't tell me."

"I saw the two of you together once. I remember you kids sitting in the back and . . ." He stopped talking as he remembered the scene.

That had been the summer before Ken showed up. It was Jared's second summer without his father. Even though people had told him that time would make it better, he'd found that time had made it worse. He'd dropped out of all school sports, he hadn't opened a textbook that whole year, and he was drinking everything alcoholic he could get his underage hands on. He'd had several after-school jobs, but he'd been fired from all of them because he rarely showed up when he was supposed to.

His family had exhausted themselves talking to him, threatening him, offering him incentives to change his ways. Even his ghostly grandfather had endlessly lectured him on how he needed to be a man and help his widowed mother, not make her life worse. But Jared's anger had no ability to reason.

Only his great-aunt Addy didn't nag him. In her very long life she'd seen a lot of death and knew about grief. Her only comment had been, "You're a good boy and that goodness will come out again when it's time." As a result of her understanding, the only place on the island Jared felt any peace was at Kingsley House with his aunt.

On the day Jared saw little Lexie and Alix playing, he had just been fired from yet another job. He'd taken a beer from his aunt's fridge — she never pointed out that he was a kid — and sat in a chair by her under a shade tree.

"Alix fits in here so well," Addy said.

"You know that Victoria will take her away. She's not the type to live here all year," Jared said. "You'd do better not to fall in love with the kid." He sounded very old.

"I know," Addy said, "but I plan to enjoy her as long as I can."

"What does Victoria do all day? The house needs a good cleaning."

"I know. There's dust everywhere." Addy lowered her voice. "I think she's reading the old Kingsley journals."

"How the hell did she find them?" Jared looked at Addy's face. "Sorry. How did she find them?"

"She knocked over a cabinet while she was dancing with a tourist." Adelaide made it sound like Victoria had consorted with an enemy alien.

Jared smiled as he drank his beer. That sounded like Victoria. She was beautiful and vivacious and —

"Earth to Jared!" Lexie was saying.

He blinked a few times. "I was just remembering you and Alix together."

"What did we play?"

"I don't remember. No. Wait. I do. You brought over some little dolls and she built houses for them."

"It's a wonder you didn't help her with the building."

"That was before Ken arrived, so I would have built it out of fishing lures."

"And we're back to Ken. So what's this about not telling Alix that her father trained you?"

"I'm caught in the middle," he said and told her about his first meeting with Alix. "I had no idea she recognized me, then Ken called and laid me out for lying to her."

Lexie slid a ham and cheese omelet onto a plate. "So that's why you're spending an entire week holed up with her? To make up for lying to her?" She poured two cups of coffee.

"I didn't want her to leave the island, because I knew I'd get blamed for running her off."

Lexie took bread out of the toaster and slathered it with the jam Toby had made. "Is that it? The whole, entire, and only reason you've not left this house for days?"

Jared cut into his omelet and took his time answering. "It started out that way."

"And now?" Lexie took a seat across from him.

He looked at her with eyes that seemed to spark flames. "Now Ken's the reason I keep my hands off her."

"Oh, my," Lexie said, leaning back in her chair. "You haven't fallen in . . . you know, with her . . . have you?"

"I've known her for less than a week," Jared said, frowning.

Lexie sipped her coffee and watched her

cousin, fully aware that he'd not answered her question. Dilys said that Jared had never recovered from his father's premature death. Lexie had been told how Jared and his mother had both nearly lost their minds when Six died. Jared had been angry at the world, while his mother had sunk into a depression that no counseling or pills could get her out of.

Then Ken Madsen had shown up and given the boy an outlet for his rage. But nothing and no one had been able to revive Jared's mother. She'd died soon after her son graduated from high school.

Since then, Jared had been the family loner, living in two worlds, even using a different name off-island.

"And you're doing all this out of respect for Ken?" Lexie asked.

"I owe him, don't you think?"

"We all do," Lexie said, smiling at her cousin. She and Toby weren't the only people Jared had helped. He'd given friends and relatives jobs, had subsidized the mortgages of two destitute cousins, and he'd stayed with Aunt Addy at the end of her life. "So when are you going to tell Alix the truth about you and her father?"

"I'm not," he said. "It's not my place to tell her. Besides, she just found out that Victoria comes here every year."

"She didn't even know that?"

Jared shook his head.

Lexie got up to get the coffeepot. "Did you tell her about Victoria?"

"No." Jared grinned. "She saw the bedroom, called it the Emerald City, and she knew it was her mother's."

Lexie laughed as she refilled their cups and sat back down. "I think you need to protect yourself here. When — not if — Alix finds out the truth about her father and you, she won't be happy that you kept such a big secret from her."

"That's a good idea," Jared said. "I'll call Ken and say I want permission to tell his daughter about his visiting here because I'm so hot for her that my fingertips ache. That when she leans over me to look at a drawing her breath smells so good I want to swallow her whole. The way her body moves inside her clothes makes me sweat." He looked at his cousin across the table. "You think if I tell Ken that truth he'll give me his blessing?"

Lexie could only blink at him.

"Is there any more toast?" Jared asked. "Toby's jam is great. Alix will like it."

Lexie took a few breaths to recover herself, then got up to get the bread. "I think . . ."

"I'm open to suggestions," he said.

"You didn't actually promise Ken to keep your hands off her, did you?"

"I did."

"Oh, my goodness. You have to get him to

come here so he can tell Alix the truth. Then you'll be released from your promise."

"That should go over well," Jared said. "Ken shows up and I immediately carry his daughter off to bed."

Lexie thought for a moment. "The question is, how does Alix feel about *you*?"

Jared grimaced. "I'm her teacher. Although she doesn't listen to me much. You want to hear what she's doing?"

"Sure." Lexie didn't let him see her surprise. She'd never heard her cousin talk about any of the women he dated, but then he didn't stay with them long enough to even remember their names. He had never brought one of them home to Nantucket, never introduced one to the family.

"While I was out on my boat, she and Izzy broke into my office."

"The one you never let anyone into?"

"That's the one." He looked up as his grandfather appeared behind Lexie.

She turned around, but saw no one. "What is it?"

"Nothing," he said, but he knew his grandfather was warning him not to tell too much. "I think Alix must have seen some of the drawings I did for small structures because she designed a chapel. She even found some card stock and made a model. I saw it hidden in a cabinet and it was great. Original. Perfect. I'm going to try to get some of my clients to build it and give Alix full credit for it. A great start to her career, right?"

"It sounds wonderful. What did she say when you told her?"

"She hasn't shown me the model," he said.

Lexie nodded. "She couldn't very well admit she sneaked into your office. Maybe you could hint that you don't just do big buildings."

"I did, but it got no reaction from her. Maybe tomorrow I can —"

"You won't have time," Lexie said. "I'm here because we need to talk about this weekend. But go ahead and tell me about the chapel."

"There isn't anything else to tell. She hasn't mentioned her design and the model's no longer in the cabinet."

"Why don't you tell her you saw it and that it's great?" Lexie said.

"It would seem like I was snooping. I think there's a reason she won't show it to me, but I don't know what it is."

"If it were me," Lexie said, "I'd be terrified that you'd think it was awful. Sounds like she wants to impress you, but what if you see something done by her and you hate it? That would really hurt."

"I pretty much told her I'd give her a job at my firm."

"She probably doesn't want to do anything to jeopardize that," Lexie said.

Jared finished his toast, picked up his empty plate, and put it in the sink. He was frowning as he thought about what Lexie had said. "What were you going to tell me about this weekend?"

"What are you going to do about Daffy Day?"

"Same thing I always do, I guess," he said.

"Stay home bent over a drawing board?"

"More or less."

"You've spent all this time with Alix, working, drinking rum, but you've not made a pass at her?" Lexie asked.

"Not a touch."

"No long, lingering looks?"

Jared smiled. "Not any that she saw."

"Even though you're very attracted to her?"

"You and Dilys! Are you two trying to make me feel bad? What are you getting at?"

"I'm just trying to see this from Alix's point of view. This pretty young woman has spent nearly a whole week being rejected by a man known for . . . what can I say? . . . having numerous women in his life. But he — you — has fed her lots of rum but not so much as made a move toward her. And tomorrow she's going out with Wes."

"Wes?"

"Your cousin? My cousin? Remember him? Young, handsome Wes Drayton who inherited two acres out in Cisco and plans to build a house because he's ready to settle down and have kids? *That* Wes?"

"Are you trying to say that Wes and Alix might get together?"

"Wes hasn't shut up about Alix since he met her. Yesterday he spent an hour with Toby planning the daffodil decorations for his dad's old car for the festival. His family is putting on a tailgate picnic meant to welcome Alix to the island. And in the afternoon he plans to take her out on his boat."

Jared leaned back in his chair and stared at Lexie. "Alix wouldn't . . . Look, she just broke up with some guy, so she's not going to run off with another one she just met and get married and live on an island. She's ambitious. She wants a career in architecture. She has to make a name for herself before she can hide away somewhere."

"Okay," Lexie said, her eyes on Jared's, "then she'll just have a lot of fabulous rebound sex with your cousin Wes. He'll make her feel like a man wants her for something besides drawing a house plan, and next year she'll leave Nantucket feeling great. She'll get a job at your big, fancy company, then she'll marry some guy who works for you, and they'll have kids. The end." She smiled sweetly at her cousin.

Jared looked back at Lexie, too shocked to say anything.

"Maybe Ken did put some limitations on you, but you need to figure out how to change things or you're going to lose her before you even get her." Lexie picked up her bag and went to the door. "Toby and I will be home all day tomorrow, so come for lunch. We'll be cooking for the picnic. Too bad Alix is going to be dining with Wes's family. Bye-bye," she said as she closed the door behind her.

Jared sat where he was, thinking about what Lexie had said. The truth was that it would be good if Alix and Wes hooked up. That would free Jared from having to escort her everywhere. And having a boyfriend on the island would make her stay. No one would give Jared hell for making her leave. Instead, they'd tell him he'd done a good job. Plus, he could give Alix the boxes of info about Valentina and she and Wes could work on that.

For a moment Jared had a vision of Alix and his cousin sitting on the floor of the back parlor, papers all around them. They would be like he and Alix had been for the last few days. Only Wes wouldn't have chains around him as Jared did. No one was going to tell Wes to keep his hands off her.

And what would Jared do? Return to New York and go back to twelve- and fourteen-hour workdays? And for the next year when he was on the island, would he be banished from wandering in and out of his own house? He could imagine Alix telling him that she and Wes needed their privacy. Would Jared accidentally walk in on them when they were . . . ?

He didn't want to take that vision any further.

He looked around the kitchen and thought of the days since Alix had arrived. They'd done such ordinary things: grocery shopping, preparing meals together, working side by side. In work, she had the ability to look ahead, to see how and why a feature wasn't going to work. It was a talent Jared also had, but he knew from experience that few people did.

But none of that really mattered.

All in all, it made sense that Alix and Wes should spend tomorrow together and let happen what may. In fact, it would be good for everyone if the two of them got together.

"Like hell!" Jared muttered as he left the house. He needed to shower and make some calls. Daffy Day started with a parade of antique cars and he knew just where he could get one.

# Chapter Ten

When Alix awoke she heard voices. One was unmistakably Jared's deep rumble and the other belonged to a woman. For a moment she lay on the couch and wondered if the voice she remembered hearing so long ago was his. She'd heard Jared laugh, but only slightly, not that kind of laughter that comes from deep within a person and is so all encompassing that it cures illnesses. That was the laugh she remembered.

She turned her head to look at the jumble of books and papers on the floor and couldn't help smiling. It had been glorious working with him! He was opinionated and knowledgeable and experienced and . . . and sexy, she thought. But she'd tried to stamp that thought down. If she got too close to him, he moved away. It looked like her original impression that he was interested in her as a woman was wrong.

She couldn't bring herself to ask him if he

had a girlfriend. That wasn't any of her business.

When she heard the back door open and close, she leaped off the couch and ran for the stairs. She knew she must be a mess and she needed time to clean up. Besides, she was dying to call Izzy and tell her everything that was going on.

Once Alix was upstairs, she phoned Izzy but it went to voice mail, which made her frown. She hadn't talked to her friend or had a response to her many emails and text messages for days now.

On the first night after she'd been to dinner with Kingsley — somewhere in there she'd dropped the "Mr." — she'd talked to her father and told him of the lavish apology she'd received, complete with flowers.

"Just an apology?" her dad asked. "Nothing else? No inappropriate innuendos or touches?" He made the last sound like his worst fear.

"No, Father," she said solemnly, "I'm still as virginal as I was before I met Big Bad Kingsley."

"Alixandra," her father said in warning.

"Sorry," she said. "Jared Kingsley treats me with absolute and total respect. Is that better?"

"I'm glad to hear it," Ken said.

Alix wanted to say "I'm not," but she didn't.

She hadn't heard from her father since

then, but she knew that he had finals to administer and grade, so he was busy.

Her concern was Izzy. Alix sent another email, left yet another long voice message, then went to the shower.

She took her time dressing and working on her hair and makeup, even though she wondered if she should bother. Would she see him today? On the first of these last four days they'd finished the plan for his cousin's house. In the end they'd compromised between her ideas and his: his dormers; her windowed addition. He had surprised her by being good at landscape design, something Alix knew little about.

"It comes from seeing a lot of gardens and drinking a lot of beer with a lot of landscapers," he'd said.

Alix had wanted to say "I like beer," but she was afraid such a remark would scare him off.

After they'd finally settled on how to remodel his cousin's house, they were faced with being *finished.* There were no more reasons to work together. No reason to stay in the same room, side by side.

It took Alix all of thirty seconds to decide to run upstairs and get her fat portfolio of school drawings. When she'd first realized that she was going to meet Jared Montgomery, actually be living near him, she'd fantasized about all the wonderful things he'd tell her about her work — just as her teachers did.

But Jared had gone through them quickly and said, "Do you have anything original?"

For a moment Alix felt like a little girl. She'd wanted to run away and hide so she could cry. And she wanted to call her best friend and tell her what a jerk Montgomery really was.

But in the next moment she became a professional and began to defend her work. When she saw a tiny bit of a smile from him she knew that's what he was pushing her to do.

One by one, they went over her drawings and tore them apart. Only if she could give a good argument for a design feature did he begrudgingly admit it was possible. What was really annoying was that Alix saw that he was nearly always right. His eye for proportion and his intuition for design were perfect. As her father often said, "You can't teach talent," and talent was what Jared Montgomery Kingsley had in abundance.

Under his guidance, she changed nearly everything she'd drawn — and they were all improved.

It was on the last day — to Alix's astonishment — that he brought out the plans for a house he had designed for a client in New Hampshire. By that time they had become quite familiar with each other through work and shared meals and even falling asleep in the same room. Even so, she was hesitant to say anything critical about his designs, but then the truth was that it was extraordinary. That he — and for all his name changes, he was *the* Jared Montgomery — would ask *her* opinion gave her a moment of speechlessness.

"You have nothing to say?"

"It's perfect," she whispered, and the exterior was. But then she saw the floor plan. She took a breath and plunged ahead. "The living room is in the wrong place," she said, and they went on from there.

Now that they were truly done with the plans, she wondered if he would retreat to the guesthouse and work on his own. Several times he'd mentioned the house in California that he had to do and Alix'd had to work not to say something about her own design. But there was something so personal about the chapel she'd drawn that she didn't want it critiqued.

On impulse, she pulled her suitcase out from under the bed, unzipped it, and removed the little model. She was still so pleased with it that she couldn't bear having someone tell her the roof angle was wrong or the steeple was too tall or too short. She liked it just the way it was.

Standing up, the model on the palm of her hand, she held it up to the portrait of Captain

Caleb. "What do you think?" she asked. "You like it or not?"

Of course there was silence and Alix smiled at the thought of receiving an answer. She turned to put the model back into the suitcase, but looked back at the portrait. "If you like it just as it is, make something move."

Instantly, the framed photo of the two women yet again fell off the table and hit the thick rug.

For a moment Alix felt a little dizzy at what had happened. She told herself that the picture falling just when she'd asked the question was a coincidence, but she didn't believe it.

She sat on the edge of the bed, still holding the model. "I guess you do like it," she said. She was glad when there was no response to her words. "And it looks like I'm living in a haunted house."

She didn't want to think about that too much. After a few deep breaths she stood up, put the model back in its hiding spot, and went to the door.

A white envelope like the one that had been with the daffodil had been pushed under the door. "Why didn't you tell me this was here?" she said aloud, then caught herself. "And don't you dare answer that. One ghostly answer a day is all I can take."

She opened the envelope and saw the distinctive lettering.

Would you like to go with me to liberate an old truck?

Alix couldn't help laughing and doing a little dance around the room. "Oh, yes, I would love to go," she said aloud as she danced over to Captain Caleb's portrait. "Are you happy about this?" she asked, looking up at him, then said, "Do *not* make anything fall down."

She was pleased when everything in the room held steady. After taking a moment to compose herself, she headed downstairs. As before, Jared was in the living room reading a newspaper. All their papers and the big prints were gone from the floor and neatly stacked on the shelves.

"Hungry?" he asked without looking up.

"Starved. Did we get any cereal?"

"No," he said as he put down the paper and looked at her.

She thought she saw a spark in his eyes, but it was quickly gone.

"If you can scramble eggs, I can make toast. Toby sent over some jam she made."

"The Toby who everyone loves does her own canning?"

"And baking. She makes a blueberry pie that'll make you weep. I think she puts cinnamon in it."

"When are you two getting married?"

"Toby is much, much too good for someone

like me. I'd feel that I had to behave all the time."

"No hijacking of old trucks?"

"Definitely not," Jared said, smiling at her.

As they started for the kitchen, Alix's phone buzzed and she looked at it, hoping it was Izzy, but it was an ad trying to sell her a used car. She deleted it.

"Something wrong?" Jared asked.

She told him that it had been days since she'd heard from her friend and that wasn't usual.

"Are you worried about her?" he asked as he went to the fridge.

"Not really, but I do wish she'd let me know what she's doing. Have you eaten?"

"I did."

As usual, they worked together like a perfectly aligned machine, getting food out and putting it where it was needed. When Alix picked up the skillet Jared handed her the butter. He'd already cracked two eggs into a blue bowl that Alix remembered seeing being used for eggs. Bread went into the toaster and Jared set the table.

Within minutes they sat down and he filled their cups with hot coffee.

"Did I hear voices this morning?" Alix asked, then said, "Even if it's a lie, please tell me that I did."

"What does that mean?"

If she told him the whole truth she'd have

to mention her chapel model and she didn't want to do that. "Just that another picture fell off a table — and don't you dare say it's a drafty old house."

Jared grinned as that was exactly what he was about to say. "Old houses always have odd things happening in them, but, yes, this morning Lexie stopped by."

"Please tell me she didn't see me passed out on the couch."

"She did and she wanted to know all about you."

"What did you tell her?"

"That you nearly worked me to death."

"You're the one who — !" She stopped and shook her head at him. "Where's perfect Toby's perfect jam?"

"How could I have forgotten it?" he said, his eyes laughing as he went to the fridge and got the jar.

It had a label with daisies on it and perfect lettering said BEACH PLUM JAM — CLW.

"CLW?"

Jared shrugged. "I guess those are Toby's real initials."

"I would have thought that you knew everything about her."

"Mortals can't aspire to reach so high."

Alix gave a groan that was also a laugh. "I'm afraid to meet this creature. Do her wings get in the way when she moves?"

"She's used to them, so she sort of tucks

them under her arms. Are you ready to go?"

"This jam is great. What are these beach plums?"

"They grow wild here, and where they are is kept secret from one generation to another."

"I guess that means you know."

"No, but the man who haunts this house does."

Alix laughed as she took her plate to the sink and rinsed it. "Where is this truck you want to steal and why do you plan to take it?"

"It's for the Daffodil Festival, for the parade."

"For Lexie and the angelic Toby to use? Will Wes drive it?"

"No, I will."

"I thought you didn't attend it."

"Lexie changed my mind. You have any more solid shoes than those? I thought that before we get the old truck I'd show you some land I own. It's been passed down from one Jared to the next."

"Who's that?" Alix asked without missing a beat.

He looked puzzled for a second, then gave a half grin. "Jared is the name that comes between the Mr. and the Kingsley."

"Before or after the number?"

"Before," he said, still smiling. "In fact, it's what most people call me. Well, except for the peons in my office, the ones who are there to gain wisdom from me."

"Ooooooh, *that* Jared. The wise one. He's above my league. Makes me nervous even to think about him."

"What about Jared Kingsley?"

"Him, I rather like," Alix said, looking him in the eyes.

For a moment they stared at each other. He was the first to break away as he put his hand on the doorknob. "Go change your shoes and meet me outside in five minutes. Don't make me wait."

"Okay . . . Jared," she said, then left the room to run up the stairs to her bedroom.

She closed the door and leaned against it briefly. "Well, Captain," she said, looking around the bed at the portrait, "what do you think of your grandson and me? Don't answer that," she said quickly.

She slipped off her sandals, opened the big wardrobe to get her sneakers out, and tied them on. When she stood up, she looked at the portrait and suddenly realized something. If there was a ghost in the house, he'd met her mother.

"I'm Victoria's daughter," she said. "I don't look like her, except maybe my mouth does, and my hair's a little bit red. I don't have her talent, but she is my mother. She —"

Pebbles hit the window and she went to push it up then leaned out.

Jared was downstairs and looking up. "Are you writing a book? Let's go!"

"I'm correcting the errors you made on your cousin's house. It takes a while." She shut the window. "Not exactly patient, is he?" She opened the door, then looked back at Captain Caleb and blew him a kiss. "See you later." She hurried down the stairs, grabbed her bag from the hall table, and kept running.

Alix got into the truck beside Jared and closed the door with a solid pull. A few days ago she would have wondered why a man as famous and probably as rich as he was didn't buy himself a new truck. But the longer she stayed on Nantucket, the more the old truck seemed to fit in.

He drove down one street after another, some of them so narrow she caught her breath. But Jared didn't seem to notice.

"Oh, hell!" he muttered.

Alix looked to see what was upsetting him but nothing seemed to be unusual. They were on a very narrow street and coming toward them was a big black SUV, but that was normal. "What is it?"

"Off-islander," he said under his breath and his tone made the term sound vile, maybe even evil.

The big car looked like all the others, so what made him think it wasn't someone who lived on Nantucket? "How do you know?"

His answer was a look that said "How do you not know?" He put his arm across the back of the seat, reversed, and maneuvered the truck into a tiny space against the curb.

Alix looked with interest as the vehicle passed. Inside was a woman with lots of shiny hair, half a dozen gold bracelets on her arm, a designer linen shirt, and a cell phone plastered to her ear. As she drove past them she didn't so much as wave a thanks to Jared for having moved aside so she could get by. In fact, she didn't even look at them.

"Answer your question?" Jared asked.

In just a few days on the island Alix had become so used to the friendliness and courtesy between inhabitants that the woman's rudeness was shocking. It was as though the beat-up old pickup didn't exist to her. "Off-islanders," Alix said in wonder. "Will there be a lot of them here?"

"Horrific!" Jared said as he pulled out of the temporary parking place. "And not one of them knows how to drive. They think four-way stops mean the other drivers stop to let them go by without so much as slowing down."

Alix hoped he was making a joke. The rest of the way she looked out the window. She doubted if she'd ever get used to the beauty of the houses of Nantucket.

At last he turned off the paved road and down a dirt path. Around them were scrubby bushes and tall, bent pines that looked like bonsai plants on steroids. "The wind's done this?" she asked.

"Yes. We're on the North Shore near where the first English settled."

"Where your ancestors lived?"

He nodded. "They built houses near here, but the harbor closed up in a big storm so they moved."

"And the harbor is everything."

"No, the sea is everything," he said, then quoted, "*Two thirds of this terraqueous globe are the Nantucketer's. For the sea is his; he owns it, as Emperors own empires.* That's what Melville said about us."

"Ah, yes. *Moby Dick.* When they glorified killing the whales."

"Not my family," Jared said as he stopped, turned off the engine, and they got out of the truck.

"That's right. Captain Caleb was in the China trade. Why didn't that continue? Or did it?"

"Opium Wars," he said. "I need to talk to you about something. How much — ?" He broke off because his cell phone buzzed. He took it out of his pocket and looked at the ID. "Sorry, but I need to take this call. The sea is that way."

"Sure," she said. There was a little path ahead of her and she walked down it. The plants around her looked fierce and tough.

Kind of like Nantucketers, she thought, and tried to imagine what the first settlers had seen. She really did need to read some Nantucket history.

At the end of the path was one of the many beautiful, sandy beaches that surrounded the island and that she'd seen photos of. She'd never been a "beach person" who longed to sit in the blistering hot sun and do nothing, but on this beach a person could, well, *think.*

"Like it?"

She looked up to see Jared standing near her, gazing out at the ocean. "Yes, I do. Was there a house here?"

"Come on," he said, "and I'll show you."

She followed him down a narrow path that had been made in between the fierce little shrubs and noticed the sand on the ground. She had an idea that if you dug anywhere on the island you'd hit sand.

He stopped at a large, cleared space that had only an indentation to show that there had once been a building there.

"Was the house moved?"

"Burned," Jared said.

"Recently?"

"Early 1800s."

As she looked at him, he walked to a tall pine tree and sat down on an area of softened needles.

Alix sat down beside him, but not too close. She thought he seemed awfully serious. "You wanted to talk to me about something?"

"Yes," he said, "but first, that call I just had? It was from my assistant in New York."

"You have to return," she said before she thought.

"No." He smiled at her. She'd sounded like she didn't want him to go.

"What did she say?" Alix was a bit embarrassed at the way she'd said that.

"He. My assistant is a man named Stanley. Wears a bow tie and is a powerhouse of efficiency. I asked him to find out about your friend Izzy."

"Did you?" she asked, surprised.

"I did, and Izzy is in the U.S. Virgin Islands."

"You're kidding."

"Stanley never kids. Or makes a mistake. He called Izzy's mother and she said that Gary's mother —"

"Glenn's mother."

"Glenn's mother is making Izzy so crazy that he took her away for a while."

"She isn't the only culprit. Izzy's mother isn't exactly easy to live with."

"So Stanley told me. It seems that after Glenn told his parents as well as Izzy's that they wouldn't be invited to the wedding if they didn't let up on Izzy, both sets of parents paid for the trip. However, Izzy's cell phone doesn't work on the island and a call using the hotel phone is very expensive."

"She and Glenn aren't rich, by any means, and Izzy wouldn't want to run up a bill that their parents had to pay."

"I guessed that, so Stanley is having a prepaid international phone delivered to your friend's hotel from a nearby shop. She should be getting in touch with you soon."

Alix sat there looking at him. He had his head turned so she saw his profile. "Yet another kindness from you," she said softly. "And I'll pay you back for the phone."

"It'll be a wedding gift and besides, it gave Stanley something to do."

"Thank you," she said. "Thank you very, very much." She bent forward as though to kiss his cheek, but he turned his head away and she sat back down. Okay, she thought. Friendship. She needed to try to remember that that's what he wanted.

"You keep doing nice things for me," she said. "Flowers and now a telephone. I don't know how I can repay you."

For a moment he didn't speak. "Did you read my aunt's will?"

"No. My mother called and gave me the number of a lawyer. She said he had some spectacularly fabulous news for me and it was going to make me wildly happy."

Smiling, Jared looked back at her. "That sounds just like Victoria."

There was so much affection in his voice that a wave of what felt very much like jealousy went through Alix. She tried to repress it, but it flashed through her mind that her mother might be the reason Jared Kingsley turned away from her. It's what Izzy had said when she'd first seen Victoria's room. But Alix pushed the thought out of her mind.

"I take it the lawyer didn't tell you about Valentina," he said.

"You mentioned her name before, but I know nothing about her."

"My grandfather —" Jared caught himself. "You know the portrait in Aunt Addy's bedroom? I mean, your bedroom?"

"Of Captain Caleb? I guess he would be your grandfather, but a little far back."

"He's five greats," Jared said. "Would you like to hear his story?"

"Very much so."

It was quiet where they were, sitting under the bent tree, the sun shining on the old house site.

"Valentina Montgomery was an off-islander," Jared said. "She came here in the early 1800s to visit an old aunt who'd married a Nantucket sea captain. The aunt was a widow and an invalid, and Valentina took care of her."

Jared went on to tell that young, handsome Captain Caleb Kingsley had been away when Valentina arrived. He'd been on one of his four voyages to China where he'd made a name for himself by bringing back exquisite goods and selling them for top prices to stores all over the East Coast.

"He had taste," Jared said. "That's what set him apart and made him rich." He explained that the others who went to China brought back the cheapest things they could find so they'd make the most profit. But Caleb had gone for beauty, and as a result, by the time he was thirty-three he was wealthy. He was the prize catch on an island that had many widows.

"He and Valentina fell in love and they were going to get married," Jared said, "but Caleb wanted to go on one last voyage."

"Didn't those trips last for years?" Alix asked.

"Anywhere from three to seven years."

"So they agreed to wait until he got back?"

"Yes." Jared smiled. "But they didn't wait for everything. When Caleb left, he didn't know it, but Valentina was expecting their child."

"Oh, my," Alix said. "What did she do?"

Jared couldn't tell Alix that he'd heard this story all his life and no matter how many times his grandfather told it, it was always with passion — and anger.

"Valentina married Obed Kingsley, Caleb's cousin. No one knows why for sure, but it was assumed that she did it to give her child the Kingsley name. Or maybe it was so she could stay on the island and raise her child here. Or . . .”

“Or what?”

“Maybe she was blackmailed or threatened in some way. You see, Valentina had the recipe for Kingsley Soap. She’d found a way to use glycerine to make a mild, transparent soap — and this was in a time when lye was used as the base.”

“Even the thought of that makes my skin hurt,” Alix said.

“Valentina had been making the soap for a couple of years and she sold it in Obed’s store. After they were married, he began making the soap on a large scale and sending it off-island to be sold. Whatever else he was, he was an excellent businessman.”

Alix noted the sneer in Jared’s voice; it was as though he were talking of recent events. “He just needed a product to sell,” she said, encouraging Jared to continue. From his tone Alix could tell that the story was leading to tragedy. But then having to marry a man you didn’t love just to give your child a name was already tragic.

“The soap . . . ?” she began, but then hesitated. Again she thought of her mother’s novel about a soap empire. It had been a clear soap scented with wild jasmine that had started the family on to great wealth. But hadn’t that novel been told from the point of view of a second wife? “What happened to

Valentina?"

"We don't know," Jared said. "She gave birth to a son, named him Jared Montgomery Kingsley, and —"

"He was the first one?"

"He was," Jared said.

"What happened when Captain Caleb returned and found his girl married to his cousin?"

"Caleb didn't return. He was in a port in South America with a damaged ship that was going to need months for the repairs, when his brother showed up on another ship."

"Nantucketers owned the oceans."

"They did." Jared's face was serious. "Caleb's brother, Thomas, was on his way home and docked to see his brother. They exchanged news and Caleb was told that Valentina had given birth to a son six months after her marriage. Caleb knew the child was his and he had an idea of why she'd married Obed. He wanted to go home immediately, so he talked his younger brother into exchanging ships. Thomas's ship was much faster than Caleb's and it was ready to leave right then. Caleb wrote out a will leaving everything he owned to Valentina and their son, then he headed home on his brother's ship. But it hit a storm and went down with all the crew on board. It was almost a year later when Thomas got home with Caleb's ship full of valuable goods from China, all of which belonged to Valentina and their son. They moved from here to the new house on Kingsley Lane, and a year later, Valentina was gone. She'd disappeared. Obed said she ran off and left him and her son. But no one saw Valentina leave the island. Some people had doubts, but then no one had any reason to disbelieve Obed. Everyone felt sorry for him, and a few years later, he remarried."

"So the child inherited it all."

"Everything. And Obed and his second wife had no children, so Kingsley Soap went to the boy too. He was a very wealthy young man."

"But with no parents," Alix said. "Not so wealthy, after all."

Jared turned to her with a sweet smile. "You're right," he said. "Nothing in the world makes up for that loss."

For a moment they looked at each other, the soft Nantucket sea breeze on them, but then Jared stood up and the moment was lost.

"You're supposed to find out what happened to Valentina," he said.

"I'm what?" Alix asked as she got up.

"You're to find out what happened to Valentina. It's the Great Kingsley Mystery."

"This woman disappeared over two hundred years ago. How am I supposed to research that?"

Jared started walking down the path and back to the truck, Alix close behind him.

"Beats me," he said. "Aunt Addy left boxes of papers collected by various relatives, but no one could find out. She always said the secret died with Obed."

They had reached the truck. "Let me get this straight," Alix said. "Your ancestors spent years trying to figure this out but couldn't and now they want me, who is — I hardly dare say this — an off-islander, to figure out what happened to her? Is that right?"

"That's exactly right. You catch on quickly. But then I've seen that you're smart, a little impatient at times so you get things wrong, but you have brains."

"Me impatient? You were throwing rocks at my window this morning and hurrying me to change shoes."

"I was afraid you were having a long conversation with the Captain you're so crazy about."

"I told him to keep quiet."

Jared's eyes widened. "You were talking to him?"

"Just blowing kisses at him. Our relationship is purely physical."

"Bet he likes that," Jared muttered as he got in the truck beside Alix.

She sat in silence, thinking about what he'd said as he turned the truck around and drove back to the paved road. She was thinking so hard about all that he'd told her that she paid little attention to where he was going.

All she could think of was the story she'd just heard. Two people deeply in love, but they'd agreed to wait for years. Alix couldn't imagine that happening in the modern age. At least Caleb and Valentina'd had some time alone. Was it the night before he left? One wild, passionate night? Maybe they'd decided to wait until Caleb returned from his voyage, but on that last night Valentina had slipped into his room and untied her corset strings and —

"We're here," Jared said. "You seem a million miles away."

Alix came out of her trance and looked out to see a house, new, fairly modern, and definitely not designed by Montgomery. The sea stretched out behind it. "I was thinking of the story you told me. My mother wrote about a man who built up a soap empire."

"Did she?" Jared asked. "What did she say about where he got the recipe?"

"I don't remember. It's been too long since I read it, but I seem to remember that there was a second wife. Sally?"

"Susan," Jared said, then gave her a sharp look. "Not that your mother was writing about *my* family."

Alix was about to make a sarcastic remark about her mother spending so much time on Nantucket yet he didn't want to believe that she wrote about the place. But she stopped herself, suddenly understanding that Jared didn't like the idea that his family's past passions and indiscretions had been published for the world to see.

"What's the name of the book about soap?" he asked.

*"Forever at . . ."* She looked at him.

"At what? Making bubbles?" He was not being funny. In fact, he looked thoroughly disgusted.

*"Sea,"* she said softly. *"Forever at Sea."*

"Great," he muttered. "And my quarterboard is . . ."

"TO SEA FOREVER," Alix said, sympathy in her voice as she thought, Oh, Mom, what have you done? "It could be a coincidence. Kingsley Soap used to be a very big deal, so maybe Mom —"

Jared looked at her with hooded eyes. "Do you really think it's a coincidence?"

Alix started to say it could be, but changed her mind. "I think my mother spent one month a year here with Aunt Addy, prying the whole Kingsley family history out of her. Then Mom spent the next eleven months writing the stories into best-sellers. That's what I really think."

Jared looked like he was about to answer that, but then he opened the truck door and got out.

Alix thought, He knows a great deal more about this than he's telling.

"Come on," Jared said. "We need to get the

old truck."

Alix had lots of questions for him but she had an idea that right now he wouldn't answer them. "It couldn't be older than your truck."

He gave a little smile. "It's even older than *me.*"

"A true antique," Alix said as she hurried forward to walk beside him.

She'd thought he would laugh at her joke but instead he gave her a look that said he'd like to show her how old he was. Truthfully, his look was a bit intimidating, but she remembered what the woman in the liquor store said, that she wasn't to let Jared bully her. Alix pulled herself up straighter and met his look with one that said "Bring it on. I can handle it."

She had the great satisfaction of seeing him smile a bit before he turned his head away. She followed his long strides across the gravel to the garage.

When they got there, he lifted the lid to an alarm box and punched in numbers, and the door began to go up.

Alix was looking at the house. "He may be your friend, but you didn't design this house."

"I did one in Arizona for him."

"The Harwood house?" Her breath caught in her throat.

"That's it."

"Oh," Alix said, blinking up at him. "That's

one of my favorites. That house seems to rise out of the desert, to be part of it."

"It should. I still have scars on my back from where I ran into a cactus. Damned things! Worse than being hit with a tuna rig."

She followed him into the garage. "So you spent time there studying the land? How long did you stay? Did you have any trouble getting the owner to agree to that slanted roof? Usually the roofs there are flat, but yours —" She stopped because Jared was glaring at her.

"We are *on* the island," he said.

"But we just spent days designing houses together and —" When he kept staring at her, Alix couldn't help laughing. "Okay, you win. No more work. I'm supposed to think about Valentina and the ghost who keeps tossing things around my room — when he's not kissing me, that is — and then there's Izzy's wedding that I'm to arrange. That I'm not a professional researcher and I'm certainly not a wedding planner doesn't seem to make any difference to anyone."

"Everybody has great confidence in you. What do you think of the truck? If you can quit complaining long enough to look at it, that is."

He was right in that she hadn't even glanced at it. It was old, with big round fenders, whitewall tires, and a large front grille. It was probably from the thirties and in pristine condition, with bright blue paint that was so shiny it looked wet. "Nice." She ran her hand over a fender. "And you're going to drive it in the parade?" She wanted to ask who would be riding with him.

"Yes, I'm going to drive," he said as he looked at her through the truck windows. "Toby and Lexie will help you with the wedding plans. And I can help you with Granddad's papers. If you want to work on them, that is. Aunt Addy's will says that you don't have to."

She couldn't help the little charge that went through her at the thought of continuing to work together. An idea hit her. "I know that what happened to Captain Caleb and Valentina was a great tragedy, but it was a very long time ago. What difference does it make *now*?"

Jared looked away and seemed to be having trouble coming up with an answer.

"Is it the soap?" she asked.

"The soap?"

"If you could prove ownership of the recipe, would that mean you still own the company?" Her eyes widened. "Or *do* you still own Kingsley Soap?"

Jared smiled. "Aunt Addy's brother, Five, sold the company, recipe and all, then he spent every penny of it." He raised the hood of the truck and looked under it.

Alix stood beside him. The engine was as clean as the outside of the vehicle, but she wasn't looking at it. Wasn't one of her mother's books about a likable scoundrel who wasted the family fortune? She brought her mind back to the present. "So why does anyone want to know what happened to Valentina?"

"Maybe Aunt Addy promised Caleb to find out. Who knows?"

"She wasn't *that* old." Alix followed him to the back of the truck. "Wait a minute. You don't believe what Dilys said about Aunt Addy talking to a ghost, do you?"

He looked up from the truck. "Would you like to see the inside of the house?"

"Are you trying to make me stop asking questions about your family? Are there *lots* of secrets?"

"Walt Harwood had me design a bedroom in this house for his grandson. It's like the interior of an old whaling ship. Or a movie version, anyway. And photos of the room have never been put in any book."

Alix very much wanted to know more about Valentina and Caleb and even Obed. And she wanted to know for sure how her mother came to know so much about all the Kingsleys. Could Aunt Addy have known so very much about the family? All the way back to the 1700s? That didn't seem likely. And why had Alix been asked to do this research? Why not her mother? But then her mom would have hired someone from the Smithsonian.

But as much as Alix wanted to ask questions, she knew this could be her only chance to see a room — an *interior*! — designed by Jared Montgomery. She knew he was trying to distract her, but still . . .

"I have a sixteen-megapixel Nikon in the glove box of my truck," he said. "You can take all the photos you want."

Alix stared at him.

"Think your friend Izzy will want to see them?" he asked enticingly.

"Okay, you win," Alix said. "Lead me to the room. Have you done many interiors?"

"On island," he said. "No questions."

"You're a rat, aren't you?"

"With a long, strong tail," he said and walked ahead of her.

Alix watched the backside of him as he walked away and agreed. Quite strong looking.

Alix thought the house's interior was very ordinary. There were big windows looking out to the sea and that was nice, but there was absolutely nothing in the house that was unique or even very interesting. The crown moldings were insipid, and what woodwork there was came from a millwork catalog.

However, she noted that the kitchen cabinets were the very expensive kind made in Germany, the granite had fossils in it, and all the tile had been handmade. To her it was odd that the walls were Sheetrock but the marble was Carrara.

She looked back at Jared. "You mind if I ask how much your friend paid for this house?"

"Twenty mill."

Alix took a moment before she could get her mouth closed. "Twenty *million* dollars? American dollars? Twenty of them?"

"That's right."

"Why in the world did it cost that much?"

"Because it's on Nantucket."

"I know that. But if it were in Indiana . . ."

"If it were in Indiana it wouldn't cost even one million," he said. "But it's on Nantucket."

"Yes, and it's on the water, but isn't twenty million a bit excessive?"

"Not if the house is on Nantucket," he said firmly.

"Okay," she said, "what would this house cost if it were on, say, Martha's Vineyard?"

"Who's she?"

"I don't know who Martha was. I'm talking about the island that's about thirty miles west of here."

"Never heard of the place." He turned and walked down the corridor.

Alix stood still for a moment, shaking her head, then she followed him upstairs to see the room he'd designed to look like a ship captain's quarters.

# Chapter Eleven

As they were leaving the house, Alix tripped on the porch and fell into Jared's arms. She had taken over fifty photos of the room he'd designed — it was charming — and she was looking at them in the viewfinder of the camera. She was so absorbed in the photos that she wasn't paying attention to where she was walking and didn't notice when she got to the edge of the porch.

Jared must have seen what was going to happen, or else he had the reflexes of a cobra. His arms went out and he grabbed her before she fell facedown onto the ground.

For a moment they stood there, Jared holding her with her feet off the ground, both his arms around her. Alix had the camera in one hand and the other was on his back.

The only thing certain in her life was that she wanted him to kiss her. Her eyes went to that bottom lip of his and words from her poem like "succulent" and "tip of my tongue" and "draw it in" came to her mind. Words and anticipated sensations floated through her mind and seemed to run through her body.

She felt his breath on her lips. Mingling breaths, she thought. She couldn't help moving her face closer to his until their lips were no more than a quarter inch apart. She looked up into his eyes and they were like blue fire, like an explosion about to happen.

Had he been anyone else she would have closed the tiny gap between their lips, but with this man she had doubts.

A seagull screeched nearby and the trance was broken.

Jared set her down on the ground with such a thunk that Alix's teeth clicked together. The second they were disentangled, he turned and quickly walked toward the sea.

Alix took a step back and sat on the edge of the porch. If he'd slapped her, he couldn't have hurt her more. She buried her face in her hands and tried to calm her wildly pounding heart.

A conversation she'd overheard a few years ago between her father and a friend of his came to her. "The real joy of youth is that you're desirable to everyone," her father's friend said. "When you get to be our age every year cuts that number in half."

"So where are we now? Down to fifteen percent of the population?"

"You always were an optimist."

Both men had laughed together.

When Alix had heard that she'd been about twenty, which made her father close to fifty. She didn't think that now, at twenty-six, she was old, but she was realizing that she wasn't desirable to every man. And definitely not to Jared Montgomery Kingsley the Seventh.

As she stood up, she took some breaths. She could not continue to carry a torch for someone who didn't want her. The sooner she stopped her lunacy of imagining something between her and this famous man, the better.

She looked toward the water and saw him standing with his shoulders raised as though fighting off an attack. His self-protective stance made her feel bad. She reminded herself that this island was his home, a place where he could get away from eager students pouncing on him.

It took courage on her part, but she walked the few feet and stopped just behind him. He didn't turn around. "I apologize for that," she said softly. "It won't happen again."

He kept his face turned away from her but he gave a sigh, as though in relief.

Alix couldn't help feeling a bit sorry for him. How horrible it must have been for him to be in an auditorium full of students, all of them wanting something from him. "Friends?" she said and held out her hand to shake.

When he turned to look at her, Alix drew in her breath. She'd expected sadness in his eyes, but instead she again saw that blue fire. Raging hot. So fiery that she had to work not to step back from it.

It was gone as quickly as it came. In the next second, he was smiling as though nothing had happened.

"I don't know about you," he said, "but I'm starving. Want to go to Lexie's house for lunch?" He started walking toward the antique truck.

"Does this mean I get to meet the angelic Toby?" Alix asked as she hurried after him. She was hoping that they could return to the easy camaraderie they'd enjoyed these last few days.

He stopped with his hand on the door handle of the old truck. "On one condition."

Alix quit breathing. Was he going to ask her to promise to keep her hands off him? "What's that?"

"That you help me with that house in L.A. that I'm late on. Tim emailed me again. They want a plan yesterday."

"Oh," Alix said as she got into the truck. "Oh."

"Is that a good oh or a bad one?" he asked, getting behind the wheel.

"I'm a student and you're . . . him. What do you think it means?"

"That I should do my own work?"

She was glad that he was back to teasing her and that the tension between them was gone. "You have any photos of the land?"

"I have a 3-D of the terrain of the twelve-acre plot, including existing trees and a big rock formation. I was thinking —"

"Of making one wall part of the stone?" she asked.

He had his arm over the back of the seat as he reversed the truck, but he paused to look at her — and the look he gave her was just as her father used to do when she'd done something that pleased him.

"You had the same thought?" she asked.

"Exactly. But I can't decide about the entrance. What do I do to match the stone wall? Maybe —" He broke off when Alix's cell phone rang.

She pulled it out of her bag and looked at the ID. "It says 'Unknown Caller,' " she said. She was always cautious about such calls.

"It could be your friend."

Alix pushed the button. "Hello?"

"I'm so sorry!" Izzy said. "So, so sorry I just disappeared, but Glenn threw a fit. It was wonderful! I was never so in love with him in my life. I thought he and his father were going to start slugging each other, but Glenn stood his ground and his mother stopped pestering me about who had to be in *my* wedding."

Alix looked across the seat at Jared and

nodded that it was Izzy. At her look of happiness, he smiled. "What about your mom?"

"My dad took care of her," Izzy said. "He was hilarious. He said that my young knight scared him half to death and that even though Mom also scared him, Glenn was bigger."

"That sounds like your dad."

"And your father too. Did you know that he called my dad and said . . . ? Well, I don't know what he said, but it started everything and — Oh, Alix, I've just talked about *me.* How are *you* doing?"

"I'm great," she said, "but I'm afraid I haven't done much about your wedding."

"That's okay. I have and I'll email you all about it. Did you know that Glenn and I are in the Virgin Islands right now?"

"Yes, I did."

"It was your dad's idea, but both our parents paid for it."

"My father helped?" Alix looked at Jared, who lifted his eyebrows.

"Yes, he did. And when my phone didn't work here, they had this one sent to the hotel."

"Actually, that was —"

"I'm pregnant."

"What?" Alix said.

"That's why I was crying so much on Nantucket. Hormones, I guess. And now all I do is throw up. I —" She stopped because Alix gave a scream of happiness.

"You're sure?"

Jared looked at Alix in question and she gestured a big curve over her stomach.

"Yes, yes," Izzy said. "But only you and Glenn know."

"You told him first?! Before *me*?" Alix said. "What kind of BFF are you?"

Izzy laughed. "I already miss you. Have you met *him* yet?"

"Jared is right here. Would you like to talk to him?" Alix held the phone up to Jared's ear.

"Congratulations, Izzy," Jared said. "Sorry I was eavesdropping but we're in a truck together so I couldn't help hearing." He waited in silence but there was no response. He looked at Alix and shrugged.

She took the phone back. "Izzy?"

No reply.

"Izzy? Are you there?"

Silence.

Alix looked at the phone. "I think we got cut off."

"I'm here."

Alix put the phone back to her ear. "You're there? Did you hear what Jared said?"

"J . . ." Izzy managed to whisper the J sound but that's all.

"Jared," Alix said. "Jared Kingsley at home. Jared Montgomery to off-islanders, but they don't count."

He gave her a smile of approval.

"You're in a truck with him now? This minute?" Izzy's voice was so low Alix could hardly hear it.

"Yes. It's an old one. Thirties?" She looked at Jared in question.

"Nineteen thirty-six Ford," he said.

"That's him talking now?" Izzy whispered.

"I can't hear you."

"Are you two a couple?" Izzy asked.

"Friends," Alix said. "Colleagues. A few minutes ago Jared asked me to help him design a house that he has a commission for. He and I are going to try to use a rock that's on the land as part of the structure."

"You and . . . and . . . ?"

"Jared," Alix said. "Or just Kingsley. But I think he's sometimes called Seven." She looked at him in question and he nodded.

"I think I'm going to have to lie down," Izzy said. "This is too much for me to take in. Alix?"

"Yes?"

"How is the plumbing in that old house?"

She remembered Izzy's fantasy of the pipes bursting and Alix and Jared being drenched with water. "The plumbing is fine, and there is absolutely no danger of any pipes bursting." As she said it she couldn't help glancing at Jared's body. He was turning a corner, his face away from her. He certainly did keep in shape! Flat stomach, heavy thighs. He straightened the wheel and Alix looked away.

"Alix," Izzy said, "sometimes old pipes can be made to burst if they have pressure put on them."

"Yeah, but pressure can also cause them to explode and blow the whole house apart. Izzy?"

"Yes?"

"I told Jared I was worried about you, so he had his assistant call your mother to find out about you. And it was Jared who had the phone sent to your hotel and he paid for it."

For a moment Izzy was silent. When she spoke, her voice was that of a commander. "Alixandra!" Izzy said sternly. "That man is a keeper. If you have to use a sledgehammer on those pipes, *do* it! I have to go. I'm going to throw up."

Alix turned off her phone, then was silent as she looked out the windshield and thought about what Izzy had told her.

"Happy for your friend?" Jared asked.

"Very. Izzy was born to be someone's mother. When I'm down, she's always there with chocolate and a listening ear. You couldn't be a better friend than that."

"Is she still planning on having the wedding here?"

"I think so, but it'll be fairly soon — if she plans to still fit into the dress we bought, that is."

"You can spend the afternoon talking to Toby about what you need." He glanced at her. "You okay?"

"Sure. Fine." She knew she needed to adjust to this new development. Her friend was not only getting married but she was going to have a baby, while Alix . . . "It's just that I'm still getting over a breakup. You ever go through that?" She waited for his answer with her breath held. It was the first really personal question she'd asked him.

"Oh, yeah," he said. "Every single one of them eventually said, 'You love your work more than you will *ever* love me.' After that, I always knew the end was near."

"That's kind of what Eric told me," Alix said. "Not about love, but that I paid more attention to work than I did to him. I couldn't make him understand that buildings have always been a big part of my life."

"I can vouch for that," Jared said. "You used to build three-foot-tall towers when you were just a kid. You and Granddad —" He stopped. His grandfather used to oversee little Alix in her placement of objects. And he told her where things in the house were. Under Caleb's direction, she'd pulled pieces of scrimshaw and little enamel boxes, and even coins from places where they'd been hiding for a century or more.

"Your grandfather and I did what?" Alix asked.

He knew she meant his most recent grandfather, but he'd died not long after Jared's birth. His mother's father had died before that. When Jared was a toddler, he'd made his father laugh when he'd been shocked that one of his friends had a grandfather everyone could actually *see.*

"Sorry. Mixed up. You and Aunt Addy used to spend hours building things."

Alix looked away for a moment as she felt like he wasn't telling the truth. She didn't remember Aunt Addy sitting on the floor and stacking things. But Alix wasn't going to push it. She was learning that if she persisted she could get whatever she wanted to know out of him. But if she asked directly, he changed the subject. "So what's Lexie's house like?"

Jared dropped his shoulders, which he'd unconsciously raised to protect himself against her onslaught of questions. He gave her a dazzling smile. "It's a new purchase, only been in my family for about seventy-five years."

"Downright modern," she said and they smiled at each other. He talked of the history of the house until they got back to Kingsley House, where he parked the old truck. They walked toward Main Street to Lexie's.

Alix couldn't help feeling nervous. What if the three women didn't like one another?

Walking beside her, Jared must have picked up on her thoughts. "Anybody gives you any problems, let me know."

She smiled at him in gratitude.

# Chapter Twelve

"They're coming up the walk now," Lexie said as she peeked out through the dining room windows.

Toby was making sandwiches for their guests. She and Lexie had been up early to start cooking for tomorrow's picnic, so they'd already eaten. When Jared had sent his text that he and Alix were on their way, the two women had dropped everything and scurried to prepare.

"They look good together," Lexie said. "She's tall enough for him and he's always liked red hair. I can see Victoria in her face, but she's built like Ken."

"Remember!" Toby said.

"I know. Don't mention Ken. I think I'll call him and tell him how annoying keeping this secret is. Better yet, I'll let *you* call him."

Toby smiled. Lexie could sometimes be rather abrupt. "What's taking them so long?"

"Jared is hovering over her like he's afraid someone's going to run up and snatch her away. Now he's pointing at the house and talking. I hope he's not boring her with words like 'crossbeams' and 'angles' and . . . and whatever else he goes on and on about."

"Alix is a student of architecture so maybe she likes that," Toby said as she put her homemade sliced pickles on the sandwiches. She didn't really know what either of them liked to eat so she put some of all of it on the bread.

"I'd feel better if he were telling her about her eyes," Lexie said.

"That they're like liquid pools of moonlight?" Toby suggested.

"Perfect!" Lexie said. "Uh-oh. She's frowning. Please, I hope he's not telling her about those little beetles that eat the wood. That's a death knell to romance."

Toby put the plated sandwiches on the dining table. "Why are you so determined to match Jared up with this young woman?"

"He needs someone," Lexie said. "Jared has had too many deaths around him. Aunt Addy was the only constant he had left, and now she's gone."

"There's you and all his other relatives, and he's friends with most of the island," Toby said.

Lexie let the curtain fall back into place. "But he's split in half. Part of him lives in America and part of him is here. Did I ever tell you that I met one of his girlfriends in

New York?"

"No," Toby said. "What was she like?"

"Tall, thin, beautiful, intelligent."

"That sounds wonderful."

"I couldn't see her on a Nantucket fishing boat and I certainly couldn't imagine her in an old house with that green stove. What would she do if Jared Kingsley slapped down twenty striped bass and told her to clean them?"

Toby sighed. "Fall in love with an elegant Montgomery and find yourself married to a sea-salt Kingsley. It wouldn't be fair to either of them."

"And then there's Jared's work habits. I can't tell you how many times Ken or Aunt Addy sent me upstairs to wake him up and I found him in bed surrounded by a dozen rolled-up drawings."

"Rather like Alix on the couch?" Toby asked.

"Exactly like that." The two women smiled at each other. "What I want to know," Lexie said as she walked to the front door, "is how Alix feels about him."

"Let's see if we can find out," Toby said.

Lexie opened the front door.

Alix took the seat that Lexie pointed to at the beautiful old dining table. Jared was next to her while the two young women sat across from them.

When Lexie and Jared started talking about things Alix had never heard of, she looked at her sandwich. It had Swiss cheese on it, something she'd never liked. Dry old stuff. And when she tasted a bit of turkey, it was smoked, another thing she didn't like.

While Lexie, Toby, and Jared talked, Alix pulled his plate next to hers and fixed the two sandwiches. She gave him the cheese and the smoked turkey, which she knew he loved, and she took his pickles and cheddar cheese. She took the olives off his plate and gave him her chips.

When the sandwich fillings and condiments were properly distributed, she cut each one diagonally and gave him back his plate. She switched drinks so she had the lemonade and he had the iced tea.

When Alix looked up, both Toby and Lexie were staring at her in silence.

"Sorry," she said. "I missed what you were saying."

"Nothing of interest," Jared said as he looked at Toby. "You have any hot mustard? Alix likes that."

"We do." Toby got up to retrieve it from the kitchen.

Lexie was looking at Alix with great intensity. The resemblance between Jared and his cousin was evident: the strong jawline, the eyes that seemed to see through a person. Alix decided she wouldn't want to be on the receiving end of Lexie's temper — something she was sure the woman had.

As for Toby, she wasn't at all as Alix had imagined. From what Jared had said, Alix had envisioned some hippie earth mother in handwoven cotton and sandals made out of old tires. But Toby was quietly elegant, very pretty but in an old-fashioned way, rather like a medieval painting of a Madonna. She wore a lovely dress that Alix thought might have come from the same store where Izzy had shopped.

"Zero Main?" Alix asked, naming the shop.

"Yes," Toby said, smiling. "My father visits me every few months, takes me there, and the owner, Noël, dresses me. Isn't that one of her tops you have on?"

"Yes, it is," Alix said.

"If you ladies are going to talk about Petticoat Row, I think it's time for me to go," Jared said.

Alix looked at him to explain that term, but Lexie answered. "When the men were at sea, the women ran the island, and where their shops were was called Petticoat Row."

"Still is," Jared said as he stood up.

"That's because the women did such a fabulous job of running everything, and still do." Lexie looked up at him. "I want you to check the heater in the greenhouse, and there are rats burrowing under a couple of the flower beds."

"Rats?" Alix asked.

Jared looked at her. "Thanks to our illustrious ancestors' world travels, we have an extraordinary variety of rats on the island."

They were all looking at Alix to see how she'd take this. Would she cringe and squeal in distaste?

"A rodent Galapagos," she said.

"Right." Jared smiled at her so warmly that Alix blushed. "Okay," he said, "I'll leave you girls to it. It smells good in here. Alix is a great cook and she has a wedding to plan and . . ."

Lexie and Toby were gazing at him in curiosity.

He looked down at Alix. "If you need anything, let me know."

Alix stood up. "I will. You'll be outside?"

"Yes, but after I fix the heater and wire out the rats, I'll go home."

"Big or little house?"

"Your choice," he said.

"Big. I'll wrap the last two fish in rosemary. I saw some growing in the back. Maybe you could put a couple of potatoes in the oven. Two fifty. Slow bake."

"Okay."

They stood there looking at each other, neither of them seeming to want to move.

Lexie and Toby sat across from them, watching Jared and Alix just standing there, gazing into each other's eyes and saying nothing. They didn't seem to know how to separate.

Shaking her head in disbelief, Lexie stood and threw up her hands. "I think I'm going to be sick. Jared! Go fix the heater. Alix! Go to the kitchen and help Toby stuff some mushrooms or whatever."

Jared looked away from Alix to give his cousin a half grin. "And what are you going to do, Miss Dictator?"

"Pop over to the church to give thanks that *I* am still sane."

"What does that mean?" Jared asked.

Still shaking her head at him, Lexie went around the table, reached up to put her hands on his shoulders, and shoved him through the kitchen to the back door. "Go outside. Breathe. I promise that Toby and I won't hurt her."

"Really, Lexie!" Jared said. "This is —" He cut off because she shut the door in his face.

Lexie went back through the pretty little sitting room into the kitchen, where Toby was at the counter. Alix was standing in the doorway looking like she wanted to run away.

"Lexie," Toby said softly, "why don't you walk down to Grand Union and get us some limes?"

Lexie grinned. "Want to get rid of me?"

"Yes," Toby said.

Laughing, Lexie left the room and they heard the front door close behind her.

"Sorry for that," Toby said. "Would you like to sit down?" The kitchen was a long galley type but on one wall a part of the counter had a couple of stools.

"I apologize if Jared and I were . . ." Alix didn't know what to say. "He's the only person I know on Nantucket and we've spent most of the time I've been here together. Well, not together-together, but . . ."

"You know how to zest citrus?" Toby asked.

"I'm not as good a cook as Jared said I was, but I can do that."

Toby nodded to a bowl full of lemons, limes, and oranges. "I need a quarter cup of each one." She held out the little multi-holed zester.

Alix was glad to get away from the topic of her and Jared.

"What do you think of Nantucket?" Toby asked.

"So far, it's great." Alix began to tell of her impressions. The word "beauty" was second only to the word "Jared." What Alix saw was beautiful. All her other senses were covered by Jared. What he said, did, thought, were all part of Alix's talk.

"Are you still going out with Wes tomorrow?" Toby asked.

"Why wouldn't I?" Alix asked.

"I thought maybe you and Jared were becoming . . ." Toby trailed off. She knew about Ken's hands-off order to Jared, but she wanted to know if they were overcoming that restriction.

"Oh," Alix said. "You think Jared and I are on our way to being a couple. We're not. I hope we're friends, but we're certainly work colleagues who are becoming friends."

Toby looked at Alix in disbelief.

"No, really," Alix said. "I think he and I gave the wrong impression."

"But you've been spending so much time together. The whole island is asking what's going on."

"That's not good," Alix said. "Jared and I just work together. That's all."

"And the sandwiches?"

"What do you mean?" Alix asked.

"Switching food that each of you likes."

"We've been working on plans, so we eat together and we've learned about each other."

"But . . . ?" Toby's eyes were wide.

"Okay, I'll be honest. At first I was interested in him in that way." Her poem came to mind. "But he clearly let me know that nothing like that was going to happen. I admit that it hurt at first, but I'm okay now. And between you and me, I'm looking forward to going out with Wes. I could stand a little touchy-feely action. I'd like to remember that I'm a girl." Alix took a breath, hoping her lie sounded convincing. She did *not* want to go on a date with another man. "Could we talk about something besides me?"

"Of course," Toby said. "I didn't mean to pry. It's just that we've never seen Jared so interested in anyone before."

Alix had no idea what to reply to that, so she changed the subject. "I told my friend Izzy that I'd help her set up her wedding here on Nantucket, but I don't know where to begin. Jared said you would know what to do."

Toby understood that Alix was politely asking her to back off. "Do you have a date set for the wedding?"

"I did, but I'm sure it's going to change." Alix didn't explain why. For right now she wanted to keep Izzy's pregnancy private. With a bit of a jolt she realized that "private" now seemed to include Jared.

Toby continued. "The first thing you need to do after you have the date is to get the colors your bride wants. Everything revolves around her colors. If she wants any special flowers I'll need to know well in advance so we can get them flown in."

"Flown in?" Alix said. "That's not the kind of wedding Izzy wants."

"Nearly everything on the island is flown in or put in a truck then driven onto a ferry. You need to be sure of what your friend wants, and be aware that brides often change their minds. I've seen girls come in wanting something simple, then later deciding that they have to have thirty grand's worth of purple orchids."

"Thirty . . . ?" Alix picked up a lime; she'd finished the oranges. "I think that kind of thing is for the people who live in the twenty-million-dollar houses."

"Or more. Right now there's a house in Polpis asking fifty-nine million."

Alix could only blink at her.

"What about you?" Toby asked.

"About me, what?"

"What kind of wedding do you want?"

"One with a groom."

Toby laughed. "But really, you haven't thought about it?"

"Not the wedding itself, no, but Izzy's happiness with her fiancé has made me think about things. What about you? You have a man in your life?"

"No one permanent."

Alix hesitated before she spoke. "I thought maybe you and Jared were . . . you know."

"That Jared and I were having an affair?"

Alix kept her eyes on the lime in her hand. "Maybe in the past?"

"Oh, heavens no! Jared's like a big brother to me. Has he been using me to try to make you jealous?"

"Of course not! We're not like that at all." But when she thought about it, she had felt jealous of the way he'd rhapsodized about the angelic Toby. "Maybe he was." Alix couldn't help smiling. "Does he have many ex-girlfriends on the island?"

"Not at all. Lexie said there was a girl in high school, but she married his cousin."

"That could be anyone on the island."

"Just about. But from what I gather, this particular cousin and Jared don't have much to do with each other even today. They live in Surfside."

"I take it that's on Nantucket?"

"It sounds like you've learned that only Nantucket exists."

Alix laughed. "To Jared, that's certainly true."

That afternoon, after Alix left, Lexie returned and the two women discussed what they'd seen and heard.

"She said that?" Lexie asked. "Alix said that she was hoping for some 'touchy-feely' time with my testosterone-laden cousin Wes?"

"When it comes to testosterone, I think Jared can probably hold his own," Toby said.

"If he weren't tied down by Alix's father, he could," Lexie said. "This is *not* going well."

"I'm afraid I have to agree," Toby said. "Who are you calling?"

"Wes. Break out the beer. I'm inviting him over for tea and talk."

"What are you planning to do?" Toby asked. "I don't think Jared will like —"

"Let me handle my cousins," Lexie said, then gave her attention to the phone. "Wes?

This is Lexie. Toby and I want you to come over." She paused. "Of course now. Next you'll be asking for a printed invitation. And, yes, it has to do with your date with Alix." Lexie clicked off the phone. "He'll be here in ten minutes."

Toby thought she might never get used to the informality of Nantucket. People popped in and out of each other's houses all day. One day she was nearly knocked down when a door opened inside the house. It was the plumber coming up from the basement. He'd entered through the exterior door — which as far as anyone knew had never been locked — fixed the dripping pipe, then had gone up the stairs into the house to make sure the toilet was no longer leaking. That no one knew he was in the house seemed to bother no one but Toby.

"Look, Wes," Lexie said. It was twenty minutes later and she and Toby were on the couch across from him. Toby had made sure the young man had been furnished with beer and pretzels, and he was waiting to be told why he'd been summoned.

"The whole island knows you're still in love with Daris Brubaker," Lexie said. Daris was the woman Wes had wanted to marry, but six months ago they'd had a big fight — which no one knew the cause of — and Daris had told Wes to get lost. Since then he'd dated nearly every unmarried woman on the island.

Lexie waited for Wes to say something, preferably to tell what had happened between him and Daris, but he just drank his beer and said nothing. "But she dumped you, probably because you've got a roving eye. You only asked Alix out to get her back and, of course, to try to show up Jared."

Wes was unperturbed by her criticism, nor was he volunteering any information. "So what's your point?"

"I don't want to beat around the bush," Lexie said. "What's it going to take to get you to call Alix and get out of this date?"

"It's not going to happen. My dad's driving his old Chevy in the parade, and —"

Toby spoke up. "Jared will design a house for that land you own, and he'll do it for free."

Lexie looked at her with wide eyes. They all knew that Jared charged a hefty six figures for his designs.

Wes couldn't conceal his shock at that. It was one thing for his cousin to sketch out a garage, but an entire house? "With an outdoor shower and a place for my boats?"

"Whatever you want," Toby said.

"I couldn't afford to build anything that Montgomery would come up with."

Lexie knew that for Wes to call his cousin Montgomery and not Kingsley was an intentional insult. She leaned back on the couch and glared at Wes. It was a game to him, but they were serious.

Toby, who hadn't grown up on the island, wasn't hindered by past relationships or subtle meanings of name usage. "Jared will act as a bank and lend you the money."

"I don't think —" Lexie began, but Wes and Toby were looking at each other. Lexie may as well not have been there.

"Interest free?" he asked.

"Half a percent lower than the current rate at the time of closing," Toby said quickly.

"One and a half," Wes said.

"Three quarters," Toby said.

"Done," Wes answered.

"Holy crap, Toby," Lexie said. "I didn't know you could negotiate a deal that way."

"I learned it from my dad."

After Wes left, Lexie dreaded telling Jared what had been done in his name. On the other hand, since he didn't seem to be taking over on his own, someone had to. She called him and told him she had to see him immediately.

Lexie had him sit in the same chair where Wes had sat an hour before, but Jared refused all refreshment.

"What's going on?" he asked. "Alix has dinner about ready and we have things to do."

"Such as?" Toby asked.

Jared smiled at her. "Not what you two are obviously hoping. Now, what's so important that it couldn't wait until I see you tomorrow?"

"Tomorrow is the whole point," Lexie said. "You seem oblivious to the fact that Alix has a date with Wes tomorrow. An all-day date."

Jared didn't reply.

"You don't care?" Lexie demanded.

"Not that it's any of your business, little cousin, but I'm planning to take care of that."

"What does that mean?" Lexie asked.

"I think you should wait and see," he said and started to get out of the chair. "Now, if you're finished nosing about in my private life, I'm going home."

"To Alix," Toby said, smiling.

Jared smiled back at her. "Yes, to Alix."

"We fixed it," Lexie said. "We arranged it all with Wes. It will cost you some, but it'll be worth it."

Jared looked at them. They were smiling and so innocent looking. Such pretty girls, he thought. And so very well meaning. But then dynamite wasn't invented to cause harm. He sat back down in the chair. "Tell me what you've done." His voice was calm.

"We made a deal for you," Lexie said. "I came up with the idea but Toby negotiated the interest rate. She was great." Lexie looked at her roommate with pride.

"Maybe you two should start at the beginning," Jared said.

Lexie did most of the talking as she explained what they'd promised Wes in return for calling off his date with Alix.

Jared's face didn't show any emotion; he was an excellent poker player. "I'm to design a house for him for free *and* lend him the money at a ridiculously low interest rate?"

"When you put it like that it does sound like too much," Lexie said. "But, Jared, you can't let Alix spend the day with Wes. Since Daris told him to get lost, he's been a wolf on the prowl. And there's always been a rivalry between you and him. We worry that he'll pounce on poor Alix."

"I think," Toby said softly, "that Jared has another plan."

"Do you?" Lexie asked of her cousin.

He didn't tell these two well-intentioned busybodies, but he'd been intending to do this after he left Alix tonight, and to do it in private. Taking his cell out of his pocket, he pushed a button to put it on speaker so Lexie and Toby could hear, then he called a number.

"Jared?" said a female voice. "Is that you?"

"Hi, Daris, how's your dad?"

"He's fine now. Did you get our thank-you notes?"

"All four of them."

"We owe you so much for helping us out."

"I wondered if I could ask a favor of you," Jared said.

"Anything!" Daris said. "Up to and including running away to elope with you."

Toby and Lexie, sitting across from him on

the couch, looked at each other with wide eyes.

Smiling, Jared's voice lowered and got slower. "Such a sacrifice won't be necessary, Daris, even though the prospect sounds delightful. I won't be able to sleep tonight from thinking about it."

"I could —" Daris began.

Lexie cut her off. "Hi, Daris," she said loudly. "It's Lexie. How's your mom?"

Daris recovered quickly from the surprise that Jared wasn't alone. "She's doing great. She lost twenty-two pounds while Dad was sick. She's thinking about writing a book called *The My Husband Had a Heart Attack Diet.* Jared, what can I do for you?"

"You have any interest in getting Wes back for whatever he did to you?"

"Is this a favor for you or for me?"

Jared smiled. "So I take it you're in?"

"One hundred percent. All the way. Should I bring weapons?"

"I'd prefer very small shorts and a tank top."

Daris was silent for a moment. "Jared, honey, are you *sure* you don't want to get married?"

"I'm not sure at all," he said softly, and Lexie's and Toby's eyes widened even farther.

Daris laughed. "Okay, now I'm understanding. Does this have to do with that pretty girl you've been practically living with since she moved into your aunt's house?"

"Maybe. I'll call you later to work out the details, but could we meet at nine forty-five tomorrow morning to ride in the parade?"

"I will shorten my shorts tonight."

"I look forward to the sight." Jared clicked off and looked at Lexie and Toby, his eyebrows raised in question. "Well?"

"Do you think they'll get back together?" Toby asked.

"That's none of my business," Jared answered.

Lexie put her hands up as a balance scale. "Daris's legs or a million-dollar loan? That's going to be Wes's choice." She looked from Toby to Jared and back.

"He'll choose legs," Toby said.

"Daris's legs?" Jared said. "Definitely yes!"

# Chapter Thirteen

Jared had shown up at Kingsley House in a beautiful custom jacket, a blue shirt, and khaki trousers. Alix took one look at him and ran back upstairs to change. "Why didn't you tell me this was a high-class event?" she said to Captain Caleb's portrait. "And if you make one thing move, I'll turn your picture to the wall."

They met Lexie and Toby and walked down Main to where the road widened and the long, double line of vehicles was waiting. Jared had left early to get his friend's truck fifth in line.

The streets were full of people, nearly all of them wearing daffodils. Some of the women had concocted outrageous hats that looked good in the morning sunshine.

"Stay with me," Jared said as soon as they got to the crowd.

"But I'm supposed to meet Wes," she said for what had to be the fourth time. Each time, Jared had acted as though she hadn't spoken.

"So much for jealousy," Alix muttered as she tried to keep up with his long legs. Last night he'd left the house just as dinner was ready, saying there was an emergency with Lexie. He'd returned forty-five minutes later but wouldn't tell Alix anything about what had happened. The most he'd say was, "There was no bloodshed. Should have been but wasn't."

They'd watched a movie together — *Mr. Blandings Builds His Dream House* — and twice Alix had mentioned that she was going to the parade with Wes. Jared had made no comment. When she'd accepted the date with his cousin, she'd hardly known Jared. She remembered how in awe of him she'd been then, and she couldn't help smiling. Now she'd much, much rather ride with Jared in the old Ford truck.

But no matter how hard she hinted, Jared said nothing.

Last night, when he'd left to go to the guesthouse, Alix couldn't help feeling, well . . . almost angry at him. She'd begun to feel that she was part of the Kingsley family, but it looked like Jared didn't see it the same way. Or maybe he did. Wes was a cousin, so what did it matter if she rode with him?

This morning, by the time the four of them got to where the cars were lined up, Alix was silent. Would she sit beside Wes and wave at the people she'd come to know?

But no one else seemed perturbed about anything. Lexie and Toby were going to drive to 'Sconset with the coolers of food that Alix had helped prepare, but first they were going to say hello to the summer people.

"Are they the same as off-islanders?" Alix asked.

"Yes and no." Jared explained that there were people who owned houses on Nantucket and came every summer. Some of them had been coming for twenty to thirty years or more.

"Do we like them or not?" Alix asked, trying to make a joke.

But Jared didn't smile. "Depends on whether they add to the community or take from it."

Once they got in the crowd, Lexie and Toby went off on their own, but Alix stayed with Jared. Yet again, he seemed to know everyone.

"When are you going to design that guesthouse for me?" one man asked. He was short and stout and looked vaguely familiar.

When they stepped away, Alix asked who the man was.

"Forbes top ten" was Jared's answer before he said hello to someone else.

She knew that meant a "richest list."

When Wes showed up, everything happened at once. Alix reluctantly left Jared's side to go to him. Her mind was frantically scheming for a way to get out of this date without offending anyone. But on the other hand, it wasn't as though Jared had said he *wanted* her with him.

When Alix took a step toward Wes, Jared made no move to stop her. But then Wes abruptly halted and stared at something behind Alix. She turned to look.

A young woman had come up beside Jared, taken his arm, and was leaning toward him in a possessive way. Fairly attractive, with short blond hair and big eyes, but what really stood out about her was how she was dressed. She had on an airy white tunic that reached to the top of her thighs — and there appeared to be nothing underneath it. Her long, beautiful legs — perfectly tanned, perfectly waxed — seemed to go on forever, down to some little gold sandals.

Alix, speechless, looked from the girl to Jared, to Wes, and back again.

"This is my date," Jared said to Wes.

Alix's mouth dropped open. No wonder he didn't care that she was going out with someone else. No wonder —

"Trade?" Jared asked his cousin.

Wes gave a curt nod and the girl left Jared's arm to go to Wes.

Alix was standing still, unable to move, and she had no idea what had just happened.

"Are you ready to go?" Jared asked impatiently.

Alix was still blinking.

"The parade's about to start and we need to get in the truck."

Alix recovered enough to walk across the cobblestones to the blue Ford and get in beside Jared. "Did you plan that?"

He started the engine. "Plan what? Oh. You mean Daris?"

"Is that the girl with no pants on?"

Jared smiled. "Best legs on the island. She and Wes were a couple until six months ago. He did something she didn't like so she told him to get lost. I guess she's punished him enough. Here." He handed her a bouquet of daffodils.

Alix took them as he pulled into place behind a gull wing Mercedes from the sixties. "So you did plan it all."

He glanced at her with a little smile. "Did you really think I was going to let you go out with Wes?"

"Yes," she said simply. "I did." She smiled at him. "Thanks for proving me wrong."

"My pleasure," he said.

He spoke in such a vain way that she couldn't let him get away with it. "It's so rare that I'm wrong that I'd begun to think it wasn't possible."

He laughed. "Wave at the people."

She did. "So what ideas do you have for

the guesthouse for the Forbes top-ten man?"

"All glass," he said. "Philip Johnson comes to Nantucket."

"That's a joke, right?"

"You're not supposed to work today. Enjoy the scenery."

They were going down Orange Street and every beautiful old house made her think of a guesthouse design. But she didn't say anything.

"His wife loves to garden and wants her own potting shed," Jared said. "Just a little one. A mere two thousand square feet."

"Really?" Alix looked at him with wide eyes. "Maybe Toby has some ideas about that."

"My thoughts exactly," Jared said, grinning, and they talked about design all the way to 'Sconset — which was only about eight miles, but it seemed longer.

When they got to the impossibly cute little town that Jared said used to be full of fishing shacks, Lexie and Toby were waiting for them. They'd unloaded an SUV full of food, utensils, and elegant picnic gear.

Jared drove the old truck into the parking area Lexie pointed out to him, then disappeared in that way males do when faced with whatever they consider women's work. Alix followed Lexie's orders and helped set up. Within minutes the back of the old truck and a table had been covered with food and drink on top of pretty Italian tablecloths. It was all very high end, very much like a picture-perfect country picnic.

Alix stepped into the street. On both sides were the beautiful old cars and trucks that had been in the parade through the town.

Since she'd arrived on the island, Alix had been gradually becoming aware of the wealth on Nantucket, but the gathering of the old cars had solidified it. They weren't just jalopies but museum-quality vehicles, and the laughing and chatting owners were decked out like models in a Ralph Lauren ad: Blazers, ascots, gold watches for men. Perfect designer outfits for the women. She looked at the lavish layouts of the picnics and smiled.

"Like it?" Jared asked as he reappeared now that the work was done.

"Truly beautiful. I feel like I've stepped onto the cover of *Town and Country* magazine."

"Come on," he said. "They're doing an ice-carving demo halfway down."

There were dancers and musicians, artists and acrobats wandering around and everyone seemed to know everyone else. When they got back to the truck, Jared talked to a group of people while Alix filled plates for the two of them. There were chairs at the front of the truck and she and Jared sat there to eat.

"I haven't been to this in years," he said. "It's grown."

"Why would you ever miss it? It's wonderful."

"Couldn't get a date," he said.

Alix could remember all too well the sight of beautiful Daris on his arm. "Ha! Half the women here —"

He cut her off. "I meant that I couldn't find a date I wanted to go with."

Alix smiled at him and for a moment his eyes held hers. But as always, he turned away. "Mixed signals" were the words that came to Alix's mind. Jared had gone through an elaborate scheme to keep her from going out with another man, but when she looked at him with something besides work in her eyes, he turned away.

She told herself to keep it light.

Thirty minutes later they were standing on the road, chatting to people, when Jared turned to her with a serious expression. "Alix?" he said. "Do you have any feeling that you owe me for anything at all?"

"Of course. Haven't I said thank you often enough? If not, I apologize for —"

"No, it's not that," he said. "It's just that my cousin is coming this way and —"

"Wes?"

"No."

"The woman from the liquor store?" His look made her stop guessing. "Okay, sorry. One of your cousins is coming toward us and . . . ?"

"His wife was my girlfriend in high school. He won; I lost. It's ridiculous of me, but —"

Alix looked through the crowd and saw a man about Jared's age who had the Kingsley jawline, the dark hair and eyes. But whereas they worked together on Jared to form a very masculine face, on this man there was something effeminate about his features. He was well dressed, in a perfect shirt and jacket, and even had on jeans. But they weren't like the jeans Jared usually wore that even when clean looked as though they'd been to Davy Jones's locker and back.

Beside the man was a tall, slim blond woman with pale blue eyes. Alix thought she was quite pretty, but she looked tired and maybe older than she really was.

When the woman caught sight of Jared, her face lit up, the tiredness disappeared, and her prettiness doubled. Alix could imagine her riding on a parade float and being the queen of the prom.

When the man beside her saw Jared, for a split second, his face clouded. He recovered enough to put on a grin that didn't make it all the way to his eyes.

"Jared," the woman said and held out her arms as though she meant to hug him.

Alix reacted on instinct. He hadn't finished his request of her, but she thought he'd been about to ask her to run interference between him and his ex. "Want me to protect you?"

she said under her breath.

"Please," he said, standing his ground and waiting for the charging woman to get to him.

Alix put her body in front of Jared's so that she halted. Her arms were still outstretched and she didn't seem to know what to do with them.

Alix reached up and shook her hand. "Hi. I'm Alix. I take it you know Jared." Out of the corner of her eye she saw Lexie punch Toby in the ribs. Of course both women stood there eagerly watching the drama unfold.

"I'm Missy," the woman said. "Jared and I have known each other for a very long time."

"Oh?" Alix said. "And here I thought I'd heard of all his friends, but he never mentioned a Missy." When she turned to look at Jared, she realized that, with his head bent, they were practically nose to nose. When she started to step away, he put his arm around her waist and pulled her full length back against him.

Alix's eyes widened, but then she got herself under control. Sort of. "I, uh . . . I . . ."

"It's good to see you, Jared," the man said as he came to stand behind the blond woman. Like Jared, he put his arm possessively around her waist. "So how is it living off-island? Did you learn lots of new things about the outside world?"

Even Alix knew that was an insult. She gave

the man a chilly smile. "Jared is still conquering the world with his magnificent designs." When the man didn't lose his self-satisfied little smile, Alix remembered her mother's books and how that family had spent centuries fighting over the family home. "And of course there's all the work he does at Kingsley House. Keeping it intact for his son-to-be, the Eighth, is a cherished legacy of his inheritance."

For a moment Alix thought she'd laid it on too thick, but then she had the satisfaction of seeing him drop the smug little smile.

Behind her, Jared buried his face in Alix's neck — and sent the hairs of her body rising.

"You are my dream girl," he said, and she could feel him holding in his laughter. He managed to recover himself enough to lift his head. "This is my cousin Oliver Collins and his wife, Missy. And this is Alix."

"How nice to meet you," Alix said, holding out her hand to shake Oliver's. "You're not named Kingsley?"

"We're related through his mother, who married an off-islander," Jared said. Then, still holding firmly on to Alix's waist, he motioned toward the truck that was loaded with food. "Come and have lunch with us."

"Thanks," Oliver said, "but we must get home. The children need us. Marriage carries great responsibilities. Alix, Jared," he said curtly, leading his wife away.

Missy glanced back as though she wanted to stay, but her husband didn't let up his iron grip.

Jared turned Alix around to face him. "You were wonderful!" he said. "Really great. Ol' Oliver hasn't been put in his place so well in . . . well, ever, I guess. You *are* Victoria's daughter!" Still laughing, on impulse, he planted a quick, hard kiss on Alix's smiling mouth.

At least that's what it was meant to be. Instead, both he and Alix were jolted as though an electrical current went through them.

"I . . ." Jared began, then stepped closer.

Again she saw that fire in his eyes, and she lifted her arms to put them around his neck.

But it wasn't to be. Frowning, Jared stepped away, the fire in his eyes doused.

Alix's first impulse was to flee. How many times was this going to happen? They'd get close, he'd look at her as though he was about to devour her, then he'd turn cold and walk away. Again and again it had happened.

Alix didn't know where she'd go if she did leave the picnic, but from the anger that surged through her she thought she could walk back to Kingsley House. And once she was there she just might pack and leave the island. She'd had all she could take of this man looking at her with lust one second and turning away the next. She backed away from him.

"Alix —" Jared began, but she moved quickly through the crowd.

Toby caught up with her.

"I don't want to hear the excuses —" Alix began.

"Go straight ahead to the store, bear left, and there's a bridge to the beach. Walk."

Alix gave a nod and hurried forward. It wasn't difficult to find the tall bridge, go down the stairs, then out to the beach. The cool weather meant there weren't many people about and she was glad of it. The water and the sand calmed her.

She wasn't sure how long she stood there. Her thoughts wouldn't come in an orderly fashion but seemed to float around in a mixed-up way. Visions of her and Jared drifted before her, laughing and eating and creating together. And through it all, he'd made it clear that there was to be nothing sexual between them. She'd assumed it was because he didn't feel that way about her.

But that kiss! As electric as a bolt of lightning. She saw that he'd felt it too, so why had he pulled away? Why had he looked at her so coldly? There didn't seem to be someone else in his life, so what was his problem?

When a shiver went through her, she rubbed her arms and turned around. Not far away, Jared was sitting on the sand in the shade. Just sitting there, waiting. He looked as though he was worried about something.

But she had no sympathy for him. She walked to stand in front of him. "I'd like to go . . ." She couldn't call Kingsley House "home." "Back," she finished.

He didn't stand up. "I'll take you wherever you want to go, but first I'd like to tell you the truth."

"That would make for a change," she said.

He took off his jacket and held it out to her, but she didn't take it. "Please," he said. "Give me twenty minutes, and if you still want to leave me or Nantucket or whatever you want, I'll arrange it."

Reluctantly, she sat down on the sand a few feet away from him and when he started to put his jacket around her, she flinched. "You'll get cold."

"Not when you're shooting laser rays at me, I won't," he said.

She didn't smile, but she did let him put the jacket around her shoulders.

"I don't know where to begin," he said. "If it were up to me I'd tell you everything, but I can't."

She turned to glare at him. "Then why am I here?"

"I don't know!" Jared said in exasperation. "I know about five percent more than you do and I don't understand any of it. I do know that people have been keeping secrets from you all your life."

"Who?"

"I can't tell you that. I wish I could, but I can't. All I can say is that I owe people for my entire life. I wouldn't have been anything but maybe a criminal if it hadn't been for . . . for some people who helped me."

Alix looked out at the sea and tried to figure out what he was telling her. "I know you didn't want me to come here."

"No," he said. "I didn't. I told you that I was angry at my aunt. I saw her will as a betrayal of me. If you hadn't come early, I would have been gone, and we never would have met."

"But you stayed," she said.

"Because I liked you," he said.

"Past tense?"

He took his time answering. "I've never before met anyone who fit into both my worlds, a woman who could clean a fish and argue about subflooring too."

"I know," Alix said softly. "We're on our way to becoming great friends."

"No," he said. "Tim, my business partner, and I are friends. He hates fishing, thinks all dirt paths should be covered with concrete, and endlessly bellyaches about money. But we're good friends."

"And you and I aren't?" Alix asked. Damn!

She could feel tears beginning to form in her eyes.

"As much as I care about Tim, I have no desire to tear his clothes off. I've not wanted to make love to him for however long it takes until this gnawing hunger inside me is fed. I haven't stayed awake thinking about his lips or his thighs or anything else he has."

Alix was staring at him. "Yet you don't touch me."

"I made a promise to someone I owe," he said softly.

"And this person has asked you to . . . what? Keep your hands off me?"

"Yes."

Alix looked back at the water. "I want to get this clear. You owe someone — or multiple people — big time and they know both of us."

"Yes, but I really can't tell you more than that."

"That's okay. I may be able to guess some of it. There have been a lot of fairly recent repairs on Kingsley House, things like the roof, and they're expensive. But I couldn't help noticing that some of the repairs were very deep, which means that at one point the house was allowed to deteriorate rather extensively. Am I right?"

Cocking his head to one side, Jared looked at her and gave a quick nod.

"To allow a house to get into that state

means either the owner doesn't care or couldn't afford the repairs. Obviously, your family cares very much about that old house."

"We do," he said.

"And then there are the other houses. You said your family owns the one Lexie lives in, and it also owns where Dilys lives, where you grew up. You told me you were all of fourteen when that remodel was done, and it was obviously your work."

He was watching her in fascinated silence.

"The year I was here with my mother, that was when you were fourteen. Now, who in the world would allow a teenage boy to plan a remodel? And who would pay for it?"

"Aunt Addy," Jared said, smiling at her.

"If she could afford that, why didn't she repair her own house?"

Jared was smiling broader. "Okay, Miss Sleuth, what's your theory?"

"I think my mother has written all her books based on your family, and for compensation she paid for the remodels, and . . ."

"And what?"

"I think she probably helped with your schooling."

Jared didn't answer, but she could tell by his eyes that she was right.

"The question is," Alix said, "why would my mother forbid you to touch me?" As a truly shocking thought came to her, her eyes widened. "It's true! You and my mother were lovers." Her voice was full of horror.

"No. Never," Jared said and smiled. "But when I was seventeen and your mother kept wandering around in the garden in a red bikini I did visit Aunt Addy more often than usual."

Alix narrowed her eyes at him.

He lost the smile. "I can assure you that Victoria and I never came even close to anything other than friendship."

She looked away from him. "What does my mother have to do with the will?"

"Nothing that I know of," Jared said honestly. "She was as shocked by it as I was."

Alix thought for a moment. "I want to be clear on all of this, since I think you're right that I've been lied to for most of my life. Is it true that you like me for something besides helping you draw plans?"

He started to protest that, but then smiled. "I think I can handle the business by myself."

She ignored his joking tone. "You did all that with Wes because . . . ?"

"You think I'm going to let a lech like him spend the day with my girl?"

"Your . . . ?" She took a deep breath. "While we're being honest, I'd like to add my own piece of truth. My father is also an architect, although he mostly teaches now, and he's been on my case about you."

"How so?"

"Your reputation with women isn't good."

"Or private," Jared mumbled.

"You're too public a figure to be private. You go through models and starlets and —"

"What's your point?" Jared asked.

"There was a time when I imagined having an affair with the Great Jared Montgomery, but —"

"But what?"

"When I was dumped by Eric it hurt, but a good cry and a few pounds of chocolate healed me. Then, seeing you, the Great —"

"Don't say it again."

"Okay. The truth is that I don't see you that way anymore."

"How do you see me now?" he asked softly.

"As a human. A living, breathing man who is impatient, who manipulates conversations and information to however he wants it to be seen, and as a designer who sometimes falters in his visions."

"Anything good in there?"

"A man who generously shares everything he has and everything he knows with others. Food, money, work, whatever is yours, you share it. I've seen that you're a man who protects the people he loves, and you love hard and with all your heart."

"An absolute saint." His words were light but his tone wasn't.

"Not quite," Alix said as she looked out at the sea. "Eric I could recover from with some chocolate and a poem, but you . . ." She took her time before she spoke. "You I could love. If I had a . . . a fling with you and you tossed me aside, I'm not sure I'd ever recover." She took a breath. "There. I've said it and I think it's much more than you ever wanted to hear. I think —"

She stopped talking because he kissed her. Gentle, sweet, a meeting of the lips that was soft and . . . and promising.

Pulling away to look at him, her hand on his cheek, she searched his eyes. She needed to find the truth within herself. Was she attracted to this man because of who he was? She'd been in awe of him for so many years.

But now she knew the man, had met his friends and relatives, had seen him in his own country, so to speak. She had an idea that she'd seen what no other woman had: the real Jared Montgomery Kingsley the Seventh. Truly and completely, without armor of any kind, she had seen *both* sides of him. There was the internationally famous man who was asked for his autograph, and there was the man an old couple sitting on the porch asked to look at their furnace before winter came.

Jared was waiting in silence, his face close to hers. He seemed to know that she was asking a question and when she said the words he'd be ready to answer.

Which man did she like better? she wondered. The brilliant designer or the man who was part of a community and family that she had an idea could sometimes be overwhelming?

"I like both of you," she said, her hand caressing his cheek, feeling his whiskers. For days now she'd been looking at him and hadn't realized how much she'd wanted to touch what she saw. The strong Kingsley jaw felt good against her skin, his whiskers soft.

He turned his head to kiss her palm — and the blue fire returned to his eyes.

The hairs on her body stood on end. She'd never before felt such desire for any human being.

"We need to take this slowly," she said as part of her seemed to scream, *This is real. This could be forever.*

Jared dropped his hand from her face. "No touching. I understand." His voice seemed to weigh a thousand pounds.

"No!" Alix said. "Touching is fine. It's great. In fact, I'm for it. The more touching, the better. It's just promises that we need to think about."

Jared smiled. "You are my kind of girl. I suggest that we go home. Now. I'll get someone to give us a ride back."

"What about the old truck?" She knew it was still covered with food.

"Lexie can return it."

Only their fingertips were touching, but it was like a current of high voltage electricity was going from Jared to her. It wasn't just that they were touching, they were *connected.* Mind, body, souls seemed to be flowing one to the other. It was almost as though she could read his thoughts and she could see, well, the future. It was the two of them. Designing, arguing, traveling. Years together. Joy shared and laughter. A great, great deal of laughter. There was more but she was almost afraid to look.

"I feel like I know you, that I know *us,*" she whispered.

"I feel the same way," Jared said as he stood up, took her hand, and pulled her to him.

She wanted to slide her arms around his neck, but she knew that if she did she wouldn't be able to stop. They'd end up rolling about in the bushes on a public beach. Not a good start to forever, she thought.

Jared seemed to understand. He stepped away, breaking contact. "Let's go home."

Alix started down the beach to the road that led to the stairs, Jared behind her. Twice she stumbled, but then her legs weren't stable. "I think maybe I saw our future," she managed to say when they reached the stairs.

"I can believe that. Was it good?"

She nodded. "Very good."

"Odd things happen to people who hang around the Kingsleys."

"Are you talking about ghosts?" She was trying to sound light but it wasn't easy.

"I think maybe we should talk before we go

any farther."

Alix stopped on the stairs and turned to look at him. His face was even with hers. "If it's all right with you, I'd just as soon not talk any more right now. Tell me the awful things later, after we — you know."

Jared laughed. "Okay, let's go home and, uh . . . later, we'll talk about our future. You know, goals and that sort of thing."

"That sounds exactly like what I'd like to do." Their eyes were laughing.

# Chapter Fourteen

When they got within sight of the crowd, they dropped hands. Touching or not, Alix knew that everything had changed. She stood back as Jared told Lexie they wanted to leave right now.

"You're kidding, aren't you?" Lexie said. "Toby and I have that big SUV with us and we have to get all this into it, and then what do we do with that old truck?"

"One of you can drive the SUV and one of you can take the truck back to Polpis." Jared's voice was of exaggerated patience.

"Great idea," Lexie said, smiling. "I assume it's an automatic, as I've never driven a manual, and I can hardly wait to take it down Nantucket's wide lanes. I saw Mrs. Ferris a few minutes ago. Think she's driving today?"

"Lexie . . ." Jared began but didn't finish his sentence. He turned back to Alix with a helpless look on his face.

"Who's Mrs. Ferris?" Alix asked.

Lexie answered. "She's our neighbor, lives

right on Kingsley Lane, and what's especially great about her is that she drives smack down the middle of every road. Even tourists get out of her way. Hope I don't pass her in your fancy old truck. Wouldn't want to scratch it, but then I'll probably tear the transmission out when I try to shift gears, so what do scratches matter?" She turned toward the food, but as she passed Jared she said, "Hate to mess up your afternoon, but you know what they say about anticipation."

"That it's a useless waste of energy?"

Laughing, Lexie kept walking.

Jared went to Alix. "Sorry, but I think I —"

"I know," she said. "You and I should take the truck back."

He smiled at her, his eyes thanking her for understanding.

They were standing close together and she reached out to touch his fingertips. "Why don't you go talk to your friends while I help clean up?" The truth was that she didn't think she could stand being around him without making a fool of herself. They'd already been on the receiving end of Lexie's sharp tongue and she didn't want to go there again.

"Good idea," he said, and in an instant he was gone.

Alix went to the truck, where Lexie and Toby were packing things away. Lexie was talking about what should go where when a man stopped behind her.

Lexie didn't see him, but Alix and Toby, standing across from her, certainly did. He was gorgeous. Not rugged-looking like Jared, but beautiful, like something off a billboard. Dark hair and eyes, high cheekbones, a sculptured mouth. Tall, slim-waisted but with broad shoulders.

Alix and Toby froze in place, staring.

"Hi, Lexie," he said. His voice was as beautiful as he was.

"Oh, please, no. Not today," she said without turning around. "Go away."

"Do you know where my belt is? The one with the whale on it?" he asked.

Turning, she glared at him. "You came all the way out to 'Sconset to ask me where your belt with the silver buckle is?"

"More or less." He gave a self-deprecating little shrug that would have made any female forgive him.

But not Lexie. She turned away, her fists clenched, and took some deep, calming breaths. She glanced at Alix and Toby standing there in frozen silence and staring at him. Oh, great, Lexie thought. More women drooling over him. Just what he does *not* need.

Turning back to him, Lexie knew that the argument was going to take a while. Her goal was to get rid of him. She was not going to mix her work with her personal life!

As soon as Lexie started lecturing the man,

Toby whispered, "I think that's her boss, Roger Plymouth."

"You've never met him?" Alix whispered back.

"No," Toby said.

"He's . . ."

"Beautiful?" Toby finished for her.

"More than that," Alix said. "He looks computer generated. She didn't tell you he was like that?"

"No. Lexie only complains about him. I got the idea he was a troll."

Alix bent her head. "Did you see his face when Lexie turned away from him?"

"You mean the way he looked at her? As though he's madly, passionately, insanely in love with her?" Toby asked.

"That's what I saw but then I thought maybe I'd imagined it. Do you think he really is . . . you know?"

"In love with her?" Toby asked. "If he is, she never mentioned that either."

Roger was no longer listening to Lexie telling him that he could find his own clothing, that it wasn't her job to track down his personal possessions, etc., etc. He'd heard it all before. He looked over her head, gave a slight smile to the two pretty women staring at him as though he were an alien being, and looked around. "What is this place?"

" 'Sconset," Lexie said, her voice annoyed. "It used to be an old fishing village. And get that look off your face. You can*not* buy anything here."

He looked over her head as the pretty blonde stepped forward. Not my type, Roger thought. Too pure and untouchable-looking. The other one, the redhead, had a spark about her that he liked, but there was an intensity in her eyes that put him off. He had a feeling she might ask him to recite the multiplication tables.

"There's a store down the road," Toby said, looking up at Roger.

"He tends to buy houses, not loaves of bread," Lexie snapped, then glared at Roger. "Listen, go walk around and look at things, but buy nothing. I'm going to get the keys to this truck from Jared and you can drive it back to Polpis for him."

"Your cousin? Jared Montgomery, the architect? I'd like to meet him."

"You can't meet him and you can't hire him to build you a bigger house. Go away!"

Roger didn't move, but just kept looking at Lexie as though he expected something more from her.

"All right!" Lexie said. "Stop looking at me like that. I'll go with you in the truck!" Her words showed that she knew exactly what he'd been waiting for.

Smiling, Roger turned and sauntered into the crowd.

Lexie looked at Alix and Toby. "Not a

word," Lexie said. "I don't want to hear anything about him and I'll answer *no* questions. Got it?"

Alix and Toby nodded, but looked at each other in wonder.

A few minutes later Jared returned and Lexie told him that Roger had shown up and he'd drive the old truck back.

"Lexie." Jared again had that patient tone to his voice. "This truck is valuable. I can't just turn it over to somebody I've never met."

"Minutes ago you were willing to give it to me and I can't even drive a stick shift."

"Yeah, but I know that you're a good driver because I taught you. But I don't know this Roger guy from any other off-islander."

"He drives Formula Ones. Races them," Lexie said. "Not to earn money. He doesn't do anything for that. He just likes to drive things. And sail them. Climb them." She waved her hand. "Whatever moves, he likes it."

"He's a race car driver and you never told us?" Jared asked.

"It seems that she didn't tell anyone a lot of things about her boss," Alix said.

"There's more to a person than the exterior," Lexie said, her eyes narrowed as she looked at Alix and Toby.

"Races, climbs, sails," Alix said. "Sounds good to me."

"All wrapped up like the best ever Christmas present," Toby said.

"I've always loved Christmas," Alix said.

"Meeeee tooooo," Toby said.

"Give me a break," Lexie muttered, then turned back to Jared. "Go! Leave. Take Alix and go home. We'll take care of the truck, the car, and the food."

"Will Roger airlift it all out of here for you?" Alix asked, her face absolutely serious.

Lexie frowned as though she meant to make an angry retort, but then she laughed instead. "You and Jared are a perfect match."

Jared grinned at Alix. "I think that's quite possible," he said. "Come on, I found us a ride." They waved goodbye to Lexie and Toby and walked down the road toward the grocery.

The ride turned out to be in the very back seat of an SUV that was more like a bus than a car. The middle was full of kids and teenagers, with tired-looking parents in the front. In their place in the back, Jared and Alix had what was very nearly privacy. "So what's this about Roger Plymouth?" he asked, his voice hidden by the noise of the kids.

"Nothing much," Alix said. "It's just that he's drop-dead gorgeous, seems to be staggeringly rich, and he wanted to meet you — or Montgomery anyway. And, oh yeah, he's madly in love with Lexie."

Jared looked at her in astonishment. "I was only gone a few minutes. How did so much happen?"

"What can I say? Roger is a fast worker."

"Should I be jealous?"

"Definitely yes!" Alix said, and Jared laughed.

"Jared!" the driver yelled over the noise of the kids. "When do you have to go back to New York?"

Jared reached up to catch a Frisbee before it hit Alix in the head, put it on the floor, and gave the boy who'd thrown it a look to cut it out. "Not for weeks," he answered.

Alix had been introduced to the couple but she couldn't remember their names. For the remaining five miles back to town the couple fired questions at Jared.

He answered everything while holding Alix's hand, and the two youngest kids looked through the seats and giggled.

They were finally let out on Main Street.

"Hope you don't mind if I don't drive down your lane," the man said. "A bit too narrow for my taste."

Jared and Alix got out, thanked them all profusely, and breathed a sigh of relief when they drove away.

"Summer people?" Alix asked.

Jared took her hand. "What gave it away?"

She laughed. "Kingsley Lane is quite wide compared to some I've seen on the island."

"Downright spacious."

As soon as they turned the corner and saw

Lexie and Toby's house, Alix felt at home — a far cry from what she'd been feeling a few hours before. It was a quiet, tree-lined street with elegant old houses, and the best of them was theirs. No, she thought, not "theirs." Not yet. But then she'd spent little time in the house without Jared so it did feel like it belonged to both of them.

When she looked up at him, the thought of what was to come sent a little thrill through her.

Jared must have felt it too because he stopped. When he turned to her, his eyes were on fire. He pulled her into his arms and kissed her. Not sweet as before but showing his longing and desire for her.

She had to stand on tiptoes to reach him and his body felt good against hers, but they broke apart and again started walking. On the way to the house, Alix began to get nervous. She and Jared had been friends, coworkers, but now . . . The truth was, she didn't know what to expect when they reached the house. Until today, touching had been taboo. And then there was the fact that he was an intellectual. He traveled in such lofty circles. Some of the richest people in the world wanted him to design their houses.

They went to the back door of Kingsley House — which was usually unlocked — and went inside.

Alix turned to look at him. "I guess I better

change —"

She didn't finish her sentence because Jared picked her up, his mouth on hers, her legs around his waist, and held her up against a wall. In seconds they were both nude from the waist down.

Passion, she thought. It's what she wanted . . . needed from this man.

When he entered her she started to scream, but he put his mouth over hers.

For all the frantic need between them, he took his time so that the sensation began building in Alix and increasing. Rising.

He put her on the kitchen table, salt and pepper shakers tumbling to the floor, and she clung to him as his slow, even strokes increased in strength.

She put her arms out, her hands against the back of the bench, as he entered her again and again. Her eyes were closed, and she gave herself over to the sensation of this man and this moment.

When she thought she could stand no more, he picked her up and pulled her to him, holding her against his body. They had on shirts but the heat of their skin blazed through.

When she felt herself reaching the peak, Alix put her head back, but Jared drew her to him closer and closer until the shudders came, both of them clinging together, silent, fulfilled. It was minutes before either of them moved.

"Kingsley," Alix said.

"That's me." Jared had his mouth on her ear.

"Good, because I was a little nervous about Montgomery."

He laughed as he stepped away from her, picked up his trousers, and pulled them on. Alix stayed on the table, her shirttail falling between her legs.

"You've stolen Daris's title," he said, smiling.

At first she didn't know what he meant but then remembered that he'd said Daris had the best legs on the island.

"Lots of leg presses," she said. When he walked to her, she slipped her hand under his shirt to run over his hard, flat stomach. "What about you? Go to the gym a lot?"

"I reel in two-hundred-pound tunas," he said as he picked her clothes up off the floor and handed them to her. Considering the way relatives walked in and out of the house, she knew it was better not to leave them lying around. She started to put on her trousers but Jared halted her.

"I like to *see* beauty." He put his arm under her legs and lifted her. "Aunt Addy or your mom?" he asked.

He was asking her which room they should retire to — and she was glad their evening together wasn't over. "Not Mom's and . . ."

"And what?"

He was carrying her up the stairs seemingly without effort. But then, Alix thought, she weighed less than a tuna. "Well, with the Captain watching us . . ."

"He won't be there," Jared said, and when Alix started to say more, he kissed her to silence. "There are some things you need to take my word on."

He gently put her down on the master bedroom's big bed and she wasn't sure how it happened, but in just seconds she was naked. He stretched out beside her, putting his mouth on her neck while his hands began running over her upper body. "You are beautiful," he whispered.

He was still fully dressed, only his jacket missing, and it felt odd for her to be naked but for him to be covered. The shades in the room were down but light filtered in, golden and shadowy.

As Alix lay there, surrounded by the silken drapes of the bed, her body fully nude, she looked at Jared, at his eyes, hooded, sultry, unfathomable. She reached up to start unbuttoning his shirt but he kissed her fingertips and took her hand away.

She started to ask why, but didn't. Her experience of sex was that it was something quickly done and finished. In school, sex had fit in between classes and assignments.

But this man — key word being man, not boy — seemed to have other ideas.

He began to caress her body as he looked at her. His lips soon followed his hands over her breasts, her ribs, down onto her stomach. She lifted her hips, wanting him to touch the center of her, but he didn't. His hands ran over her legs, down to her ankles.

He kissed her mouth as his hands wandered over her and Alix felt the urgency building inside her. There was something intensely erotic about being bare while he was clothed, something she'd never felt before as his hands touched and caressed her.

When he did reach the center of her, she arched up to meet him. It didn't take long for her to reach a crescendo, to come against his hand.

She buried her face in his shoulder. "Where did you learn *that*?" she asked.

"Made it up. I'm very creative."

She laughed and for a moment they were still, then she began unbuttoning his shirt. She'd never seen him in anything but long sleeves. They'd been rolled up to expose strong, tanned forearms and she'd wondered what the rest of him looked like.

It took only seconds to get his shirt off and she gasped at the sight of him. He was tanned all over, a deep, golden brown, and there wasn't an ounce of fat on him. She put her mouth on his skin and it was as warm as it looked.

It was an hour later that Alix, exhausted and sublimely happy, heard him say, "You have beautiful lips." When a laugh escaped her, he drew back to look at her. "Why is that funny?"

"I don't know you well enough to answer that."

"After what we've just done you can't tell me what about your lips causes you to laugh?"

"Not mine. Yours. Specifically your lower lip."

He ran his teeth over his lip. "What does that mean?"

"Someday I'll tell you. Show you, I guess."

"Are you keeping secrets from me?" he asked.

"A few. What about you? Weren't you going to talk to me about something?"

"Not now. Later."

She could tell that he was falling asleep, and that meant the part of sex that Alix hated was about to happen. The man either left or he turned away and started snoring. "You're going back to the guesthouse?"

"I will if you want me to, but I'd rather stay here. If it's all right with you, that is."

Smiling, she snuggled up to him. "I don't understand why some woman hasn't snatched you up."

She meant it as a joke but he seemed to

take her comment seriously. "Since you've been here, what have we spent most of our time doing?"

"Working."

"That's what they don't like about me."

"Foolish women."

"I agree," he said.

They didn't sleep much. They woke at midnight, both hungry, first for each other and second for food. They satisfied the first one right away, then Jared put on trousers and Alix slipped on his shirt and they went downstairs to the kitchen. To their delight, the fridge was full of leftovers from the picnic. Cold crab salad, chicken slices, bread, four kinds of cookies. But as nice as it was to find the food, it also meant that while they'd been upstairs someone had come into the house. Alix didn't want to think about what they might have heard.

"Now you see why I never leave underwear on the kitchen floor," Jared said, his mouth full.

"Does that mean you've had a lot of practice in leaving undies on the floor of your great-aunt's kitchen?" she asked primly.

"Not mine. Hers," Jared said. "Aunt Addy's. I had to pick it up often."

Alix laughed at his joke. "So what were you like as a kid? Other than kind and generous?"

"Do you think that because I gave you some old Legos? I was protecting my inheritance.

Aunt Addy let you play with things that should be in a museum."

"Speaking of which, maybe tomorrow I could see the papers about Valentina."

Jared stopped with a fork full of food on the way to his mouth. "Say that name again and the ghost arrives."

"Are we talking of the beautiful Captain Caleb? Then I'm on board."

"What is it with you and so-called beautiful men today?"

"There's you and who else?"

"Good catch," he said. "First Lexie's boss and now my grandfather."

Alix's face lost its smile. "You've mentioned him before. Maternal or paternal? Still alive?"

"If I remember correctly, I changed that reference to Aunt Addy."

"So you did." She looked at him and could see that he wasn't going to say any more. "Could I see the papers?"

"Sure. They're in the attic. Can I stand on the floor and watch you climb up those steep stairs?"

"With or without undies?"

Jared's look made her shove the last bite in her mouth. Without a word spoken between them, they jammed the rest of the food back into the fridge and ran up the stairs to the bedroom.

An hour later, Jared suggested that they try out the big bathtub in Victoria's room.

"I don't think I looked in her bathroom. Please tell me it isn't green."

"Then I'll have to be silent," Jared said.

Groaning, Alix let him pull her along the corridor to her mother's ivory and green bathroom.

In the hallway, Caleb was smiling.

# Chapter Fifteen

"Alix? Are you here?"

The voice was familiar and comforting and seemed to come from far away. She snuggled against Jared. Light was filtering into the room so it was day, but she had no intention of getting up. With the way she felt, she might stay in bed forever.

She felt him kiss the top of her head and move even closer. "Last night you earned the name of American Living Legend," she murmured as she fell back asleep.

"Alix? Are you upstairs?"

She heard the voice again, so very familiar. "Just another minute," she said, her eyes still closed.

But then they opened abruptly. "It's my dad," she whispered.

"So it is," Jared said, his arms holding her tightly.

She turned over to face him. "It's my father. You have to leave. He can't see you and me . . . together. You have to climb out the window."

Jared lay back in the bed but he didn't open his eyes. "When I was sixteen I was too old to do something like that. And now . . . Besides, we have to tell your father sometime."

At that thought, a feeling of panic ran through her. If her mother found her in bed with a man, it wouldn't matter. But not her father. He believed in honor and integrity and . . . and *not* finding his daughter in bed with a man she wasn't married to. She tried to conceal her anxiety from Jared. "I know you'll meet him," she said with as much patience as she could manage. "But not yet. Let me soften him up first. Please?" She put her hand on his face.

When he opened his eyes, he saw the fear in her eyes. "All right," he said, "but later we need to talk about a few things."

"Isn't that what women usually say?" she whispered.

"They do, and in my experience, those words mean that she wants a declaration of undying love."

"Oh? And how many times have you given it?"

There was a tap on the door. "Alix," Ken said, "unless you're like your mother, I'm coming in."

"No!" she said loudly. "I mean, I am." She lowered her voice to Jared. "He's referring to the fact that my mother sleeps —"

"In the nude," Jared said as he got out of bed. "Every male on this island knows that and dreams about it." He pulled on his jeans and picked up his other clothes off the floor.

Alix slipped on a T-shirt and went to the window. She was about to unlock it when Jared, on the other side of the bed, reached behind Captain Caleb's portrait, unlatched something that made a click, then swung the big frame out.

Alix was aghast — mainly because the architect in her hadn't seen that the portrait was hinged and covering an exit. It took a moment to recover from her shock, then she rolled across the bed to get to him. Behind the portrait was a doorway with a narrow, dirty staircase leading down.

"Alix?" her father said, louder this time.

"Just a minute, Dad, I'm getting dressed." She looked back at Jared and whispered, "Is that so the Captain could sneak in and out of Valentina's room?"

"It was put in so the maid could empty the chamber pot and nobody'd have to see her do it." After a quick kiss, Jared started down the stairs and Alix pushed the door shut, but she didn't lock it in case he wanted to return.

She looked up at Captain Caleb's portrait. "The secrets you hide!"

"Alix," her father said from the other side of the door, "I just got a call that I need to answer. Take your time getting dressed and meet me downstairs."

Alix let out a sigh of relief that showed how tense she'd been. How in the world was she going to tell her father about her and Jared? And *what* would she tell him? That they were lovers and she had no idea what would happen in the future?

At that thought, she could imagine her dad's groan, see his look of hurt, and worse, feel his disappointment. "So you've added yourself to the entourage of the Great Jared Montgomery," he'd probably say.

She listened at the door and could hear her father talking quietly, then his footsteps went down the stairs. Good, she thought, as she needed time to think — and to shower. As much as she didn't want to, she was going to have to remove all evidence of last night from her body. She wanted to savor her memories of the night, but right now she couldn't indulge herself. Dealing with her father came first.

She spent a long time under the hot water and thinking about how she was going to present Jared to her father. "If you'll just get to know him as a man and not by his reputation," she'd say. Or "Maybe he can be quite arrogant in America, but —" No, that wasn't right. She'd have to explain that remark. She'd just say "off-island." "Off-island, he might be so arrogant that he tells clients to take what he designs or get out, but here on Nantucket . . ." No, that wouldn't work either. "Arrogant" was too strong a word.

She shampooed her hair. What if she reminded her father that she was a grown woman and could make her own decisions? Great, she thought. Start off with everyone angry. Her dad would hate Jared if Alix suddenly became belligerent and demanding.

When she got out of the shower, she was no closer than she had been to figuring out how to deal with this.

"Maybe they'll like each other," she said aloud as she picked up the blow-dryer, but then gave a little laugh. Her gentle professor father and tuna fisherman Jared? No, that would never happen. But maybe Montgomery and her father could . . . But then there were all those women Jared had been seen with. No, that wouldn't work either.

As she took her time with her hair and in dressing, she couldn't help wondering what Jared was doing. Had he run away on his boat? Anything to escape having to face a girl's father. But he'd seemed to be utterly unafraid, so maybe . . .

Alix smiled into the mirror. "My girl." That's what Jared had called her. Maybe if she could make her father believe that there was more — or going to be more — between her and Jared Montgomery Kingsley the Seventh that would make it all easier for him to swallow.

When she was at last clean and dressed, she opened the bedroom door. It was time to face reality.

Jared went down the old stairs, and as he'd done many times, he vowed to run an electric cord up the wall and put in lights. It was pitch-dark in the downward tunnel and cobwebs were all over him.

He was looking forward to seeing Ken. It had been months since Aunt Addy's funeral, when they'd last seen each other. Of course there was that call when Ken had blasted Jared within an inch of his life. But he was used to that. When they'd first met, Ken had been so angry at the world that he could only talk in loud bursts. But back then, Jared wouldn't listen to anything said in a normal tone.

Jared's big concern was Alix. How was she going to take finding out that her father had also spent so much time on Nantucket and concealed it from her?

The stairs ended in the front parlor, behind what appeared to be paneling — and yet again he doubted the family chamber pot story. The maid could have shown up in the midst of a tea party. He'd have to ask his grandfather for the truth — which he had *no* hope of getting.

Jared wasn't surprised to see Ken standing

in the room waiting for him. Many years ago the two men had repaired the old stairs. As they had been tearing out the dry-rotted treads, Ken said, "Don't want Addy's ghost lover to hurt himself, do we?"

At the time, Jared had looked at him sharply, wondering what he knew, but Ken had only been making a joke.

Now there was a second of hesitation between them because it was obvious that Ken knew where Jared had been. Ken was the first to react as he opened his arms and Jared went to him. He was so grateful that Ken wasn't angry that the reunion was like a son coming home from war. They held on to each other for a long moment.

"Come on," Ken said, his arm still around Jared's shoulders, "let's sit down. I made coffee and I brought doughnuts from Downyflake."

Jared had never been one to postpone bad news, so he said, "You know where I was?" It was better to get this about him and Alix out in the open.

"I always believed that you and my daughter would like each other."

Jared's smile showed his relief. It would have been bad if Ken disliked the idea of his precious Alix hooking up with a man who used to be less than an upstanding citizen. Forget all the success he'd had since then. Jared knew that Ken saw inside him.

The pretty little front parlor was where the good furniture was, including several pieces that his grandfather had sent back on the ship with his brother. After that time, no more children in the family were given his name, as a lot of Nantucketers were angry that Caleb Kingsley, in his rush to get home, had gone into dangerous waters and sunk the ship. Family, friends, and crew had gone down with him.

Ken took the couch and Jared sat on a chair across from him. To Jared's great annoyance, his grandfather sat down in the big wing chair. His shape and substance were stronger in this room and it amazed Jared that Ken couldn't see him.

"How's Celeste?" Jared asked as he picked up a chocolate-covered doughnut.

"Gone," Ken said. "And Avery?"

"Stormed out months ago," Jared said. "She wanted a ring."

The two men smiled at each other. It was humor and understanding based on many years of shared confidences about the women who'd been through their lives. That neither of them had ever settled with one had been a bond between the men.

While eating one of the delectable doughnuts, Ken took a moment before speaking. "What does Caleb say about you and my daughter?"

"He's always thought —" Jared began, but

then halted, his eyes wide.

Ken smiled at Jared's shock. "Don't bother trying to cover it up. I used to practically live with you, remember? You were always arguing with an unseen person. I figured you were either crazy or talking to a ghost. Of course I meant the last as a joke."

"So you decided I was insane?"

"More or less."

Jared refused to look at his grandfather — who, no doubt, knew that Ken was aware of the Kingsley Family Secret — or one of them, anyway.

"Besides," Ken said, "I found out that if Addy drank enough rum she'd tell me anything."

"But she didn't know I could . . ." Jared couldn't bring himself to say the truth out loud. Secrecy had been preached to him by every male in his family since he could understand words.

"No, she didn't tell me about you, but she did tell me about my daughter and your ghostly ancestor. I assume Alix's ability to see the . . . the man is what this year is about."

"I think so," Jared said. He wasn't quite able to control his discomfort in talking of this matter.

"Has she . . . ? Has my daughter . . . ?"

"Seen him? Not yet," Jared said.

Ken frowned. "I worry about that. In fact, it's the real reason I came here — and I plan to stay until it . . ." He looked at Jared. "Until he shows up. I don't know how my daughter will react to seeing a ghost."

Jared didn't know either. If he were alone he'd demand an answer from his grandfather, but Ken's presence made that impossible. "I'll be here," Jared said. "Alix won't be alone, and I don't think she's going to be too upset." He thought it was better not to mention all the things his grandfather had already done to ease Alix into actually seeing him. Pictures falling, cheek kisses. Caleb had never stopped.

Jared wanted to change the subject. "How is the beautiful Victoria?"

Ken understood that Jared wasn't going to say any more about the ghost that, supposedly, Alix could see. Or could when she was a child. "Victoria is telling her editor that her next book is half done."

Jared groaned. "When she gets here, she's going to want to take this house apart looking for Aunt Addy's journals."

"What do you want to bet that she's going to try to get Alix to leave the island so she can search in peace?"

"Under *no* circumstances is Victoria going to stay in *my* house alone," Jared said. "For all I know, Aunt Addy may have hidden them under some hand-carved molding."

"Victoria would tear out the wallpaper to get to those journals." The men, both architects, both lovers of old houses, looked at each other in mutual horror. Some of the wallpaper had been made specifically for Kingsley House, hand-painted in France in the early nineteenth century. It was one of a kind. Irreplaceable.

"Which is yet another reason why I plan to stay here." Ken looked at Jared. "Is it possible that *you* could ask your . . . uh, ancestor where the journals are hidden?"

Again, it took all Jared's strength not to glance at his grandfather sitting just to the left of Ken. It was one thing to speak of a ghost in a general sense, but quite another to be told one was sitting just a few feet away. Jared and his father had talked openly about Caleb, and when Jared was a teenager there were many times when he'd also wanted to confide in Ken. "My grandfather" — Jared said the name pointedly — "knows, but it's his sense of humor not to tell. He probably believes that if the journals are found, no one will look for Valentina."

Jared watched Ken struggle to not show his discomfort at this outright mention of a man who had died long ago. Maybe he'd thought Jared would deny the contact — and maybe he should have.

"Oh, right," Ken said, then cleared his throat. "The missing Valentina. I read about her in the will."

"The one Victoria so very carefully didn't

let Alix see?"

Ken smiled. "And we keep coming full circle, back to my daughter." He paused. "I think I was a little rough on you when I called."

"I deserved worse. She's . . ."

"Go on," Ken said. "What were you going to say about her?"

"That she's not like I thought she would be. I'd heard so much about her from you and Victoria over the years that I thought she'd be a spoiled brat. She had two parents who competed for her attention. To my eyes, she had everything. A real princess." He took a sip of his coffee. "I think I was jealous."

"There's no need to be. We didn't mean to, but I see now that her mother and I tried to split Alix in half. Victoria wanted her to write, and I . . ." He shrugged.

"Wanted her to follow you," Jared said. "Alix told me that she hadn't inherited her mother's talent, that she could write but couldn't plot. I couldn't tell her that she had exactly inherited Victoria's talent. And yours."

"Alix is better than I ever was." Ken's voice was full of pride. "She has her mother's ambition and my — No, I'm not going to take anything from her. Alix has her own talent. She is unique."

"When she speaks of you she goes into a rapture."

Ken smiled. "That's an odd choice of word."

Jared took his time before speaking. "Will she . . . ? Do you think she'll forgive me?"

"You mean when she finds out that you haven't told her about my part in your life?" Ken asked.

"Yes."

"Is it important that she does forgive you?"

Jared answered immediately and there was passion in his tone. "Yes, it is." He looked Ken in the eyes. "It is *very* important to me."

Ken didn't try to hide his pleasure at the words. Alix and Jared were the two people he loved most in the world, and right now he was *very* glad that they hadn't grown up together. Chalk one up for Victoria, he thought. She'd always said that it would be a mistake to let the two of them spend a lot of time together when they were growing up.

"He'll never see her as anything but a kid," Victoria had said.

At the time, Ken thought it had been just another of Victoria's excuses for getting what she wanted, but it looked like he was wrong.

Ken smiled at Jared. "It's me Alix will be angry at, but I'm not too worried. She's forgiven Victoria for a thousand things."

"But not you?"

"She's never needed to forgive me for anything." Ken's smile and his lack of worry made Jared relax. "Until now."

Jared laughed.

When Alix got downstairs, she tried to calm her jangled nerves as she walked into the big back parlor, tried to prepare herself for the coming argument. This is ridiculous! she thought. I'm twenty-six years old and I have a right to . . .

The room was empty and she didn't know if she was glad or disappointed. The problem wasn't that she had a boyfriend, it was a matter of *who* he was. Jared Montgomery's designs were shown by her father in his classroom. And a quarter of his students, especially the females, had turned in papers about Montgomery's work. More than once Alix had heard her father complaining about what they wrote. "Why they feel compelled to include whole pages about Montgomery's sex life is beyond me. Listen to this!" He'd then read aloud something about how the man had been seen with half a dozen females in the last year.

How was Alix going to counteract that? How would she be able to make her father believe that Jared had changed?

And for that matter, what made Alix so sure that he *had* changed? Just because she'd made some statement about not wanting to be hurt didn't mean that the two of them had a future together.

For a moment she thought of running back

upstairs and hiding. Maybe she'd send her dad an email.

"Coward!" she said and started walking again.

When she got toward the front of the house, she heard two male voices. Had someone come to visit and her father was entertaining him? But as she got closer she recognized the voices — Jared and her father.

Oh, no! she thought. This is a disaster. Please, please don't let Jared tell my father the truth. Alix needed to talk to him first.

The sound of laughter made her stop just outside the door and listen.

"It's good to hear that Dilys is well," her father was saying. "Think I can persuade her to have me out to dinner?"

"I think she'll be hurt if you don't go. She'll make those scallops you like so much," Jared answered. "And Lexie always wants to see you."

"Oh, no," Ken said. "Lexie is going to bawl me out for not telling Alix everything."

"Get in line!" Jared said. "I try to go over there only when I'm sure Toby is home."

"And how is that beautiful girl?"

"The same. Her dad bought her a big fridge for her flowers."

"Barrett! I haven't seen him in over a year. In college, we were such close friends. Is he still playing tennis?"

"Last I heard, he was. Great Harbor." He

was referring to the yachting club that cost over three hundred grand to join.

"How's Wes? He and Daris get married yet?"

"He tried to take Alix out," Jared said.

Ken snorted in derision. "I guess you took care of *that.*"

"I certainly did." There was laughter in Jared's voice. "I got Daris to show up half naked. Wes couldn't resist her and besides, she was ready to forgive him."

"Ever find out what he did to her?"

"Not a word of it."

"Poor guy. How can he know what not to do again if he doesn't know what he did wrong in the first place?"

"It'll be good for him. Daris will keep him on his toes." Suddenly, Jared looked to Ken's left and his face seemed to drain of color. "Oh, no," he whispered, then put down his mug.

"What is it?" Ken asked, alarmed.

"Granddad said Alix overheard us. She went back upstairs." Jared crossed the room in three strides and left.

Ken leaned back in his chair. He didn't like that his daughter had just had a bombshell dropped on her, but he *hated* that Jared had just talked to a ghost.

■ ■ ■ ■

All Alix could think of as she ran up the stairs was that Jared and her father had known each other for years — which meant that her father had spent a lot of time on Nantucket. But he'd never told her. Alix would not have believed that her father would keep a secret like that from her. Her mother, yes, but not her dad. They had a special bond. Or she'd thought they did.

She shut the bedroom door, leaned against it, and thought, Now what do I do? Try to act as though this information doesn't hurt?

Turning, she tried to lock the door but the key for the old door plate wasn't there. "It's Nantucket!" she said aloud, momentarily annoyed that nothing ever seemed to be locked.

She moved a chair under the knob, then, in anger, started stripping the bed of sheets. What else was being kept a secret from her? she wondered. Her mother and now her father. Everyone had been lying to her for what looked to be her entire life. But then hadn't Jared said that? Secrets kept all her life, is what he'd said. Alix threw the sheets on the floor and looked up at Captain Caleb's portrait. "Do *you* have thousands of secrets too? Like *all* the Kingsleys do? And don't answer that or I'll drag your picture up to the attic and nail boards over your chamber pot staircase."

"Alix?" came Jared's voice through the door. "Could we talk? Please?"

"Go away," she said.

"I never lied to you. I told you there were secrets being kept from you. Please open the door and let me explain. I didn't want to hide anything from you, but I'd made promises. Please let me in so we can talk."

She started to tell him to leave, but she knew he was telling the truth. She moved the chair away and he opened the door, closing it behind him, but he didn't come inside any farther. It did help that he looked deeply worried.

"You let me guess that everything had to do with my mother," she said. "But then I didn't think my father would . . . would . . ."

"Betray you?" Jared asked. "Would it help if I told you that it was all your mother's doing? She made Ken swear to say nothing to you about Nantucket."

"But *why?*"

"She —" He broke off. He had no right to tell about the journals that were the basis for all Victoria's novels.

"Are you trying to decide how much to lie to me?"

"I'm not going to lie, but some secrets are not mine to reveal." He took a step closer to her. "I'm sorry that I can't sit down with you and tell everything that I know, but I owe all that I am, all that I have, to your parents. If it weren't for your father I'd probably be in prison now — or dead. And as you so shrewdly guessed, your mother paid for the bulk of my very expensive schooling. Your dad helped with that but . . ."

"Mom has the money," Alix said.

"Yes, she does. But I learned everything that's made my career from your father."

Alix's eyes widened. "Master builder. You said a 'master builder' let you design a remodel when you were just a kid. Was that my father?"

"Yes, it was. That was right after your mother took you away from Nantucket. Ken was very depressed because his wife was divorcing him and he wasn't going to get to live with his beloved, and may I add, his adorable, daughter."

"And you'd lost your father not long before that," she said softly.

"It had been two years but I still didn't believe that Dad wasn't going to walk through the door and force me to give up my evil ways." Jared gave a tentative half smile. "Not that I would have relinquished *all* of them."

"I'm glad of that." She paused, knowing that everything he was saying was true and actually, she liked that he'd honored the vows he'd made. But his vows weren't hers. She was going to find out all that she could. "I just don't understand why my mother didn't want me to know about Nantucket."

"You expect me to explain Victoria to you?"

"Are you evading my question?"

"Completely. I'll tell you a secret. Your dad can yell at me until his face turns purple, and an hour later I'm fine. But Victoria . . . She can make me feel like a worm."

"Really? It's the opposite for me." She looked at him. "This whole thing is very strange. To think that you know both my parents so well . . . It's difficult for me to comprehend."

"They were like second parents to me. Well, actually, your dad was like a father to me, but Victoria doesn't seem like anybody's mother."

"She does to me," Alix said, then her head came up. "You don't think this makes you and me brother and sister, does it?"

At her ability to make a joke, Jared looked greatly relieved and pulled her into his arms, her face buried against his chest. Alix could hardly breathe, but she didn't mind.

"I would have been a horrible older brother," he said.

"Ha! You were wonderful with the Legos."

"Come on," Jared said. "Let's go downstairs and talk to your father. He'll want to go out to get some seafood for lunch."

"Did *you* teach him how to clean fish?"

"I did," Jared said. "When he first got here, he didn't know top from tail." He had his arm firmly around Alix, as though he was afraid to let her get even inches away from him.

Alix halted at the top of the stairs and looked up at him. “How many more huge, enormous secrets are you keeping from me?”

“Two,” he said.

“And they are . . . ?”

Jared gave a groan of pain. “If I promise to go with you to get whatever Izzy needs for her wedding, will that make you pre-forgive me for not telling you now?”

Alix thought about that for a moment. “Are you saying that you will go with me to pick out flowers?”

“Sure. Toby can —”

“No, you and I will go to a florist together. You’ll have to look at photos of flower arrangements that I can send to Izzy.”

Jared winced but he nodded.

“And you’ll help me choose the cake to show Izzy?” she asked.

“You mean one of those tall things?”

“Yes,” she said. “It’ll have tiers.”

“Tears?” He ran his fingertip down from his eye.

She gave him a look.

“Okay. Wait! How about making a cake that looks like a Gaudi building? Or I could design something —”

“No buildings in sugar,” Alix said. “Izzy is very traditional. She’ll probably want pink and lavender roses."

With a look of horror, he grabbed the newel post for support. "What else?"

"Tent, food, a band. A dress for me."

"I see a ghost," Jared blurted out as he broke under the pressure.

"Who wouldn't, living in this house?" Alix said as she started down the stairs, then looked back up at him. "Come on, it won't be that bad."

"I'd rather swim in a pool of sharks," Jared mumbled as he followed her down the stairs.

"Good idea," she said. "Hey! Maybe we can get some reproduction lightship baskets and fill them with flowers."

"Reproduction?" Jared whispered, the word catching in his throat as though it were poison. "You're going too far."

Laughing, Alix slipped her arm in his. "Where can I get shoes suitable to wear to a wedding? You like kitten heels?"

Jared looked like he might start to cry.

# Chapter Sixteen

Three weeks, Ken thought. He'd been on Nantucket for three whole weeks and he didn't think he'd ever been happier in his life.

At first he'd stayed in the guest bedroom of the big house. Not Victoria's Palace of Green but in the one across from Addy's, now Alix's, bedroom. Over the years, he'd often stayed there. He liked being near Addy in case she needed him during the night. Smiling, he thought of the many times he'd heard her voice when she was alone in her room. He'd thought she'd been talking in her sleep, but one night over their rum drinks — she could easily drink Ken under the table — she mentioned Alix and Caleb. He knew she was talking about his daughter, but who was Caleb? Another Kingsley relative he'd yet to meet?

It took several nights and multiple bottles of rum before he got Addy to tell him the whole truth.

It seemed that his dear daughter, Alix, at four years old, used to regularly converse with a ghost. If Ken had known back then what was happening, he would have . . . The truth was he didn't know what he would have done. At that time he'd been so angry and depressed that he wasn't rational. If he'd been given any reason to do so, he feared that he would have taken his wrath out on Victoria, which could have meant that the rage would have filtered down to little Alix.

As it was, Ken had shown only Jared his fury at what life had done to him. Oh, but the shouting matches the two of them used to have! Never before or since had Ken yelled like that. Cursed like that. But then he'd never again been so unhappy. Nor had Jared.

There was one night when Ken found Jared crying. He was a six-foot-tall teenager who had an attitude of Don't Mess with Me, but he was sitting by a pond on land his family owned, and crying. Ken reacted naturally and put his arms around the boy. They didn't say a word but Ken knew of the boy's continuing grief. Jared's mother had told him what a good and loving man her husband had been, and how he'd doted on his son.

"I couldn't have any more children after him," she'd told Ken. "I begged Six to divorce me and get some healthy girl who could give him a lot of babies. But he said that one perfect son was all he needed."

When Ken met Jared — or Seven, as his mother called him — the last word he would have used to describe the boy was "perfect."

Somewhere in there, he and Jared stopped fighting. Ken was sure it was when the boy showed his extraordinary, dazzling talent for architectural design. Only by accident did Ken see Jared drawing in the dirt. No one else paid any attention to the marks, but Ken recognized them as a rudimentary floor plan.

Ken discussed it with Jared's mother, and she showed him a whole drawer full of sketches her son had made. "He and his dad were planning to add a big room to this old house. Six told him that he could design it. But after . . . afterward, Seven put it all away."

Ken had to push Jared to get him to show his ideas. As Ken looked at the drawings, he acted as though he was just thinking about them rather than ready to set off cannons in praise. Slowly, Ken showed the boy how to put on paper what he saw in his mind. And since Jared knew nothing about construction, over the years Ken taught him how to build what he envisioned.

But no matter that Ken had made a life for himself on Nantucket, he knew that if he wanted to see Alix regularly he had to leave the island. He felt torn in half. He had a daughter in America and an honorary son on Nantucket — and his ex-wife was decreeing that Ken couldn't openly have both of them.

The day Ken left, he saw in Jared's eyes that he didn't think Ken was coming back. But he had. Every holiday he wasn't with Alix, Ken was on Nantucket. Vacations, accumulated sick days, playing-hooky days, whatever time he could manage to scrape together, he spent on the island.

Even after Jared left for school, Ken still visited as often as possible. By that time he and Addy were good friends and he knew a lot of other people on Nantucket. It was natural that he began to look after the houses owned by the Kingsley family. He'd tell Addy what needed to be repaired, then she'd tell Victoria, who would pay the bills. At first Ken hadn't liked that arrangement, but Addy said that all Victoria's money came from the Kingsley journals, so why shouldn't she pay? Ken didn't argue. Roofs that didn't leak took precedence over his pride.

All in all, Ken thought everything had worked out well — except that Alix had been left out. Victoria never budged on her rule that her daughter was not to go to Nantucket, not even to hear about it. At first Ken had fought her, argued with her, questioned her, but she never showed the slightest weakness in her resolve.

It was on a snowy night when the big old drafty house was colder than the outdoors and Ken had made a roaring fire that Addy had told him about Alix and the ghost.

"Does Victoria know about this . . . this person?" Ken asked, not sure whether to believe or not.

"No," Addy said, smiling. "Victoria thinks I'm a boring old woman. She thinks I'm . . ." She leaned toward Ken. "Victoria thinks I'm a virgin."

Laughing, he told Addy that she was much too sexy for men to be able to stay away from. She'd laughed in delight, poured them both more rum, and told him that none of the other women had written about Caleb. "They could see him but they never told about him." She took a drink. "They wrote about their affairs and even about murders, but they told no one about seeing and talking to a ghost."

"But you did," Ken said, smiling as the rum coursed through him.

"Oh yes, I did," Addy said. "And when Victoria finds out, she's going to look hard for my journals."

"Where are they?" Ken asked.

"I've hidden them quite well," Addy said, smiling. "And Caleb and I worked out a plan so that someone who can see him will be told many things. But that will be after I'm gone."

At the time Ken had been too mellow to question her, and he'd only found out at the reading of Addy's will that "someone" was his daughter.

It was after that conversation that Ken thought about what he'd been told. Years before, even if Victoria didn't know about a ghost that Alix could see, she'd known *something* was wrong. After that, Ken quit badgering her to tell Alix about Nantucket. They never spoke of it, but it seemed they had reached an understanding.

When Addy died and her will decreed that Alix could stay in the house for a year, Ken was fairly sure he knew why and he hadn't liked it at all. As a father, he wanted to protect his daughter.

But Victoria hadn't felt the same way — and Ken thought it had more to do with her quest to find Addy's journals than it did with Alix. When he told her so, they'd had one of their blistering fights. Years before, he'd stopped beating himself up with thoughts that his neglect of his beautiful young wife was what had driven her away. It had taken a few years after the divorce, but he'd realized that Victoria's strong personality was more than he could take. If they'd stayed together, they probably would have murdered each other. But then during one of their arguments Victoria had admitted that she'd only married him to escape her small hometown. That had hurt more than Ken allowed her to see.

After Addy's will was read, Victoria had begged Ken to stay away from the island and let Jared and Alix have some time alone. And it had all worked out. Ken had shown up to find Jared and Alix very much together. And he'd stayed to . . .

Ken wanted to think that his reasons for staying were altruistic. First, he wanted to protect his daughter from a ghost. And he needed to be there in case Jared got a wandering eye and hurt Alix. And he should . . .

Ha! Ken wasn't fooled by his own lies. He was staying because for the first time in his adult life he had a feeling of family. True, deep down, delicious *family.*

By the end of the first week he'd moved into the guesthouse and Jared was back in his own home, staying with Alix in the big bedroom that should have gone to him when his great-aunt died.

How comfortable the three of them were together! Ken had taught both Jared and Alix about architectural design and building, so they tended to agree on everything. Jared had taught Ken about the sea and its inhabitants. In turn, Ken had relayed it all to his daughter.

As for Alix, she bound the men together. She looked out for them, made their lives comfortable, and above all, she put new life into them.

Several times in the past weeks, the three of them had been out on Jared's boat. They liked the same food, baited hooks the same way, enjoyed the same scenery.

When they were home, Ken made sure he gave the couple time alone. He often went to visit Dilys. One lovely summer long ago, they had been lovers. Dilys was older than Ken and he'd enjoyed her quiet company — and the sex she'd learned in the freewheeling seventies. But he knew he could never stay on Nantucket and she was never going to leave, so they'd used that as their excuse to break up. They'd quit being lovers — except for one stormy night in 1992 — but had remained friends.

In these last weeks, Ken had spent a lot of time with Dilys and had taken over Jared's repair jobs in his old neighborhood. Ken had also properly fixed the greenhouse heater for Lexie and Toby. He had let Toby cook wonderful meals for him, had listened to Lexie complain about her "horrible" boss, and had later puzzled with Toby about the matter of Lexie and her employer.

All in all, Ken had never felt so good. He was going to retire in a few years and he was now sure that he'd do it on Nantucket. Maybe he could persuade Jared to give him a long lease on one of the houses he owned on Kingsley Lane.

Right now it was raining outside and the old house was cool, so Ken had built a fire in the fireplace of the big parlor, and the three of them were in there together. Alix and Jared were working on the design of the movie stars' house. It was going to be the first official collaboration between Madsen and Montgomery. The pride Ken felt at the uniting of those names was immeasurable.

Two weekends ago Izzy and her fiancé, Glenn, had come to the island to talk about the wedding. It had taken twenty-four hours for Izzy to get over her awe of Jared. For a whole day she'd just watched him, not even blinking.

Glenn took it all well, but then he was so in love with Izzy he could hardly see straight. On the first night Jared told Ken, "Granddad says that in another life Glenn was the local wheelwright and he was in love with Izzy back then too."

No matter how many mentions of the ghost there were, Ken was still shocked. He tried to hide it, but when the reference to reincarnation was added, he wasn't successful. Jared must have seen it because he didn't mention his grandfather again.

And Alix certainly hadn't said anything about seeing a ghost. Her mind was fully occupied with Jared's California house, the remodel for his cousin, and her best friend's wedding.

Izzy'd had a lot of trouble deciding on flowers and cake flavors, and the music for the wedding. For most of the weekend she'd visited, all anyone talked of was tents and Porta Potties and seating and anything else they could think of. Jared had been the telephone man, calling people he knew and booking things. With Izzy's pregnancy they'd moved the wedding up to the twenty-third of June. Very, very soon.

"What would *you* do?" Izzy asked Alix on Sunday night when they were all at the dining table, a feast of their own making before them.

"About what?" Alix asked.

"If this were *your* wedding, what would you do?"

Everyone at the table paused and stared at Alix. Ken was happy to see that Jared's face was as intent as the others.

"About the flowers?" Alix asked.

Ken could see that his daughter was avoiding Jared's eyes. It was too soon to think of a wedding, but then when you knew, you knew.

He decided to help his daughter out. "Victoria has been planning Alix's wedding since she was a baby. Everything is set. Alix doesn't have to make even one decision."

Alix groaned. "No, no, please don't tell that story."

"Now you have to," Izzy said.

"I'd like to hear it too," Jared added.

"A dress." Ken smiled. "What was it your mother said about a candle lighting up the world?"

Alix shook her head. "Okay, this is from my mother and you all know her, right?"

"I don't," Glenn said.

"You will," Alix said. "Mom told me that I'm to wear a wedding dress with so many crystals and faceted beads on it that I can carry one candle and the thousands of reflections will light up the whole church." She looked at Glenn. "And now you know my mother."

He laughed. "I think I'm going to like her."

Jared was looking at Alix. "Not to your taste?"

His face was so serious that Alix turned pink. "I'm more of a cotton girl."

Izzy spoke up. "Alix doesn't care about the dress or the flowers. She just wants to be married in a building of architectural significance."

That made everyone laugh.

"In *your* chapel," Izzy said over them. "You should get married inside the chapel that *you* designed."

"I don't think —" Alix began.

Ken cut her off. "I forgot about that. You told me on the phone you were designing one but I've not heard any more about it."

"It's nothing really. It's just —"

"She made a model," Izzy said.

"Could we see it?" Ken asked.

"No," Alix answered. "It was just for fun. We've been working on a house, with a rock in one wall. It's —"

Jared put his hand over hers. "I would really and truly like to see the model you made."

Ken knew his daughter well enough to see that she was worried about criticism of the design, but with everyone staring at her so expectantly she couldn't say so. He nodded at her in encouragement and Alix left the table to go upstairs to get the model.

When she returned she looked so apprehensive that Ken wanted to warn Jared to make *no* criticism. But he needn't have worried.

Jared just looked at it and said, "It's perfect."

Ken didn't think Jared had ever thought that word, much less said it before. Certainly not about anything that had to do with a building.

"Do you really like it?" Alix asked, and everyone at the table was quiet. It was the first time she'd ever sounded like a student asking for praise.

"You're asking Montgomery, aren't you?"

"I guess I am."

He put his hand over hers. "I wouldn't have said it if I didn't think it was. I'll tell you how much I like it: I don't want to change a thing."

"The steeple isn't too tall?" she asked.

"No."

She opened her mouth to speak.

"And it's not too short either," Jared said.

She closed her mouth.

He squeezed her hand. "Where do you think it should be built?"

"When I designed it, I was thinking of Nantucket."

It was Izzy who interrupted what had become a private conversation. "Too bad that chapel isn't here now. If I got married in it, we wouldn't have to try to cram a hundred people into the back garden."

"Amid the portable toilets," Glenn said.

As Alix joined the laughter, she turned to look at Jared in question and he seemed to understand. Could they build the chapel on the land Jared had shown her?

Jared shook his head. "It can't be done. The permits would take weeks, if not months. We Nantucketers are fierce about what we allow to be built on our island."

She leaned back in her chair. "Too bad. It would have been nice for Izzy to get married in . . ."

"Something of architectural significance?" Jared asked. "A building created by her best friend who is about to set the world on fire with her designs?"

"And built by the world's greatest living architect," she said, smiling at him with adoring eyes.

"I'm going to be ill," Izzy said as she leaned over to kiss Glenn's cheek. "I'm glad you and I don't act like that."

"You've got to be kidding!" Alix said. "I remember the night after your third date with Glenn. You were so mad about him that you —" She kept talking, delighting in the telling of Izzy and Glenn's story — and deflecting attention away from her and Jared. It was much too soon for them to even think of discussing the future.

Alix was so engrossed in her story that she didn't notice the way Jared and her father looked at each other over her head. Based on many years of time spent together, they easily communicated silently. All Jared had to do was raise his eyebrows and Ken nodded. Before anything was built on Nantucket it had to pass the HDC, the Historic District Commission — and Dilys was on that committee.

When Alix finished her story of Izzy and Glenn dating, Jared and Ken were smiling extraordinarily widely. They had just made a plan and they were going to do everything they could to make it happen.

Now Ken was smiling at Jared and Alix. They were sitting on opposite ends of the couch, the floor before them littered with papers. Over the last weeks, the three of them had been using the office in the guesthouse to draw the plans for the remodel of Jared's cousin's house in town.

Years ago, the office had been Ken's. He'd set it up when he'd arrived on Nantucket and it was where he'd taught Jared how to use a triangle and T-square. It had made him feel good to see Jared and Alix bent over the big drafting table.

Each of them had a story about the old-fashioned office. Ken told what he'd gone through to get Addy to lend him the mermaid that had once been a ship's masthead.

"There it was, sitting in the attic amid all those old trunks, covered in dust, and she acted like I wanted to take it out and use it for firewood."

"So what did you have to do to get her to let you move it over here?" Jared asked.

"I tried logic, but that didn't budge her. Finally, I told her I was in love with the memory of the woman who'd sat for it back in the eighteenth century. That worked."

Alix had nearly choked on her drink in laughter, then she embellished her story of how Izzy and she had broken into the place. "But that was before we knew you were a real person," she told Jared.

He gave her a serious look. "I have to admit that there's a part of me that misses that student admiration."

"I know just what you mean," Ken said with a pointed look at Jared.

They all laughed together.

Jared's story was simple. He had never allowed anyone into the room except the two of them.

Ken smiled. Coming from Jared, the statement meant so very much.

As Ken was smiling at the two of them, thinking that life was good, outside there was a quick flash of lightning, startling them with its ferocity. Seconds later came a huge crash.

They looked at one another. As people involved in the building trade, they knew what that sound was. They nearly tumbled over each other as they ran toward the kitchen and out the back door.

Outside it was dark and raining hard. Jared had grabbed a big flashlight from a drawer and he shone it around the garden. When he came to the rose arbor, he stopped.

The arbor, still covered in prickly stems, had fallen to the ground — and it had taken the rose bushes with it. Where there had once been a beautiful covered archway was now a mess of broken wood and uprooted plants. The ground was muddy and grassless.

"Oh, no!" Alix shouted over the rain. "How can Izzy use that?" She looked up at Jared. "Izzy will be so disappointed. You can fix it, right?"

With rain running down his face, Jared smiled at her. She was looking at him as though she thought he could do anything. If there was a hole in the earth, she seemed to think he could repair it. Reaching out, he put his arm around her and drew her to him. When he did, he glanced upward and saw his grandfather at the upstairs window.

Suddenly, Jared knew without a doubt in the world that, somehow, his grandfather had done this. From getting Alix to design a chapel, to this strong, sturdy cedar arbor lying in the mud, to the wedding, he *knew* that Caleb Kingsley had done it all.

"Come on," Jared said to Alix. "Let's get you inside. You're wet and you don't have on any shoes."

"I'm just concerned about —"

He kissed her forehead. "I'll fix it. Okay?"

She nodded and they went back inside the house, while Ken went to the guesthouse to dry off.

Once they were inside, Jared told Alix to go upstairs and fill the bathtub with hot water. "I'll join you in a few minutes."

It would have been a sexy invitation except that Jared was frowning deeply.

"Is everything all right?" she asked. Her teeth were beginning to chatter.

"Yes," he said. "I just need to . . . to get some towels. Go on, I'll be there in a few minutes."

Alix wanted to ask him what was going on, but she was too cold to think clearly, and her mind was on Izzy's wedding. What were they going to do now? Of course they'd rebuild, replant, and drape cut roses everywhere. It could be done. She ran up the stairs to her bathroom — *their* bathroom, she thought — and began filling the tub.

•

# Chapter Seventeen

Jared went straight to the stairs that led up to the attic. He knew from experience that his grandfather was strongest at the top of the house. The large attic room was packed with trunks and boxes and old furniture, some of them containing items that had been owned by his grandfather. These earthly connections, here and in the front parlor, made Caleb more visible.

Jared also knew that his anger would draw his grandfather to him. Sure enough, when he opened the door to the attic and pulled the string to the overhead lightbulb, there his grandfather stood, hands clasped behind his back, fully ready for the coming argument.

"You did it, didn't you?" Jared said, his jaw clenched. "You made the arbor collapse."

"What makes you say that?"

"Don't evade my question," Jared snapped.

"I thought you had perfected question-evading."

Jared glared at him, but then his face

changed. All his life he'd seen the shadowy figure of his grandfather. One of his earliest memories was of seeing him bending over his childhood crib and smiling. Jared had never thought it was strange that he could see through the man. It was years before he realized that semitransparent men weren't part of other people's lives.

But right now he couldn't see through his grandfather. At least not totally. He was clearer than Jared had ever seen him before. "What's going on?" The anger was gone from his voice.

"What do you mean?"

Jared knew his grandfather understood him, but he motioned his hand up and down his body. "Why do you look like that?"

Caleb took his time in answering. "On the twenty-third of June I'm going to leave this earth."

It took Jared a moment to understand what his grandfather was saying. "Leave?" he whispered. "As in die?" For all that Jared often made cracks about his grandfather finally leaving the earth, he couldn't imagine a life without him. "I . . . I . . ." Jared began but couldn't go on.

"You'll be all right," Caleb said gently. "You have a family now."

"Of course I'll be okay." Jared was doing his best to recover from the shock. "And you'll be . . . be happier."

"Depends on where they send me." Caleb's eyes were twinkling.

Jared didn't smile. "Why on Izzy's wedding date?" Jared's head came up. "Or did you make her set it then?"

"Yes, I did. I seem to be able to do more . . . things than I could. And I know considerably more. Something is going to happen. It's . . ." He trailed off.

"What?!" Jared half yelled.

"I don't know. It's just that I can feel things changing. Every day I get stronger." He held out his hand. "I can see my own body. Yesterday I saw myself in a mirror. I'd forgotten how handsome I am."

Jared still didn't smile. "*What* is going to happen?"

"I told you that I don't know, but I feel . . . a sense of anticipation. I just know that my life . . . your life . . . the lives of *all* of us are going to change soon. You need to tell Alix what you and Ken have been plotting. You *can* build it in time for the wedding."

"I'm not sure," Jared said. "There's not enough time."

"You need to do it!" Caleb said, his voice adamant, fierce. "You know where her chapel goes, don't you?"

"On the old house site."

"Yes, you have it right." Caleb listened. "Alix has the bathtub full. Go to her." Caleb's body was beginning to fade away. Not disappear in an instant as usual, but more like the sun beginning to set. "You need to find —"

"I know!" Jared said impatiently. "I'm supposed to find out what happened to Valentina."

Caleb's body was little more than a shadow. "I think that before you can find her, you should look for Parthenia." He was gone.

Jared stood there a moment staring into the dim length of the attic. "Who the hell is Parthenia?" he muttered.

Shaking his head, he pulled the light string and went down the stairs. When he got to the bathroom, Alix was already in a tub full of hot water, six-inch-deep bubbles across the surface, her head just peeping above. She gave Jared a smile of invitation, but when he didn't seem to notice, she sat up straighter in the tub. "What happened?"

Distracted, Jared removed his cold, wet clothing and put a leg into the water. "Damn! But this water is hot."

"I think you need it. You're white as a glacier." As soon as he was in the tub she moved between his legs, her back to his front. "Tell me what's bothering you. And don't even think of saying that nothing is."

Jared took a while before he spoke. Even though his life had been one of secrets and keeping things to himself, right now he wanted to tell Alix what his grandfather had told him. On Izzy's wedding day, Captain Caleb Jared Kingsley, who'd died over two hundred years ago, was at last departing this earth. It would *not* be a joyous day for Jared.

He couldn't tell Alix that. But what he could tell her was what he and her father had been secretly working on for the last two weeks.

"I think we can build your chapel," he said.

"What do you mean?"

"Ken and I've been working on this in secret and he should get building approval very soon. It hasn't been easy."

Alix was silent as she listened to Jared tell what they had accomplished. Her father had taken measurements from Alix's sketches and her model, and he'd spent an all-nighter drawing a floor plan and elevations.

"Then he sent them to New York to be made into blueprints. Stanley rushed it all through."

"Your assistant," Alix said.

"Sometimes I think Stanley is the boss."

She turned to look up at him. "Now, why do I doubt that?"

He kissed her and she turned back around. Her heart was pounding. She was going to see one of her own designs built? She couldn't really believe it.

"Of course Ken knew we had to make two designs."

"What do you mean?" she asked.

"Committees *never* accept the original proposal, so the first time around your dad turned in a caricature of your design, and with Dilys's help —"

"What does she have to do with this?"

"She's on the board. My name can't be on the plan because she's my cousin, but she and Ken aren't related, even if they once were . . ."

"Were what?" Alix asked, then held up her hand. "Don't tell me. I can guess. So what did she do?"

"Raised a ruckus, said the plan was horrible, and threw it out. Then the next week Ken put on his meek face and presented the real one. Dilys led the group in saying the new one was much better."

"And it passed?" She held her breath.

"Yes, but to get it through so fast there are strings attached."

"Oh," Alix said, deflated.

"It's to be an accessory building, meaning that it has no kitchen or bath, no plumbing at all. It can't be seen from any public road or path but that's not a problem. Later we can . . ." He trailed off. He'd been about to say that later they could build a house there. A rental maybe. Or . . . He hardly let himself think this, but maybe it would be a house for the Eighth and his family to live in.

"Where exactly on the land would it be built?"

"On the old house site," Jared said quickly.

"You think that's a good idea? It might be like building on a Native American burial ground."

Jared thought that was probably exactly why his grandfather wanted it built there, but he didn't say so. When they started digging, he'd make sure Alix wasn't there. If his guess was right, they might find a centuries-old body there, and he didn't want Alix seeing it. "Maybe we'll find some artifacts and donate them to the NHS."

The only word Alix heard of that was "we." "Do you actually think this could be done in time for the wedding? That Izzy could get married in a chapel?"

"In *your* building?" Jared said. He was finally beginning to recover from what his grandfather had told him, but it did cross his mind that Caleb was leaving the earth because Jared had found Alix.

He kissed her cheek as his hands began to move over her body. "Excited?"

"Of course."

He took her shoulders and turned her to face him. "How do you feel about your own creation going from paper to something you can see and feel? That you can walk inside of? Be surrounded by?"

"It feels . . . wonderful!" she said, her head back. She turned to put her legs around his waist. "It feels like I've climbed the highest mountain, leaped toward the stars, that I've gone from the moon to the sun. It's like I'm tripping across rays of sunshine."

"Speaking of mountains . . ." Jared said as he kissed her neck and set her down before him, letting her feel how much he desired her. "I'll go off-island." He kissed her throat. "And get the materials and bring them back in a truck."

"What kind of bricks will you get?" she whispered.

"Handmade."

"Oooooh," she said. "You certainly do know how to turn a girl on."

His lips went lower. "I know a blacksmith in Vermont who can make door hinges like the ones you drew. Celtic meets thirteenth-century Scotland."

"You're driving me mad with desire. What else?"

"A bell."

She pulled away to look at him. "A bell?" she whispered.

"Hand-cast. I have a warehouse full of things I've collected. I always knew that someday I'd need a bell." He was kissing her breasts.

"The door!" she whispered urgently. "What about the door?"

"Seasoned oak. Three inches thick."

"I can't stand any more. Take me. I'm yours."

His hands began exploring her body, the smoothness of the soapy water making each touch a caress. He roamed over her thighs, always moving upward, his hands going to the center of her. Alix put her head back, her neck on his shoulder, and his lips touched her cheek.

"You are beautiful," he whispered. "All pale, golden skin. Sometimes, I feel as though I've known you forever."

Alix liked his words, but she sensed that there was more involved in his words. For the first time, she felt that the great and powerful Montgomery *needed* her. Turning, she put her arms around his neck, her bare chest against his. "I'm here," she said as she kissed his chin. "I'm not planning to leave." She kissed his mouth, her tongue just touching his lower lip. "Soft and succulent," she whispered.

He pulled away from her. "What did you say?"

"Luscious and firm." She pulled his lower lip between her teeth. "Beguiling, enticing, calling to me." She ran her tongue over his whiskers, feeling the stiff prickles of them. "A Siren's song, Pied Piper's flute." She kissed his mouth, then moved her lips to his lower one. "I dream of it asleep, awake. To touch it, caress it, kiss it." She put her lips to his. "The tip of my tongue," she whispered and followed the words with action. "Breaths mingling." For a moment she opened her mouth under his, then pulled his lip into the warm cavity of her mouth. "To draw it in, to caress it, to feel it against my own. Ah," she said in a throaty whisper. "Jared's lower lip."

When he looked at her, his eyes were dark with lust. That blue fire she'd come to love. In the next second he stood up in the tub, lifting her with him, his arm tight around her as he took her out of the tub and carried her into the bedroom. He stood over her, nude, and looked down at her warm, wet body, and the smile he gave her made her grow even warmer.

"There are parts of your body that I especially like too," he said as he stretched out beside her.

"Such as?" she asked as he began kissing her neck, his hand at her waist.

"I'm better with action than words."

"Are you?" she whispered. "Then perhaps you should show me."

"I would love to." He began to move down her body, his mouth following his hands.

# Chapter Eighteen

"You're sure you'll be all right without me?" Jared asked Alix for what had to be the twelfth time. It was seven A.M. on a Wednesday and they were at Downyflake awaiting their breakfast. The very pretty Linda had waited on them and the always cheerful Rosie had stopped by to chat. It was the fifth or sixth time they'd been to the restaurant and Alix had run into a few acquaintances that Jared didn't know. Knowing people separately from him made her feel like she was beginning to belong on the island.

"I'll be fine," she told him again as she moved her hand across the table to touch his fingers. She was still in a daze after the night before. They'd made love for hours, taking their time with each other. Even though Alix knew that something had happened, she couldn't get him to tell her what it was, but all last night and this morning he'd acted as though Alix might walk out the door and never come back. She was concerned about him and didn't want him to worry. "Dad will be here, and Lexie and Toby. What are you so afraid of?"

He wanted to say, "My grandfather and your mother," but didn't. This afternoon he was going to board JetBlue and fly to New York to begin making arrangements for the purchase and shipment of the materials to build Alix's chapel. "Sure you don't want to go with me?" he asked.

"I'm not sure at all, but . . ." She didn't really understand why she felt that she *had* to stay on Nantucket but she did, and she went with her instinct. "I'm going to learn what I can about Valentina. And who was the other woman you asked me about?"

"Parthenia."

"And you don't know her last name?"

"With a first name like that she doesn't need another one." He looked down at his coffee and thought that it was his grandfather who'd put this idea of remaining behind and working on the papers into Alix's mind. If it was, Jared knew *why* he was doing it. One month from today Captain Caleb Kingsley would depart from this world forever. The last close attachment of Jared's life was going away. Forever.

Alix reached across the table to put her hand over his. "I wish you'd tell me what's bothering you."

"I would if I could." He gave her a half

smile. "What have you heard from your mother?"

"She's finished her book tour and is back home now. The last time we spoke, I started to let her know just what I thought about her lying to me all these years."

Jared genuinely grinned. "How hard did she laugh?"

Alix groaned. "I hate that you know both my parents so well. Mom said it was all done for art and therefore was permissible."

"Did you tell her I was going off-island?"

"I did, actually."

Jared took a drink of his coffee. "Then she'll be here within twenty-four hours after I leave."

Alix started to speak but paused when Linda appeared and put their food before them. When they were alone, Alix leaned toward Jared and said softly, "Why would my mother need to wait until you left before she came here? What other secrets do you two have?"

"You mean like sex on the chamber pot staircase, like you and I had last night?" he asked, eyebrows raised. "My back still hurts."

Alix didn't like his joke.

Jared realized his bond with Alix was much more important than any loyalty to her mother. "Victoria wants the last of the Kingsley women's journals, specifically Aunt Addy's, so she can make a novel out of them."

Alix ate a few bites of her breakfast quesadilla as she thought about what he'd said and how it fit so well into what she already knew. "Then it wasn't Aunt Addy's storytelling — there are journals."

"Yes. Lots of them."

"Is this one of your two secrets?" she asked.

"It is."

"And the other one is that you've seen Captain Caleb as a ghost?"

"More or less," he said.

"Is that it? I now know *all* your secrets?"

"I guess maybe you do," he said, but his eyes were laughing. He hadn't exactly told the extent of his ghostly encounters.

"And you think Mom is going to wait until you're not around to come here to look for Aunt Addy's journals?"

"I do," Jared said. "And since no one knows where they are, I'm a little concerned that she could . . ." He'd been about to say that Victoria might take a chain saw to the old house, but he didn't think Alix would like to hear that.

"You're worried that she might damage your house in her quest to find the books, aren't you?" Alix asked.

"Exactly." Jared was relieved that she understood. "You think your dad can . . . you know?"

"Make her behave?" Alix asked. "No. She terrifies him. He stands up to everyone else in the world but my mother turns him into a wimp. Dad says there is no man on earth strong enough to handle her."

"I have to agree with him on that," Jared said. "I would never want to go head-to-head with Victoria. Ready to go?"

She nodded, he left money, they said goodbye to everyone — including Mark the owner/cook — and went out to get into Jared's truck. They were heading out to the North Shore to look at the chapel site again. The building permit had yet to come, but it would be there soon and they wanted to be ready.

Alix was looking at the people standing outside of Downyflake, waiting for an available table. She'd been on the island long enough that she could distinguish locals from tourists — and watching them, she felt as though she were an observer at a zoo. They seemed abnormally clean and thin, as though they'd been extruded from a machine and were not quite real. Jewelry and cell phones dangled from their arms.

She was about to make a derogatory remark, when three pretty girls with long, glossy hair saw them.

"Jared! When are you going to come play with us?"

"I'm too old for you kids," he said out the truck window.

"You didn't say that *last* summer," the prettiest one said.

"And that's what aged me."

The girls laughed.

"Sorry about that," he said as he turned onto Sparks Avenue. "I know their dads." He was looking at her intently, wondering how she'd handle the bit of flirty wordplay.

"Does that mean you think *I* am old enough for you?"

Jared laughed. "You *are* Victoria's daughter — and you look like you're planning something."

"I was thinking that Mom would love to write about Valentina and Captain Caleb. Maybe I can get her so involved with those two that she won't need to search for Aunt Addy's journals. Besides, what could possibly be in them? In my memories of Aunt Addy, she's hardly a wild woman, or a possible murderer."

Jared said nothing as he looked at Alix.

"Oh, right. Captain Caleb's ghost," she said. "But surely my mother couldn't think that she'd be able to write an entire novel based on a few ghostly encounters. A foggy figure standing at the top of the stairs then vanishing. That's not much. I vaguely remember stories Aunt Addy told me about Captain Caleb, but romantic daydreams aren't the same as the truth. I'll tell Mom that it would be better if she tried to find out what catastrophic thing happened to Captain Caleb that made him into a ghost. Isn't there always some romantic tragedy that results in a ghost?" Alix looked at him. "That, of course, will lead her to the story you told me about Valentina and Caleb. I know Mom hasn't seen the papers, but has she heard the story?"

"I don't believe she has," he said. "If she had . . ." He looked at Alix.

"Mom would already be here asking to go through your attic."

They exchanged smiles of understanding. At the hint of a romantic story, no doubt Victoria would have quickly been on the doorstep cajoling, sweet-talking, doing whatever it took. It would have been nearly impossible to resist her.

"You know," Jared said, "I think this might actually work."

"It probably will," she said. "I can be a good salesman when I need to be. Too bad you and Dad didn't tell me about all this earlier. If you two hadn't spent your lives keeping secrets, I could have helped from the beginning." For the rest of the drive to the North Shore, Alix quietly — but firmly — told Jared where he'd made his mistakes in handling Victoria.

He just smiled and didn't defend himself. He knew there was a lot more to the Kingsley ghost than just a vague vision standing at the head of the stairs, and he wondered what Alix was going to say after she found out all of it. Would she be so sassy then?

When he got to his land on the North Shore, he parked and turned off the truck. "Want to see the site again? If you can stop bawling me out, that is."

"You can't blame me for feeling left out, can you? I missed out on an entire *life.*"

Leaning across the seat, he said, "From my point of view, whatever it was that made you what you are was done right." After a quick kiss, he got out of the truck.

All Alix could do was smile.

They spent a couple of hours at the site. In the toolbox in the back of the pickup Jared had construction flags, stakes and string, and a two-hundred-foot tape. With no need for discussions, he and Alix got right to it, both wanting to see the outline of the chapel laid out on the ground.

As though they'd been working together for years — which, thanks to Ken, in a way they had — they temporarily staked and strung the foundation, then stepped back into the shade and looked at it.

"Can you envision it?" He'd pulled a couple of bottles of cold water from the cooler and handed one to her.

"I can." Her voice changed. "I want to tell you that this is very generous of —"

"Don't say it!" he said.

She knew he didn't want to hear her gratitude yet again. "All right. Just so you know." She looked around. "Did Valentina live here or in town?"

"Both. After Caleb built the new house, he gave the old one to his cousin Obed."

"*Gave* it to him?"

"For one dollar. It's still a common practice on Nantucket. Check the local newspaper, the Inky, for property transfers and you'll see it being done nearly every day. Nantucketers often inherit their houses." He made a scoffing noise. "Otherwise, we couldn't afford to live on our own island."

Alix thought of the rather ordinary twenty-million-dollar house she'd seen. What he said certainly made sense. "So Caleb went away on a ship, leaving the love of his life behind carrying their child. But she married his cousin — probably because she had to — and at first Valentina and Obed lived here in the original house."

"That's right," he said. "After Caleb's death, when his brother returned with the will, Obed and Valentina moved into the big house on Kingsley Lane."

"With Caleb's son, the first Jared," Alix said. "Then Valentina disappeared and this house burned to the ground." She thought for a moment. "Do you think there's any connection between her disappearance and the fire?"

They were both looking at the depression in the earth that was in the center of where the chapel would be. When he didn't answer right away, she looked at him.

"I think," he said slowly, "that there is a *strong* connection between the two events."

He was saying that he thought Valentina had died in the fire, but she didn't want to believe something so terrible could have happened to the young woman Captain Caleb had loved so much.

They looked at each other, and understanding passed between them. There was more to this building than giving Izzy a place to get married. It had to do with Jared's family. And righting a wrong, she thought.

"I do have a question," she said. "Who is Parthenia and where did you hear of her?"

"What time is my flight?"

Alix groaned. "And I thought you had no more secrets."

Smiling, he lifted her off the ground and swung her around. "I wouldn't be very interesting if I had no secrets, now, would I? Come on, let's go into town. I have to buy ten pounds of chocolate-covered cranberries to take with me."

"You can't get them in New York?"

"Only if I want low quality and tasteless," he said as they started back to the truck. "The ones I buy are made with *Nantucket* cranberries. Besides, they're not for anybody in New York. Stanley got the truck I keep off-island and I'm driving to Vermont to see the lovely Sylvia. They're for her."

On their way back to town, he teased her about Sylvia — who turned out to be the blacksmith he'd mentioned before. She was married to a farrier and they had two little girls. Jared said that if he was going to coax Sylvia into doing the big hinges for the chapel for them right away, rather than six months from now, he needed to show up bearing gifts. They parked at the house, walked back to town, got the cranberries at Sweet Inspirations, then crossed the street to Bookworks. They bought four children's books set on Nantucket, and the latest edge-of-your-seat nonfiction book by Nat Philbrick — who lived close by. By lunchtime all the shopping had left Alix exhilarated, but Jared was exhausted. They went to Languedoc for lunch.

After they ate, they walked back to the house and carried their purchases upstairs. On the bed was Jared's half-packed suitcase. He had an apartment in New York so he didn't take much, but he needed to pack the gifts.

"Is that all of it?" Alix asked as she closed the case.

"No, one thing is missing," Jared said as he took her in his arms and kissed her.

She clung to him.

"Think you'll miss me?" he asked, his face buried in her hair.

"Stop it or you'll make me cry."

He moved back to look at her face. "I could stand your tears if I knew they were for me."

She put her head back down on his chest and the tears began to come. "You'll go back to being the Great Jared Montgomery and forget all about me."

He kissed the top of her head. "Haven't you yet realized that there is no Jared Montgomery? He's not real. The real me is here in this house, on this island." He started to say, With you. But it was too soon for that.

Alix put her arms around his neck and kissed his mouth. "Your beautiful lower lip," she whispered.

"Is that the only part of my body you like?" He was kissing her cheeks, her temples. Soft, sweet kisses.

"I like your mind. You're fairly intelligent. For a man, that is."

Jared laughed. "I'll show you how smart I am!" He swept the suitcase onto the floor.

"Please do," she said. "I like anything you can show me or tell me or ask —" She broke off because he kissed her into silence.

# Chapter Nineteen

The day Jared left, they drove to the airport in silence. Alix seemed to be full of thoughts and worries — and maybe even a dread of the future. No matter what Jared said about this separation not changing anything between them, she was still concerned.

"Will you put on a suit?" she asked as he stopped at the token machine at the airport parking lot.

"Yes. I don't want to but it's New York."

"Will you shave and get your hair cut?"

"No," he said, smiling. "Unless you want me to, that is."

"No, I don't. Will Tim yell at you for being away so long?"

"All he cares about is that the California house plans are finished." Jared pulled into a parking place, turned off the engine, and looked at her. "What's really bothering you?"

"Nothing," she said. "It's just that we've known each other such a short time and you're —" His look made her say what she didn't want to. "You'll be *him* again."

"And 'he' is a bad guy? An exploiter of women? Love 'em and leave 'em?"

"I didn't mean that," she said, then grimaced. "Maybe I did."

"If I did that to you, your parents would kill me."

"Great," she said. "Glad to hear that it's fear that keeps you with me."

Jared just shook his head. "Words aren't going to prove anything. Call me, I'll call you. Text, email. All of it. I'll let you know where I am at all times. Will that make you feel better?"

"Only when you return will I be sure. Return to *me,* not just to your old house and your beloved island."

Jared laughed. "I think you know me too well. Come on, let's go."

In the airport he was about to go out the door to the small jet, but he turned back, took Alix in his arms, and kissed her yet again. He put his lips near her ear and whispered, "Within four hours everyone on this island will have heard that we're a couple."

There was another kiss goodbye, then Alix watched him walk across the tarmac and go up the ramp to the plane. His seat was by a window on her side and he waved to her as they took off.

When he was gone, Alix turned to leave the

airport and saw that a number of people were smiling at her. Not the tourists who traveled in packs and had a frantic look in their eyes, not the summer people in their linen and bracelets. These were the Nantucketers, the men and women who lived and worked there. The *real* people. The people who mattered. The women smiled and the men nodded to her — just as she'd seen them do to Jared. It was almost as though his public kiss had been an announcement that Alix was now . . . What? she wondered. Somehow related to the people who'd settled the island? That she *belonged*?

Alix couldn't help returning the smiles. As she walked outside toward the truck, a man loading luggage nodded at her. Word was spreading outward.

The next morning Toby showed up asking Alix if she'd like to see some of Nantucket, and she readily agreed.

Toby drove around the island, to beaches and moors, altar rock, and the oldest house with its beautiful herb garden. They walked behind the lovely old house to Something Natural to have lunch.

They drove back to Kingsley Lane, parked, and walked into town. Since Toby hadn't been born on the island, she had a clearer idea of what was unusual about it. "Everything is named Nantucket — the town, the island, the county." She went on to say that Nantucket had recently been given the dubious honor of being declared the richest county in the U.S. "Although a lot of us are struggling to put food on the table," she added.

Alix couldn't believe such a predicament was true of Toby. She had an air about her that could only be described as elegant. Her clothes were the best quality, but understated. She didn't wear a dozen bracelets or a gold necklace as big as a horse collar, like the off-islanders did. And no cute little hat with an upturned brim that you knew cost a normal person's monthly salary. With Toby, everything was simple and refined. By the end of the day, Alix found herself standing straighter and vowing to toss out her oldest pair of sweatpants.

Later, Lexie showed up at Kingsley House with a bag full of fresh vegetables for dinner, just harvested from her boss's garden. "Heaven knows *he* never picks any of them. He just likes to watch the girls bending over and weeding."

Toby and Alix looked at each other with raised eyebrows.

"What does Roger wear while he's watching the girls?" Alix asked.

"As little as he can lawfully get away with," Lexie answered.

Toby and Alix smiled at each other. It was

a nice image.

After dinner the three women sat in the living room and finished off a bottle of wine. As usual with Lexie, she got right to the point. "So how are you and Jared getting along?"

Alix was very aware that Lexie was Jared's cousin, so how could she tell of her worries about his departure? "Great. Fine," she said.

"Anything we can help with?" Toby asked. Obviously she wasn't fooled by Alix's bravado.

"It's just a matter of time," Alix said, then took a breath. She *did* have worries and her best friend wasn't here to talk to, so cousin or not, she needed to get her thoughts out into the open. "I know Jared likes my designs and my work ethic, and the sex is truly great, but I think he's happy the way he is. And . . ." She took a breath. "He has a life in New York as well as here, so maybe I won't fit into his world there." She looked at Lexie. "Why are you smiling?"

"Because Jared isn't like you think he is. He isn't the famous public guy that people see. Here on Nantucket is the real him."

"I guess we'll see, won't we?" Alix said. "Okay, that's more than enough soul searching from me. I want to know about you two. What are you looking for in life?"

Lexie grimaced. "My problem is that I *know* my future and what my life will be like. I'm sure I'll marry Nelson within the next couple of years. I know where we'll live, even the house we'll live in. All of it. Everything."

"Who is Nelson?" Alix asked. She'd seen no man near Lexie except her boss, and it was clear that she wanted nothing to do with him.

"He's my Eric."

"But I was dumped by him," Alix said.

Toby nodded. "If Lexie doesn't marry him soon he's going to drop her."

Lexie took a drink of her wine. "I just want a life where I can't see straight down the road. I want some hills, mountains even. I want an adventure. Actually, I'd settle for something that's merely out of the ordinary."

Alix turned to Toby. "What about you?"

Lexie spoke first. "Toby has more than boyfriend problems. She has a mother."

Alix looked at Toby in question.

"My mother," Toby said, "was — is, I guess — obsessed with being . . . I don't know how to explain it, but the most accurate thing to say is that she wants to be considered upper class. You see, my dad is . . ."

"Blueblood," Lexie said. "Or as close as America can get. Golf clubs, private schools, a family tree back to . . . What is it?"

"It doesn't matter." Toby looked away, embarrassed.

"What's your mother's side of the family like?" Alix asked.

"I don't know. I've never met any of her

relatives or anyone who knew her before she married my dad. It's like she was born on the day she got married." Toby looked at them. "However . . ."

"What?" They leaned forward.

"One time my mother was quite angry at me and —"

"That's her usual state from what I've seen of her," Lexie interrupted, her tone showing her disapproval.

Toby continued, "One night after dinner, Mother wanted Dad and me to hurry up to go somewhere. She grabbed our half-full plates and put one on her forearm and one in her hand. It was very efficient. I said, 'Mother, you do that like an experienced waitress.' I wouldn't have thought anything about it except that she immediately dropped the plates and stomped off — and my dad couldn't stop laughing."

"Very interesting," Lexie said. "That sounds like a mystery worth pursuing."

"Lexie loves mystery novels," Toby said.

Lexie grimaced. "In this mystery, the only man your mother would approve of for you is Prince Charming."

"Too late," Alix said, her face serious. "I already got him."

Toby laughed and Lexie groaned.

"We want to know about *your* mother," Toby said. "What's it like to live with someone who is as unique as she is?"

"Unique?" Lexie said. "Toby is being polite. Victoria Madsen is an international sensation, beautiful, successful, and those books!"

"You do know the Great Secret of the origin of them, don't you?" Alix asked.

"That they're about my family?" Lexie said. "Of course. Everyone on Nantucket knows that." She waved her hand in dismissal. "I know about my family. I want to know about *yours.*"

"Well," Alix said slowly, thinking how to explain her mother in a way that wouldn't take hours. "She is a mix of practical and flamboyant, vain and selfless, naive and very sophisticated."

"That sounds either horrible or wonderful," Lexie said. "But what we want to know is what it was like to be with her on a daily basis."

Alix thought for a moment. "All right, I'll tell you a story that might illustrate my life with her, and I only know the details because years later so many people told me what happened. It was my fifth birthday, and Mom and I were living in an apartment on the sixteenth floor of a building way downtown in New York City. It was after her first book had been accepted for publication, but before it came out and hit the best-seller lists. But what was important to me was that my parents had recently separated and I was missing my dad a lot."

Alix looked away briefly. "Anyway, on the morning of my birthday, I woke up looking into the eyes of a real live pony."

Lexie smiled. "That's nice. Your mother took you to a stable while you were asleep."

"No," Alix said. "I was in my own bed in our apartment in New York. My mom had brought the pony up in the service elevator. She had so charmed the doorman — I think she even wept a bit at her failed marriage — that he'd looked the other way."

"I wonder what the neighbors thought," Toby said.

"You hit it there. My mother couldn't have cared less that the floor was permanently damaged by the hooves, but when the neighbors complained about the noise, she had to *do* something."

"What did she do?" Lexie asked.

"She turned it all into an impromptu party. She chose the ugliest little man there, who was standing silently by his angry wife, and asked him to go buy some booze. And of course my mother had no money so he paid. Then she got some big, good-looking teenage boy to make drinks for everyone who showed up to complain."

"I don't think using an underage boy like that was legal," Toby said.

"My mother doesn't believe that laws apply to her. When school let out, even more neighbors showed up with their kids and they rode the pony around inside the apartment."

"What about the mess?" Lexie asked.

"My mother went to two teenage girls who couldn't take their eyes off the boy at the bar and told them *he* wanted them to help out."

"They got the poop scoop detail?" Lexie asked, grinning.

"Exactly," Alix said. "And you know what? Years later my mother told me that one of those girls married that boy."

Both Lexie and Toby laughed. "Your mother is a matchmaker."

"She loves romance in any form," Alix said.

"What happened to the pony?" Toby asked.

"At the end of the day, when the owner returned, he was livid! Mom had lied, telling him she had a farm in the country and a trainer. She'd been so convincing that he'd turned the pony over to her. When he found out the truth, he was furious, but Mom flirted with him so much that by the time he took the pony back down in the elevator, he was smiling. And by that point, Mom had to push everybody out of our apartment because they were drunk. She gave me a bath, then snuggled down with me in bed and read me a book. That it was the galleys of her own novel with the sex skipped didn't matter. I was asleep instantly. And after that I was the most popular child in the building. Everybody cried when we moved to the suburbs."

For a moment Lexie and Toby sat in silence,

taking in the story.

"How wonderful!" Lexie said with a sigh. "I could stand some adventure in my life."

"Doesn't your boss —" Alix began.

"He's too in love with himself to matter," Lexie said.

Alix and Toby looked at each other. From what they'd seen of Roger Plymouth, he was madly in love with Lexie, not himself.

After that first evening, the young women became a threesome — when they could, that is. Both Toby and Lexie had jobs, and Alix was trying to complete her sketches for Jared's clients.

And then, of course, there was Izzy's wedding to work on. Without the rose arbor and with the inclusion of the chapel, everything changed. Alix came up with a theme of wildflowers based on the dishes in Kingsley House. She showed Toby a place setting and Toby made an arrangement that looked like the china pattern. They planned everything around small flowers, many of them on a stem, all of them light and airy, nothing heavy.

"I think you're onto something," Toby said to Alix as she began to sketch the flowers for the table settings.

For the chapel they designed swags of robin's-egg blue ribbons that hung from the ceiling along the wall. At every loop would be a bow with bouquets of blue larkspur and tiny white daisies dripping down. They put them on a background of ornamental grasses.

"I think it's beautiful," Alix said, looking at what Toby had done, and Lexie agreed.

Alix photographed everything and sent it all to Izzy, but she couldn't focus very well. Her morning sickness was bad, and she told Alix that she kept falling asleep. "You know what I like," Izzy said. "What would you like for *your* wedding? That's what I'll take."

Alix didn't allow herself to think of her own wedding; if it did happen, it would be years in the future.

On the evening after Jared left, Alix got on her computer and began searching for Parthenia. With only one name to go on, it wasn't easy. But she added a place — Nantucket — and she found a Parthenia Taggert Kendricks. The name Taggert led to the Montgomerys of Warbrooke, Maine.

"Bingo!" Alix said, then began searching to see if she could find any contemporary Montgomerys or Taggerts who might still be living in Maine. To her joy, she saw that there were a *lot* of them.

By the time Jared called that night, she had a great deal to tell him. "She was Parthenia Taggert, Valentina's cousin, and they both came from Warbrooke. Parthenia married a Nantucketer named John Kendricks, but I couldn't find much about him other than that he was a schoolmaster. I'll email you the dates." She hesitated.

"What's on your mind?"

"I think you should drive to Maine and talk to those people," she said.

"And ask about something that happened two hundred years ago?" Jared asked.

"Why not?" she said. "Maybe the family is like yours and they have a big old house full of junk that no one has thrown out in centuries."

"There couldn't possibly be two of us."

Personally, she didn't think there was anyone on earth like him.

"So you think I should go?" he said.

She loved that he was asking for her encouragement and maybe even her approval. "Yes, I do."

"I have to go to Vermont to get the hinges so maybe I'll just drive up to Warbrooke, Maine," Jared said.

Alix was smiling broadly. It made her feel good that he'd taken her advice. "Were they glad to see you in New York?" She wanted to know how he was feeling about being back in his office, but she'd long ago learned to never directly ask a man about feelings.

"Tim and Stanley were ecstatic, but I ripped apart eight designs of the employees. They wanted me to go back to hell, where they think I live when I'm not in the office."

Alix laughed. "Wouldn't they be shocked to hear what a nice man you really are?" she said, then took a breath to get up her courage. "Miss me?"

"Ferociously. I showed three of your hand sketches to one of the morons Tim hired. The kid now hates you."

"Really?!" Alix said with so much enthusiasm that Jared laughed.

"Yes, really. You know, you should invite Dr. Huntley of the NHS over and ask him to find out what he can about that guy Kendricks. Besides, Huntley probably misses Aunt Addy's tea parties. And he's great friends with your mother, so if you talk about her, no doubt he'll do whatever you want him to. Just be sure you don't let him near the attic. Those historians can be kleptos if you give them a chance. If it's old, they want to put it under glass and charge admission to see it."

"Gladly," Alix said, laughing.

"I have to go. Think you can find me a name and address of who to see in Warbrooke?"

"Sure."

"I have to go now but I'll call you about nine and we can talk about sex."

"Great idea!" she said with enthusiasm and they hung up.

Alix tossed her phone on the bed and went to stand in front of the portrait of Captain Caleb. "Did you hear that? The Great Jared Montgomery showed *my* sketches to an employee! I am in heaven!" She danced around a bit, then pulled out her sketchbook. She had an idea for the guesthouse and she wanted to get it down before it faded.

A few days later, the permits for the North Shore chapel came through so Alix's father, with contractor Twig Perkins and his men, broke ground. From the first day Ken had forbidden Alix to help. "You have enough to do for Izzy," he'd said. "Let me do this."

She knew he meant to make the building as a gift, but still, she wanted to stay the day of the ground breaking. What would they find in the ruins of the old house? Bones?

There was nothing. Some charred timbers, but nothing else. She didn't know whether to be relieved or disappointed. So far, they'd found out nothing that could be used in solving the mystery about Valentina.

Alix knew she should go to the attic and start her research, but something inside her said, Not yet. Besides, Jared kept discouraging her from delving into it. "Just stay on the Net and wait until I get back and we'll go through all of it together," he'd said. It was too enticing a suggestion for her to turn down.

When Ken heard from Alix that Jared was driving north into what he called "antiques country," he immediately called him. Alix had to conceal her laughter when she heard her father tell Jared what he was to buy somewhere between Vermont and Maine. "A stained-glass window," Ken said. "And I don't want one of those cheap, modern ones with heavy lead and big sheets of glass. Get something old and well made. Nothing later than about 1910. After the war, all that craftsmanship and attention to detail fell apart."

What was funny was that he was talking to a man considered to be one of the greatest . . . etc. But Ken treated Jared like a fourteen-year-old kid who knew more about hot-wiring cars than how to choose a stained-glass window.

"Did you write down the dimensions?" Ken asked. "Good! Just don't lose your phone. When you get to Maine ask someone where you can get antiques of quality." Ken listened. "Yeah, yeah, architectural salvage will be fine. What? Oh, yeah, she's right here." Ken handed the phone to his daughter. "He wants to talk to you."

"Your father!" Jared said in exasperation and she understood. "Heard from your mom?"

"No. You thought she'd show up here right away."

"The only reason she hasn't is because I called her and said I was hot on the trail of Aunt Addy's journals. But I added that if Victoria showed up on Nantucket she'd so dazzle my informant that I'd lose my contact."

"And you made all that up on your own?"

"I did," he said.

"Don't tell Mom you're so good at lying or she'll want you to plot her next novel. I bet she loved hearing that she'd dazzle someone," Alix said.

"I think she took it as her due. She certainly wasn't surprised by the accolade," Jared said. "By the way, if your dad doesn't like what I buy he can damned well shove it."

"I'll give him your message."

Jared lowered his voice. "You tell him I said that and I'll tell your mother *you* have the journals."

"You are cruel," Alix said. "Really cruel."

She invited Dr. Frederick Huntley to tea on Sunday afternoon. Alix was surprised at how much she remembered about Aunt Addy's tea parties. She knew where the good set of Herend china was hidden. Getting on her hands and knees, she rummaged far back inside a cabinet to pull out the beautiful green and white teapot, the sugar and creamer, and two cups and saucers.

Toby helped Alix make petit fours, even putting the yellow rosebuds on top. They made little sandwiches with the crusts removed and filled them with thinly sliced cucumbers. And Lexie entertained them with more stories of Roger Plymouth's escapades.

When Dr. Huntley arrived, Toby and Lexie

slipped out the back, and Alix opened the front door.

Alix's first thought when she saw him was that he was a very unhappy man. He stood with his shoulders hunched a bit forward, and his eyes tended to dip down at the outside corners.

It took only minutes for Alix to ask for his help in finding out about John Kendricks. He wrote down the name and dates, said he'd look into it, then sat there as though waiting to hear what else she needed.

"Won't you have some tea?" Alix asked as she began to pour. "My mother speaks so highly of you." It was a flat-out lie but she thought that in this case it was allowed.

Dr. Huntley gave a bit of a smile and Alix thought the man might be younger than he seemed.

He stayed for over an hour. They drank two pots of tea, ate all the food, and Alix got to hear a lot about the charm of her mother, and how Dr. Huntley and his wife had so enjoyed the company of her and Adelaide.

"They were such interesting women," he said. "There was Victoria's extensive travel to research her wonderful novels, and Addy knew everything about the island. Her details were so vivid it sometimes seemed as though she'd actually known the people who lived in this lovely old house centuries ago."

Captain Caleb's ghost probably told her

everything, Alix thought but didn't say. As for her mother! Travel indeed. She was more of an armchair explorer. Alix now knew that the descriptions of foreign places that ran through her mother's books were from the journals of women who had actually been there. Her mother certainly wasn't going to go traipsing across some remote South Sea island trying to find where some awful event had happened so she could describe it. Alix used to think she made it all up. Now she knew that she just transposed it.

Dr. Huntley remembered when Alix was a child and spoke of how she'd built towers out of museum-quality artifacts. "When I got home, my wife had to revive me with a shot of brandy."

"You'll have to bring her with you the next time," Alix said.

It had taken an hour to get the sad look from the man's face, but in an instant it was back.

Quickly, and in a way that sounded rehearsed, as though he couldn't bear the pain of actually telling it, he said that his wife had died two years before. He had been diagnosed with cancer and while she'd been with him throughout his treatment, her own illness had been neglected.

"By the time I was in remission, it was too late for her." When he looked back at Alix, the grief in his eyes was horrible to see. "Well, now," he said as he stood up, "you're young and you have your life ahead of you, and I mustn't keep you any longer."

Alix was glad that she'd never experienced anything like what this man had. She stood up and put her hand on his forearm. "I very much wish I could have met your wife."

"She would have liked you. She adored Victoria, so alive and energetic and always looking ahead. And Victoria never stopped talking about her wonderful daughter."

"Did she?" Alix asked, surprised.

"She said it was one of the hardships of her life that you always chose to spend the time she was on Nantucket with your father." He gave her a chastising look. "You should have visited us at least once."

Alix somehow managed to keep her smile even as she vowed to give her mother a piece of her mind — not that it would do any good, but it might make Alix feel better.

On Monday, Ken took the fast ferry to Hyannis to greet the truck the superefficient Stanley was escorting to the port. He'd outdone himself in so quickly getting together all the building materials.

"Give me some men and a fleet of pickups and in two days I could assemble a cathedral," Stanley had told Ken, who reported the brag back to Alix. When she twisted it around that Stanley was proof of how good Jared was at hiring people, Ken was glad the phone hid his eye rolling.

He bought extra tools in Hyannis and, like all Nantucketers, he went to the local wholesale warehouse and loaded up on household supplies. The truck drivers, who weren't local, were shocked at the sheer number of things, like giant packages of paper towels, they were expected to jam between the lumber and nails. When they asked what was going on, the ferrymen looked at them like they were crazy. "They live on Nantucket" was the answer for every question, as though that explained it all — and to an islander, it did.

When Jared got to Warbrooke, he called Alix. She'd found the names of Michael Taggert and Adam Montgomery online in the town directory. Based on their involvement in the community, she guessed that they were patriarchs of the family. "It looks like the family owns most of the town," she told him.

"It's a nice place," he said about the town in Maine. "Reminds me of Nantucket."

"High praise indeed."

On the day Jared was to meet the men Alix had tracked down, she found she was a bit nervous and had trouble concentrating on what Toby was saying. They had nearly all the wedding preparations done, including reservations for all of Glenn and Izzy's guests. A few were staying in hotels — which cost a fortune — but most of the guests were being put up in the houses of the Kingsley relatives. Lexie had organized that, as well as persuading Roger Plymouth to let her use his six-bedroom house for guests.

"Will he be there?" Toby asked.

"No!" Lexie said. "He's promised to stay at his house in Taos then."

"Darn!" Alix said. "Toby and I were thinking of taking over the master suite."

"And if he showed up . . ." Toby said.

"We'd lock him in with us," Alix said.

"You guys are crazy," Lexie said. "And you have no idea what that man is really like."

"So tell us," Alix said, and she and Toby leaned forward, chins in hands, ready to listen avidly.

Frowning, Lexie started to say something, but then shook her head. "You two are hopeless. So how's Jared doing with the new relatives up in Maine?"

"I haven't heard about them yet. Just the town, which he likes a lot," she said. "He's going to meet the men today and call me tonight."

He didn't call until nearly ten P.M.

"Tell me!" she said. "I want to hear every word."

"They are . . . unusual," he said.

"What do you mean?"

"There are two families, the Montgomerys and Taggerts, and they intermarried a long time ago."

"How long have they lived in that town?"

"It seems that they arrived here a few centuries ago." He paused. "Are you laughing because it sounds like my family?"

"Exactly like them. Do they have any documentation about Valentina and Parthenia?"

"As a matter of fact, they do."

"You're kidding."

"No, I'm not. There's a woman who has sort of become the family historian, and she's going to fly in from Colorado and bring me letters between Valentina and her cousin."

"That sounds great," Alix said. "So do you like your new relatives?"

"Yeah," he said, but there was hesitation in his voice.

"What's wrong?"

"Nothing. In fact, it's all good. They're so much like me that I feel as though I've known them forever, especially the Montgomery side. They even sort of look like me. The truth is that I'm trying to get them all to spend time on Nantucket. The Harper house is for sale."

"Isn't that the big place on the corner? And isn't the asking price of that house seven and a quarter million?"

"I think so," he said. "But they can afford it."

"Rreeeeaaaallllyyy?" Alix said.

"Really. I have to go. I'm meeting Mike in a few minutes. Tomorrow I'm going fishing with a couple of my new cousins. And I may stay a few days longer than I originally planned. Do you mind?"

Alix smiled. She wouldn't tell him so but it felt great that he'd asked what she thought. It was as though they really were a couple. "I think you deserve time off, so go have fun. And by the way, what do they have that needs designing?"

Jared laughed so loud that Alix had to hold the phone away from her ear. "There's a huge old house set on a rock bluff and it needs a major remodel, but they've not trusted anyone to do it."

"Until now," Alix said.

"Until a blood relative came along. It's a distant connection, but the time element of family doesn't seem to bother them."

"You'll fit right in with them since you talk about Captain Caleb as though you saw him yesterday."

Jared was a bit taken aback by that, but he smiled. "I miss you," he said. "Are you getting along all right?"

"Well enough." She was pleased with the sweet tone in his voice. "Dad doesn't want me to see the progress on the chapel, Izzy can't seem to stay awake long enough to make a decision, and this house is big and empty with only the Captain and me here.

Other than that, I'm great."

Jared drew in his breath. "Have you been talking to him?"

"Yes. Lots, but, alas, he never answers back."

"Not even any cheek kisses?"

"None," Alix said. "So what do I do to get the legendary Kingsley ghost to talk to me?"

"Now that I think about it, it might be good for you to move in with Toby and Lex until I get back."

"Is that jealousy I hear?"

"You're wanting to talk to a ghost and I'm jealous?"

"Yet another question evaded."

Jared laughed. "Yeah, okay, so I'm more than a little envious that he's with you and I'm not. What are you wearing?"

With a look at her sweatpants and old T-shirt, Alix lied completely.

It was a few days later that Jared called and talked to her about Jilly Taggert. She was the family historian who'd flown to Maine especially to see Jared. "Is it all right if she returns home with me?"

Alix replied instantly. "How old is she and what does she look like?"

"She's pretty in a quiet, Sunday-picnic way, intelligent, and she's in her forties, I guess. She said she's always wanted to see Nantucket, so I thought . . ."

"That the island is so beautiful that she *needs* to see it," she finished for him.

"Exactly!" He paused for a moment. "Alix, would you think I'm crazy if I told you that something about her reminds me of your father?"

Was Jared matchmaking? she wondered. If he was, then Alix was pleased. Her father deserved to find someone. "I take it Jilly isn't like my mom?"

Jared gave a guffaw of laughter. "Jilly is the complete opposite of your mother. She never demands attention and she's very thoughtful of others."

"It does sound like my dad will like her, so yes! Bring her back with you. Are you going to drive or fly back?"

"Drive." He gave her the date of his reservations on the slow boat. "I should see you in the early afternoon," he said and his voice lowered. "So have you written any more poems?"

"No, but I've a good idea for one."

"Tell me," he said softly.

# Chapter Twenty

It was early Sunday morning and Alix was in bed listening to the rain. It seemed that today everyone she knew on the island was away or busy. Toby was doing the flowers for an afternoon wedding, and Dilys and Lexie were off-island shopping. Her dad was at the job site at six A.M., seven days a week, and Alix knew he didn't want her hanging around there.

Alix had work to do on the sketches for the guesthouse for the man from the Daffodil Festival, but she didn't want to do that. At long last, this morning she awoke with an overwhelming, impossible-to-deny urge to go to the attic and see what she could find. In spite of Jared's offer of help, Alix knew that the time had arrived to begin searching through the papers about Valentina.

Getting up, she opened the bedroom curtain and saw the rain coming down in a steady stream. It was dull outside, colored by a mix of rain and fog. "The Gray Lady" was a nickname for the island and she saw why.

Alix dressed quickly — no need for careful attention to her hair and face if Jared wasn't there. She hurriedly ate a bowl of cereal, then started up the stairs to the attic. A couple of days ago she'd asked Lexie what she knew about the attic and its contents.

"That place is a mess," Lexie said. "Although Jared likes it. He goes up there and hangs out for hours."

"Interesting," Alix said. "I need to work on this mystery. Besides, if I wait until Jared returns we'll get wrapped up in designs and I'll never get up there. So where are the documents about Valentina?"

As Lexie had told her to do, Alix left the door open "for the hall light," then pulled the string on the single bulb. Even though Alix hadn't been in the attic before, she'd figured it would be full. But nothing could have prepared her for what she saw. The huge room covered the whole house and whereas the downstairs had been continually repaired and remodeled, the attic looked to be just as it was when Captain Caleb built the house. There were big, exposed beams overhead and a wide plank floor. However, Alix was glad to see that every inch was dry and even fairly clean. It was obvious that Jo Costakes's Domestic Goddess team, who came in every other week to clean the downstairs, also sometimes took care of the attic.

Not that they could do much besides dust. In front was a space with a little couch, a rickety old coffee table, and a threadbare wing chair. Behind them, stretching out until they disappeared into darkness, were rows of boxes, trunks, baskets, furniture, and suitcases that were stacked nearly to the ceiling. Narrow walkways wove between the objects and she saw a couple more bulbs in the ceiling, but all in all, the idea of trying to find anything in the huge expanse made Alix want to turn and run.

She opened the door of an enormous armoire and found old clothes that looked to be from the twenties and thirties. In front was a fur-collared wool coat, some cotton dresses, and a sparkly gown, perfect if they were invited to a costume party.

So where was the info on Valentina? she wondered. Lexie had said it was all together, "to the right of the door." But when Alix looked near the door she'd entered, she saw only a stack of tables.

"Maybe she meant to go down the aisle on the right," she said aloud and started edging her way through it. About halfway down was another light and she pulled the string. The weak bulb made the place even gloomier. Any documents she found would have to be taken downstairs, as it was much too dark to read.

To her right was a six-foot-tall stack of storage boxes, the kind for files. On the end of each one, written in large letters, was VALENTINA. Alix stepped back as far as she could — about eight inches — to look at them. There had to be twenty boxes, all of them looking to be packed full. She climbed on the top of a steamer trunk on the other side of the aisle and stretched across to pull off the top box. She got it in her hands, but then lost her balance. For a second she thought she was going to fall. With her feet slipping, she held on to the box and made a leap to the floor. She landed on her seat on the hard surface. As she hit, the overhead bulb went out.

"Perfect!" she said, getting up. Just yesterday she'd noticed that the house's supply of lightbulbs had run out and that they needed new ones. Grumbling, she picked up the box and started toward the front.

"Hello?"

It was a male voice that seemed familiar. For an instant, she thought it was Jared returning early, but then she realized the voice was deeper and sounded older.

At the end of the aisle, she stopped in her tracks. Standing there was a modern version of Captain Caleb. He had on jeans, a denim shirt, and heavy brown lace-up boots, but other than that, he was the Captain.

"I think I've startled you." His voice was very much like Jared's. "I'm terribly sorry. I better leave and return after we've been properly introduced." He turned toward the door.

"No!" she said. "You don't need to leave. You look too much like Captain Caleb to be anything but a Kingsley."

"I look like Captain Caleb?" he said and even in the dull gray light she saw his eyes twinkle. "I couldn't possibly be that handsome. No man today could be."

Smiling, Alix put the box she was holding down on the floor. "I have to agree, and perhaps you do look somewhat different from him. Your eyes are less serious."

"Ah, but then when that portrait of him was painted, the Captain had a lot on his mind. He was trying to win the beautiful Valentina."

"From what I heard, he had no trouble with that." As Alix plopped down on the little sofa, a spattering of dust went up around her and she gave a sigh. "Sorry," she said as she looked up at him. "It's just that I'm feeling overwhelmed at all the boxes I'm supposed to go through."

"Do you mind?" he asked, motioning to the chair across from her.

"Please."

He took a seat in the big wing chair, the flanges casting his face in deep shadow. He really did look like the Captain, she thought, but then maybe it was because she looked at Caleb's portrait every morning and evening.

Whatever the reason, he seemed very familiar. "Who are you?" she asked.

"Jared didn't tell you about me?"

"No, he didn't," she said. "But then he didn't volunteer any information about his cousin Wes either."

When the man laughed, Alix was almost sure she'd heard the sound as a child. "I think I've met you before, but you're . . ." From the look of him he was a bit younger than Jared, which meant that he wouldn't have had that deep, adult laugh when she was so young.

"We did meet when you were a child," he said, smiling. "But you've met so many of my family that perhaps you can't place me. I'm Caleb."

"That seems appropriate," she said.

His smile made her relax. "I take it that the great cache of material isn't making you want to dive in and explore?"

"No, it's not."

"I will tell you a secret," he said. "I have read every word on those papers in the boxes."

"Have you?"

"Oh, yes. In fact, I am directly responsible for a great deal of the information stored here. Would you like for me to tell you the true story of Valentina and Caleb? The one the rest of my family doesn't know?"

Alix hesitated. Perhaps she should wait until Jared returned and Caleb could tell both of them. But she couldn't resist. She nodded.

He looked around the attic. "For this story of great and deep love, we need to create the proper atmosphere. I have a . . . What do you call it?" He made a small circle with his hands. "It plays music. Do you have a gramophone?"

She smiled at the image of the old-fashioned machine, which fit right in with the artifacts surrounding them. "No, but I have an excellent laptop and it will play your CD."

He smiled at her as though she were the most intelligent of people. "I remember seeing a gown in a box down the first aisle. Its owner was rather tall, like you, and I believe the garment will fit you. Perhaps you'd like to put it on and while we talk I could teach you a dance from Valentina's time."

"Oh," Alix said, her eyes wide. As a woman in a modern world that rarely bothered to dress up for anything, she started to protest. But then she glanced at the window. The rain was still coming down hard and she had nothing else really urgent to do, so why not dance with Jared's handsome relative? "Where is the dress?"

Caleb smiled at her with such warmth that Alix felt herself take a step toward him. Good grief! she thought, stepping back. If the real Captain Caleb had this magnetism, she could certainly understand why Valentina ended up pregnant before they were married. He seemed to understand Alix's thoughts, but didn't comment as he gave her directions to find the box containing the dress.

She found it easily but getting it out was difficult. She had to remove six other objects off the top and drag it out. It was a dress box, dark green, with the name of a store in Boston on the lid.

When she got it to the front, Caleb was standing by the chair and smiling. She wondered why she hadn't been introduced to him. Did he live nearby?

"That's it," he said.

It took Alix only moments to open the box. Inside was what looked to be a white cotton dress. Pulling it out, she held it up under the single bulb of light. It was beautiful: crisp, clean cotton, with a deep square neck, long sleeves, and a floor-length skirt done in folded-over layers. It was, without a doubt, a wedding dress. She looked at Caleb. "1950s?"

"I believe so." He paused. "Would you like to try it on?"

She looked at the long white dress. There was really no reason for her to put it on, but then lately her mind had been so full of weddings and all that goes with them that she felt drawn to the gown. And then, of course, there was Jared. Hadn't she said that her wedding dress would be cotton? "I think I'll go downstairs to put it on."

"Then you'll come back to me?" he asked in a way that took her aback. He sounded as though he'd be devastated if she said no.

"Yes, I will," she said as she ran down the stairs to her bedroom.

Once in the room, she couldn't help going to Captain Caleb's portrait. The man upstairs really did resemble his ancestor! "He's not *quite* as handsome as you are," she said. "But he's a close second."

In the next minute she'd stripped off her clothes. On impulse she rummaged in a drawer to find her best white lacy underwear and put it on. She started toward the gown but instead went to the bathroom and put on makeup. She was glad her long hair was clean. She pulled off the tie for her ponytail and managed to sweep it up into a soft chignon. It wasn't a professional job but it was more fitting for the elegance of the dress.

At last she returned to the bedroom, wearing just her underwear, and picked up the dress. As she stepped into it, she had to struggle with the tight, narrow sleeves, then work to fasten the buttons up the back. Only when she had it on did she look in the mirror. If the dress had been made for her, it couldn't have fit better. The neckline was low, showing rather a lot of cleavage. She made a halfhearted attempt to pull it up, but then smiled. Her breasts had never looked better!

As she went up the steep, narrow attic stairs

wearing a wedding dress and carrying a laptop, she was hesitant, but the moment she saw Caleb her reluctance vanished. He wore a tuxedo, one of that utterly perfect kind, like out of a Cary Grant movie. It fit him exactly, curving in at the waist and showing his long, heavily muscled legs. She didn't know what gym he went to, but it should be given an award.

The look he gave Alix made her stand up straighter. "Goddesses must envy you," he whispered.

His words were flattering and of course untrue, but they made all Alix's doubts leave her. She set her laptop down and inserted the CD that he'd put on the table. The first tune was a combination of Scottish and Irish reels, with a lot of violins. It was fast-paced but also lyrical.

Smiling, he held out his hand to her.

When she took it, an instant warmth went through her. His touch wasn't as electric or sexual as Jared's, but it was calming — and invigorating at the same time. Her concerns about the work she needed to do fell away. All that seemed important was this moment and what this man had to tell her.

Stepping back from her, he bowed, and even while Alix didn't know the dance he was leading her into, she did seem to know. She curtsied, then turned and walked forward four steps, Caleb beside her. She stopped, turned back toward him, and lifted her hands to touch his.

"How do I know what to do?" she asked.

"Past memory," he said, turning her around once more. "But now is not the time for thought. Just feel, and I will tell you the story. Valentina was extraordinarily beautiful. She had red hair and green eyes, and a waist the width of a man's hand."

They were moving to the music toward the far wall. "She sounds like my mother."

"She is exactly like her."

"Then she must have caused a stir among the young men on the island."

"Oh, yes," Caleb said in a voice that sounded faraway. "They all made complete fools of themselves when she was near."

"Did she and Captain Caleb fall in love immediately?"

"He did. He didn't know it then, but he did. As for Valentina, at first she despised him."

"Isn't that always true of Great Romance?" Alix turned full circle, then came to face him.

"Perhaps to read about, but not to experience. Their meeting came about because the Captain returned from his long voyage earlier than expected."

"Just as Izzy and I did," Alix said. "And if we hadn't shown up early, I wouldn't have met Jared."

"Are you referring to your sister?"

Alix laughed. "I can believe Izzy was my sister in another life. I guess that next you'll be telling me that an alternate me knew Jared."

"You made buildings together," Caleb said. "Many of the houses on this island are yours. You drew them; he built them."

Alix found herself laughing again. "What a marvelous prevaricator you are! You *must* meet my mother. With your plotting and her writing you'd be a perfect match."

"We were," he said.

"Yes, of course. You couldn't be anyone other than Captain Caleb. But how could Valentina ever despise *you*?" Alix couldn't help flirting with him. If there was ever a man made to flirt with, this was him. His eyes had a soft, bedroom quality, and combined with the beautiful dress, she was beginning to feel like the most desirable woman in the world. Long ago, Alix had found that with a mother like hers, she needed to be smart and talented and accomplished. When it came to pure sex appeal, no one could compete with Victoria. But right now this man was making Alix feel like she was a temptress.

"You see," Caleb said, "when the Captain arrived back on Nantucket, he didn't know who Valentina was. She'd come to the island after he left on a voyage to China, so he hadn't seen her." He turned about, then came back to Alix with a look that said he'd been away from her much too long.

Her face was close to his. He was clean shaven and she could smell his skin. It was salty and oh, so very male.

A new tune played, this one softer and slower. Caleb held out his arms to her. It seemed the most natural thing in the world to slip into them. He led her into a waltz that was so light she wasn't sure her feet were touching the ground. Around and around they went, higher and higher.

Alix put her head back and closed her eyes. When she opened them she was glancing *down* at the window, *down* at the stacks of artifacts. She and this man seemed high, high up, above the floor. As an architect, she knew it wasn't possible, the ceiling was too low, but right now she didn't feel like a businessperson of any type. The beautiful white wedding gown swirled around her body, nearly surrounding the two of them in a soft mist. Within her, she could feel a deep sense of herself as a woman. All the enticing, alluring touches that made her who she was were coming out of her, radiating.

And this man, this beautiful man, was making it happen.

Alix let the sensations and feelings seep into her body. The music grew louder, as though there were an orchestra in this vast room. She smelled food and perfume. She heard laughter and people talking. When she looked down, there was light: golden, glowing, and warm. It was candlelight, flickering and radiant, illuminating the flushed and rosy skin of a hundred people.

Alix seemed able to see beneath the floor. The entire downstairs was awash with light and laughter. "I see it," she whispered, clasping Caleb's hand tighter.

"Who do you see?" he whispered back.

"My mother! The men are around her. She looks like she does in the mornings before she puts on makeup. I've never seen her eyebrows unplucked."

"That's Valentina," Caleb said softly. "Who else is there?"

"Many people. That man looks like my father."

"He is John Kendricks, a widower and the schoolmaster, but he also built this house while the Captain was away," Caleb said. "Do you see yourself? Perhaps you're John's daughter. There on the window seat."

"Oh, yes. The girl with the sketch pad reminds me of myself. What is she drawing?"

"A house, of course," Caleb said. "Do you see Parthenia? She would be with your father. They were deeply in love."

"There!" Alix said. "Is the pretty woman beside him Parthenia?" The woman was standing to one side, smiling, but not laughing and chatting as the other people were. "She seems very quiet."

"She is."

"Who is the gray-haired man? He looks like Dr. Huntley."

"That's the Captain's father," Caleb said. "He will do *anything* for his son."

Alix closed her eyes again and the music grew louder. Opening her eyes, she smiled at Caleb. "Yesterday I was calculating how much cement to order for a job. Now I'm wearing a beautiful gown and dancing on air. Literally. By the way, where is the Captain?" Still breathless from the dance, she looked for him.

"You won't see him down there. He's just coming home from his long voyage; he felt like he'd been at sea forever. He's tired and hungry and he wants to see his new house."

"So the luscious Captain Caleb was coming home that night?"

Caleb smiled. "Luscious. I like that word. But this evening he was anything but. As he stepped onto Kingsley Lane he saw his new house lit up — and he didn't like it. You see, John and Parthenia were getting married that night and half the island was invited. But the Captain didn't know that. All he saw was that there were a thousand candles, and many carriages and horses outside. The manure was ankle deep."

"What a romantic image," Alix said, laughing. "Did the Captain run the people out?"

"No, he was never like that. But he didn't

yet want to see anyone, so he sneaked inside and made his way up the stairs to his bedroom. Unfortunately, he found his bed covered with ladies' cloaks, so he went up to the attic."

"To hide away and sulk."

"No!" Caleb said, sounding affronted, but then he twirled Alix even harder and gave a little smile. "Perhaps it was so, but for whatever reason, he was there when Valentina came upstairs."

"With a young man?" Alix asked.

"No. She wanted to remove her shoes and be quiet for a moment. She had been danced off her feet."

"Was this a romantic meeting?"

"Hardly," Caleb said, a smile in his voice. "You see, he didn't know her and from the look of her, he believed it was quite possible that she was a lady of the evening."

"It sounds to me like Captain Caleb had just returned from exotic ports, took one look at the gorgeous, voluptuous Valentina, and made a serious pass at her. I don't think it was his *mind* that was involved in that first meeting."

"Perhaps," he said, grinning. "I think the schoolmaster's daughter is too clever. You'll never get a husband that way."

Alix returned his smile. "My mother is also very clever and *she* got Captain Caleb."

His laugh rang out and indeed it was the

one Alix remembered so well, so deep, coming from way inside him, rumbling upward like rich, dark, sweet molasses. "I swear I have not laughed so well since you were last here. Now, where was I in my story?"

"John Kendricks's daughter was too smart for any man to handle."

Caleb smiled. "It is true that on that first night Captain Caleb tried to persuade the beautiful Valentina to kiss him. But that's all there was."

"How much rum was involved?" Alix asked.

"Measured in gallons or flagons?"

Alix laughed. "Did Valentina slap him?"

"No," Caleb said. "She . . ."

Alix looked at him. "Are you blushing?"

"That is a female condition," he said. "Men do not blush."

"What did Valentina do to the Captain? Who, by the way, might have been a bit tipsy."

"She played a trick on him. You see, she pretended to invite him to make love to her."

"What does that mean?"

Caleb kept dancing, holding on to Alix, and took his time in answering. "She got him to remove his clothing."

"You mean he was naked and she wasn't?"

"Yes." Caleb gave a sheepish grin. "Once the Captain had disrobed entirely, Valentina took his clothing and left the attic. She locked the door rather securely behind her."

"Oh?" Alix began to laugh at what she was

visualizing. "If the house was new there probably wasn't much up here, was there?"

"There was only a half-empty jug of rum." Caleb's look seemed to be a combination of remorse and embarrassment. "And it was a cold night."

Alix couldn't repress her laughter. "How did he get out of this room?"

"The next morning Kendricks heard . . . well, some fairly strong words coming through the floorboards. It had been very difficult to raise the household after the night's revelry."

"Not to mention that it was the schoolmaster's wedding night. I don't mean to laugh at the Captain, but he really did deserve what he got."

"He did," Caleb said. "Although he certainly didn't think so at the time. When he was finally released from the attic he put on his most impressive uniform and went to Valentina's washhouse, where she was stirring her big pots of soap. He demanded an apology from her."

"Did she give it to him?"

"She told him to make himself useful and grab a paddle and stir."

"Not the way a ship's captain was used to being treated?"

"No," Caleb said, smiling. "Not at all how he was used to being treated."

They smiled at each other and kept dancing.

# Chapter Twenty-One

Jared was in the beat-up old truck he kept in Hyannis, driving back from Maine. In the summer it was difficult to get a reservation for a vehicle on the slow boat. What with the sixty thousand or so visitors who came and left the island, and their many vehicles taking up room on the ferry, a lot of Nantucketers kept a car or truck off-island.

Beside him was Jilly Taggert Leighton, just one of the many relatives he'd met over the last few days. There seemed to be hundreds of them!

There were some, mostly Montgomerys, in the little Maine town that had been founded by their ancestors and he was told of more, Taggerts, who lived in Chandler, Colorado. He saw photos of an enormous house in Colorado built by a robber baron back in the nineteenth century. As far as Jared could tell, the house hadn't been updated in many years. He didn't say so, but he very much wanted to get his hands on the place and bring it up to code. He couldn't imagine how dangerous the electrical probably was.

As Jared looked at the pictures, he'd imagined Alix's face when she saw the mansion in Colorado. And he thought of what she'd say when she saw the big house in Maine. Besides the buildings, he wondered which member of the family she'd like the most and who she'd never be close to. Would he and Alix have the same opinions of everything and everyone? Or would they disagree?

The truth was that Jared had thought of Alix the whole time he was away. And he'd talked about her. He thought maybe that's what surprised him the most, that he'd spoken of her out loud. Off-island, he'd always been a very private person. His grandfather said the contrast was good. On Nantucket you couldn't get a girlfriend, break up with one, or even flirt with a girl without half the town knowing about it. Which was one of the many reasons why Jared had only gone out with tourists while at home — and why he'd kept his New York girlfriends in the city.

But Alix was different. Never in his life had he felt so comfortable, so at ease, with anyone. From fish filleting to designing a house, they just seemed to know how to . . . well, actually how to *live* together.

A couple of times before Jared had lived with women, but each time it had been a disaster. For one thing, all his girlfriends had seemed much more aware of his success than his passion for his craft. He was a famous architect who moved in elite circles, and they wanted to be part of that. They wanted to wear gowns that cost thousands, jewels that cost even more, and go to parties every night of the week. They wanted to be seen with the famous Jared Montgomery, wanted to be associated with him. Jared felt secondary to that man, whom he often thought of as a media creation.

Over the years he'd tried dating women from different social strata. There was a pretty young woman from Indiana who worked as a receptionist. But she'd been overwhelmed by Jared's high-flying life and one day he'd found her crying in his apartment. He paid for her ticket home. The women who'd grown up rich were annoyed that Jared could spend so little time with them. Those with ambition tended to use Jared's contacts as stepping stones on their way to the top.

Whatever their origins, all the women he'd dated had been far more interested in Jared the Famous than in the Jared the Man. Not one of them had grasped the concept of the *work* behind what he did. Sheer, huge volumes of *work*.

But Alix did. He could hand her the end of a measuring tape and she knew what to do with it. He could talk in shorthand to her and she understood. But work wasn't all of it, or even the main part. Alix saw him as a man. She saw both sides of him and liked them both.

"Are you missing her?" Jilly asked from the passenger seat beside him.

Jared smiled. "Did I make a fool of myself talking about her so much?"

"Not at all," Jilly said. "Most of us have been there and the ones who haven't hope to be someday. Did you tell Alix that we'll be arriving today?"

"No. She doesn't expect me until tomorrow." He was grinning at the thought of seeing her again. Two days ago he'd gone with Jilly's older brother Kane and his identical twin grown sons, in search of the stained-glass window for the chapel. At the second store, they'd found the perfect one. Made in the 1870s, it portrayed a knight leaning on his sword and looking wistful. Jared didn't say so, but the man looked uncannily like his grandfather, Caleb.

After he'd purchased the window, Jared started to help put it on the back of the truck, but Kane said, "You're a Montgomery so you better let us do it." Jared had soon learned about the rivalry between the two families. The big Taggerts said that the taller, thinner Montgomerys were weak and scrawny, while the Montgomerys said the Taggerts had no brains. Of course it was all untrue, but Jared enjoyed the ribbing.

All in all, he fit in with the family and, yes, he was more like the Montgomerys. They were the relatives who encouraged him to talk about what he'd designed over the course of his career, and who enjoyed puzzling out how they were related.

Of the Taggerts, Jared especially liked Kane and Mike, men in their early fifties who had amassed great fortunes — but were as down-to-earth as could be. They were identical twins, so alike Jared couldn't see a difference between them — but their wives could. And none of their children were fooled.

Kane's wife, Cale, was a famous writer and she made everyone laugh with her witty little remarks, some of them quite sarcastic but always right on target. She could nail a situation perfectly in just a few words.

"So what's Nantucket really like?" she asked on his second day there. She'd walked out to a point on the Maine coast where he'd been sitting and watching the ocean. As always, she had a notebook in her hand.

"It's quiet," he said. "If you ignore the visitors, that is." She was small and pretty, her eyes full of curiosity. It was a look he'd often seen on Victoria's face. Were writers always looking for ideas? he wondered. "And we have lots of ghosts on the island."

Her eyes widened.

He'd also seen that look on Victoria's face. "Some of the stories of how they came to be ghosts are long and complicated, and quite fascinating."

"Oh," she said, but didn't seem able to say anything else. As a professional writer she was always on a quest to find more material. Like an alcoholic craved booze, writers were addicted to *stories.*

"I better let you get on with your writing." He nodded toward her notebook as he stood up, but then turned back to look at her. "There's a house on Kingsley Lane that's for sale. It's big and old. It's called BEYOND TIME because there's a legend that the ghost in it can take you back to his time." Jared waved his hand. "But that's just hearsay. I don't know if anyone has actually done it. Though I wonder how the rumor got started? But then it's been around for centuries. I hope to see you at dinner." He'd walked away, smiling. Unless he missed his guess, that old house was as good as sold.

Jilly flew in from Colorado a few days after Jared's arrival. She was a widow, and her two grown children were in summer camps in their home state. It was their last summer before they left for college.

Jared had been told that after Jilly's husband died, she'd been hired by the family to become their genealogist. She'd spent years going through the mass of family documents and writing histories of everyone. Recently she'd posted a detailed family tree online, which was where Alix had found Valentina and Parthenia.

Jilly brought with her from Colorado three big boxes of photocopied papers. "The originals are in a vault," she said at dinner at the huge table that first night. In one of the boxes were the letters from Valentina and Parthenia to each other. She recapped them for Jared.

As she told him what the letters said, of the two young women missing each other and planning to visit, he watched her. She was sweet and gentle while the other Taggerts were big and rough.

"She looks like her maternal grandmother," Cale, sitting on his other side, said. "Or else she's an alien from another planet."

Jared laughed. Jilly, so fragile-looking, so soft-spoken, sitting amid her great, hulking brothers, did indeed look as though she were from another dimension.

Seeing that she had an audience, Cale kept on. "What do you think her planet looks like? All pink and cream?"

Jared didn't miss a beat. "I think it must look like Nantucket, with mists and sunsets over the ocean, sun-warmed sand, and houses grayed by centuries of life."

Cale blinked at him for a moment, then looked across the table at her husband. "I need your checkbook."

"Yeah?" Kane said, his eyes alight. "What are you going to buy?"

"A house on Nantucket."

Kane looked from Cale to Jared and back again. "Let me guess. It has a great story attached to it."

"Maybe," she said and everyone laughed. They knew how much Cale loved stories.

It was after dinner, the night before he was going to leave, and Jared was sitting outside in a swing with Jilly beside him. Since the first moment he met her, she'd reminded him of someone. At first he'd thought it was Toby. They both had a quiet elegance about them, but at dinner there was something about the way she held her fork — in that tines-down European way — that made him realize that she reminded him of Ken. A gesture here and there, a tone to her soft voice, made him want to call Ken and say he'd met the perfect woman for him.

But Jared knew that would end it before it started, so he only told Alix about his idea of returning home with Jilly. On the last night, he sat with her and listened as she told more about the letters. "After the first visit to Nantucket, Parthenia returned to Maine and their letters started again. But this time they wrote about the men they cared for. Parthenia had fallen in love with the schoolmaster, and Valentina with —"

"Caleb," Jared said. "But what happened to her?"

"We know no more than you. When Valentina disappeared, Parthenia was married to her schoolmaster and living on Nantucket, so there were no more letters between them. A Montgomery ancestor wrote home that after Valentina disappeared three men from her family went to the island to search for her. They discovered a couple of sailors who said they'd taken her to the Cape, but no trace of her was found there or anywhere else. She certainly never came home to Maine. After Parthenia's death, all the letters between her and Valentina were sent back to Warbrooke. I've read everything and an explanation for Valentina's disappearance is nowhere to be found."

Jared was frowning. "I was told . . . heard, anyway, that no one had seen Valentina leave the island."

"Perhaps it was kept quiet. A woman leaving her child behind wouldn't have been looked on favorably, and I doubt if her relatives would have spread that information. It was all so long ago. Do you have many family documents at your house?"

Jared could tell by her voice that she'd like to see them, so he took the opening. "I have acres of them. Nothing is ever thrown away in my family. We own several houses and all of them are packed to the top of the mast with yellowing old papers, letters, and books."

"It sounds fascinating."

"Not to hear Alix tell it." He smiled in what

he hoped was a persuasive way. "Why don't you come back with me and spend the rest of the summer going through them?"

"I couldn't possibly," she began, then sighed. "On the other hand, both my children will be leaving home soon and I've nearly finished with our family papers. I'm afraid I have a serious case of empty nest syndrome." Her head came up. "Actually, I'd love to go to Nantucket with you. Should I make reservations to stay somewhere?"

"There's an apartment upstairs in my house. You can stay there as long as you like."

"But you and Alix need your privacy."

"We'll enjoy the company," he said, thinking again of Ken.

She looked at him in speculation. "I don't know you very well, but you have a look in your eyes that my family, the Taggerts, says means a Montgomery is up to something and you'd better watch out."

Jared gave a laugh that could be heard all the way to the inside of the old house. "Does this mean you're not open to a bit of adventure?"

Jilly smiled. "I have raised two children on my own since they were three years old and my job has been to delve into eight-foot-tall stacks of old papers. The truth is that if a pirate asked me to go sailing with him I would probably say yes. What time should I be ready?"

"Is daylight tomorrow too soon? It'll take five hours to drive down to Hyannis. I found someone to deliver the stained-glass window I'll be taking back, so we can catch the noon fast ferry to Nantucket."

"I will be ready by four A.M."

"You're my kind of girl," he said.

"I'm hardly a girl but thank you for the compliment."

That had been last night and he'd spent the evening helping Jilly pack. Or rather, he saw the women scurrying about getting her ready. Jared had stayed with the men and watched sports on TV. One by one the women came in to make a comment.

Mike's wife told Jared how pleased they all were that he was adding to Jilly's life. "She's the sweetest of all the Taggerts."

"That doesn't take much," a Montgomery said and the Taggerts threw popcorn at him.

"You men are cleaning that up," she said as she left the room.

Cale came in with a laptop, squeezed beside Jared on the couch, and showed him the real estate listing she'd found for a house on Kingsley Lane. "Is *this* the house you told me about? The one with the time-traveling ghost?"

"It is," he said.

"This house costs rather a lot."

"It's Nantucket," Jared said.

Cale didn't ask what that meant, just

glanced at her husband. "This is going to take some persuading."

"Do a time-share," Jared said. "Three or four months per family. Share the cost." He leaned toward her. "Writers love winter on the island the best. That's when it's quiet and the ghosts show themselves."

"You really are a Montgomery, aren't you? A true snake oil salesman." She was smiling. "I like this idea and I'll propose it to them." She put her hand on his arm. "I'm glad you joined the family, and I look forward to meeting Alix."

"What's going on with you two?" Kane asked from across the room.

"I'm planning to run off with your new cousin," Cale said. "Where's Kane?"

Jared looked up in surprise. "He's Mike?"

"Yes," Cale said. "He's fat; my husband isn't."

Mike grunted at that and looked back at the TV.

Jared smiled at the absurdity of her words. He knew that both Kane and Mike used their basement gym to keep in shape with workouts that would be tough for an Olympic athlete. Their muscular bodies showed the results. Neither was the slightest bit overweight.

As she'd said, Jilly was ready to leave as soon as it was daylight — and every family member over the age of two was there to see her off. Jared had never seen so much hugging and kissing in his life! One of the biggest Taggerts pulled him into a death grip and said, "You let her get hurt and you answer to us." Jared nodded in reply. It was a concept he understood and approved of.

Hours later, when they reached the dock at Hyannis, one of Jared's cousins was waiting for them. He was going to take the truck with the stained-glass window in the back on the slow boat — the ferry that carried vehicles — the next day, then he'd stay on the island to help with the chapel.

Jared and Jilly got out their overnight cases and went to the fast ferry. On the hour-long ride over, they sat at a table. Jilly looked at a copy of the newspaper, *Yesterday's Island,* while asking him about who she'd be meeting.

He leaned back in the long bench seat, coffee cup in hand, and talked about the people on Kingsley Lane. "Ken is staying in the guesthouse for now. He's Alix's father." Jared didn't want to ruin anything by saying he thought Jilly would really like the man, but he did run on a bit about how Ken had helped him get started, and how if it weren't for Ken he'd probably be in prison now, and how Ken and he had built Jared's final project at school, and how Ken was unmarried and looking. Just a few facts.

Jilly listened politely, never making a comment, and said, "What about Alix's mother? I know she's a writer like Cale, but what's she like personally?"

Jared smiled. Physically there couldn't be two more different people. Cale was small and trim while Victoria was tall and hourglass curvy. "Victoria isn't like anyone else," he said, "but she isn't there right now. Ken is building the chapel for Alix's friend's wedding." Jared told about Alix's design and the approaching nuptials and all that was being done for the wedding.

"I guess you know your whole face lights up when you talk of Alix," Jilly said.

Jared looked away for a moment to restore his New England reticence. "We seem suited to each other."

"Then I hope you don't lose her," Jilly said. "So tell me about your other neighbors on the lane."

A minute later Jared had her laughing about Lexie and her mega-rich boss, and how Alix and Toby teased Lex about him. "The girls say he's not bad to look at, but personally, I don't see it. The pictures I saw of him look kind of girly to me."

Jilly laughed.

When the ferry docked, Jared carried their luggage and they walked up Main Street. He'd always liked being around first-timers. Seeing Nantucket through their eyes renewed his vision of the island's beauty.

"Oh, yes," Jilly said. "My family will love

this place." There were beautiful buildings, perfectly proportioned, with tall windows with elegant panes. Brick crosswalks ran through the cobblestones to make walking easier. She was turning one way then the other as she looked at the old houses. When they came to the Three Bricks, she paused a moment to take in their majestic beauty before starting down Kingsley Lane.

At the first house on the right, she stopped. "BEYOND TIME," she read on the quarterboard above the door. "Is that the house Cale was talking about? The one that's for sale?"

"You have it right. Is she already campaigning to get your family to buy it?"

"She is, and after I report back to them, she'll win. Besides, Kane is so mad about his wife that he'll do anything for her."

"Good," Jared said, then quickened his pace. He was eager to see Alix.

Just three buildings down was his old house and he didn't think it had ever looked so good to him. They went through the side gate toward the back and by one of those cosmic coincidences, Ken was just coming out of the guesthouse, a rolled-up drawing in one hand, a steaming mug in the other.

But Jared knew the meeting was no coincidence. Turning, he looked up at an attic window and there stood his grandfather. He was staring down at Jilly as though he were studying her.

Frowning and not liking the idea that his grandfather could have made this happen, Jared looked back at Ken. He was looking at Jilly with wide eyes, as though he were seeing a divine vision, an angel come to earth — and she was looking right back at him with the same expression.

Jared felt like congratulating himself but he only indulged in the smallest of smiles. "Ken, Jilly; Jilly, Ken," he said and stepped toward the house. "Mind if I go see Alix?"

No one answered. They just stood there looking at each other.

"Okay," he said. "I'm going." When he turned away, he smiled broader.

As soon as he was inside, he thought of calling out to Alix, but didn't. His grandfather was in the doorway.

"Where is she?"

"Front parlor," Caleb said. "But first, we need to discuss a certain matter."

"Later," Jared said, walking through his grandfather and to the front room. He thought Alix would be curled up with a sketchbook, working on a plan for a guesthouse, but she wasn't. She was sitting on the floor, cross-legged, and was surrounded by boxes of dusty old documents. Papers and tied-up bundles of letters covered the couch, tables, and chairs. There was a foot-tall stack of yellowed sheets on Alix's lap.

"Hi," he said softly.

When she looked up, the way her face lit up, as though she'd just seen the most wonderful vision on earth, showed her happiness at seeing him again. She jumped up, papers falling to the floor, leaped across two boxes, and threw her arms around him as her mouth landed on his. Their kiss was deep — and joyful. They'd missed each other a great deal and their lips and tongues told how much.

"Did you think about me?" he asked as he moved to kiss her neck.

"Yes and double yes!" she said, leaning her head back. "I have so much to tell you. Dr. Huntley found John Kendricks and brought me some papers about him, but I haven't read them yet. Toby and Lexie and I did tons for the wedding. And Caleb told me about the Captain and Valentina and about her cousin Parthenia and —"

Jared put his hands on Alix's shoulders and held her away from him so he could look into her eyes. "Caleb? When did you see him?"

"Yesterday, on Sunday. He and I . . ." Alix wasn't sure how to tell about what she and Caleb had done.

"What did you do?"

"I'm sorry, but we danced together. You won't be angry, will you? It really meant nothing."

Jared worked to calm himself. "It's all right. I know that Caleb can be supernaturally charming."

Alix sighed in relief. "And he's an excellent historian. His storytelling was so overwhelming that it was almost as though I saw the inside of this house on the night John Kendricks and Parthenia Taggert got married. I saw beeswax candles and smelled delicious food. I heard music too, but then I was playing a CD on my laptop, and — Why are you looking at me like that?"

"I want us to leave this house. Now."

"I can't." She stepped away from him. "Caleb told me about how the Captain and Valentina met. It was really rather funny, but what happened later was so tragic. I *must* find out the *truth* of what happened to her." Alix motioned to the boxes and papers surrounding them. "I need to go through everything and find out — Hey! What are you doing?"

Jared had bent, lifted Alix, and put her over his shoulder. He turned toward the door. His grandfather was there and wearing an apologetic look for taking things so far with Alix.

With a glare that ignored the man, Jared walked through Caleb and headed toward the back door.

Alix, with her head down and fanny up, said, "I don't mean to interrupt your *Shrek* moment here, but the bedroom is upstairs."

"We're not going to bed. At least not now. We're going to stay at Dilys's house for a few days."

"Then I need to pack some clothes."

"You won't need any," he said as he carried her out of the house.

"Ooooooh," she said. "I was looking forward to your coming home but this gets better by the second."

After Jared left Ken and Jilly together, she was the one who spoke first. "So you're the man who fathered the most beautiful, intelligent, talented young woman on earth."

"I did," Ken said, pleased by her words — and her voice. He didn't think he'd ever seen a more beautiful woman. She was quite slim, with an oval face, and she was wearing a pink and white dress that looked so fragile it could have been made of rose petals. A big sun hat was in her hand. "Is it Jared who agrees with me?"

"He does. He told my entire family about Alix, even showed us designs she'd drawn."

For a moment Ken just stood there smiling, but then he seemed to come to his senses. "Where are my manners? Would you like to come inside and I'll make us some tea? I have some doughnuts."

"From Downyflake?"

Ken laughed. "Did Jared tell you *everything* about Nantucket?"

"He said nothing but good things. In fact, he wants our family to buy a house here. The one on the end."

"BEYOND TIME?" Ken asked.

"Yes, that's the one."

"Then we must discuss it." Stepping back, he opened the front door to the guesthouse.

A few minutes later, Ken and Jilly were sitting outside at the beautifully aged cedar table, munching on doughnuts and waiting for the tea to steep. Their heads were bent toward each other so closely that they were almost touching.

It was Ken who first saw Jared walking toward them with Alix tossed across his shoulder.

Jared stopped by the table, with an expression on his face that implied that nothing was out of the ordinary. "We're going to Dilys's for a few days," he said. "She's off-island so we'll have the place to ourselves." He looked from one to the other. "You two don't look like you'll miss us."

"No, I don't think we will," Ken said, standing up. Jared's suitcase was on the ground and Ken picked it up. He walked over to put it in the back of the pickup.

Jilly followed them. "I feel that I should ask: Alix, are you all right? And by the way, I'm Jilly Leighton, a Taggert before I married."

Jared turned around so Alix could get an upside-down view of her. "It's nice to meet you, and I'm fine. Jared is just jealous because I spent yesterday morning dancing with one of his relatives."

Ken smiled. "And which relative was that? Wes?"

"Caleb," Alix and Jared said in unison.

"Oh" was all Ken could reply, then he lowered his voice and looked at Jared. "Please, take my daughter away, and keep her away for as long as you want. As long as you *can.*"

"Betrayed!" Alix said. "I am betrayed by my own blood." Her tone said that she was quite pleased by it all.

Jared set Alix in the truck, shut the door, then got in the driver's seat.

"Call me," Ken said through the window.

"You can be sure that I will," Jared said, his eyes betraying his anger at his grandfather. He backed onto the lane.

When Ken and Jilly were alone again, she said, "Jared told me about a lot of people, but I don't believe he ever mentioned a Caleb. Is there a problem with this man?"

Ken ushered her back to the table. When they were seated, he said, "I guess that all depends on how you look at it. You see . . ." He looked at her. He'd met her less than an hour ago but he liked her. The look of her, the way she moved, the sound of her voice appealed to him. But he feared that if he told her the truth, it was quite possible that she'd run away. But sometimes, he thought, you needed to risk something to gain everything.

"Caleb . . ." he said slowly.

"Yes?"

"Caleb died about two hundred years ago."

"Oh, my," Jilly said as she picked up a chocolate-covered doughnut. "Now you must tell me all of it. From the beginning."

Ken couldn't help smiling at her. A woman who didn't freak at the mere mention of a ghost! Where had she been all his life? "More tea?" he asked, smiling even broader.

"Yes, please, but I think we're going to need a second pot because I want to hear every detail."

"I think you're right. You see, it all started when I found my wife, Alix's mother, in bed with my business partner."

"How awful for you."

"Worse than I can describe."

"I imagine that it was," Jilly said, thinking of her own unfortunate marital experience, but she didn't mention that. This was Ken's time for telling.

He looked into her eyes. There had been other women in the many years since Victoria, and twice he'd been close to marriage. But at the last moment he'd chickened out. Never, not with anyone, had he come close to telling the truth about Victoria, or even about his time on Nantucket. And he'd never told of his connection to the famous architect Jared Montgomery. Most of all, he'd never told about a ghost who haunted the old

Kingsley House, a ghost his daughter had seen clearly when she was a child — and seemed to have danced with on a rainy day.

Pretty Jilly was looking at him patiently. It was as though she had all the time in the world and the only thing she wanted to do was hear his story.

And Ken realized that all he wanted to do was tell her.

In the upstairs window, Caleb smiled down at them. "Welcome home, Parthenia," he whispered.

# CHAPTER TWENTY-TWO

Jared was doing his best to remain calm — and to protect Alix. He could see that she had no idea that she'd been dancing with a ghost, and he didn't want her to ever know. If she did find out, he didn't think she would go into hysterics, but who could be sure? He just had to make it until Izzy's wedding, then Caleb would leave and . . . He didn't want to think about that.

What was really bothering Jared was that his grandfather seemed to have so much more power than he used to have. Rules and facts about Caleb had been passed down through the Jareds for centuries. "Don't tell the women you can see him." "Don't mention him to outsiders." "He can't leave the house." "He can stand in front of people but they can't see him." On and on, never ending.

But never, ever had anyone hinted that Caleb could *dance* with someone. Touch them. An odd hand on a shoulder, a cheek kiss, yes, but not actual full-body contact.

And what about his apparent ability to provide Alix with glimpses of the past? He'd never experienced anything of the sort with his grandfather, nor had his father told him of such a thing.

Beside him, Alix was talking about what she'd seen. "Of course it was all my imagination. Probably from having seen too many movies, but I completely envisioned what he was telling me about. Such an amazing storyteller! It was as though I could see and hear it all. Like I was *there.* Or hovering over it and looking down at it, anyway. And the people he spoke of I imagined looking like people I know. My dad was there and —"

"Is everything in place for Izzy's wedding?" Jared asked. "How's she doing? Is she feeling better?"

Alix understood that Jared didn't want to hear more about her and Caleb. When she'd said he was jealous she was teasing, but maybe it was true. He had no reason to be, but she didn't want to upset him, whether he was being entirely reasonable or not. "Izzy is doing well. We exchange half a dozen emails and texts a day and call every other day. She's almost stopped throwing up, but now she says she's eating everything in sight."

Jared pulled into the parking lot of the Stop and Shop. "I have to make a quick call to the office," he said. "Would you mind getting groceries, enough to last for at least three days?"

"No clothes but lots of food?"

"I'll eat it off your bare belly," Jared said, and Alix laughed as she got out of the truck. As soon as she left, he phoned Ken.

"How is she?" Ken asked as he stepped outside to take the call. Jilly was in the guest-house making tea and sandwiches.

"She has no idea what she saw," Jared said.

"My daughter danced with a ghost but she doesn't know it?"

"That's right," Jared said. "And it seems that my granddad showed her some vision of the past. She saw Valentina's cousin getting married."

Ken was still trying to adjust to the idea of the ghost being real. He looked up at the back of the big house, his eyes searching every window. But he saw nothing — and he was glad of it. He didn't think he'd much like seeing a ghost. "Are you going to tell her the truth about what happened?"

"Hell, no!" Jared said. He didn't want to say that his grandfather was leaving the earth on Izzy's wedding day. It was too painful to think of, and he doubted Ken would understand. Outsiders loved phrases like "eternal rest," as though that solved everything. Get rid of the ghost and everyone would be happy — except for the people who love him, that is. "I don't want her seeing him again, so I'm going to do my best to keep Alix by my side every minute."

"That's what you're doing with my daughter anyway," Ken said, sounding like the father he was.

"Don't get on my case!" Jared snapped, then calmed himself. "I need something to distract her. As much as I'd like to be alone with her, that's not going to keep her from talking — and thinking. If she keeps on like this she's going to figure it all out."

Ken knew he was right. "All she needs to hear is that the name Caleb was used only once in your family and she'll know. My girl is smart."

"Too smart," Jared muttered, looking around at the packed parking lot. Cars were on the grass, in the roadways. During the summer season, getting groceries meant taking your life in your hands. "What do you think of Jilly?" When Ken didn't answer, Jared said, "Are you still there?"

"I'm here," he said. "Do you believe in love at first sight?"

"A month ago I didn't," Jared said. "You ought to get Jilly to talk. Cale said her late husband was — and I quote — a 'lying, thieving monster.' It seems the bastard stole Jilly and her kids' entire inheritance."

"I hope he rots," Ken said under his breath. "Wait a minute! Are you talking about Cale Anderson? Victoria says she makes a nest on the *New York Times* best-seller list, then sits on her eggs until they hatch into movies."

Jared chuckled. "Thanks, I needed a laugh, and that's the right Cale. Listen, I need help distracting Alix. She's really digging at this."

When Ken spoke, his voice was cautious. "Don't forget that at the end of the year she'll leave your house. After she's gone, you won't have to worry about her ever again seeing the ghost."

"I'm going to pretend you didn't say that," Jared said. "I just have to keep Alix occupied until Izzy's wedding, then everything will change — and, no, I'm not going to tell you why. After that, Alix is mine. Forever. Not just for a single year."

"Okay," Ken said, his voice full of his joy at hearing that. "I'll talk to Jilly and see if she has any ideas on what might take my very curious daughter's mind off your ghost."

"You told Jilly about my grandfather?!"

"I did," Ken said, "and don't give me any grief about it or I'll call Victoria and tell *her* about Caleb."

Jared took a moment to imagine that horror. "I have to go. You and Jilly need to come up with something *fast.*" After he hung up, as he waited for Alix, he tried to come up with a distraction, but couldn't. When he saw Alix approaching with a full grocery cart, he went forward to help her.

At Dilys's house, they'd just unloaded the

last of the groceries when a car pulled in behind the truck. A pretty blond woman was driving and in the backseat was a little boy, about two, belted into a car seat and crying at the top of his lungs.

Jared bent down to look at the woman through the passenger window. Alix stood behind him.

"Jared! Thank goodness I caught you!" she said over the noise of her son. "Dilys isn't here so I have no sitter. I hate to drag Tyler around and you know how much he hates shopping, but I have no one to look after him. With his dad away fishing, fighting the seas to earn money to support us, it's hard for Tyler and me to —"

"All right!" Jared said. "You don't have to beat me up."

Alix had no idea what he was talking about, but she watched as Jared opened the back door, unbuckled the car seat, and the child nearly leaped into his arms. From the way the boy immediately stopped crying, it was obvious he and Jared were well acquainted.

"You better get the bag," his mother said. "There are phone numbers in there and clean clothes and you should take the seat too. Just in case. And, oh yes, I think he needs . . ." She trailed off with a little smile.

"You think?" Jared's voice was sarcastic.

She smiled even broader as she put the car in reverse. As she pulled away, she called out,

"Jared, I love you."

Alix watched the car until it turned the corner, then looked at Jared comfortably holding the boy. He was cute, with dark blond hair and big blue eyes. "Old girlfriend?" she asked in a tone that she hoped sounded unconcerned. Inside she was screaming. Please don't let her be an ex-anything and this be Jared's love child.

"Naw. Her brother and I went to school together. She loves me because this is one fragrant kid. Want the job?"

For a moment, Alix had no idea what he meant. "Oh! You mean he needs changing?"

"And right away." He slid the heavy bag off his shoulder and handed it to her. Alix took it, but when Jared started to give her the boy, she stepped back.

"Scared?" he asked, teasing.

"Not really. It's just that I've never changed a diaper before. I don't know how."

Jared blinked at her a few times. "What are they teaching in that fancy school of yours these days?"

"How to earn a living," Alix said, smiling.

"But obviously not what to do with what you earn. Come on in and I'll teach you the great art of nappy changing."

"If you're teaching again, this must be Montgomery."

"That guy? He wears a tux to dinner."

When they got inside the house, to Alix's

disbelief, the boy didn't want to have his diaper changed. Didn't movies and TV have the kid crying if its diaper was soiled even a little bit? But not Tyler.

"Should we put him on the bed?" she asked.

"Dilys would kill us if we got it dirty," Jared said, holding on to the boy who was now struggling to get down.

"Go! Go!" he yelled as he kicked Jared in the ribs.

"Look in the closet and get out that old blue blanket and spread it over the rug," Jared said. "And I'm going to need a wash-cloth — no, two of them — wet with warm water."

Alix got the blanket and spread it out, then ran to the bathroom to get some wet cloths. All this to change one messy diaper? she wondered.

When she got back to the living room, Jared had Tyler's shorts off and Alix saw that they weren't clean. She rummaged in the bag and got out a diaper, then sat on the arm of the couch and watched. Tyler was laughing as Jared held him down with one hand and removed his very dirty diaper with the other.

Alix's first thought was how could someone so small produce that much? Jared used the diaper and the cloths to clean him but . . .

"Look," Alix said. When Tyler rolled over, she saw that it was all the way up his back, almost to his hair.

"Okay, buddy," Jared said, "let's get you into the shower."

"Wouldn't a tub be better?" Alix asked.

"You want to clean it?"

"No, thanks."

With Jared holding the half-naked boy at arm's length, they went to the master bath. Alix was going to get the blanket and shorts up, but Jared called for her.

"Help me undress, would you?" he said as he reached in and turned on the shower. "I can't let him loose or he'll spread it all over the house, so I'm going to get in with him." With his arm securely around Tyler, Jared bent so Alix could pull his shirt off over his head.

When Alix started to help with Jared's jeans, the child almost escaped, but Jared caught him. Unfortunately, the mess on Tyler was now also down the front of Jared's bare chest.

Alix couldn't help laughing.

"Don't encourage him," Jared said, but he was smiling. Still holding Tyler, he got into the shower with the boy and grabbed a bar of soap.

Alix looked at the two of them, both naked, both beautiful. Never in her life had she seen a sight that affected her more. No building on the face of the earth equaled the perfection of this man with this child. The tenderness, the kindness, the love between them seemed to create a glow around them.

For a moment she had to hold on to the sink to keep from collapsing. “I’ll . . .” she began. “I’ll get the . . .” Vaguely, she pointed toward the living room.

“No eating the soap,” Jared told Tyler. “And keep your eyes closed. I have to shampoo your entire body.”

Alix left the room to get the blanket and clothes in the washer, and put the diaper in the outside trash.

When she got back to the bathroom, Jared held a wet and slippery Tyler out to her. “He’s yours to dress. I’ve got to wash my hair.”

“I don’t know how —” Alix began, but Jared wasn’t listening. Grabbing a towel off the rack, she took the boy.

Tyler didn’t like having his diaper changed but he *hated* being put back into clothes. Alix managed to get him onto the bed where he promptly rolled off and ran for the door. She caught him, put him back on the bed, and held him down with one hand on his chest while she got clothes out of the diaper bag.

Tyler was laughing hilariously as he struggled to free himself from Alix’s grasp. Figuring out how to put on a diaper while holding him down wasn’t easy. As soon as she’d get the diaper under him, he’d roll away and she’d pull him back. She got the diaper in place, then the sticky tab glued itself to her left thumb and she couldn't get it off. She had to get the other tab in place before the first one gave way.

When she finally had it on, Tyler looked at her with eyes of mischief, but she caught him before he made another run for it. "Oh, no, you don't. Now come the clothes!" She made a cackling sound like an evil witch — which made Tyler go into hysterics with laughter.

When Alix finally got him into his shirt and shorts, she looked at him in triumph. "There, now. Doesn't it feel good to be clean? Let's get your sandals on."

Seeing an opening, Tyler did a lightning-fast roll and was off the bed in less than a second. He ran past Jared, who was standing in the doorway. He wore only his jeans with a towel around his neck.

Alix sat on the edge of the bed, then flopped back onto it, her arms spread wide. "I am *exhausted.*"

Too bad Tyler didn't feel the same way. Jared nabbed him as he ran out of the room, then tossed him onto the bed beside Alix. When Jared stretched out on the other side of them, Tyler immediately began yelling, "Press! Press!"

Jared groaned. "He only knows about six words, so why does that have to be one of them?"

"What does it mean? Is it someone's name?"

“I should be so lucky,” Jared said as he began to stack pillows on top of each other then lay down on them.

Alix watched as Jared stretched out on the pillows so his body was a foot above the bed. With a howl of laughter, Tyler flopped across Jared’s chest and stiffened his sturdy little body. Jared began to bench press the boy. The pillows were for Jared’s arms to go down by his ribs.

“I think I’ll go make dinner,” Alix said, laughing as she got up and left the room.

When Jared and Tyler got to the kitchen, with Jared saying his arms were aching, Alix was stirring shrimp and rice in one of Dilys’s big skillets. Jared fastened Tyler into a sturdy wooden high chair that he said had been made by his great-grandfather, and began to feed the child cheese and crackers.

Alix was eager to tell Jared what Caleb had told her about Valentina’s journal. At the end, just as the rain stopped and the sun started to come out, Caleb had told her where it was probably hidden. A minute later, Caleb had glanced toward the attic window and said he had to leave.

“Are you a vampire and the sun makes you sparkle?” she’d asked, teasing.

“Something like that.” After Caleb left, the attic no longer seemed magical. It was just big and full of too many boxes filled with too many secrets. For a moment Alix sat on the little couch wishing the candlelight and music would return. The ladies at the party had looked so beautiful in their long dresses.

Not long after, hunger drove Alix downstairs. As she ate at the kitchen table, she thought of all she'd seen and heard. And as the hours went by, the idea that it had all been real faded. She began to remember the experience as though it were a movie she'd seen.

"Caleb said Valentina kept a journal," Alix said to Jared as she stirred the rice.

"Did she?" Jared asked but didn't seem interested. "Pass me that box, will you?"

Alix handed him the water crackers. Jealousy was one thing, but this was information that needed to be told, so she kept on. "Caleb said he believes Valentina's journal was hidden in an oven in the basement of the washhouse where she used to make her soap. He said that building burned down when the house did."

"I never heard of any outbuildings there."

Alix spooned the shrimp and rice onto a plate. "Caleb said that Parthenia drew a map of the property that shows where the washhouse was. That's what I was trying to find in those boxes I lugged downstairs to the living room. If I can find Parthenia's map maybe we could excavate the journal and the mystery of Valentina would be solved. But it's going to take weeks to go through all that material in those boxes. I was thinking that maybe you could help me."

"Could you watch Tyler a sec and make sure he doesn't leap out of that chair?"

"Sure," Alix said as Jared got up. "Where are you going?"

But he didn't answer. Instead, he returned with his laptop and opened it. "Maybe Parthenia drew a map to show the people in Warbrooke and maybe it's in the letters Jilly has."

"What a good idea," Alix said, smiling at even the prospect of being relieved of having to go through all those old boxes.

Jared sent an email to Ken to ask Jilly about a map. He closed the computer and looked at Alix. "So now maybe we can stop talking about Caleb for a while?"

"Sure," Alix said, but she turned away to hide her frown.

After dinner, Tyler's mother called and asked if they would please, please keep Tyler overnight. "It's fine with me," Jared said, "but let me ask Alix." He told her of the request and Alix readily agreed. She was becoming attached to the happy little boy.

"I had no idea," Alix said, looking out at the water. They'd put Tyler down for the night in a crib that Jared took out of a closet. Every door and window of the house was open so if he made a sound they could hear him. She was leaning against an old wooden rowboat, one of three turned upside down in the sandy backyard. Jared's head was in her lap and she was stroking his hair. "I don't think I've ever been so tired in my life," she said.

"Good tired or bad?" he asked.

"Very, very good." She looked at the back of the house and again marveled at the beauty of a Jared Montgomery design. "How did it happen that you were given the remodel of this house to design? You were so young."

Jared kept his eyes closed as he smiled in memory. "For years my father complained about our old house falling apart, but he wasn't sure what to do about it. Add onto the side? Or go up a floor? Hire an architect? He liked that idea the least because it would cost too much."

"But he had you."

"I don't know what made him say it, but one day he turned to me and said, 'Seven, why don't you save me a truckload of money and *you* design the addition?' He was only joking, but I took him seriously."

"How old were you?"

"Eleven," he said as he looked up at Alix.

She knew what his eyes were saying. It was the year before his father died. "What did you do?" she asked softly.

"I became obsessed with the idea. Didn't sleep for three days. I didn't know how to draw or measure, nothing — but I started making sketches."

"It was all there inside your brain."

"I guess it was. Mom knew I wasn't sleeping and that I was hardly eating, but she didn't tell on me to Dad. Instead, on the fourth day she made our favorite dinner of scallops and grilled corn on the cob, then she told me to show Dad what I'd drawn."

"Were you nervous?" She couldn't help thinking of how she'd felt when she'd first shown him her chapel model: thrilled but also scared.

"Very nervous. I knew I was doing an adult thing and I don't know what I would have done if he'd laughed at my primitive drawings."

"But he didn't."

"No. Dad thought they were great and he said that next year we'd start building it. But . . ." Jared shrugged.

Neither of them had to say what they were thinking, that Jared's father had died and the house wasn't remodeled until years later when Ken showed up.

When she looked back at him, his eyes seemed to bore into hers with that blaze of blue fire, but this time it wasn't lust that she was seeing. "What?" she asked, not understanding exactly what he was trying to tell her.

"It's just that sometimes things are right and you know it. This old house was little more than a shack but I could see it as it was in the future. All I did was draw what I could see. Does that make sense?"

"Perfect sense," she said, but he seemed to be leading somewhere else, and she didn't know where.

He closed his eyes. "I've had a lot of girlfriends," he said softly.

Alix drew in her breath. Was this story really about them? About *her*?

When he looked at her, his eyes were so intense that the hair on the back of her neck stood up. "Sometimes you just *know.* You know about buildings and you know about people."

"Yes, you do," Alix whispered.

She didn't know what would have happened next if Tyler hadn't let out a scream.

Jared was on his feet and running inside, Alix right behind him. In the bedroom, she stood back as Jared picked up the boy and soothed him.

"Bad dreams, little man?"

Tyler pushed back from Jared, looked at him as though he'd never seen him before, then fell to the side. He wanted Alix to hold him.

"Ah, the comfort of women," Jared said. "I understand perfectly. There's a big rocker in the living room. He's not too heavy for you?"

"Not at all," Alix said, loving the way the heavy child clung to her.

When she and Tyler were settled in the chair, Jared stepped back and looked at them snuggled together. "Can I take it that you want kids?"

Alix's first thought was to sidestep that question, to make a joke about it. Usually men asked something like that in an attempt to trap a woman. If she said she wanted children someday, he took it to mean that she was after him. But Jared wasn't like the boys she'd dated. He was a *man,* one who didn't run from responsibility, wasn't afraid of being an adult. She took a breath. "Once I have my license and a job, I think I would like to jump on the baby wagon."

He didn't say anything but she saw his smile as he turned away.

It was over an hour before they got Tyler back to sleep. Jared took him from her and carried him back to bed. It wasn't really late and Alix had visions of glasses of wine and lovemaking, but the light on her cell was flashing. It was her dad and she read his message as Jared came back into the room. "Dad says Jilly sent you a copy of the map."

"Did she?" Jared said. "In the morning I'll . . ." He trailed off as he looked at Alix's face. She wanted to see it right away. "Okay, where's my laptop?"

Alix already had it in her hand. It took a while to print out a copy of the map. Dilys had a new printer and they couldn't find the disk for it, which meant that they had to download the driver — and of course the first two times they tried it didn't work. Alix had already learned that she was much better at computers than Jared was, and she was the one who found the upgrade that made it work. By the time they were able to print out the map, they'd drunk two glasses of wine each, it was nearly midnight, and they were yawning.

Jared held up the piece of paper. "All that for this." It was just a simple sketch, drawn with a quill pen by a young woman writing home to her family. It vaguely showed the whereabouts of the North Shore house and three outbuildings. "Why didn't she get a cartographer to do the coordinates? There were certainly enough men on Nantucket at that time who could have made a proper map. Any first mate worth his salt could have charted it for her. How's anyone supposed to find anything with this thing?"

Alix took it out of his hand and put it on the table. "Parthenia drew it for her family. She didn't think that someone was going to need it two hundred years in the future. Come on, let's go to bed. You can complain about women and maps all day tomorrow when we go to the site and try to find where the washhouse was."

"Maybe we should wait on that, and I'm not complaining. I'm —"

She stood on tiptoe to kiss him to make him stop doing what he said he wasn't doing, then led him into the bedroom. It took only seconds for Jared to strip down to his underwear and for Alix to pull on one of his big T-shirts. She didn't have any of her own clothes and she was too tired to think of rummaging through Dilys's closet.

"Now, where were we?" Alix began as she started to kiss him, but she drew back and looked at him. There was no blue fire in his eyes. In fact, it was more like a hazy bluish-gray fog. But he was putting his arm around her as though he was about to make love to her. Gently, Alix pushed him back down on the bed, tucked the quilt around him, and kissed his forehead.

"Thank you," he whispered and was asleep instantly. Before Alix fell asleep she couldn't help but think that this snuggling was even more romantic, more intimate, than all their lovemaking.

# Chapter Twenty-Three

Alix awoke when a small hand hit her in the mouth. At first she didn't remember where she was. As the sleep cleared from her mind, she saw that sometime during the night Tyler had escaped the confines of his crib and climbed into bed with them. He was in the middle of the two adults, sideways, so his body was over both of them. Jared was on his side, facing Alix, his arms out, encasing both her and the child, as though he were protecting them.

Smiling, Alix carefully extricated herself, then stood for a moment looking at them. They looked so sweet together that she picked up her phone and snapped a photo. She made her way to the kitchen, pulled one of Dilys's cookbooks off a shelf, found a recipe for biscuits, and set about making them.

She patted out the fluffy dough. Even through her pleasant thoughts about where she was and who she was with, she couldn't help feeling frustrated. She had so much to tell Jared about what Caleb had told her and what she'd seen, but she couldn't seem to find a time. But then Jared wasn't making it easy for her. Every time she mentioned Caleb, it was as though a shutter closed on Jared. His expression became distant, as though he was refusing to listen to what she had to say.

But she knew it was important. If the family considered Valentina's disappearance significant enough that the house was willed to an off-islander for a whole year, then what Alix knew *needed* to be told.

And besides, Alix had a lot of questions she'd like to have answered. Number one was, Who was Caleb? Why hadn't she been introduced to him? He looked enough like Jared that he was obviously a close relation, but she'd not heard him mentioned. Did he live on the island?

The *big* question was, Why hadn't Caleb told his family what he knew? Jared hadn't been told that Valentina kept a journal and that Caleb might know where it was hidden. Nor did Jared know about Parthenia's map. Why had Caleb told all this to Alix, an outsider? Was there some family feud? But if that were true, Caleb wouldn't have felt free to wander about Kingsley House. Or did he show up because he'd known Jared was away?

If Alix hadn't been so absorbed in the old

documents the morning after she met Caleb, she would have called Lexie and found out more of the particulars. As it was, the first chance Alix got, she was going to bombard Jared with every question running through her mind. She needed answers!

By the time the biscuits were done, Alix had strengthened her resolve to force Jared to answer her questions. The will said that Alix was to look for Valentina and doing that had to include Caleb.

As she removed the biscuits from the oven, she looked up to see Jared, shirtless, with a sleepy Tyler snuggled against him. It was a truly beautiful sight.

"The smell woke us," Jared said. "At first I thought I'd died and gone to heaven."

At the sight of the two of them, Alix's steely resolve left her. Feeding a child was more important than Caleb and his mysteries. "Think Tyler eats bacon and eggs?"

Jared was putting the boy into the high chair. "From the heft of what he put in his diaper yesterday, I think he eats whole roast rhinos for breakfast." He took a biscuit off the sheet, tossed it from hand to hand to cool it, broke it apart, buttered it, and gave it to Tyler. After the first bite the boy laughed and banged his heels in appreciation.

"That's the way I feel too," Jared said as he sat down and took another hot biscuit. "I was thinking," he said as he slathered it in Dilys's homemade strawberry jam, "that you and I ought to drive up to Warbrooke and spend a few days there. We could even go before Izzy's wedding. We need to take a look at that old Montgomery house and get its floor plan on paper. I could send some of the kids from the office up there, but . . ."

What he was saying sounded so wonderful — especially his frequent use of "we" — that Caleb and Valentina seemed to fly out of Alix's mind. "But you'd like to get to know your new relatives."

"I would. Mike Taggert and I hit it off, and I told you that his twin brother, Kane, is married to Cale Anderson."

"Don't tell Mom, but I love her books."

"Okay, but only if you promise not to tell Lexie I met her. She'd be hysterical. One time Lex made a trip to Hyannis just to get Cale's latest novel on the day it came out."

"What's she like in person?"

"Smart, funny, perceptive. She's little and her husband is the size of a bear. All the Taggerts are big, heavy men while the Montgomerys are like me."

"Tall, lanky, and beautiful?"

Jared laughed. "You didn't think that yesterday when I was covered in the offerings of young Tyler here."

"*Especially* then. In fact, I don't think I've ever seen a more beautiful sight."

"Yeah?" That blue fire returned to his eyes

— but then Tyler laughed and threw a chunk of buttered biscuit, hitting Jared on the nose. "Talk about a mood killer!"

Alix walked over and kissed Jared long and lingeringly. "It didn't kill *my* mood."

Jared looked at Tyler and shook his head. "You're going to learn that any man who says he understands women is a liar." He looked back at Alix. "You ready to go find Valentina's journal?"

Alix's smile was deep. He *had* been thinking about Caleb. "Give me about ten minutes. I thought we'd take a whole package of diapers. Think it'll be enough?"

"Are you kidding? Those packs are so big that if I run my truck into the sea it'll float."

"True, but will it be enough for Tyler?"

They looked at him, at the egg, milk, jam, and buttered biscuit on his face, in his hair, and down the front of him.

"We'll take the second pack just to be safe," he said.

"I'm on it and I'll get some towels too."

"Great idea," Jared said as he pulled the child out of the chair and headed for the kitchen sink. "Can you get him a clean shirt?" he called to Alix.

But she was ahead of him and handed him one before he finished speaking.

"Thanks, Mom," he said as he kissed her forehead.

Alix went away smiling.

■ ■ ■ ■

It took longer to get all the things needed for Tyler into the truck than it did to drive to the site. They decided that figuring out how to strap in the car seat required a degree in engineering.

"I used to think my education was worth something," Alix said as she stood on the ground and leaned across the truck seat to hold the safety belt for Jared. Tyler was trying to start the engine.

"There were too many long-legged girls in school for me to think mine mattered."

"Give me a break!" Alix said, groaning. "Tyler, sweetie, don't eat that."

Jared pulled the boy away from the gas pedal, put him in the car seat, and fastened it. "Everybody ready?" he asked as Alix got in and shut the door.

"All of us long-legged creatures are ready to go. Right, Tyler?"

He laughed, kicked his stubby little legs, and said, "Go! Go!"

"Aye, aye, Captain," Jared said and pulled out of the driveway.

When they got to the North Shore, Twig's men were there working. Right away, two of them gathered a stack of scrap wood, put it in the shade, and Tyler ran to it.

Alix hadn't seen the chapel for a while and

she stood there transfixed. To see her own design come to life was almost more than she could bear. The structure wasn't yet complete, but enough of the chapel was done that she could envision the finished product. The exterior, the windows, the doors, the steeple, were all just as she'd seen them in her mind.

"Like it?" Jared asked from behind her.

"Very much."

He put his hands on her shoulders and squeezed. As a fellow architect, he knew how she felt.

"Okay," he said, "enough daydreaming. Let's get to work." He was holding Parthenia's map. "Not that anyone could find anything from this thing, but —"

"What's that?" Alix pointed to a rectangle drawn beside the washhouse. Last night she'd been too sleepy to do more than look at the drawing.

"It says SOAP. I guess Valentina stored her soap there."

Alix took the sketch, pointed the front of the house toward the sea, then looked to her right where the washhouse was drawn. There was no distance given, so it could be fifty feet or a hundred yards, as the property was quite large.

The only thing near the washhouse was a funny little icon of two round circles with a rectangle connecting them with the word SOAP written beside it.

Alix and Jared looked at each other, having no idea what the symbol meant, but it was west of the house so they walked that way. The centuries had covered the ground with fierce little bushes and it was slow moving through them.

A short distance from the house, Alix saw a chest-high rock and another near it. There were some boulders on the island, left over from some long-ago glacier, and these two were only about six feet apart.

"They've been flattened here," Alix said, running her hand across the top of the first rock. Someone had chiseled out a place on the top surface and a matching one was on the other rock. It was subtle, not something a person would notice, but a tabletop could be held in the chiseled places.

Jared looked at the map. "If this was a table —"

"Or open shelves to hold the drying soap molds," Alix said.

"Right. Then the washhouse was . . ." He stepped over about three feet. "Here." Reaching down, he scraped out a stone from the sandy soil. It was a round rock, the kind used in a fireplace, and under it was a very old piece of rusty metal. It looked to be the handle of a big washtub.

Alix smiled. "Looks like Parthenia *did* draw a good map."

Jared gave a one-sided grin.

"Petticoat Row rules again!"

Jared laughed. "Stop bragging and let's go get some shovels. This has to be dug out by hand."

Twig's men stopped work on the chapel to help find the washhouse. Over the years they'd found many artifacts — coins, ivory, buttons — in the old houses they'd remodeled, but no matter how many things they discovered, each one was of interest.

It didn't take much digging to see that a building had once been on the site. There were a few pieces of charred timbers, broken china, more scrap metal. After about an hour, they had the stone of the basement outlined. They could see where the foundation of the big fireplace had been and started digging there.

The men took turns, filling the bucket, then the wheelbarrow. Alix stayed under a tree with Tyler, trying to keep him occupied so he wouldn't get in the way. At first she'd tried to keep him clean but soon found out that wasn't possible. They broke for lunch and started again an hour later. It was slow going, as the old stones needed the dirt to hold them in place. Three times they had to stop to construct forms to fortify the stones. Two trips were made to Island Lumber to buy reinforcing materials.

It was late afternoon when Jared called to Alix. "I think we have something."

She picked up Tyler and went to what was now an impressively large hole. Jared and Dennis, the tile setter, were at the bottom. Some stones had fallen out of the thick walls and the men were standing in rubble. Jared stepped back to expose what they'd uncovered. Just behind him, set deep into the stone, was a rusty iron door. All the men were standing over the hole, looking down, and watching. Dave, the cabinetmaker, passed down a crowbar to Jared. After a look at Alix, he pried the door open.

She held her breath as he reached inside. Slowly, he pulled out a corroded metal box, the kind used for holding tea.

He started to open the box, but then held it up to Alix. Bending, she took it, and waited until Jared was out of the hole and beside her. It took several minutes and a putty knife to loosen the lid. Even then Alix had to stick her fingertips under the rim and pull hard before the old box opened. Centuries were holding it together.

When the top came up, she took a breath, glanced at Jared, then back down at the box. With a creak, the lid moved back on its hinges.

Inside was a leatherbound book. Considering where it had been for the last two hundred years, it was in good condition. The cover was a little moldy but the pages hadn't crumbled. But then it had been protected by the stone enclosure and the box.

Alix reached inside as though she meant to take out the journal, but then she looked at Jared. Their eyes met and they seemed to speak in silence to each other. There were other people who deserved a first look at this book.

With a smile, she nodded at him, and Jared closed the lid and took the box from her.

"I think we should save this for your . . . relative, Caleb." She was teasing because she had yet to find out who the mysterious Caleb was. "He's the one who told me how to find the journal, so I think he should see it first."

"Hey, Jared," Dave said, "isn't Caleb the ghost in your house?" He was grinning. "Didn't he cause a lot of people to drown and that's why your family's never used the name again?"

Jared gave Dave a look to shut up but that didn't quell him in the least. All the men were looking at them, waiting for Jared's answer.

He looked back at Alix, whose face had drained of color. *She knew!* "It's time we got Tyler home," he said. "Ready to go?"

All Alix could do was nod.

Tyler, who'd missed his nap, seemed to know his day's adventure was about to be over, and he started running around like he'd drunk two cups of espresso. Jimmy headed him off, Eric blocked him, and Joel, who had twins, picked up the boy and handed him to

Jared. Tyler acted like he was being imprisoned and wrestled against Jared, but he held the child tightly as he took Alix's hand and led her to the truck.

He opened the door, then nudged her inside. As soon as she was seated, Jared reached across her to strap Tyler into his car seat, then closed the door and walked to the other side. By the time he got into the driver's seat, the boy had twisted around to face Alix and was sound asleep. She was staring straight ahead, holding on to the boy's hand as though he were a life preserver and they were alone at sea.

Jared glanced at her but Alix didn't look away from the windshield. He started the engine.

"Did I . . . ? Is he . . . ?" Alix's voice was barely a whisper.

Jared thought about going into a long-winded explanation, something that would calm her down. But he knew that in the end the answer would be the same. "Yes."

Alix took a deep breath, trying to grasp all of it. When Tyler moved in his sleep, she leaned over to put her cheek against his sun-warmed hair. "You told me about him, didn't you?"

"Yes, I did."

"But I thought you meant a . . . a . . ."

"Foggy light at the top of the stairs?" he said.

Colorful visions ran through Alix's mind. Dancing, laughing. What she saw, heard, even smelled. "I think maybe I really did see a scene from Parthenia's wedding. Oh!" She looked at him. "Parthenia looks just like Jilly Taggert. I was upside down when I met her and I didn't realize it then. And my father looks like her husband, John Kendricks, which probably means that —" Her voice was rising.

Jared reached across the seat to take her hand and squeeze it. "It's okay. Everything will be all right. I'm sorry you got pulled into this. Usually, only we Kingsleys can see him, and then only a few of us can. No off-islander has ever . . ." He trailed off.

"Just me," she said. "An outsider. What is that term I heard? Something about arriving on a beach?"

"A washashore."

"That's me. I just floated into everything."

Jared was still holding her hand as he pulled into the driveway. He shut off the truck, then turned to look at her. He knew he should start at the beginning and tell her about his grandfather from the shipwreck forward. But he didn't. She didn't need anything heavy right now. He looked from her to Tyler. "You two look good together. Still think you want kids of your own?"

"What does that have to do with — ?"

Bending across the long seat, Jared kissed

her sweetly on the mouth. "Did Granddad scare you?"

"No. Not at the time. We danced and flirted outrageously. I didn't mean to, but he was, well, rather persuasive."

"I'm jealous and my rival is a two-hundred-year-old ghost. How do I compete with that?"

"He's not really a rival!" Alix said. "I like you better than —" She stopped because Jared's eyes were dancing with merriment. He was teasing her! Alix gave him a look of disgust. "You're a lot like him, you know that?"

"So I've been told." His face got serious. "Alix, what I know is that right now you have a choice. You can go the horror movie way and be scared out of your mind. You can even leave Nantucket forever if you want to. Or you can take my haunted house with its meddling old ghost in stride and I'll help you deal with it. I can answer any questions you have, tell you any stories you want to hear. Whatever information I know, I'll share with you."

With the engine no longer running, Tyler began to wake up. Jared took him out of the seat and got out of the truck. But he stood there, holding the child, looking at her, waiting for her decision.

Alix opened her mouth to ask questions, but there were too many of them. Where to start? Finally, she said, "Do *you* want children?"

Jared gave her a smile of such complete and total happiness — and joyous relief — that Alix's bones seemed to start melting.

"Yeah," he said. "At least three of them." His eyes were boring into hers. "But Granddad says I'm so late getting started that no woman will have me."

The last part of that sentence was so absurd she didn't consider it. "This is *that* grandfather?"

"Same one you spent the day dancing with," Jared said. "Why don't you go make us some drinks while I take Tyler home? And break out the good rum that Dilys hides in the back of the cabinet over the fridge." He turned away, but then looked back. "Alix, you're not a washashore. I don't understand it, but I've never met anyone who belonged to Nantucket more than you do. You see the Kingsley ghost, guzzle rum like a whaler, and you move about my old house like you were born there."

His words were making her calm down and she gave a small smile. "I belong here even if I'm not actually a Kingsley?"

"Oh, well," he said. "The last name's easy enough to change in a woman. See you in a few minutes."

Alix sat back in the truck. What did that mean? Change a woman's name? She knew but she couldn't possibly be right.

# Chapter Twenty-Four

Alix sat at the breakfast table watching Jared at the stove. Last night she'd been too tired and too overwhelmed to think clearly. He'd grilled fish and made a salad while she took a shower. When they'd returned from the construction site there'd been a stack of clean clothes and a bag of toiletries for Alix on the bed. A note said:

> I hope these are all right. Ken helped me choose them. Jilly

Even the evidence of her father with someone hadn't interested her. As soon as Alix had eaten, she went to bed. Between the exhaustion from Tyler, the excitement of finding the journal, and the shock of hearing that she'd been dancing with a ghost, she slept heavily.

When she awoke, Jared was already up and dressed and in the kitchen making breakfast. The wonderful aroma of coffee filled the house. In the middle of the table, on a folded dish towel, was the box with the unopened journal inside. But what Alix had found out about Caleb had overridden her interest in the book. Jared kissed her good morning, held her for a long time, and said they could stay there all day if she wanted to. He again said that he'd answer every question she could come up with.

"Can Dilys? See him, I mean?" Alix asked, but then she put her fingertips to her temples. "No, Dilys was asking me about Caleb, so she can't . . . But then everyone seems to have been in on this secret so maybe she can." She looked at Jared as he poured batter from a carton onto a grill. "Can Lexie see him?"

"I'm certain Dilys can't, but I don't know about Lexie. She keeps things to herself. All of the first-born men in each generation have been able to see and speak to him. The men with numbers for nicknames, that is."

She thought about that continuity and the longevity of the man she'd danced with. "I assume you know that in most families the numbers at the end of a name are dropped when someone dies."

"True," Jared said as he turned a pancake. "Which means that by off-island standards I'd be back to number one since none of the others are alive. But Granddad needed help distinguishing one from another so we kept the numbers."

"I see," she said, looking at the back of him, trying to take it all in. "Do you think my mother knows about him?"

"I have no idea, but she and Aunt Addy were awfully chummy, so my guess is yes."

Alix nodded. "What happened to the man Valentina married?"

"He . . . I don't think you want to know."

"Go ahead and tell me. I can take it."

"Obed beat Caleb's son severely because the boy was talking to someone Obed couldn't see."

"Was he talking to his father? To Caleb?"

"Yes, he was, and that night Obed died. It's been passed down in my family that the expression of terror on his face was so horrible that he could only have died of fright."

Alix drew in her breath. "So Caleb can do bad things."

"I don't think that's correct. Granddad said it was guilt that killed Obed. The man woke up, saw Caleb standing there, and was so afraid of what might happen that he died instantly. There wasn't even time for Granddad to ask him what happened to Valentina."

Alix looked down at the table. "Has he danced with many people?"

Jared gave a little laugh. "As far as I know, that's the only time my grandfather has danced with anyone."

Alix heard the love in Jared's voice at the word "grandfather." She wondered what it was like to grow up with a ghost for a relative. But right now she wasn't ready to nonchalantly discuss such things. She glanced at the metal box. "What are we going to do with Valentina's journal? We can't very well hand it over to a ghost. Well, maybe we could. But . . ." She looked at him for help.

"I think there's only one thing we can do with it," Jared said, his face absolutely serious.

At first she didn't know what he meant, then she saw the sparkle in his eyes. Her face was just as serious as his. "We must use it to protect the floors."

Jared grinned. "My thoughts exactly. Do you think that if we give Victoria *this* journal, we could prevent her from tearing up Kingsley House looking for Aunt Addy's diaries?"

"I don't know. Sometimes Mom is easy to persuade and sometimes she's impossible. She might insist on writing Aunt Addy's story first."

"There goes the wallpaper," Jared muttered as he put a stack of pancakes in front of Alix.

"These look good. I was beginning to think you only knew how to fry fish."

"And you'd be right. I found this carton in the fridge and told myself I *could* do it. How much harder could pancakes be than a skyscraper?"

Alix gave her first smile of the day — a small one — as she took a bite. "These are quite good."

"Thank you," he said, putting another plate on the table and sitting down. He motioned with his fork to the box. "What *are* we going to do with this thing?"

"Give it to Mom on the condition that she swear a blood oath not to dismantle anything in the house looking for Aunt Addy's journals?" Alix's head came up. "Maybe Caleb knows where —"

"Don't even say it. Of course he knows where they are. I've asked him a thousand times. Maybe you could ask him —" He broke off as Alix's face seemed to lose color. "Too soon?"

"Oh, yes," she said. "Much too soon. Too bad Mom can't see him. I'm sure he'd tell *her.*"

"Probably. He likes pretty women."

"It's more than that. Mom is a ringer for Valentina."

Jared paused with the fork on the way to his mouth. "What?"

"I told you all of this," Alix said. "Or as much as I could before you changed the subject. I saw Parthenia's wedding. She looks like Jilly and the man she married looks like my dad. It's interesting that he was named John Kendricks and now he's a Kenneth. He —"

Reaching across the table, Jared put his hand over hers. "What about Valentina and

Victoria?" His eyes were intense.

"My mother *was* Valentina. I saw her at the wedding and Caleb told me how they met. It was quite funny. He —" When Jared abruptly stood up, she could see that he wasn't listening. "What's wrong?"

He turned away so Alix couldn't see that he was shaking in fear. He could clearly hear what he'd said to his grandfather just before Alix arrived. He even remembered his tone of sarcasm mixed with anger.

"You're waiting for the return — or the reincarnation, whatever — of the woman you love, your precious Valentina. And you've always been faithful to her. I've heard it all before. Heard it all my life. You'll know her when you see her, then you two will go off into the sunset together. Which means that either she dies or you come back to life."

"Jared, are you okay?"

He took a breath and turned back to her. Above all else, he didn't want Alix to figure out what he was thinking. He tried to look cheerful. "I hate to do this but I have to go back to the house for an hour or so. For work. Want to go with me?"

"Not yet," she said.

"I can't leave you alone. I'll call Lexie and —"

"No!" Alix said. "I'm not an invalid and I'm not going to imagine that I'm seeing ghosts everywhere." She paused. "There aren't any in this house, are there? And can Caleb . . . ?"

"There are no ghosts here and he can't leave Kingsley House."

"I'll be fine, really. Jilly put my eReader in with the clothes and I saw that she and Dad have filled it with Cale Anderson books. I'll be fine. Actually, I could stand some time alone."

"Sure?" he asked.

"Absolutely sure." She looked at him. "Did you take any photos of that house in Maine?"

Jared laughed in relief. "You *are* my girl! There are a couple hundred of them in the photo file on my computer under Warbrooke, and I made a rudimentary floor plan. Go through all of it so you can tell me your ideas."

"If you give me access to your computer, I can't guarantee that I won't snoop around in your most private files."

"Snoop all you want. The computer with all the juice on it is in New York."

Alix laughed. "Okay, go do whatever you're not telling me about. I'll be fine. Any drawing paper around here?"

"In the upstairs bedroom closet is a box of my old supplies."

"That paper is probably as old as Valentina's

journal."

Jared put his hand to his heart. "You crush me. And when I get back, I'll show you how old I am."

"I can't wait," she said sincerely.

Alix would have liked for their kiss goodbye to be longer, but she could tell that something was bothering him and he wanted to leave and take care of it. A few days ago she would have pestered him to tell her where he was going and why. But not now. For the time being, her curiosity was sated and all she wanted to do was focus on a design project. No more ghosts! Or dancing with men who didn't exist. Or supernatural glimpses of the past.

She needed peace and quiet and to lose herself in a project.

# Chapter Twenty-Five

At Kingsley House Jared threw the back door open so hard that the old glass rattled. Usually, he treated the house with the respect it deserved, but not today. He slammed the door just as hard.

He glared at the doorway, hoping to see his grandfather, but he wasn't there. Jared went up the back stairs to the attic, two at a time. He pulled the string on the light so hard it came off in his hand. Angrily, he tossed it away.

"Come out!" he demanded, and turned full circle, but Caleb wasn't there. "Are Valentina and Victoria the same person? I know you can hear me so you can damned well answer."

"I am here," Caleb said softly from behind him.

When Jared turned, he gasped, for his ghostly grandfather looked almost solid. No wonder Alix thought he was real! Jared almost reached out to touch him, but didn't. He just stood there, glowering and waiting for him to answer.

"Yes, Valentina and Victoria are the same spirit."

Anger raged through Jared so strongly that he thought his head might explode. "You are going to leave the earth! Are you planning to take Victoria *with* you?"

"I don't know," Caleb said in a quiet, calm voice. Only his eyes betrayed his worry.

"You can't do that to Alix — or to Victoria," Jared shouted. "She deserves *life.*"

"It's not up to me," Caleb said, raising his voice. "Do you think I want to be a . . . a . . ."

"Go ahead and say it. You're a ghost!"

"Yes, I am," Caleb said and his own anger started rising. "Do you think I *chose* to stay in this house for two hundred years and see people I love die? I see them as babies, watch them grow, laugh with them, cry with them, but always — always and always — I have to stand back and watch them *die.* It happens over and over, and no matter how many times I see it, the grief is the same. Each time it hurts just as much."

Jared didn't relent in his anger, but when he spoke he wasn't shouting. "And now you're going to leave the earth and take Victoria with you. All because you love her. Is that love to you?"

"Is that what you think of me?"

"I don't know what to think anymore.

Please don't do this. If you leave, you can*not* take her with you!"

Caleb tried to calm himself. "I told you that it's not up to me. All I know for sure is that the same people who were involved when I was last on this earth are assembling again. And I know that on the twenty-third of June I will depart this place. Where I go I don't know." Caleb's body seemed to be fading. "I must leave you now. I am tired."

"Since when do you get tired?" Jared shot at him.

"The closer I get to the time, the stronger and the weaker I get."

"That makes no sense."

"None of this half life of mine makes sense." He looked at his grandson with eyes that showed his misery. "Please believe me when I tell you that I don't know what is going to happen. If it is at all possible, I will leave alone and I will *not* take Valentina with me."

"She is *Victoria,* she lives in *this* century, and she has people here — on earth — who love her very much." Jared was too upset to think clearly and his grandfather was fading quickly. "Can Victoria see you?"

For a moment he was brighter, less transparent. "If I allowed it, she could. But I've never wanted her to love half a man." He began to grow dimmer. "Don't let Alix get away. Don't be the fool that I was. If I'd stayed with Valentina none of this would have happened, but I wanted one more voyage. I thought I needed to be richer than I already was." There were tears in his voice and his eyes. "Learn from me. And talk to Parthenia. Her spirit has always been able to see inside you."

He was gone.

Jared flopped down on the couch, feeling like he was single-handedly trying to stop a freight train.

It was only minutes later that he knew he had to get out of the house. As he needed to breathe, he *had* to leave. The thoughts were so strong that he was sure his grandfather was controlling them. "Stop it!" he growled, and immediately the overwhelming feelings stopped.

He stood up, calming himself, and more fully comprehending what Alix had been through. With these new powers his grandfather had, it was believable that he could show Alix visions of the past.

Jared looked around the attic, at the familiar sight of too much left over by his family, then went down the stairs and out the back door. He thought of returning to Alix, but he had an idea that she was happily buried in the plans for the Montgomery house. How he wished he could join her! But the thought that Victoria might die soon was too strongly in his mind for him to relax, and he didn't want Alix to pick up on his fear.

He walked down the lane toward Main Street. Maybe Lexie or Toby was home. Alix's questions had made him wonder who else in his family could see Caleb. Jared had grown up being told all the rules about his grandfather, but this morning he was questioning them. Maybe if the women had told the men and vice versa, they could have done something long ago. An exorcism?

While Jared couldn't imagine having grown up without his grandfather — especially after his father died and before Ken arrived — at the moment he wished someone had long ago sent the man away.

Jared went to Lexie's house, opened the back door, and called out, but no one answered. They were at work. He turned to leave, but then heard a noise in the back. Maybe one of them was in the greenhouse.

It was Jilly. She'd just dropped a huge flowerpot, it had smashed, and she was trying to pick up the pieces.

"Let me do that," Jared said as he bent and began gathering the pot shards.

Jilly stood up. "I was trying to help but I did this. I should probably quit, but the girls are so busy and I needed something to do."

Jared looked about the greenhouse. He wasn't a gardener but even he could see that the place needed a good cleaning. "How about if I do the heavy lifting and we work together?"

"You must have other things to do," she said. "I'm sure Alix needs you."

"She's working on a remodel plan for that big old house in Warbrooke, and besides, she's glad to be rid of me."

Jilly looked hard at him for a moment and deep into his eyes. Something was bothering him. "How about if we start at this end?"

"Perfect," he answered.

Cleaning the big greenhouse was hard, physical labor. Everything had to be moved, weeds pulled from under the benches, gravel raked. Two of the tables needed repair since they were always wet. Plants needed repotting, which meant dealing with big bags of compost, peat moss, and vermiculite.

Jared needed the labor, so he carried fifty-pound bags, sawed new cedar boards, and hammered them into place. He picked up heavy pots of shrubs and took them outside so Jilly could prune them, then carried them back inside. When the back of his hand was torn by rose thorns, he didn't seem to notice.

It was late afternoon before Jilly could persuade him to stop work and eat something. Besides, there wasn't anything left to do. She suggested they walk back to Kingsley House but Jared said no. The truth was that he didn't even want to go to the guesthouse, so they went inside Lexie's. Jilly looked at him, dirty, sweaty, and with eyes that seemed to be haunted, and said, "Why don't you take a shower while I make us some sandwiches?"

"That sounds good," he said. "Lexie stole a pair of my sweatpants and she has a dozen of my T-shirts."

"I'll find them," Jilly said. "You go get clean."

By the time she had sandwiches made and the clothes he'd tossed out the bathroom door in the washer, Jared appeared at the table. He looked a bit less worried than when she first saw him, but whatever was upsetting him was still there.

"Is it Alix?" she asked, hoping that he wouldn't do that infuriating male thing of making her drag it out of him.

"There's nothing wrong between us," he said as he looked down at his plate.

"Then is it Caleb?" she asked, and when Jared looked at her she drew in her breath. His eyes looked as though something deep inside him — his soul, maybe? — had been mortally wounded. She put her hand over his. "Tell me," she whispered.

"I think maybe Caleb is going to kill Victoria."

Jilly didn't say a word. Long ago she'd learned that the first rule of listening was to do just that: to *listen.*

It took Jared nearly an hour to tell the whole story. He told of his grandfather leaving Valentina behind for one last voyage, then finding out that she'd married his snake of a cousin, a man who'd practically stalked her. "When Caleb heard that she'd given birth to his son, he traded ships with his brother and led them into a storm with the sails up. The crew was mostly Nantucketers and they all went down," Jared said. "For years after that, it was a bad time to be a Kingsley on this island."

"But Caleb came back," Jilly said.

"Yes, he did."

"Did Valentina ever see the ghost of the man she loved?"

"No. When he first showed up at Kingsley House, it was six years after his ship went down. By that time Valentina was gone and Obed had remarried. But Granddad's son was there and he could see and talk to his father."

"Was the boy's stepmother nice to Caleb's son?"

"Yes, she was. She had no children of her own so young Jared was greatly loved by her."

"And the snaky cousin?"

"Died young," Jared said quickly, then gave a look that said he didn't want to talk about that. He quickly brushed over the next two hundred years to get to Alix and what she'd seen — and what Caleb had told him about at last leaving the earth.

"But he must not take Victoria with him," Jared said, his eyes showing his fear. "She is so *alive.* She takes care of people and was such good company for Aunt Addy. They used to walk into town and have meals together and talk about how Victoria could tell the stories she'd read in the journals. Aunt Addy was quiet and hardworking, while Victoria holds court, like some queen of old. She draws people to her. They were perfect for each other."

Jared looked at Jilly. "Granddad talks about people resembling each other and reincarnation, and that he *knows* he's going to leave the earth on Izzy's wedding day. But if he does really love Victoria, he won't take her away with him. If Alix . . ."

"If Alix what?" Jilly asked.

"If I had to leave the earth, I wouldn't be selfish enough to take her with me. I wouldn't think that my happiness was more important than her *life.*"

"What does Caleb want to do?"

"He says he has no choice in the matter. He didn't choose to be a ghost and he isn't going to be able to choose what happens when he leaves." He looked at Jilly as though asking for her advice.

"I think you need to keep Victoria away from here until after the wedding," Jilly said.

"I agree," Jared said, "and I believe I've done it." He told her about Aunt Addy's journals that Victoria wanted but couldn't find. "As long as she thinks staying away from here will get her access to the precious Kingsley journals, she won't come near Nantucket."

"Good," Jilly said.

Neither of them said the obvious: that death could find you anywhere.

# Chapter Twenty-Six

It was nearly six when Jared and Jilly left Lexie's house. Neither she nor Toby had yet returned from work. Jared had changed back into his own clothes and he was feeling better after having talked to Jilly. Now he wanted to see Alix. Maybe he could clear his mind enough to think about a design project.

"Mind if I walk back to the house with you?" Jilly asked. "Ken will be home soon and I promised to make dinner."

"You two seem to have hit it off," Jared said.

"Very well," she said, smiling.

"I'm sorry for dumping so much on you today. You must think —" He stopped talking as he looked out onto Kingsley Lane. It was usually a quiet little street. The only busy house was Sea Haven Inn and parking for it was entered through another street.

But now Kingsley Lane was anything but quiet. Delivery trucks were bumper to bumper and side by side. They had to drive over curbs to be able to pass one another.

The signs on the trucks were of florists, caterers, a seafood shop, a wine merchant.

The deliveries could mean only one thing. Victoria had arrived!

In a state of shock, Jared just stood there and looked at all the chaos. He had no idea how she had managed to get all these places to deliver to a private residence. In between the trucks were half a dozen cars with male drivers. Two kids on bicycles had baskets full of flower arrangements.

"Hey!" one of the boys on a bike yelled at Jared. "You know where Kingsley House is?"

Jared was frowning too hard to answer.

"It's number twenty-three," Jilly answered and pointed. "The big white house."

"Thanks," the boy said as he got back on his bike and rode away.

Jilly looked up at Jared. "Is someone having a party?"

"Yes and no," Jared said. "Only Victoria arriving could cause this much commotion."

Wide-eyed, Jilly looked at the long line of vehicles. In the distance there were two men angrily shouting at each other. She looked at Jared, who was standing in place, staring at the trucks and seeming to be immobile. "Will there be a fight?"

"Probably," Jared said. "There usually is around Victoria." He turned to her. "Why don't you go through that fence to the back and walk to the guesthouse that way? Let me deal with Victoria first."

"Good luck," Jilly said as she crossed the street.

Jared stood there for a moment as he tried to collect his thoughts. They had just over two weeks before the wedding. He knew Victoria well enough that there would be no way he could get her to leave before the wedding of a young woman she cared about. And besides, distance wasn't going to stop what might happen.

Jared looked up at the sky. Such a beautiful day, but each thought he had was more dismal than the one before it. What if he told Victoria what he feared? Right away, he knew that wouldn't work. If he told Victoria the truth about his grandfather, there was no doubt that she'd want to *see* Caleb. Talk to him, interview him, ask him how he *felt* about everything. "How did you *feel* when you drowned?" "How did you *feel* to know you'd caused the deaths of hundreds of your friends and relatives?" Victoria would say her painful questions were for her novels — as though that was all the justification she needed.

And then there was the magnificent love story. All his life he'd heard of the love between Caleb and Valentina. His father had told the story, Aunt Addy had, and his grandfather had told him. Each telling had contained different elements, but they'd all been the same when it came to the great, deep love that Caleb and Valentina had for each other. A love so deep, so *true,* that nothing on earth could break it. Neither death nor time had been able to stop their love.

As Jared watched the trucks moving slowly, dropping off their deliveries then leaving, he wondered if he'd ever seen his grandfather with Victoria. Caleb often occupied a chair nearby when Ken was there, but what about when Victoria was near? Jared couldn't remember. He did remember his grandfather saying that he'd watched Victoria undress. "But only Victoria," he'd said.

As another boy rode past with yet another bouquet in the basket on the front, Jared ran his hand over his face. He had no idea how to handle this. He took his phone out of his pocket and held it for a moment. What he wanted to do was call Alix and suggest that they fly up to Maine. Now. Maybe he could persuade her to stay with him there until after Izzy's wedding. Lexie could be the maid of honor. They'd return when it was all over.

He put his phone away. Kingsleys weren't known for cowardice and he wasn't going to start.

He put his shoulders back and slowly walked to his house, pushing his way through the many delivery men. There were three of them waiting inside the kitchen. Jared took out his wallet, gave them all tips, and told them to leave the flowers, booze, food, whatever, and go.

It took a while, but he got rid of them. He could hear Victoria's laughter drifting in from the front parlor and he grimaced. How in the world was he going to get her to go away without telling her the reason?

After Jared put the food that had been delivered in the fridge, he looked at the cards on some of the flowers. "Now the summer can truly begin," one said. "Same place, same time?" It wasn't signed. A huge bouquet that took up the whole table was from Lexie's boss, Roger Plymouth. Jared didn't know Victoria even knew him. "My jet is yours." "Could you please do an autographing for us?" "I dream of you . . ." was another one that wasn't signed.

Jared didn't know whether to be impressed or disgusted. He was leaning toward the latter.

He tried to fortify his courage as he started down the hall toward the front parlor. He and Aunt Addy used to laugh about people who marveled that Jared was never intimidated by anyone in the business world. Even when he was a young architect just starting out, he'd never been nervous when going into a meeting.

"That's because you've spent so much time around Victoria," Aunt Addy said. "She has a way of making most people do what she wants. If you can handle Victoria, you can handle the world."

When Jared got to the doorway, he halted and looked at the scene. Sitting in the center of the couch was the beautiful Victoria. As always, she was perfect. Her glorious red hair was artfully messy, arranged to look as though she'd just stepped out of a breeze. Her green eyes, with their thick black lashes, managed to look at once seductive and innocent. And her body . . . He knew from having spent a lot of his life near her that to keep the shape she'd been born with she worked out as hard as a professional bodybuilder. But she managed to look as though she was unaware of her extraordinary figure.

Four men surrounded her, all of them leaning forward as Victoria lounged back on the cushions. Aunt Addy's good tea set was on the table, the cups filled, and there were pretty plates full of tiny sandwiches, cakes, cookies, pastries. Jared would have bet his next year's salary that Victoria hadn't done anything to prepare the tea.

He was about to step forward when, turning, he saw his grandfather standing to the side. To Jared the man was as clear as sunlight, but no one else seemed able to see him. When Caleb looked up, what Jared saw made him draw in his breath.

On his face was an expression of absolute love. Melting, soul-touching, raw, unbridled love, the kind a person dies for, sacrifices and suffers for. It was the kind of love that a person would wait two hundred years to see fulfilled. It was True Love in its purest form.

Jared's face must have registered what he'd seen, because in an instant, Caleb removed that love-struck look from his face. He showed his grandson his devil-may-care half smile, then was gone in a flash.

"My darling Jared," came Victoria's voice. "You're here at last."

Jared cursed his luck and his life, and gave a prayer for help, all at the same time. When he turned to face her, he was smiling.

When Victoria engulfed him in her arms, he couldn't help feeling glad to see her. She was kissing his whisker-stubbled cheeks and running her pretty hands over his long hair.

"Is all this for my Alix?" Victoria asked. "She has always liked the motorcycle-gang look. Or is it Nantucket fisherman that she's grown to like?"

"I think it's dirty architect," he said as she slid her arm through his and he let her lead him toward the couch. Reluctantly, the other men made way.

"Yes, my Alix would love that. You know everyone, don't you?"

Jared looked from one man to another. Yes, he knew them all. He gave looks to the three married ones to let them know they should leave — which they did, leaving only Dr.

Huntley, who looked as though he'd taken root.

"What a bad boy you are," Victoria said to Jared after she'd said goodbye to the other men, her eyes laughing. "Freddy was just telling me how he and Alix had such a lovely time together. I had no idea you and she were looking into the family history."

Jared swallowed. He was going to tell Victoria as little as possible.

Freddy — a.k.a. Dr. Frederick C. Huntley — sipped his tea. "Young Alix was looking for Valentina."

"Oh, yes," Victoria said. "The elusive Valentina. Did she make any progress?"

"None at all," Jared said, putting a large cream tart in his mouth.

Victoria smiled at him in a way that said she would eventually get everything out of him. She made Jared want to run upstairs and hide. Or maybe to grab Alix and fly back to New York.

She turned to Dr. Huntley. "Freddy, you'll have to tell me everything on your next visit."

"Oh," Dr. Huntley said and it took him a moment to realize he was being dismissed. Quickly, he put his cup down, took one more sandwich, and stood up to say goodbye.

As soon as they were alone, Jared gave a yawn. "I've been up for hours, I think I'll —"

"Jared, darling," Victoria said, "we need to talk."

He stood up. "Sure, it's just that your visit was unexpected and I have a lot of things I need to get done. If you'd told me you were coming — as you seem to have told the entire island — I could have blocked out some time. As it is . . ." He couldn't think how to lengthen the lie. He took a step toward the doorway.

"I want to know what your intentions are toward my daughter."

Jared looked back, his face showing surprise. "You want to know about Alix? And me?"

"Yes, of course. That's why I came. I know you warned me not to and I plan to be a quiet little mouse while I'm here, but I absolutely must know about my dear daughter."

Jared gave a pointed look at what had to be half a dozen flower displays about the room. *This* was being "a quiet little mouse."

"Oh, well," she said with a wave of her hand. "I didn't arrive on a yacht."

"Not this time."

Victoria smiled sweetly and patted the seat beside her. "Please sit down, Jared darling, I haven't seen you in months and Kenneth has been his usual beastly self and won't tell me anything about my own daughter. And look at this." She reached under the couch and pulled out a white box that he recognized. "I saved these just for us, and . . ." She removed a bottle of twenty-five-year-old rum from behind a cushion. "This is to spice up Addy's blasted tea. What do you say? Downyflake doughnuts and rum?"

Jared shook his head. "Victoria, I swear you could charm the devil." He sat back down on the couch beside her.

"From what I've been hearing about you with my daughter, that's just what you are. You aren't planning to run back to New York and leave her behind, are you? Alix isn't like me. She's as serious as her father."

"No," Jared said as he took the cup of tea she offered. It was half rum. "I'm not planning to leave Alix."

Victoria smiled. "Does she know that?"

"I've dropped enough hints, so she should."

"Hmmm," Victoria said as she broke off a tiny piece of doughnut and delicately nibbled at it. "We women aren't good at hints. We like solid declarations of love and forever."

Jared put his cup to his mouth.

"And we like rings," Victoria said. "Anything but an emerald, and size five."

"Victoria," Jared said, "I think I'm old enough to make decisions about certain aspects of my own life."

"Of course you are, darling, it's just that I love you and Alix so much. You know that, don't you?"

"Yes, I do," Jared said. "I'll take care of Alix, I promise."

"Isn't she wonderful?" Victoria said. "I

don't know how Ken and I were able to produce a child who is the best of both of us. Are you impressed with her talent as an architect?"

"Very much so."

"Ken said he's building a chapel that Alix designed. Here, let me fill your cup, and have another doughnut. You do look tired and now that I'm here I'm going to help you with whatever you need."

Between the rum and the sugar Jared was beginning to relax. "Victoria, I don't know where Aunt Addy's journals are."

Victoria took in a breath, her hand to her remarkable bosom with its six inches of cleavage showing. "Is that why you think I came here? Jared, my dearest boy, I thought you knew me better than that. You're looking at me as though you're afraid that I might . . . Well, that I might tear apart the house searching for them. Pry up the floorboards or something dreadful like that." There were tears gathering in her eyes, which made the emerald green of them shine even brighter. "Did you think I could spend years in this beautiful old house and not love it nearly as much as you do?"

"Well, I did think —" He broke off because Victoria was looking hurt. "I knew that you'd want to see them."

"And of course I do," she said, blinking away the tears. "I'm sure they'll turn up.

Kenneth said he'd met some little . . ." She waved her hand. "A researcher or some such, and he's going to hire her to go through the attic. I just hope he can afford it. Of course Kenneth never was any good when it came to money, but who am I to complain? Are you really allowing this strange woman to stay here in your house?"

Jared picked up his fourth doughnut and filled his mouth. He was *not* going to give Victoria any information about Jilly. "So did you come over on the fast ferry?" he asked, his mouth full.

She smiled sweetly. "No, this time I brought a car. I thought Alix might need it. She can't very well drive that awful old truck of yours, now can she? And by the way, where is she?"

"At Dilys's house. I gave her some plans to work on."

"How odd that you'd go out there to work when your office is right here. I wonder what made you do that?" She waited for Jared to reply but he didn't. "Are the plans for anyone I know?"

Jared had an idea that Victoria knew of Jilly's connection to the Taggerts and the Montgomerys, probably knew the net worth of each of them, but right now he didn't want to get into that. Telling her of looking for Parthenia would lead to Caleb. "I doubt it. Look," he said as he stood up. "I need to take Alix some paper so I better go. I'm sure you have invitations for dinner."

"Several of them." She walked to the other side of the coffee table and put her arms out to him.

He couldn't help hugging her.

"Jared, my dearest, dearest boy," she said softly, "you can't imagine how pleased I am about you and Alix. I've always thought you two were meant for each other. Kenneth fought me on it, but I persevered. Both of you are truly fine people and I love you both very much." She pulled away, her hands on his arms. "I couldn't have created a better man for my daughter than you are. Do you know how much I admire you?"

Jared softened at her words. "And I owe you so much. I wouldn't be where I am today if it hadn't been for your help."

"I just supplied financial aid and encouragement now and then. Not so much."

"It was everything to me," Jared said.

"And now I'm giving you my most precious possession, my beautiful, brilliant daughter."

"She's both of those things," Jared said, smiling warmly at the memory of Alix. They'd been apart only hours but he was missing her.

"I'm glad you think so," Victoria said as she leaned forward and put her warm, soft cheek next to his. "So now you can give me Valentina's journal," she whispered.

It took Jared a moment to react and he

stepped away from her, his eyes wide. "We just found it yesterday! Who told you about it?"

"Twig's wife, Jude, sent me an email. We've been such good friends for years. I adore her chickens and —"

"Victoria!" He'd been planning to give her the journal but it went against his grain that she had already slick-talked her way to it.

"Yes, dear?"

He turned away. "I'm going home to Alix." All he could think about was seeing her. He wanted her sanity, her calmness, the way she didn't try to manipulate everyone she met. He just wanted to *be* with her.

# Chapter Twenty-Seven

Alix leaned away from the computer, put her arms behind her back, and stretched. It was getting late and Jared hadn't returned. But then it was as though a little electrical current went through her and she looked toward the door. She wasn't surprised when Jared threw it open.

What was surprising was the look on his face: raging, hot desire.

He had a bag in his hand that he dropped on the kitchen counter, then, without a word, he opened his arms to her.

Alix didn't hesitate as she ran to him. He bent a bit as he caught her, his hands going under her seat to pull her up. Her legs went around his waist as he opened his mouth over hers, tongues touching, arms, legs, bodies intertwining.

She pulled away a moment. Over the pounding of her heart, she said, "Mom wants us to meet her for lunch tomorrow."

Jared gave a brief nod and put his mouth

over hers as he started for the bedroom. When a chair got in his way, he threw it to one side.

"Oh, my," Alix said, but then Jared began kissing her neck and she forgot about words.

He tossed her onto the bed so the covers and pillows went flying upward.

Wide-eyed, she began unbuttoning her blouse, but Jared tore it apart, his lips following his hands. The rest of her clothes came off in an instant and for just a moment he paused long enough to look at her. "You are so beautiful," he whispered.

Alix pulled him down to her, smiled at the weight of him on top of her, loved the way his clothes felt against her bare skin. His hands ran down her body, came up the inside of her legs, his fingers entering her. She gasped, her head back, eyes closed, as his lips touched her breasts.

He brought her to a crescendo of desire, kissing her, his hands and lips working together. Just when she thought she could bear no more, he rolled off her and in an instant was nude.

It was Alix's turn, as her hands and lips wandered over his body, settling at last at his core. Jared leaned his head back as she moved downward. Minutes later, when he could stand no more, he pushed her onto her back and entered her with all the force of his desire. Alix put her hands up to brace herself against the headboard and gasped at each of his vigorous thrusts.

When they reached the peak, she clasped her legs about his waist, her arms around his neck, and let him lift her high. She couldn't help the scream she gave.

He collapsed on her but didn't move away, just held her so tightly she could hardly breathe. But who needed air with a sweaty, heavy man on top of you?

"You okay?" he whispered in her ear, his voice soft and concerned.

"More than all right."

He rolled off her, but held her close, moving her leg so it was between his.

It took her a while to recover from what they'd just done. There had been an urgency to his lovemaking, a *need* that had never been there before. She wanted to ask him questions but she didn't. Instead, she waited for him to speak.

"I didn't hurt you?"

"Far from it," Alix said.

"I missed you a lot today."

She didn't want to point out the obvious, that he'd only been away a few hours, but then she'd missed him too. Working on plans without him wasn't nearly as much fun as with him. "What did you do?"

He hesitated. "I had a fight with my grandfather."

"Oh," Alix said, trying to be calm even

though she knew that his grandfather was a ghost. She swallowed. "What about?"

Jared couldn't tell her about his fears for Victoria. "I didn't like that he showed himself to you that way."

"He wanted to tell me about Valentina," Alix said, then gave a little laugh. She was defending a ghost.

Jared kissed her forehead. "He could have told *me* what he had to say."

"I guess so," Alix said. "But, actually, that day was very nice. It was only later that I was upset. Did I tell you about the dress I was wearing?"

"He had you put on some historic monstrosity?" Jared sounded like he was about to get angry again.

"No," she said. "It was a beautiful white cotton wedding dress."

He calmed down. "The skirt's kind of folded?" He made a motion with his hand. "And it's packed away in a green box?"

She drew back to look at him. "That's the one. Who wore it?"

"No one. It was Aunt Addy's wedding dress. She showed it to my mother one day when I was there. They were trying to get some cousin to wear it at her wedding, but she wanted something with big sleeves and shiny."

"Well, I would wear —" Alix began, but stopped herself. It wasn't good to talk of your bridal gown with a man you weren't engaged to, who you hadn't even exchanged "I love you" with.

"Would you mind telling me exactly what happened on Sunday?" he asked. "I want to hear every detail."

Alix started at the beginning, from the rainy morning when she woke up with an overwhelming urge to go to the attic, to when the vision of the wedding disappeared.

Through it all, Jared listened intently, nodding as she told of the people she'd seen at the wedding.

"I felt like I actually saw them, but now I'm not sure I really did."

"Who else was there? Where was Valentina?" Jared asked.

When Alix told him the story of how Captain Caleb and Valentina met, she couldn't help laughing. "It all sounded so much like something my mother would do. Caleb told me about that meeting. He didn't show it to me."

"Granddad would have been too embarrassed to let someone see him being bested by a girl," Jared said. "And he's never told anyone that story before. That certainly would have been passed down."

"He said I was the first one he'd told." She snuggled her head on his shoulder. "Did you see Mom?"

"Oh, yeah," he said, and told her of the

trucks and bikes and men who'd shown up. "Even Roger Plymouth sent flowers."

"Ooooooh," Alix said.

"I need to meet this guy," Jared said.

"Can I go with you?"

With a groan, he rolled over on top of her. "You deserve punishment for that remark."

"I agree completely," she said as she opened her mouth under his.

This time they made love leisurely, savoring each other's bodies, kissing and caressing, exploring. An hour later, when they lay in each other's arms, sweaty and sated, Jared's stomach growled.

"I forgot to make anything for dinner," Alix said.

"That's all right. I raided Victoria's fridge before I left. I have meals from the best restaurants on the island." He got out of bed and headed toward the bathroom.

"My mother does believe in eating well."

As he stood in the doorway in all his naked glory, their eyes met. They didn't have to say what they were thinking. Now that Victoria was there, things would change. If nothing else the big old house would no longer be theirs alone. Jilly was so quiet, and spent so much time with Ken, that her being in the apartment hadn't bothered them. But Victoria would be in the room across the hall, and she always had people around her. As a teenager, Alix had been the one to complain that the music was too loud and on too late at night.

Jared gave a sigh, then smiled. "We'll be all right. She wants Valentina's journal so maybe if we give it to her she'll . . ." He shrugged. "Want to take a shower with me?"

"Love to," Alix said and threw back the covers.

By an unspoken agreement, they didn't talk more about Victoria. They wanted to enjoy their time alone. After their shower together, they spread the feast on the floor and did what they so loved: looked at architectural plans. Alix was pleased with what she'd come up with, but Jared didn't agree with a lot of it, and told her so.

"Kingsley," Alix said, "you don't know what you're talking about."

It was what she'd said the first time they worked together, which now seemed so long ago. They looked into each other's eyes and laughed. Back then, Alix had been almost afraid of him, but now it was hard for her to remember that he was the Great Jared Montgomery.

They seemed to understand each other because he pushed away the plates and they made love on top of the sketches of the old Montgomery house. It was an especially sweet lovemaking, as both were realizing the changes in store for them.

Afterward, Alix peeled three sheets of paper

off Jared's stomach and said, "We could stay here."

"Dilys comes home tomorrow. She'll want her house back."

"Lexie and Toby's house?" Alix asked.

"No privacy."

"We'll just have to be firm with Mom," she said. "And we'll lock the bedroom door."

"Want to go to my apartment in New York?"

For a moment Alix's eyes lit up, but then she shook her head. "Maybe after Izzy's wedding."

"Right," he said. "After the wedding." He looked away so she couldn't see the fear that crossed his face. That's when his grandfather would leave the earth and maybe Victoria would go with him.

Jared looked back at Alix. "If you can keep your hands off me long enough, I'd like to show you a much better idea for that east wing."

"Different maybe, but not better. And as for hands off, you promised me a meal eaten off my stomach. What happened to that?"

"You didn't see the chocolate mousse I brought back with me? It's made for smearing across your bare belly. But first I have to teach you about remodeling a house."

"I am your pupil and eager to learn. Did you bring any whipped cream?"

"A whole bowl full of it."

"Get those papers and let's get started,"

she ordered — and Jared obeyed.

The next morning Victoria was sitting at the kitchen table and for the first time in the big old house, she was feeling lonely. How strange it was to be there but not to see and talk to Addy. Over the years they'd developed ways of doing things, who they'd see, where they'd eat. Now the house seemed enormous and empty.

Last night at dinner, Victoria had loved seeing some of her old Nantucket friends — but it hadn't been the same. Addy wasn't there. Victoria'd always had to work hard to get Addy to go out with people, but she enjoyed it once she was there. As for Victoria, she'd loved having someone nearby who knew the truth of whatever she was saying. She'd look at some man and say, "How very interesting!" then at home she and Addy would sip their drinks and laugh about how dull and pompous the man was.

But last night there'd been no one to look at with raised eyebrows and suppressed laughter — and Victoria had missed Addy horribly.

Standing at the kitchen sink and pretending she was washing dishes was Jilly Taggert. Victoria knew there was a married name but she didn't remember it. She'd met Jilly's sister-in-law, the writer Cale Anderson, at several functions and had liked her. That they wrote in different genres and their sales were fairly equal prevented the jealousy writers so often had for one another.

Victoria looked over her coffee cup at Jilly and knew there'd be no deep friendship there. At least not now. Right now all Jilly could do was stare out the window toward the guesthouse, her eyes searching the garden for any sign of movement. She was waiting for Ken to appear.

She and Jilly had chatted some this morning about inconsequential things, nothing important, but Victoria could see that Jilly was ready for a life change. She'd been widowed many years ago and now her two children — twins, a boy and a girl — were leaving home to go to college — which made Jilly free to go wherever life took her. And she was *ready.*

Victoria knew that Ken was going to be a problem. She'd learned through long, painful experience that her ex-husband had to be pushed to *do* things. It was so bad that after their five years of marriage Victoria'd had to jump into bed with another man to try to make Ken listen about how miserable she was. He'd been oblivious to the way his parents snubbed Victoria, of how they'd constantly reminded her that she'd been a waitress at the country club where Ken played tennis every day — as if she could forget! No matter what Victoria did, it wasn't good enough for his parents. But worse was how they watched little Alix as though they were judging her. They seemed to be waiting to see if she was going to be like them or become like her mother and take life without the seriousness it deserved.

Victoria had cried, pleaded, and threatened in an attempt to get Ken to listen to her complaints, but he'd just talked to her like she was a child and said she was exaggerating everything. In an attempt to placate her, he'd said that what he liked about Victoria was that she was the opposite of what he'd grown up with. The truth was that Ken didn't believe in displaying emotion — but then up until he met Victoria, his life had been so perfect that he'd had no reason to feel anything deeply.

From Victoria's point of view, going to bed with Ken's business partner was something she *had* to do. It still amazed her that Ken had never wondered why she'd done it in their house, their bed, and just when he'd said he'd be home.

But Ken's anger and hurt didn't have the effect Victoria'd hoped it would. Afterward, he *still* wouldn't listen to her. He just wanted to yell or sulk, with nothing in between.

Frustrated beyond her ability to cope, Victoria decided to give her husband time to calm down. She took little Alix and ran away to Nantucket, but she'd never thought of staying away. She just wanted Ken to know how it felt to be truly miserable — which she knew he would be without them. And also, she wanted to put him in a place where he *had* to listen.

But an afternoon of dancing and an old cabinet falling down had changed everything.

Since then, Victoria had felt some guilt that Ken had never seemed to recover from his hurt of the divorce. Over the years, as she'd seen him with one ghastly woman after another, she'd tried to keep her mouth shut. It hadn't been easy.

Victoria had seen that each of Ken's former girlfriends had all been the same: outspoken, almost gaudy, ambitious. Victoria couldn't help being flattered that the women were poor copies of her — which meant that they weren't right for Ken.

From her perspective, she thought he was afraid to love again. He didn't want to risk having his heart ripped out a second time, so he'd taken up with women who liked him for what he could give them. But then they made breaking up an easy choice.

As always, Addy had been quite perceptive about what was going on. "If you hadn't kicked Ken in his very heart," Addy said one night, "he would have become a mediocre architect struggling to stay in business. And he certainly wouldn't have so much as canceled a tennis game to help some kid stay out of jail. But you showed him what rage can do."

It took Victoria a moment before she could laugh at that backhand compliment, but it was so true that she did.

"Too bad Ken let his heart turn to stone," Addy added and Victoria couldn't help nodding in agreement. Yes, much too bad.

But now, as Victoria looked at Jilly standing by the sink, constantly looking out the window to see Ken, that old feeling of guilt ran through her. This woman was right for Ken, but would he be smart enough to act on it? Or would he be so damned scared that he'd spend years making up his mind?

When Jilly looked as though she'd seen something heavenly on earth, Victoria knew that Ken was coming. She got up, went to Jilly, and kissed her on the cheek. "I like you," she said. "Remember that."

When Victoria saw Ken walking toward the house, she threw open the door and hurried out to greet him. She had to admit that he looked better than he had in years. The usual hangdog, melancholy sadness that lingered in his eyes wasn't there.

"Darling," Victoria said loudly as she threw her arms around his neck and kissed both his cheeks.

Pulling away, he glanced at Jilly standing in the doorway. "What's going on?"

"Nothing," Victoria said. "Can't I be glad

to see the father of my child?" She slipped her arm in his and moved to the side, but kept him where Jilly could see them. "I met your newest and I must say that she's adorable. She's so sweet that I think even you can handle her."

"Victoria, you can emasculate a man in a sentence. I need to go."

"No," she said, smiling and holding firmly on to his arm. "You and I have to talk about our daughter. I'm sure your bland little doll won't mind waiting for a few minutes."

Ken, his face already angry, pulled out of Victoria's grasp, and glared at her. "Jilly is far from bland. She —" He waved his hand. "What do you have to say about Alix?"

"I was just wondering about her and Jared. You know what he's like, and I'm afraid he's going to cast her aside and break her heart."

"You read too many of your own novels. Jared and Alix are well suited. I need to —"

"You mean they *work* together? I hear he has her doing all his drafting for him. What's he doing while she works? Picking up girls at a local bar?"

"Victoria, I don't have time for this! Jared is a good man and you know it. He and Alix —" Ken took a breath to calm himself. "Look, I need to get to work myself. I'm late as it is." He turned away.

"Thank you for letting this Julie live in the house with me. She's so docile and eager to please that she's doing all my washing and she cleans up the kitchen for me. I wonder if she irons. Can she cook? I want to have a dinner party on Saturday, so your Julie can take care of it for me. Thank you so much for lending her to me."

"Victoria!" Ken growled, his teeth and fists clenched. "If you —"

"If I what, darling?" She smiled at him sweetly.

Ken was so angry he couldn't speak. He gave his ex-wife one more look of rage, then stomped off into the house, slamming the door behind him.

Victoria watched as Ken stormed over to Jilly, who was still standing by the window. Ken grabbed Jilly and kissed her so hard and with so much passion that when he stepped away, she looked dazed. Ken held tightly onto her shoulders and Victoria saw him speak to her with such force that all Jilly did was nod yes.

Moments later, Ken slammed out of the house. He didn't so much as slow down when he went past Victoria, but he said, "Get your own damned maid!"

Turning, Victoria looked at Jilly through the window. She still looked to be in a state of shock. She disappeared for a moment, then opened the back door and practically ran to Victoria.

"Ken said that I wasn't going to be your

maid so he wants me to pack and move into the second bedroom in the guesthouse. With him." She was blinking rapidly. "Victoria, I don't know what to say except . . ." She took a breath. "I love you. Really, I do. If there's anything I can ever do for you, please let me know. Ken —" She broke off at the sound of quick footsteps coming toward them.

Victoria put her finger to her lips as she said loudly and in an arrogant tone, "Of course my undies have to be washed by hand. And my sheets are from Lion's Paw so they're ultra luxurious. I need them ironed as I *must* have crisp sheets."

Ken stopped by the two women and glared at Victoria before turning to Jilly. "Why don't you spend the day at the site with me?"

"I would love to," Jilly said. "Just let me get my bag."

Left alone with Victoria, Ken gave her a look of contempt before going to his truck.

Moments later, Jilly hurried out of the house, big bag over her shoulder. She slowed down long enough to kiss Victoria's cheek. "Thank you, and I owe you," she said, then hurried after Ken.

Victoria listened for the truck leaving the drive, then, smiling, she returned to the house.

In the upstairs window, looking down at her, Caleb too was smiling. "You had to do the same thing the first time they met," he said, chuckling.

Victoria spent the rest of the morning returning calls and emails and setting up her beloved green room. It was Addy who'd encouraged her to so thoroughly indulge herself with the color scheme.

"Why not please yourself?" Addy said. "It's what I do every day." She was referring to the fact that she only accepted invitations to events she really wanted to attend. When Victoria wasn't there, she mostly stayed home.

Victoria had agreed and done her beautiful room all in green. At home she never dared do something like that since, even as a child, Alix was as critical as her father.

"Mother," Alix had said when she was just six years old, "you have to think of the overall concept."

Victoria hadn't known whether to be horrified or amused. She chose laughter. But then so much of the time Victoria felt like she was the child and Alix was the adult.

Just before noon, Victoria began preparing lunch for three. That meant she took packages out of the refrigerator and arranged the contents on platters. Alix had shown her how to use a microwave but Victoria hadn't yet mastered it — not that she'd let anyone see, that is. She found it rewarding to let other people feel needed.

As she moved about, she kept looking out

the window, as nervous as Jilly watching for Ken. It hadn't been easy for her since Alix went to college. Leaving her writing studio to return to an empty house had sometimes left her dizzy with yearning. There were always invitations and Victoria was good at throwing parties, but she still missed her daughter.

When Alix came home, it was as though the world could start turning again. They talked and talked, with Victoria telling her about her books, people she'd seen, places she'd traveled. She was well aware that Alix often left out tidbits about her own life, but Victoria knew how to get them out of Ken. All she had to do was start a sentence with, "I'm worried about Alix," and Ken blabbed his guts out. But then Victoria had never thought it was fair that their daughter told him more than she did her.

Victoria got everything ready for lunch, setting the big old dining table up beautifully. She and Addy had put on many dinner parties there. Victoria had been the one to scour the closets and even the attic for beautiful old china and tablecloths. Addy had made up the guest list. "No, no," she'd say. "Those two hate each other. Their great-grandfathers were in love with the same woman." Or "Who knows about them? Their family only moved to the island in the 1920s." Sometimes she'd say, "They're summer people, but they're still respectable."

As for the food, someone else cooked it and they poured it into the eighteenth-century Chinese import dishes that Captain Caleb had brought back.

So now Victoria set the table for Alix and Jared, two people she loved very much.

That first summer when she'd met Addy's nephew, she'd seen a tall, surly boy who was so angry he was a bit frightening. That summer Victoria'd had her mind full of the journals and had stayed away from him. Besides, he'd made it clear that he didn't like an outsider in his family home.

But the next summer she'd seen a different person. There were still vestiges of that first boy, but Jared had spent most of a year under the tutelage of a very angry Ken. It had taken some work on her part but she'd managed to elicit a few smiles from the boy.

By the time Jared graduated from high school, he was completely changed, and when Ken approached Victoria about helping pay to educate him, she'd readily agreed.

Sometimes Victoria had felt bad about keeping Alix from knowing about Nantucket, but she also knew it was for the best. Early on, Ken had shown her that Jared had a talent for architecture, and Alix had been scribbling pictures of houses since she could pick up a crayon.

That first summer, one afternoon Victoria had walked into the big family room to find a fourteen-year-old Jared and a four-year-old Alix sitting on the floor building some great, tall structure out of Legos. Alix was looking at the boy with eyes filled with stars, while Jared saw her as a kid.

In an instant, Victoria saw Alix's future: She'd crush on the big, handsome boy so hard that she'd forego her own life. Victoria wanted more for her daughter. She didn't want Alix to do what she'd done, marrying too young and taking on responsibilities too soon. And when you were settled with a man you had to deal with his family, something Victoria had been too young to handle. No, Victoria wanted her daughter to find out about herself first, then later, if she met Jared again and they liked each other, that was another matter.

All this led Victoria to her present worry. For all that she'd used Jared to goad Ken into an argument, she was concerned about how Jared felt about Alix. When it came to women, he really was a bit of a scoundrel. Every August they'd laughed about his girlfriends. He never had time for them — and he kept his work life separate from his personal one. "Half of them don't know what I do for a living," he'd said just two summers ago. "And the other half don't care."

Victoria wanted to know if Jared was temporarily using her daughter or was serious about her. As for Alix, was she starstruck or could she see past Jared's fame in the architecture world?

A little after noon, Victoria heard the back door open and her heart soared. They were here! She took a step forward, but then her cell rang. There was only one person whose call she'd take even if it meant postponing seeing her daughter and that was her editor. The ID said it was.

"I have to take this," Victoria called out and headed up the stairs. She needed quiet to be able to formulate her lies to her editor. She wasn't about to tell the truth, that she hadn't even started her overdue novel. At least this time she could say she was "almost" finished and it wouldn't be a total lie. After she'd spent a month reading Valentina's journal and writing the detailed outline, she would be on her way to turning in a finished product. "Almost" was a relative term.

Victoria spent twenty minutes exaggerating everything to her editor — not quite lying, but not honest either. She used words like "complicated" and "best I've ever written" and "dealing with deep emotions in this book." They were phrases editors loved to hear.

When she got off the phone, her first impulse was to run to tell Addy about it. She would have laughed hysterically.

A tear came to Victoria's eye, but she wiped it away. She couldn't tell Addy, but she did have her dear daughter. Alix had always loved her mother's stories.

Smiling, Victoria went down the stairs to the dining room, preparing to make a grand entrance. But they weren't sitting at the table. Alix's cardigan was folded across the back of a chair and Victoria picked it up as she went toward the front of the house.

She found Jared and Alix sitting side by side on the little couch, leaning toward each other, just their fingertips touching. Victoria was about to announce her presence, but didn't. Instead, she stood and watched in shock.

Since Alix had been on Nantucket they'd talked on the phone often, and her daughter had riddled her conversation with what Jared said and did. Victoria had known that Alix was beginning her first real love and she'd been glad of it.

But Victoria was not prepared for *this.* Alix and Jared were looking at each other as though only they existed. There were no other people in the world, just the two of them.

Victoria stepped back out of the doorway, leaned against the wall, and closed her eyes. It was the way she'd always wanted a man to look at *her.* There'd been hundreds of men through her life as she'd attracted them, but she'd always held back. They looked at her as a prize to be won, something to conquer. And if she let them get too near, they ran away.

Victoria wasn't at all helpless, as they'd assumed.

She peered around the doorway. They were kissing now. Sweetly and gently, smiling, utterly content to be together, needing no one else. Certainly not a mother who wanted to tell them about some novel she was trying to write.

Victoria was still holding Alix's sweater and she buried her face in it. She had lost her daughter! As completely and totally as though Alix had flown away to another planet, she was gone.

Victoria knew she had to calm herself before she appeared. Quietly, she went back up the stairs, but she didn't go to her own room. She went to Alix's bedroom — what had once been Addy's. That one of Jared's shirts was on a chair seemed to drive a nail into Victoria's heart.

She put Alix's sweater on the foot of the bed. I can stand this, she thought, but then she looked at the big portrait of Captain Caleb and went to sit on that side of the bed. Was the man's ghost really in the house or was it something Addy had made up?

"Now what do I do?" Victoria whispered as she looked at the portrait and more tears came to her eyes. "Do I help them? Do I make it easier for them to leave me?" She took a tissue out of the box on the bedside table and blew her nose.

"Ken just met this woman Jilly but already her eyes light up when she sees him. And he was ready to do battle to protect her. Alix and Jared . . . those two look like they've merged into one being. My daughter . . ." The tears came stronger. "My beautiful, precious daughter is leaving me. How do I live without her? She keeps me sane; she is always *there.* She is . . ." Victoria swallowed.

"She is *his.*"

She looked at the portrait. "What do I do? I need some advice. Do I go back to my big empty house and learn how to bake cookies in hope that I'll get a grandchild soon? Do I . . . ?" She took a breath. "Do I now get *old*? Is that what's left for me? To sit on a porch and grow old *alone*? Where is *my* True Love?" She was crying hard.

Suddenly, Victoria was overwhelmed with sleepiness, and it was as though someone was gently pushing her down on the bed. The bed was so very comfortable and the instant her head touched the pillow, she fell asleep.

When she awoke, it was an hour later and she was smiling. She knew what she had to do. It was almost as though someone had instructed her while she was sleeping. It was a man's voice and it sounded very familiar. "You have to help them," the voice said. "Now is not the time to think of yourself. Love can't be selfish; it can't be one-sided. This is Alix's time and Jared's, and you're going to give it to them."

Smiling, she got up and went to the bedroom door, but then she turned back and looked at the portrait of Captain Caleb. "If you want to show yourself to me, please do. I may not be your Valentina, but I could use some of what you gave to her."

She left the room, closing the door behind her. She had a plan, and the very first thing she was going to do was call Izzy. Everything depended on being able to persuade her.

# Chapter Twenty-Eight

"Mother, I really can't," Alix said for what had to be the third time. It was just three days after her mother had arrived, but already Alix's life was upside down. "Jared needs me to help him with the plans for this new commission in Maine."

"Is that the job you told me that he doesn't have yet?"

"Well, yes, it is, but I'm sure he'll get it." They were at breakfast in the kitchen of Kingsley House and Jared had already run off to the chapel site. This morning he'd decided that Ken couldn't possibly do without him. "Coward!" Alix had hissed at him. Instead of being embarrassed he'd winked at her and scurried away.

"I'm just saying, Alix, that I think you need to put some more time into Izzy's wedding, that's all."

"Everything is under control." She'd given her mother the fat folder that contained all the arrangements for the wedding, from the flowers to the cake.

Victoria leaned across the table to her daughter. "If this were World War Two and everyone was on rations, this would be the perfect wedding."

Alix looked at the clock on the wall. It was nearly eleven and she'd done no work all day. She and Jared had spent one last night at Dilys's house, then they'd cleaned the place, filled the refrigerator for her, packed up, and left.

It was when they returned to Kingsley House that the problems began. Her mother had behaved like someone out of a Victorian novel, acting shocked that Alix and Jared were planning to stay in the same room.

"Mother, I've had boyfriends before," Alix said.

"But not in front of *me,*" Victoria said, her back abnormally stiff.

"What is wrong with you? You're acting very strangely."

Jared had picked up his duffel bag and looked at Victoria. "Have it your way. Now that you've moved Jilly in with Ken, I'll stay in the maid's apartment." He was looking at Victoria with a great deal of amusement, but also clearly trying to figure out what she was up to. "Mind if I stay in the room Aunt Addy decorated with Alix? Or is that too risqué for your new delicate sensibilities?"

"I thought that was my room!" Alix said.

She looked back at her mother. "But why were you and I staying in there?"

Victoria gave Jared a look to cut it out, then put her arm possessively around her daughter's shoulders. "Come on and let's get you settled. You haven't seen any old journals around here, have you?"

"Look out, wallpaper!" Jared said as he went down the hall to the apartment.

That had been yesterday and Alix hadn't liked sleeping alone. She'd hoped Jared would use the chamber pot stairs to sneak in, but he didn't. Today as he'd kissed her good morning, he'd whispered, "Your mother put a lock on the old door." He seemed highly amused by her action.

"I'm glad you find this funny, but I don't," Alix said.

Now he was at the chapel site and Alix was with her mother, being told that she'd done a poor job on Izzy's wedding. "It is *not* like a wartime wedding and I resent your saying that."

"It's just that I thought Izzy was your very best friend. Doesn't she deserve more than *this*? Was your mind on Jared so completely that you forgot about your good friend?"

"Mother! That's not fair. Izzy is on a strict budget and she doesn't want anything elaborate. But even so, it's going to be beautiful. The wildflowers and the blue ribbons are lovely. It's everything I'd want for my own wedding."

Victoria leaned back from the table, looking as though the very idea horrified her. "*Your* wedding? You are my only child and I have a fan base to satisfy. They'll expect a show from me. For your wedding . . ." She waved her hand, as though it were all too big for her to speak of. "That doesn't matter now. You don't even have a groom."

Alix glared at her mother. "In case you haven't noticed, Jared and I are —"

"Yes, yes," Victoria said as she stood up. "You've become one of Jared's ladies. Now go put on one of those nice tops from Zero Main and let's go look at cakes."

Alix stood up. "The cake has been ordered and what do you mean that I'm one of Jared's 'ladies'?"

"Nothing," Victoria said. "A slip of the tongue. I saw the cake you ordered. It's quite simple and much too small. Alix, dearest, can you *only* design buildings? Couldn't you come up with something more fitting for a future architect? Why don't you think what you'd like for your own wedding, then scale it down to a quarter of the size and use it for Izzy?" She went to the door. "I'll be ready in ten minutes. Why don't you start the car?"

Alix stood in the kitchen, took a few breaths, and looked down at the folder full of orders and photos. Maybe it all was a bit spartan, and maybe Alix had been so involved in her own life that she had neglected Izzy's wedding.

She ran up the stairs, changed her shirt, grabbed her sketchbook, and went outside to the little car her mother had brought over for her. It was a small BMW, not new but nearly so, and the interior was pristine.

Of course her mother took thirty minutes to make sure her hair and makeup were perfect, and by that time Alix had made some drawings of possible cakes. When her mother got into the car and opened her perfectly lipsticked mouth as though to issue another order, Alix said, "Did you know that Valentina looked like you?"

"How do you know that?"

"When I danced with Captain Caleb, he told me." Alix had the deep, soul-fulfilling satisfaction of having rendered her always-confident mother speechless.

It took Victoria only seconds to recover. "When? How? Where? You didn't really dance with him, did you? It was just a dream, right?"

Alix smiled. "What if the bottom layer of the cake is square, next one up is round, then put in some risers so there can be an outdoor area, then a three-layer round tower?"

"Alixandra," Victoria said slowly, "I want to hear about you and Captain Caleb."

"Jared moves back in with me?"

Victoria took a breath so deep she almost choked. Jared spending nights with Alix did not fit in with the plan that had come to her when she'd fallen asleep on her daughter's bed. She recalled the night Addy had told her of the ghost. It had been Addy's last night alive. Since then Victoria had nearly gone crazy with waiting and waiting for Jared to stop telling her his idiot stories about people being too dazzled to be able to speak and let her return to Kingsley House. But after hearing that Valentina's journal had been found, Victoria refused to wait any longer. She was on the next ferry.

But since her arrival, Victoria's priorities had changed. Her daughter came first.

Victoria swallowed hard. Saying this was going to hurt. "Izzy's wedding is more important than whatever it is you believe you've seen," she said with her back teeth clamped together, and as a result she sounded rather prim. "You are an adult and you can, of course, do whatever you want, but I don't think it is appropriate for you to live with a man you've known for such a short time. Alix, dear, you really have neglected your friend most dreadfully."

It was Alix's turn to be silent. If her mother was willing to put aside a story she'd wanted for so very long, then Izzy's wedding must be really important to her. "You're right," she said. "I have thought much more about Jared than my friend. Are the wedding plans really awful?"

"No, of course not," Victoria said. "They're just a bit subdued and I'd like to do more for Izzy. Do you mind temporarily giving your friend precedence over Jared?"

"Of course not!" she said.

"Good!" Victoria said. "Now, tell me again about this design of yours and what in the world is an 'outdoor area' on a cake?"

It was a couple of hours later that Alix and her mother were at lunch in the beautiful Sea Grille restaurant. Victoria was looking down at her plate and pushing her food around.

"What's wrong?" Alix asked.

Victoria sighed. "I've been sworn to secrecy about something but I feel that I *must* tell you."

Alix drew in her breath. "Is someone ill?"

Victoria waved her fork about. "No, no, nothing like that. It's Izzy."

"The baby!"

"No," Victoria said. "This isn't health related. Remember that I said I called her?"

"Yes."

"I spent over an hour on the phone with Izzy and she's very upset. It's her in-laws and her mother."

"I thought that had been taken care of," Alix said.

"That's what Izzy wants you to think. What woman doesn't want to choose her own wedding cake? But Izzy is so stressed out she doesn't care. The truth is that she's dreading her own wedding."

Alix fell back against the restaurant's cushioned seat. "I had no idea, but then . . ." She grimaced. "Just as you said, I've been too involved with Jared and all things Kingsley to take care of my friend."

Victoria put her hand over her daughter's. "I know how that is. When I first came to Nantucket all those years ago, I too was overwhelmed. That's why I never wanted *you* to be taken up, swallowed whole, by the family and all their ghosts and stories of lost loves. If I'd had an ability to make a living and support my child some other way, I wouldn't have come here every summer." Victoria prayed to be forgiven for her blatant lie, but then it was all for the greater good.

"I'll go to her," Alix said. "I can take a ferry this afternoon and —"

"No!" Victoria said. "I shouldn't have said anything. That's exactly why Izzy didn't tell you that everything is still awful. She's such a good friend that she wants you to stay here with your latest boyfriend and —"

"I think Jared is more than that."

"I'm sure you do, dearest, but he's not the point. What I think we should do is work together to give Izzy a really fabulous wedding."

"I'm sorry about the cake," Alix said. "I should have taken the time to design something."

Victoria waved her hand. "I'm thinking bigger. Not as big as *your* wedding will be, but larger than it is now."

"Mother," Alix said firmly, "I wish you'd stop saying that. I don't want a huge wedding. If — when — I do get married I want people I know and care about to be there. And I already know that I want to be married in the chapel I designed. It's special to me."

"Alix, dear, I think you're getting far ahead of yourself. For one thing that chapel is on Nantucket. Unless you plan to have a destination wedding there's no reason for you to get married here. It's so much trouble and expense to fly people in, and of course my entire publishing house will want to attend, so how do they get here?"

"Your — ?" Alix broke off. "Let's keep this about Izzy, shall we? What are you thinking of doing for her?"

"Inviting the Kingsleys. And Kenneth's new girlfriend is a Taggert and they're related to the Montgomerys, so we'll invite some of them too."

"Are you talking hundreds?"

"Three-fifty anyway," she said. "We'll invite enough people that they'll drown out the disapproving relatives of the bride's and groom's families."

"You're paying?"

"Of course," Victoria said. "Izzy's like a

second daughter to me, and besides, when you get married in a cathedral in New York in a dress with a fourteen-foot-long train we don't want Izzy eaten up with jealousy."

"I can assure you that no one in her right mind would be jealous of a circus like that! Mother, as I've said before, I am *not* going to wear a dress with a train of any length. In fact —" She quit talking because mentioning Aunt Addy's pretty wedding gown could lead back to Caleb, and right now Alix was feeling deep guilt about neglecting her friend. She didn't want to tempt her mother a second time and get more guilt dumped on her.

Victoria looked at her watch. "We need to go. Freddy is taking me out to 'Sconset for the afternoon."

"Are you two serious?"

"Heavens, no! He's a sweet man but since his wife died, he doesn't seem to care about anything anymore." She leaned forward. "The local gossip is that he's soon to be relieved from his position at the NHS because of his lack of leadership ability. He still looks divine in a tuxedo, but he can no longer manage people." She slipped her credit card into the folder and the waitress took it away. "What are you thinking about so hard?"

"Lexie," Alix said. "She would know who to invite to Izzy's wedding. And Toby would know how to perk up the decorations."

"Those darling girls! How are they? Let's

have them over for dinner tonight."

"I still forget that you know everyone here. They're fine."

"Is Lexie engaged to Nelson yet? Has Toby lost her virginity?"

Alix raised her eyebrows. "No to the engagement and I couldn't say about Toby."

Victoria signed the check, leaving a generous tip, and smiled at the waitress. "Don't tell anyone about Toby. It's not something she confides in people. She's such a choosy girl. She doesn't want to make a mistake." Victoria looked pointedly at her daughter.

"Unlike me who meets a gorgeous, famous architect and immediately pounces on him."

Victoria shrugged. "Jared does that to women, but he's great experience. I'm sure that later you'll use all that you've learned from him. In your real life. Are you ready to go? The wedding is two weeks from today so we can't waste any time. Roger is in California right now so Lexie might be free to start working today."

"Do you mean Roger Plymouth?"

"Of course," Victoria said as she stood up.

"How do you know him?"

"Darling, while you were away at college I didn't just sit home and do my nails. Roger is everywhere. Did you see the pink and cream bouquet in the family room? That's from him."

"Is that the one covering a six-foot round table?"

"That's it. Roger never does anything in a small way. Is he still in love with Lexie?"

Alix shook her head. "Do you know every secret on this island?"

"I don't know where Addy's journals are, how you came to dance with a man who's been dead for two hundred years, or even where you've hidden Valentina's journal."

Alix smiled at her mother. "Good to know there are some things people can keep from you."

"But eventually I'll find it all out," Victoria said.

Alix didn't reply because she knew her mother was right.

# Chapter Twenty-Nine

Jared had never been so frustrated in his life. He was frustrated mentally, physically, psychologically — any way it could be thought of, he was feeling it.

He'd always liked Victoria. Well, maybe not that first summer, but back then he'd hated nearly everyone. Since then he'd enjoyed her visits. But right now he wanted to wring her neck.

In the nearly two weeks since Victoria arrived, Jared had hardly seen Alix. They'd gone from living together extremely comfortably to not being together at all. In the past this wouldn't have bothered him; he would have just gone fishing. But he'd found that working, babysitting, socializing, everything he did had been easier and certainly more pleasant with Alix around.

Yesterday his business partner, Tim, had called and said that he'd had enough of Jared's absence and he needed him to get back to New York. "Everybody in the office likes me so much they're standing around the watercooler and chatting. Sharing. Making playdates with one another. Since you left, two office romances have started and I can hardly wait for everyone to take sides when they break up."

"Tell them to go back to work," Jared said, but there was no real interest or conviction in his voice.

"I tell them, but they pat me on the shoulder and show me their kids' photos. And Stanley! Without you here, he doesn't have enough to do. Last week he sent out a memo saying that from now on all files were to be color coded."

"Couldn't hurt," Jared said.

"You think not? Stanley has twenty-one categories and twenty-one colors. What the hell color is cerise? Jared! You have to return and put this place back in order. I'm the money guy, remember? You're the tyrant."

Jared snorted. "If I'm a tyrant, how come I'm being run over by a little woman in high heels?".

"Do you mean Alix?"

"Hell, no! I never even see Alix. It's her mother who's driving me insane."

Tim rolled his eyes. "I know about girls' mothers. Before I got married my mother-in-law was a monster. Now she's . . . Actually, she's still a snake. I bought a book about a tribe that doesn't allow the wife's mother to speak to her daughter's husband. Want me to send you a copy?"

"No, thanks," Jared said. "After Izzy's wedding, I'll return. It's less than a week away now."

"Are you planning to bring your new girl back here with you?"

"Alix is not just my 'new girl,' " Jared half shouted. "She's more than that."

"Don't take my head off! Save it for the kids around the watercooler. Maybe I should start handing out balloons when they do their work correctly. Think that will inspire them?"

"I get your point. The wedding is this Saturday. I'll be in the office on Monday."

"Is that a pinky promise?"

"Go count your coins," Jared growled and clicked off.

After that call Jared felt worse — which he wouldn't have thought possible. At first he'd been amused by what Victoria was doing. Ken had arrived at the chapel site with Jilly and he was in a fury over what Victoria had tried to do.

"She wanted to use Jilly as her maid! Can you imagine that?" Ken was steaming in anger.

"And your solution was to move Jilly in with you?" Jared asked.

"I had to protect her, didn't I?"

Jared had turned away to hide his smile, but the next day he was frowning. Victoria had banished him from Alix's room. At the time it hadn't bothered him as he thought he'd go up the secret staircase later, but he'd underestimated Victoria. She'd locked the downstairs door from the inside. It was annoying that she knew the house so well, and he wished he could let his aunt Addy know what he thought of her telling an outsider about that staircase. That Jared had shown it to Alix, and that Ken had been allowed to help repair it didn't matter to him.

Worse than physical locks was what Victoria had done to Alix's mind. Victoria had made Alix become obsessed with Izzy's wedding. Everything she'd done before had to be redone and presented to Victoria for approval.

"Perhaps just a few more roses," Victoria would say as she looked up over a cup of tea, then Alix would go back and do it all over again. As far as Jared could tell, Alix was having to do each task about four times.

This morning he'd tried to talk to Alix about it all, but that hadn't worked out well.

"It's just until the wedding is over," Alix said, "then things will go back to normal."

"What does 'normal' mean?"

"I don't know." She looked at her watch. "I have an appointment with the tent people in ten minutes. I have to go."

He caught her arm. "Alix, after the wedding your mother will hunker down with

Valentina's journal and she'll probably start searching for the ones Aunt Addy wrote." If Victoria is still alive, that is, he thought but didn't add. That secret was gnawing at him more every day.

"I don't know why that's a problem," Alix said as she started down the stairs.

"It's just that you give in to your mother and obey her like you're still four years old."

She stopped on the stairs and glared at him. "What *exactly* are you saying? That I shouldn't give up some of my time to help my friend have a *happy* wedding?"

"No, of course not. It's just that I'm at the end of the hall and you're not there with me." He gave her a little smile.

"This is about sex, isn't it? You want me in bed with you and my friend can take care of her own wedding. Is that what you're saying?" She took another step down but Jared extended his arm and blocked her. She stopped but didn't look at him.

"Alix, I didn't mean that the way it sounded. It's just that I miss you." He leaned forward to put his lips near her ear. "I miss our talks, how we work together. I miss seeing you."

She turned to face him. "I miss you too, but I'm also a realist. You're going back to work in New York soon and I'm going to stay here with Mom for the rest of my year in your house. She's asked me to help her with her outline. She's been having trouble with her eyes so I'm going to read Valentina's journal aloud to her."

For a moment Jared couldn't speak. "And you believed that story?!"

"Believe that my mother has trouble with her eyes? Really, Jared, why would she lie to me about something like that?"

"To keep us apart," he said.

"That makes no sense! I'm in this house because of *your* aunt's will, my mother is here because she needs to earn a living, and you *won't* be here because you have a business to run. How is *any* of that my mother who is keeping us apart?"

"I mean *now.* Today, tomorrow."

"Oh," Alix said. "I see. You're angry because I'm not jumping into bed with you right *now.* You'll be fine when you're in New York wearing a tux and dating your supermodels, but now, today, you want me because . . . well, because I'm *here.*"

"That's ridiculous! I have a week before I go to New York and I *always* come home. Often."

That statement made Alix so angry she was afraid to reply. She gave him a look up and down. "I have to go!" She hurried down the stairs.

It took all Jared could do to keep from ramming his fist into the wall. *This* is why he never brought his girlfriends to Nantucket, he thought. Start being nice to them at home and —

And what? he thought. They run off and help their friends instead of spending every minute with him? "So who's the four-year-old?" he mumbled and plodded back up the stairs.

Standing at the top of the staircase was his grandfather, so solid, so *real,* that Jared knew that if he touched him he'd feel it. The man was wearing a smirk that screamed "I told you so!"

Jared hadn't seen his grandfather for weeks — and he missed him almost as much as he did Alix. "I want to talk to you."

"Everything has been said," Caleb answered, then walked away. He didn't vanish in a poof, but *walked.* Jared was sure he heard the creak of the old floorboards, which was impossible since Caleb's ghostly body had no weight.

By the time Jared got to the top of the stairs, the wide hallway was empty and Victoria was just leaving her bedroom.

"Jared, you gave me a start. Did I hear you and Alix arguing?"

"Of course not. What would we have to fight about? What have you got planned for her to do today? Arranging dolphin rides?"

Victoria smiled sweetly. "Why no, dear, I thought we'd have the guests go on a Nantucket sleigh ride." She swept past him.

A Nantucket sleigh ride was when, long ago, the sailors harpooned a whale from their rowboats, then the enormous creature would drag them across the sea in a terrifying, life-threatening rush.

Gritting his teeth, Jared watched her until she went down the stairs. When he looked back, he saw his grandfather again, but this time he was smiling broadly. "Do *not* leave!" Jared ordered, but Caleb just laughed and walked away.

Jared leaned back against the wall. This wasn't his day!

"Are you all right?" Victoria asked her daughter. It was evening and they were sitting in the family room. Victoria was on the couch with a stack of printed papers on her lap, a rum cocktail in her hand.

Alix was on a cushion on the floor, her legs under the coffee table, and she was tying little green ribbons into bows. Yesterday her mother had declared that they absolutely, positively must give Izzy a baby shower on the day before the wedding. Since then, Alix had been drowning in baby things. "I'm fine," Alix said.

"You don't look happy. If you don't want to do this, I can get Lexie or Toby to help. I'm sure they'd be willing."

"No, it's not that. It's just . . ."

"It's Jared, isn't it?" Victoria said.

"Actually, it is. We had an argument this morning and I was pretty harsh. He was saying he missed me."

"I'm sure he does. When does he return to New York?"

"Next week. After the wedding, I guess." She grimaced. "But he says he'll visit Nantucket often. I guess I'll see him then."

"Alix . . ."

She put up her hand. "It's all right. I knew this was coming. I hoped it wasn't, but . . . I don't know what I expected." She ran her hand through the box of bows. "Do you think this will be enough?"

"More than enough." Victoria was studying her daughter. "Why don't you walk down to see Lexie and Toby? Maybe they'll cheer you up. And I think Jared's outside with his head under the hood of his truck. Maybe you could hand him tools."

"No, thanks," Alix said as she got up. "Seeing him now will just make the inevitable harder. I think I'll go upstairs and read for a while. I suddenly feel very tired." She kissed her mother's cheek and left the room.

Victoria put her manuscript pages on the coffee table and sat there frowning. So far, the plan that had come to her in her sleep wasn't happening as she'd envisioned. "Jared," she said aloud, "you're an idiot."

Outside, Jared looked up from his truck to see the light in Alix's window. He'd calmed down from this morning enough to see that she was right. He'd promised Tim that he'd be back in the office on Monday and he planned to be there. Then after that, well, he would start working toward keeping Alix with him forever. He smiled at that idea. It would take a while and they'd have to work out some things together. For one thing, there was New York. His office and his work life were a big part of him and Alix needed to realize that.

He glanced back up at the window and saw her shadow moving about. Who was he kidding? Alix could probably run his office better than he could. And she got along with people better than he did, so that wouldn't be a problem.

The truth was that he couldn't think of any aspect of his life that Alix wouldn't improve.

His question was how she felt about him. She certainly hadn't seemed upset about his going off to New York while she stayed here on the island.

Jared picked up a wrench. Tim was going to be furious because in the coming year his business partner was going to be out of the office a lot.

# Chapter Thirty

It was two days later when Victoria saw Jared walking up the path to the kitchen door. It looked like he had just stepped out of the shower and he had a big bouquet of flowers in his hand. Obviously, he was coming to apologize.

Ken said Jared had been out on his boat all day yesterday. "The chapel's almost done but we could have used his help. And what have you done to Alix to make her look so gloomy?"

Victoria put her hand behind her back and crossed her fingers. "This time it wasn't me. Jared and Alix had a rip-roaring fight."

"I can't imagine that," Ken said. "They act like they've known each other forever."

"You'd like to think that they're clones of you," Victoria said in disgust, but Ken smiled.

"So what did they argue about?"

Victoria shrugged. "He told her he's going back to New York and Alix is staying here. Looks like it's over between them. Actually, she's so down she's hardly speaking. You think I should take her to a doctor to get her some pills?"

The hot blood of anger crept up Ken's neck to his face. "I'll murder that boy!" he said under his breath, then turned and stomped out of the house.

As Victoria watched him go, she could only shake her head. "So *now* you listen to me? I lie, you listen. I'm honest and you run off to play tennis with Toby's dad. Men!"

Now, coming toward the house with his arms full of flowers was a contrite-looking Jared. Maybe Victoria should be glad of the sight but she wasn't. What happened next? He and Alix would make up? That would change nothing. After the wedding Jared would go to New York and Alix would still remain behind. Stay to read Valentina's journals to her mother?

Deliver me! Victoria thought. She'd never be able to concentrate with someone reading aloud, and besides, Alix would be lovesick. She'd be looking at her phone constantly, waiting for HRH to call.

No, it would be better if Victoria hurried this whole thing along. Jared was nearly at the door, so she opened it a bit so it wouldn't make any noise, then she went into the family room.

Alix was standing by the window looking at some house plans, but when she heard her mother's footsteps she shoved them under three bridal magazines.

"You must be relieved to be done with a man like Jared," Victoria said rather loudly.

"We just had an argument. Nothing is 'done.' Mother, sometimes I think you don't really like him."

"But, darling," Victoria said, as she saw Jared come to a halt, flowers in hand and just out of sight, "I adore Jared. I always have, but do you think he's right for a girl like you?"

"What does that mean?"

"He's a man of the world, dear. He's used to yachts and all-night parties and those plastic girls who remind him that he's famous."

Alix felt the blood rushing through her body, and just like her father, it was moving upward to her face. "Jared also likes to work and I do too. And that man who sails on yachts also takes care of a lot of people on this island. If anyone needs help, Jared is there to give it."

"But how do *you* fit into this?" Victoria asked, an eyebrow raised in skepticism. Her tone implied that Alix didn't know what his life was really like.

"He *needs* me," Alix said, half shouting in her anger. "I see the person underneath the public man, behind the *famous* one. You know something? I think that before me Jared led a very lonely life, with people wanting him for what he could give them or do for them, not for who he *is.*"

"But isn't that what *you* want from him? To further your career? To become a great success on his coattails?"

"No!" Alix shouted, then just as suddenly the anger left her. "I did. When I first met him all I wanted was to work for his firm, but not now. Now I want to share my life with him. If he wants to go build huts in Africa, I'll go with him."

"And give up setting the world on fire with your designs? Do you love him *that* much?"

"Yes," Alix said softly. "Yes, I do. I love him more than all the buildings in the world. More than I thought it was possible to love."

Victoria's beautiful face lost its haughty look and once again she was Alix's mother. "That's what I wanted to hear." She opened her arms and Alix ran to her to be enclosed in a loving embrace. Victoria looked over her daughter's head at Jared, who was silently standing in the doorway.

With a smile of such warmth that it seemed to illuminate the room, Jared turned away and went outside.

Jared started to get into his truck, but what he'd heard had left him a little too dazed to be able to drive. When he realized that he was still holding the flowers, he tossed them in the open window and kept walking. He went down the streets of his beloved town, oblivious to the tourists pointing and staring at the perfection of the old houses.

He went down Centre Street to the JC house, took a right past the bookstore. It was a short walk to Jetties Beach, a place where he could see and hear the ocean.

He'd just reached the edge of the water when his cell rang. Maybe it was Alix, he thought, but it was a number not in his contacts list. Usually, he wouldn't pick up, but this time he did. A woman's nervous voice said, "Mr. Montgomery? I mean, Kingsley. I mean, Jared?"

"Yes?"

"It's me, Izzy."

"Alix is okay," Jared said, "and I'm sorry I made her so miserable."

"Oh," Izzy said. "I don't know anything about that, but I'm sure you are. That's not what I called about. Do you have time to talk right now?"

"Sure," he said. "What's the problem?"

"I don't want to upset Alix, but I'm going to do a terrible, awful thing to her. I'm not going to show up for my own wedding."

"You're going to leave Glenn at the altar?" Jared asked.

"No, no! Of course not! He's going to be with me. The people I'm leaving behind are our parents and relatives who do nothing but constantly bicker and fight."

"I don't understand what you want to do."

"Wait, here's Glenn and he can explain it better."

When her fiancé got on the phone, his voice was firm. He was a man protecting the woman he loved. "It's been bad here, with both our families fighting all the time. I thought for a while it was solved, but it wasn't. It was just brewing under the surface and it's erupted again. I didn't know how awful it was since Izzy usually handles everything, and she could now if she weren't pregnant."

He paused, then began again. "Izzy hasn't even been able to get rid of those repulsive bridesmaids that were chosen for her. She tried but . . . Anyway, I feel like a jerk because I didn't pay more attention to all this, but I thought it was what women did so . . ." He took a breath. "That's not what's important. Yesterday the doctor said that the stress she's under is causing physical problems. If Izzy doesn't get some relief from all this, it's possible we could lose the baby."

Instantly, Jared said, "What can I do? Name it and I'll do it."

Glenn said they wanted everything to go ahead as planned, that their relatives would go to Nantucket, but that at the time of the ceremony someone would tell the guests that there would be no wedding. "You — or someone — can say that Izzy and I have eloped to the far ends of the earth. They're paying for everything so let them enjoy the food and music. It's just that they won't have my bride there to torture."

"I understand," Jared said.

"There's another thing. Izzy's afraid to call Alix because she knows how hard she's worked on this wedding, especially since Victoria showed up. Izzy's also afraid you're going to think she's a bad person for letting everyone down."

"Could I speak to her, please?"

"Yes?" Izzy asked tentatively.

"Izzy," he said slowly, "I think this is the wisest thing I've ever heard in my life. And any woman who'd choose her child over a wedding is at the top of my list of best people."

Izzy promptly burst into tears and Glenn took the phone from her.

"Is she all right?" Jared asked.

"She's fine. Everything makes her cry, but then for the last couple of days my mom and hers have made me close to crying. Izzy's kept most of it from Alix so she'd . . ." He trailed off.

"So she'd what?"

"So Alix would stay on the island with you. Izzy knows that if she told too much of the truth Alix would be here in an instant — as Izzy would do for her. Izzy didn't want Alix to miss out on . . . well, on you."

Jared couldn't help feeling a pang of guilt.

"Listen, Glenn, don't worry about anything. I'll lie to everyone about everything. I'll tell them Izzy is hidden away in my house and ready to come down the aisle. They won't know until the last minute that there won't be any wedding. And I'll make sure there's so much booze that the guests won't care. As for the mothers, I'll sic Victoria on them."

"Thank you," Glenn said, and Jared could hear the relief and gratitude in his voice. "I don't know many famous people and Izzy says you're the top of the heap in the architecture world, but if they're all like you . . . Well, thanks a lot. Maybe Izzy can relax now. We're going to fly to Bermuda to get married."

"Send us a postcard," Jared said.

"Us? As in you and Alix?"

"Yes. Alix doesn't know it yet, but I'm going to ask her to let me finish the process of making a Kingsley of her." In the background Jared heard a high-pitched squeal, which showed that Izzy had been listening in.

"Okay," Glenn said, "now you've done it. I'm going to have to drug Izzy to keep her from calling Alix and telling her."

"Are you guys going to be around today? Can I call you later to work out some details?" Jared asked.

"We're here," Glenn said, "and again, thanks."

They hung up and Jared put the phone

back in his pocket.

He stood there looking out at the water. Until he'd said aloud what was going through his mind, it hadn't solidified. But he liked it. He very much wanted to spend the rest of his life with Alix.

His first thought was that he wanted to talk to his grandfather, but he knew that wouldn't happen. Besides, Jared knew what the man would say. "First, you have to ask her," he could hear his grandfather say. The smile that came with that thought reminded him that his grandfather was going to leave on the same day that Jared was going to start his new life.

As he walked back to town, he thought about how to ask Alix and where. There was only one place this could happen. He had a friend who was an interior decorator and she could help with the first part of this plan. He went to the flower shop where Toby worked and told her what Izzy and Glenn had said and how Jared had come up with a whole new plan.

"Saturday?" she said. "Lexie and me?"

"That's right. I have some things to work out with Izzy, but most of it has already been set up. It's just a few people who will be different."

"Just a few," Toby said, joking at his simplification of what would be an enormous project.

Smiling, Jared kissed her cheek. "I know you can do it. I have to go. I have a lot to do."

"I'm sure you do. By the way, congratulations."

"She hasn't said yes," Jared said.

"Her eyes have and that's what counts."

He paused by the door and looked back at Toby. "Do you think we can pull this off?"

"Of course," she said. "Lexie and I will do everything."

The minute the door closed, Toby wanted to indulge in a few tears of exasperation — but she didn't have time for that. Jared had said that under no circumstances was Victoria to find out about this, but this secret wasn't going to be easy to keep. Tell one wrong person and everyone on the island would know.

Toby had only met Jilly once, when she'd thanked her for tackling the greenhouse, but the good thing was that Jilly didn't know anyone on Nantucket to tell. Toby called her. Without preamble, she asked, "Can you keep a secret from Ken?"

"Probably not."

"Then we'll have to include him in everything, as I don't have time for cloak and dagger. At least not for the dagger. Sorry, I'm rambling. Ken is all right but Victoria is another matter. Do you think you can keep Ken from telling Victoria a really big secret that has everything to do with Alix?"

"I think Ken might sell his soul for that opportunity."

Toby laughed. "That's good. Sort of. First of all, we're missing a man. Could you possibly supply one?"

"Give me year, size, make, model, color, and I can find exactly what you need from my relatives."

Again Toby laughed. Maybe what Jared had asked her and Lexie to do wasn't going to be so difficult after all.

As soon as she hung up, Jilly called Ken.

"Have you seen Jared?" he immediately asked.

"No, but I've heard what he's doing."

"So have I!" Ken said fiercely.

Jilly could tell by his voice that he was angry. "You don't approve?"

"Of Jared leading my daughter on? Of slick-talking her, then dumping her? You're damned right I —"

"Ken!" Jilly said loudly. "I think you better listen to what I have to tell you — and do you have a tuxedo?"

That question shut him up long enough to listen to what Jilly had to say.

As for Jared, he only walked a block before opening the door to a jewelry store. "What do you have in size five?" he asked the man who owned the shop.

# Chapter Thirty-One

Alix spent the day with her mother, going from one store to another and looking at everything from cheeses to bridesmaids' gifts to cuff links for the groomsmen.

"Mother, I think Izzy is doing all this. You seem to forget that it's her wedding and not mine."

"How could I forget something like that? When you get married, I'll need a year to plan."

"Good," Alix muttered. "By the time I get married, I'll be too old to shop for myself."

Victoria took her daughter's arm. "Jared still hasn't called you?"

"No, not a word. No call, text, email, carrier pigeon, nothing."

"Ken said Jared went out on his boat yesterday so maybe he's still there. No! Wait. He got back last night. Maybe he's been busy with some new commission."

"Without me."

"Oh, heavens, Alix! You must cheer up. It

isn't the first time you've been in love and it certainly won't be the last." Victoria stopped to admire some shoes in a window, then looked across the street at Sweet Inspirations. "How about some chocolate?"

"No, thanks," Alix said, and looked at her mother. "What did you do when the man you loved didn't call?"

"Never happened," Victoria said.

"No man has ever not called you?" Alix asked with interest. Never before had she asked her mother about something like this.

"That's happened. It's just that I've never been in love. At least not the kind you mean." She started walking.

Alix hurried after her mother. "You never told me that before."

"I've never told anyone. I write books of great passion and of everlasting, undying True Love. If I ever get hold of Valentina's journal, and if I should be so lucky as to meet the Kingsley ghost, I plan to write a great saga about a love that was so deep it survived death. It's all wonderful to read and write about, but outside my books I've never felt it."

Alix was blinking at her mother. You could live with a person all your life and not know fundamental facts about them. "What about that guy Rockwell? You liked him a lot."

"That was pure sex."

"Oh." Alix was torn between wanting to

hear and not wanting to hear from her mother. "I did think that was why you liked that young man André. I never told you that he made a pass at me. I was about sixteen then."

"Darling, André made passes at everyone. At your seventeenth birthday party I found him in a closet with one of the male waiters. He asked me to strip from the waist up and join them."

"Just the waist up?" Alix put her hand up. "Don't answer that. What about Preston? I liked him."

"You liked the gifts he gave you. When I saw him folding your laundry but leaving mine in the basket, I told him to get out."

Alix took her mother's arm in her own. "I'm sorry. I had no idea, but then I've seen so many men make fools of themselves over you, I always assumed there was love involved."

"I seem to attract the wrong kind of man. They don't look at me and see a two-story colonial and three kids."

"But Dad did," Alix said, then grimaced. "Please don't tell me anything horrible about my father."

"There's nothing bad. He grew up in an easy, sheltered world where everyone knew their place. I was young and from a very different world. I think I was exciting to him. For a while, anyway. When it got bad between his parents and me, he ran away and hid." Victoria squeezed Alix's arm. "All that was long ago and doesn't matter now. Besides, your father is in love."

"With Jilly?" Alix had been so overwhelmed with wedding and shower plans that she'd spent little time doing anything else. She certainly hadn't seen that her father was in love.

"Yes. They're mad for each other. I can see it already."

Alix sighed. "Well, Mom, I guess it's just you and me. Again. Jared offered me a job at his firm, but I don't know if I should take it. If I had to see him with another woman, I would probably fall down dead."

"You're going to find that you can stand a lot more in life than you think you can. Of course you'll take the job." They were near the wharf now, at the Juice Bar. "Do you still love peanut butter ice cream?" Victoria asked.

"I do. And do you still like cherry chocolate chip?"

Victoria smiled. "Still my favorite. Shall we indulge and forget about men?"

"Gladly!" Alix said.

At about four that afternoon, Alix got a text from Lexie. TOBY AND I ARE GOING TO DRESS UP AND GO OUT FOR DRINKS. PICK YOU UP AT 7:30? She read it to her mother. "I'm not sure I'm in the mood to go out."

"I want you to," Victoria said. "Freddy is coming over and we'd like some time alone."

Alix still looked hesitant.

"What if I lend you my blue silk Oscar de la Renta?"

"With the Blahnik heels?"

"The black ones with the rhinestones on the side?" Victoria put her hand to her heart. "The sacrifices one makes for her child."

Alix pushed three magazines — all bridal — and two rolls of wrapping paper off her lap and started for the stairs. "And your silver earrings with the pavé diamonds," she called as she ran up the stairs.

Victoria gave a loud, melodramatic groan, which wasn't easy considering she was smiling broadly.

When Lexie appeared at the back door, she looked at Alix and said, "Wow! You look like —"

"Cinderella," Toby said from behind her.

They were dressed nicely but Alix looked like she was about to step onto a runway. "Mom did my hair. Like it?" Victoria had pinned it up, with soft tendrils framing her face.

"You look wonderful," Toby said. "I wish we'd hired a limo."

"But my truck will have to do," Lexie said.

Victoria kissed all three of them, wished them a good evening, and waved goodbye.

The three young women got into the front of Lexie's pickup. Alix had no idea where they were going, but she was surprised that they were heading toward where the chapel was being built. She hadn't been there since they'd found Valentina's journal, which right now seemed like a long time ago. When Lexie pulled onto the dirt drive, Alix began to suspect something was up. "What are you doing?"

It was Toby who answered. "We're sorry, Alix, but Jared asked us to bring you here. He's in the chapel and he wants to talk to you."

Alix frowned. "If he wants to talk to me, he didn't need to put on this charade. He could have —"

Toby put her hand on Alix's. "Please go. He's been quite upset since your argument."

"Does everyone on the island know about that?"

Toby looked at Lexie, then back again. "Pretty much, yes."

Alix couldn't help laughing. "Whose side are they on?"

"Yours," Toby said.

"Most definitely yours," Lexie said.

"In that case I'll go." She opened the truck door and stepped out — and sank into Nantucket sand. She removed her heels and walked barefoot toward the chapel as Lexie backed the truck out.

She could hear the ocean in the distance, and the chapel silhouetted in the bluish dusk was beautiful. Alix couldn't help a feeling of pride at the sight. To see something that had existed only in her mind in solid form was inspiring. It made her want to create more buildings.

The windows were in now and she could see candlelight flickering inside. She paused before the big doors, touched the hinges that she had designed and Jared'd had made, and got her shoes on before the door swung open.

Standing there was Jared, all six-feet-plus of him, wearing dark trousers and a soft linen shirt. He still had his beard but it had been trimmed, as had his hair. With the candlelight behind him, he took her breath away.

"Please come in," he said, sweeping his arm back and taking her hand. "And may I say that I've never before seen anyone as beautiful as you are tonight."

There was no furniture in the chapel yet. Instead, a large, beautiful rug of blue and gold had been spread on the floor. Around two edges were what looked to be a hundred pillows of silk and cotton, embroidered and plain. On the other side were a couple of chairs and a little table with champagne in an ice bucket, two crystal flutes, and plates with cheeses, crackers, and chocolates.

"It's beautiful," she whispered as Jared went to the table to open the wine. She looked around at the chapel with its hundreds of candles, some on tall stands, some suspended from ropes attached to the overhead beams, and many of them on the floor.

At the end was the stained-glass window that Jared had bought in Maine. She'd seen photos of it but hadn't seen it outside its crate. Since there was no electricity, she saw that there were candles behind the big window, which meant that it had been set forward in its frame. That hadn't been in her drawings, and it was something she should have specified. She turned to him. "Did you extend that?"

He handed her a flute of cold champagne. "It's my single contribution. Do you mind?"

"No," she said. "Maybe you can teach me more about lighting. You could —"

"Not tonight. No teaching. Tonight is for . . ." He looked up at the knight in the stained glass. "Tonight is for the future." They clicked glasses and took a sip.

It was when she looked back at the window that she realized the knight looked like Captain Caleb. "Ancestor of yours?"

"Could be, couldn't he?" He paused. "Alix, I have something I want to talk to you about."

She took a breath. Was this about New York? About who would live where? Work where? Would he tell her how often he would visit the island?

He took her hand and led her to one of the

chairs. She sat but he stayed standing. "First of all, I want to apologize for our argument. I was being a jerk."

"No," she said. "You were right. I've been following my mother around like I haven't done since I was a kid." She glanced around the chapel, at the candles, the rug, the table, the food. "I must say that no one apologizes better than you do. Daffodils and now champagne. But in this case, half the apology is mine. It's just that I've felt so guilty about neglecting Izzy's wedding that I was overwhelmed — still am, for that matter."

He was standing over her looking down and smiling. "That you care about people is one of my favorite things about you. Tyler's mom said he was asking for you."

She smiled. "I've missed him these last few days. I'll have to invite him and his parents to Izzy's wedding. Did you hear that Mom is inviting lots of island people? And that Jilly has asked some of her relatives from Warbrooke? She and Cale are trying to get the family to buy that big house at the end of the lane and —" She looked at him. "Why are you smiling at me like that?"

"Because I've missed you and because I love you."

Alix just sat there and looked up at him, blinking, not sure she'd heard him correctly. It was so very beautiful around them, with all the candles flickering and the brilliant colors of the rug and the pillows — and Jared. To her eyes, he was by far the most beautiful thing in the room.

Still smiling, Jared reached inside his jacket and pulled out a ring box.

Alix was sure that her body stopped: heart, lungs, brain, all came to a halt.

He went down on one knee before her. "Alixandra Victoria Madsen, I love you. With all my heart, with all my being, now and forever, I love you. Will you marry me?" As he picked up her left hand and prepared to slip a truly gorgeous ring on her finger, he waited for her answer.

But Alix was too stunned to react. She just sat there, not moving, not breathing, a human statue frozen into place.

"Alix?" Jared asked, but she didn't answer. She just stared at him. "Alix?" he asked louder. "Are you thinking of saying no?" He looked worried.

She managed to take a breath. "No. I mean yes. Yes and yes! And —" She threw her arms around his neck. Since he was still on one knee and not expecting her leap, he fell backward onto the rug, his body between Alix and the floor.

"Yes, I'll marry you," she said. "A million times yes." She punctuated her every word with a kiss to his face and neck. "I can go with you to New York?"

Jared was laughing. "Yes, of course you can.

Who's going to tell me that my every design is wrong if you aren't there?"

"I thought you were going to leave me behind."

He put his hand to the side of her face. "Not ever. I'll never leave you."

Alix began to unbutton his shirt.

He put his hand over hers. "No, not now."

She pulled back. "The chapel hasn't been consecrated yet, so —"

"It's not that. I just think that we should wait until after we're married."

She drew back to look at him. "But that could be a year. My mom says —"

Jared kissed her to silence. "You don't want to see the ring?" he asked. "It's rather nice, if I do say so myself."

"The ring! I'm an idiot." She rolled off him and started searching for it on the rug.

Jared held up his hand. A platinum ring with a large pink diamond was on his little finger. "This what you're looking for?"

She lay down on the rug beside him, her head on his shoulder, and held up her left hand for him to slip the ring onto it.

"With this ring," he whispered as he put it on her finger.

Alix held up her hand to look at it. Nothing sparkled like a diamond in the light of a hundred candles.

"Like it? If not, we can get something else."

Alix closed her hand. "It's perfect. The best

ring I've ever seen. Even Mom is going to approve."

"About that," Jared said as he rolled away, stood up, and held his hand out to her. "You can't tell your mother until after we're married."

"I agree!" she said as she got up. "Let's elope. Mom's been saying that my wedding will involve a cathedral and a dress with a fourteen-foot-long train."

He led her to a chair, she sat down, and he sat across from her. "I couldn't live with myself if I cheated a girl out of a real wedding."

"I don't mind," Alix said. "If it's a choice between an elopement and Mom's extravaganza, I'll take a Las Vegas drive-through with Elvis."

He sliced a bit of brie, put it on a cracker, and leaned across the table to put it into her mouth. "You see," he said as he scooped up some hummus and ate it, "it seems that Izzy doesn't want her wedding, so I thought that you and I would take it."

"Oh, no! Please don't tell me that Izzy and Glenn have broken up."

"Not at all," Jared said. "They're going to Bermuda to get married and I'm flying his two brothers and her little sister down there to be with them. If you agree to everything, that is."

When Alix realized what he was saying, she

just sat there, holding a slice of cheese on a cracker outside her mouth. Just holding it, not moving. Jared reached across and guided her hand to her mouth.

Alix chewed for a moment, then said, "I can wear Aunt Addy's dress?"

"I'm sure she'll smile down from Heaven and thank you."

"Lexie and Toby — ?"

"Will be your bridesmaids — if you approve, that is."

"Very much so." She ate another cracker. "We're talking about *this* Saturday, right?"

"Yes," he said and reached across the table to take her hand.

Alix grinned so wide her face almost split. "Tell me more."

"I would love to," he said.

# CHAPTER THIRTY-TWO

It was early morning, just three days before he was to get married, and Jared couldn't sleep. Toby had sent him an email with details, such as getting the marriage license, the rehearsal times, and that she and Lexie were flying to New York for the day to buy new dresses. She said she'd sent Alix emails of more information.

Jared lay in the bed with his hands clasped behind his head, looking at the ceiling. Last night he and Alix had stayed in the chapel and talked until midnight. It hadn't been easy to keep their clothes on but they'd done it. But then they'd been feeling the solemnity of what they were planning, their lifetime together.

Neither of them liked the secrecy of their plans, but they did like getting it done. They'd made up their minds and were now determined to go forward into their lives together. In other words, they wanted to continue in the way they had been, living and working with each other, with no further interference.

Last night as Jared was getting into bed, he sent an email to Tim to come to Nantucket on Friday and bring his tux. Jared would only tell him in person that he wanted him to be his best man. In other circumstances, it would have been Ken, but he would be escorting Alix down the aisle.

It wasn't yet dawn but Jared got up, pulled on jeans, a T-shirt, and sandals, then quietly went up the stairs to the attic. As he stretched up to reach the light chain, he remembered why he'd been so angry that he'd torn off the pull string.

For a moment he stood still, looking out the window. His anger about his grandfather and Victoria was gone now, replaced with a sense of *What will be, will be.* Somewhere in the last few days he'd come to terms with a feeling of destiny, that no matter how angry he became, he couldn't change the future. He couldn't stop what might happen — and he doubted if his grandfather could either.

When he heard a sound behind him, he didn't turn, but he knew he was no longer alone. "Do you know what I did?"

"Came to your senses and asked dear Alix to marry you?"

"Yes," Jared said as he turned around — then drew in his breath. His grandfather was sitting in the big wing chair and he was as solid looking as any human.

Walking toward him, Jared reached out to touch his grandfather's hand. It was real, almost solid and almost warm — and it was the first time in his life that Jared had ever touched him. Jared drew back and sat down heavily on the threadbare couch. He had a horrific vision of Caleb putting his arm around Victoria and the two of them walking into the fog and never being seen again. All Jared could do was stare at his grandfather.

"I still don't know," Caleb said in answer to the unasked question. "I don't know how or why or what will happen. Everyone is here now. Did Alix tell you that she saw my father at Parthenia's wedding?"

"No," Jared said, still staring.

"His spirit is in Dr. Huntley's body. My father was a man of great integrity and kindness, and my mother was his strength." Caleb sighed. "I've had to see them die four times, and three of those times were just alike. First my father went, and he was followed soon by my mother. But this time your modern medicine has made them leave each other out of order."

"What does that mean?" Jared asked.

"It's yet another thing that I don't know, but I hate to see him the way he is now. He misses my mother so much that he's only half alive."

Jared was studying his grandfather, very

aware that in a few days he would no longer be there. "Have you been spying on Victoria?"

"Not in the way you mean," Caleb said with a bit of a smile. "A bit of talk while she's asleep, but nothing more." He waved his hand. "If I got near her the way I am now, she'd see me. However, I've been considering allowing that. One last time."

"You won't get to see number eight," Jared said, meaning the son that he and Alix would have. "But then I guess we should drop the numbers."

"Perhaps you'll name a son Caleb."

"I would be honored," Jared said. "Maybe on that last day you would be allowed out of this house long enough to come to our wedding."

"I wish I could!" Caleb said. "With all my might, I wish I could be there. I would like to hold Valentina in my arms one last time, see her smile at me." He sighed. "I have paid for my greed." He gave a little laugh. "The irony is that the treasure I thought I had to have was left behind on my ship and my brother brought it back to Nantucket."

"Are you talking about the shipload of goods you bought in China?"

Caleb waved his hand. "It doesn't matter now. Are you going to let Victoria in on the secret of your wedding?"

"Absolutely not!" Jared said. "You know what she's like. She'll want to take over everything." He looked sharply at his grandfather. "Have you had a hand in this? Did you persuade Izzy to step out of her own wedding?"

"How could I have done that when I'm not allowed to leave this house?"

"What you *can* do is answer questions directly."

"Can I?" Caleb asked. "I hear someone. I think your Alix is coming up the stairs."

Jared watched, fascinated, as Caleb got out of the chair and walked across the room. When he reached the wall, he kept walking.

As his grandfather vanished, Alix appeared at the doorway. Jared opened his arms to her and she snuggled beside him on the couch.

"Is this your hiding place?" She didn't want to tell him that Lexie had ratted on him.

"Since I was a kid."

"Did you sleep well?" she asked.

"Not much," he answered. "Too much on my mind. Did you get an email from Toby?"

"I looked at my phone and I had five of them, so I turned it off. I'll read them later. You look like something's bothering you. You still have time to change your mind."

He kissed the top of her head. "My only worry is that you'll wise up and run away. You sure you want to take on all the Kingsleys?"

"I guess you mean Captain Caleb." When Jared didn't say anything, she turned to look at him. "Has he been here?"

Jared could hear the apprehension in her voice, but he wasn't going to lie. "Yes, he was here. I came up to talk to him. He's going to leave the earth very soon."

Alix didn't know what to reply to that. She'd never heard of anyone saddened because a ghost was leaving. Weren't people always trying to get rid of them? "Why is he going?" she asked.

"I don't understand it. People reincarnated from the past have gathered, so Granddad's leaving."

"It has to do with my mother, doesn't it? She was Valentina."

Jared nodded, afraid to say more.

"Maybe now that he finally gets to see her again he can leave."

"He's been seeing your mother off and on for the past twenty-two years. So why now?"

"Is there someone different here now?"

"Actually, there is. Jilly."

"Parthenia!" Alix said and turned around to look at him. "Maybe it's not just one person who mattered, but all of them. And think how it happened, from designing the chapel to Izzy's relatives fighting, even to finding Valentina's journal. Maybe now that all of us have gathered together, he can leave. We're a sort of séance of spirits from the past."

"I like that idea very much," he said, thinking that if she was right, it meant that Victoria was in no danger. He kissed Alix firmly. "Thanks. You've made me feel better. But then you always do." He glanced out the window to see the growing daylight. Victoria would be up soon. "I was thinking that we should turn Valentina's journal over to your mother now, before the wedding. It might keep her occupied enough that you and I can do all the things Toby has planned."

"Good idea. Izzy's guests will start arriving day after tomorrow and we have to meet planes and ferries, then we have to get them settled. How angry do you think they're going to be when we tell them that Izzy isn't here?"

He caressed her cheek. "Do you care?"

"No," she said. "Because of the way they've treated Izzy, I don't. I do feel bad about not letting Mom know, but she'd —"

"Put you in a dress with a train so long that you'd have to attach a caboose?"

Laughing, Alix put her arms around his neck. "I love you."

"Nice to finally hear it," he said. "I thought maybe you said yes just to get near Montgomery."

"I would *never* do that," she said. "However . . ." She kissed his neck. "Maybe he could give me a short course on lighting. Just a little one."

"Yeah, okay," he said as he pushed her

down on the sofa, "but I get a poem for each lesson. In the meantime, tell me that one about my lower lip again, especially the *soft and succulent* part."

"I rather like the *to draw it in, to caress it, to feel it against my own* part better."

"Recite the whole thing again and let me decide." He was kissing her deeply.

# Chapter Thirty-Three

It was five A.M. and this evening Jared was to get married. He should have been the happiest man alive, but all he could think was, Was Victoria alive? Would she be alive at the end of the day?

He was sitting on the little couch in the attic, his hands in his pockets, and sporting a never-ending frown. For one thing, the attic felt empty. The great heap of boxes was still there, but something was missing — and he knew what it was. All his life, anytime he'd entered the attic, his grandfather had appeared. It was one of the constants of his life. An hour after Jared had been told of his father's death, he'd run up to the attic. His grandfather had sat by him while Jared stared into space, unable to comprehend what had happened.

Today, for the first time, he didn't feel the presence of his grandfather. The room felt hollow, empty, as barren as a sea with no wind.

Had his grandfather already left the earth? It had been the twenty-third for five whole hours, so maybe Caleb had departed at midnight. If so, Jared hadn't said goodbye to him. Their last time together had been too abrupt. Things were left unsaid. When they'd last spoken, Jared hadn't thought of pleasant goodbyes. He'd only been concerned for Victoria.

And if Caleb had left the earth, it could mean that Victoria was gone. Right now she could be lying in her bed and . . . and not alive, he thought.

When he heard someone on the stairs, his heart leaped. His grandfather? Alix? Maybe even Victoria? But Alix had spent the night at Toby and Lexie's house so she and Jared wouldn't see each other. They'd all worried about keeping the wedding a secret from Victoria, but she was now so engrossed in Valentina's journal that she wouldn't have noticed an earthquake. The only person she was interested in speaking to was Dr. Huntley, as she spent hours picking his brain about Nantucket history. Last night the poor man had fallen asleep on the big couch. Jared had volunteered to drive him home but Victoria said to leave him. Poor man, Jared thought. Victoria meant to start all over again first thing in the morning.

If she was still alive, he couldn't help thinking.

Saying goodnight to her last night had been difficult. When she was heading to bed, Jared kept hugging her.

"Jared! What in the world is wrong with you?" she'd asked.

"Nothing." He stepped back and looked at her, noting that her hair was a darker auburn than it had been when he'd met her so many years before. He always gave credit to Ken for saving his life, but Victoria had been there too. It was Victoria who had helped Jared after his mother died. Victoria hadn't been a bottomless well of sympathy as his relatives had been. Poor Jared, they'd said, an orphan who now bore the entire burden of the Kingsley family.

Instead, Victoria had made Jared laugh. While she was on Nantucket she'd thrown parties and invited people he liked. When she was off-island she'd sent him funny little postcards and emails, and they'd often talked on the phone.

"Jared?" Victoria asked. "You're looking at me very oddly."

"I'm just remembering things. Are you sure the doc will be okay on the couch?"

"He'll be fine. I want to get up early for the wedding, so I'll check on him then."

Alarms went off in Jared's head. "Why do you have to get up early? I mean, aren't Lexie and Toby handling everything?"

"And Alix. She's the maid of honor, but

you're right. Maybe I should go over there and check on them now. Is it too late now to call and talk to Izzy?"

"Yes!" Jared said. He knew Izzy and Glenn had made it safely to Bermuda, as they had sent him a long email thanking him for flying their siblings and three friends there. Jared felt it was the least he could do since he and Alix were taking over Izzy's beautiful wedding. "I mean it is much too late. The girls said they were going to be . . . uh, polishing their toenails tonight."

"Really, Jared!" Victoria said. "You can't possibly be that naive. They're going to go out to drink a lot and flirt with boys."

"You think so?" Jared said, sounding as naive as Victoria seemed to think he was. "But, yeah, I'm sure they are."

"I still don't understand why Izzy wanted to stay with Lexie and Toby and not here. This house is larger."

"They don't want to be around Tim and me." His business partner had flown in early yesterday with a tux and a diamond tennis bracelet. "It's for the bride. I thought it would be a better gift than a toaster."

Jared had stared at the bracelet in puzzlement. "It's an expensive gift for someone you've never met. Izzy is —"

"Izzy? This is for Alix. It's you and her getting hitched, right?"

"How did you figure that out?"

"You wouldn't invite me to an unknown person's wedding, would you? Certainly not with a tux."

For Jared it was a relief to have another man to talk to about the coming wedding. Ken was busy during the day putting the finishing touches on the chapel and his evenings were spent with Jilly. Jared thought perhaps they were no longer in separate bedrooms.

Jared talked with Tim, a great money person, about the arrangements for the wedding, and about how the gifts would go to Izzy and Glenn, who needed them. "Kingsley House certainly doesn't need anything added to it."

Tim, who was married, had set Jared straight on that issue. "Alix may not want a new blender, but there must be something that she truly wants."

Jared realized what that was. "Her own office here on Nantucket."

The only place that made sense as an office was the two-bedroom maid's quarters. Victoria was out for the day so they could do it.

"You'll need the other bedrooms for the kids," Tim said. "In my experience they start coming about six months after the ceremony."

"Alix might like that," Jared said.

"You two have talked about kids?"

"It was either that or ghosts, so we went with kids."

"Wise choice."

Jared called a couple of cousins, who called some more, so they had enough people hired to remove the old wallpaper and paint the rooms. While they worked, Tim and Jared went shopping the Nantucket way, meaning that they raided the attics of the old houses the Kingsley family owned. They found everything they needed except for a drafting table.

Jared and Tim looked at each other and said, "Stanley." It took only one call and Stanley said he'd fly over with the table the next day and would install it during the wedding.

By ten that night they had it done. They'd moved Jared's office in from the guesthouse so he and Alix would be together. They'd found some magnificent artifacts hidden in the attics, from scrimshaw to whale bones, and they hung them about the rooms. The only thing they didn't have was the table. Stanley had managed to find an ex-client who was going to Nantucket on his private jet, and he was giving a ride to Stanley and the table.

All in all, Jared was glad for the physical labor of the day. It kept him from thinking about what might happen the next day.

It was late when the house was finally quiet, and, with Tim asleep upstairs, Jared found Dr. Huntley on the couch. Poor man, it looked as though Victoria had exhausted him.

There were circles under his eyes and his skin had a gray pallor to it. Tomorrow after the wedding Jared was going to tell Victoria to let the man rest.

At that thought, all Jared's anxiety came back to him. Tomorrow was the twenty-third, and his grandfather would leave the earth forever. The question was whether Victoria would go with him.

He saw her in the hallway and was afraid to leave her. When they finally said goodnight, he wondered if he'd ever see her alive again.

As soon as she went into her bedroom, Jared started toward the attic stairs. He meant to go talk to his grandfather, but he took one step and was so overcome with sleepiness that he almost fell. He had no doubt on earth that Caleb was doing this, using his new powers to control and manipulate.

Jared fought the feeling of being drugged, but it was no use. The door to Alix's bedroom was open and the bed — tidily made and so very soft looking — pulled him in. He barely made it to the bed before he fell across it and was sound asleep.

That had been last night, and now he was sitting in the attic, where he'd always gone when he was upset. He wasn't sure whether this was going to be the happiest day of his life or the worst. Tim appeared in the doorway. His friend had visited Nantucket often and knew that Jared often hid out upstairs.

"Please tell me you're not changing your mind," Tim said as he sat down in the wing chair.

"Change my mind? What are you talking about?"

"You look like a man who's going to be executed, not a happy bridegroom."

Jared tried to remove the frown from his face, but it wouldn't leave. "Everything is great with Alix. It's just . . ." He trailed off. "If I asked you to do something with no questions, would you do it?"

"Does it involve firearms?"

"Only a beautiful woman."

"I agree. No questions asked. Don't tell the wife."

Jared didn't smile. "I want you to go downstairs, open Victoria's bedroom door, look inside, and check on her."

Tim had met Victoria yesterday and had made some jokes about his own mother-in-law not looking like that. "Peeping in her bedroom? That's a bit invasive, isn't it? Illegal, maybe?"

"No questions, remember?"

Tim raised his eyebrows but stood up. "This isn't a question, but is there anything special I'm supposed to see? And if she asks what the hell I'm doing, what do I say?"

"I only care that she's still breathing and you can tell her that you got the wrong room."

"Breathing? As in alive?"

Jared didn't answer, just looked at his friend, and Tim left. While he was gone, Jared didn't think he took a breath. He could feel his heart pounding in his throat.

It seemed like an hour before he heard Tim on the stairs again, and Jared's right hand gripped the arm of the couch so tightly he probably left fingerprints in the wood.

"She's fine," Tim said as he came through the doorway.

"What does that mean?"

He sat back down in the chair. "It means that she's all right. She's sound asleep."

"Are you sure she's breathing?"

"What is *wrong* with you?" Tim asked, exasperated.

"I just want to know for *sure* that Victoria is well and healthy."

"Yes, she is breathing, and she certainly looked healthy to me. When I opened her door, she turned over in the bed. I guess you know that she sleeps in the raw."

Jared took a relieved breath of air. Caleb Kingsley hadn't taken his beloved Valentina's spirit with him when he left the earth.

Jared took a few more breaths, the frown left his brow, and a smile followed.

Tim was watching him. "What in the world happened to make you think your bride's mother wouldn't be alive this morning?"

"If I told you, you wouldn't believe me,"

Jared said, a full-fledged smile on his face now. "You're my best man, so tell me what we need to do to get ready for this shindig."

"First, we have to choose some poor sucker to tell the crowd that Izzy and Glenn have been replaced by a couple they don't know. That crowd is going to be pretty angry at having gone to all this trouble just to see someone else's kids get married. Not to mention the expense."

"Tim, old friend, your job is to get an accounting from each of them and reimburse them. The point of all this has been to keep them away from Izzy and let her have some peace. They won't be out any money."

Tim sighed. "I'm glad you're getting married, but I guess this means you won't be in the office on Monday. Honeymoon and all that."

Jared stood up. "You haven't met Alix. Her idea of a honeymoon will be to get her hands on every commission my company has and scrutinize every line of every plan. Those kids you hired are at last going to see some real talent — and precision. Ken taught her well."

"She won't hand out balloons and gold stars?"

Jared snorted. "I drew a wall four inches off and she told me — me! — that I needed to improve my observation skills."

Tim was looking at him with wide eyes. "If I weren't already married and you weren't marrying her, I'd call her right now and propose."

"Naw, this one is mine and I'm keeping her. Let's go to Downyflake and get something to eat. After we tell Ken he's to inform the crowd of the change, that is."

"We better invite him to go with us. Poor guy," Tim said in sympathy.

"Don't worry about him. He owes me big time. You see, I brought Parthenia to him."

"I thought the woman I met was named Jilly."

"Victoria, Valentina, Parthenia, Jilly, it's all the same."

Tim stopped at the head of the stairs and looked at him. "You really *need* to get back to New York. This island is doing something to your mind."

Jared was grinning. "What can I say? It's Nantucket."

It took both her bridesmaids to get Alix into Aunt Addy's dress, which made her wonder how she'd put it on the first time by herself. She paused with her hand on her cuff and wondered if Captain Caleb had somehow helped. That thought made her suppress a giggle. "Has anyone seen Jared today?" she asked.

They were in the house Lexie and Toby shared and the young women were wearing the dresses they'd bought in New York: a simple style but in glorious colors of sapphire and ruby. The hairdresser and makeup man had been and gone and it was less than two hours until Alix was to walk down the aisle.

Lexie stood up, scrutinizing the crisp, clean skirt. "He went with Tim and Ken to Downy this morning. I don't know what they've done the rest of the day, but I think they're planning to give Ken the job of telling the guests that Izzy and Glenn aren't here."

"You know," Alix said, "I feel bad that Izzy's mom won't see her get married."

"So they'll have a second ceremony later," Lexie said. She was always sensible.

Toby picked up the veil. "Alix, you only feel bad about Izzy's parents missing out because you have a great mother. Those of us who don't would look forward to a peaceful wedding, however we could get it."

"I do have a great mother, don't I?" Alix said softly.

"Do *not* cry!" Lexie ordered. "You'll have mascara all down your face."

"Okay," Alix said and sniffed as Toby handed her a tissue. "Tell me again what the plan is."

"We go to the chapel and you're to wait in the small tent with Jilly until your dad has dropped the news bomb," Lexie said. "After the blood from the ensuing battle is cleared out, Toby and I will walk down the aisle first, then Ken comes with you. After that we eat and dance. Simple."

"Mom's going to be really hurt," Alix whispered.

For a moment the two women just looked at her, unable to reply, but then Lexie said, "Let's leave. We need to get this show going." She glanced at Toby. At first it had seemed like a great idea to not let Victoria boss everyone around, but when you got down to it, Victoria was Alix's mother.

Lexie had borrowed her boss's driver and Bentley for the day and they helped Alix get inside. She was so quiet that no one else spoke on the short drive to the North Shore.

There were a lot of cars there but only a few guests were outside, all of whom Lexie shooed away so they wouldn't see the bride. They quickly ushered her into one of the two tents that were set up with tables and chairs. It was a beautiful sight, with white tablecloths and bouquets of blue hyacinths, cream-colored roses, and sprigs of grasses, all tied with pale blue ribbons. Big ribbons of a darker blue were on the backs of each chair and draped around the top of the tent.

"Toby," Alix said, "it's all incredibly beautiful. Thank you."

"No tears!" Lexie ordered again. "Now come through here and wait until we return to get you. Jilly should be here by now."

A little tent had been set up beside the large one. The only thing in it were two chairs and

Alix carefully sat down, spreading her skirt out so she wouldn't crease it. She could hear people outside, but so far there'd been no shouting. Obviously, they hadn't been told yet. The truth was that she dreaded being married in the midst of anger. There would be the guests' disappointment and her mother's hurt. *Not* a good way to begin a marriage! She truly hoped the guests would be understanding.

When the tent flap moved, Alix expected to see Jilly, but there her mother stood in an emerald green silk suit and a little pillbox hat with a short veil. Alix didn't think she'd ever looked more beautiful. A light about her face made her glow.

"Mom," Alix said, sounding like a lost five-year-old. She stood up and flung her arms around her mother's neck — and the tears came from both of them. "How did you know? I thought I wouldn't see you. I waited —"

"Ssssh," Victoria said, pulling out of her daughter's embrace. "Now look what we've done to our faces. It's a good thing I brought a repair kit. Now sit down and let me fix you."

Obediently — and very, very happily — Alix sat back down. Her mother took the other chair, pulled a full makeup kit out of her bag, and began to work on her daughter's face.

"How?" Alix whispered.

"Oh, my goodness, Alix! You and your

father are so much alike. Did you really think you could pull off something like this and I wouldn't know about it? All that whispering, all that sneaking around. So where's the ring?"

Alix proudly held up her left hand.

"Not bad." She paused with the makeup sponge in her hand. "Who do you think told Jared your ring size?"

"You?"

"Of course it was me." She smiled at her daughter. "When I got here and saw that you and Jared had already settled into what, by all accounts, was a married life, I knew I had to break up that overly comfortable arrangement."

"Why on earth would you do that?"

"Darling," Victoria said, "what's on your finger right now? What dress are you wearing? Sometimes men need a nudge to get them going. Look up."

Alix was trying not to blink as her mother reapplied mascara, and thought about what she was hearing. "No cathedral? No fourteen-foot train?"

"Really, dearest, give me credit for having some taste."

"Mom, I didn't want to leave you out. I mean . . ."

"No more tears," Victoria said, smiling. "Now, aren't you glad I made you design a larger cake and choose better flowers and invite more people?"

"I am, actually. But Izzy —"

"Is happy. I talked to her in Bermuda this morning, and she's calm and peaceful, and the baby is no longer under stress. Later, after the baby is born, she and Glenn are going to have another ceremony and all the relatives will be there. You'll be her matron of honor. It's all going to work out. You'll see."

Alix was looking at her mother. "You seem extraordinarily happy and I'm glad, but is there something else?"

It didn't seem possible, but Victoria's face got even brighter, even more lovely. "Well, dear, I know you're a virgin until tonight, but —"

Alix laughed.

"I had a rather interesting night."

"How so?"

"Oh no, it's not something I can tell you about. At least not now. This is *your* day." Victoria was redoing her own makeup and she looked at her watch. "I'm going to have to leave you. Your father has the job of telling everyone of the bridal switch and I know he's going to make a mess of it. I can hardly wait to see it!"

"Mother, be nice."

"I'm being extraordinarily nice to your father. I haven't said anything but sweet words to him all day. He's beginning to look downright terrified."

Alix knew she shouldn't laugh, but she did.

"I have to go meet Caleb," Victoria said as she stood up.

"What?!" Alix said.

"You and Addy and your ghost! It's not Captain Caleb, it's Freddy, you know, Dr. Huntley. And I can assure you that his body is quite solid." She paused a moment to smile. "Anyway, this morning he told me that from now on he wanted to be called by his middle name, Caleb."

"That's odd," Alix said.

"What's odd is the energy of that man." Victoria held up her hand. "But you're still a virgin so I can't tell you about that."

"Later, I want to hear every word about what's been going on."

Victoria looked outside. "I will. I promise. Jilly is coming, and I'm going to sit in the church with Caleb and watch your father make a fool of himself. What a divine day this is!" She threw a kiss to Alix and left the tent.

"There he is!" Lexie whispered to Toby. They were hidden inside a tent in their pretty jewel-toned dresses, and peeping out at the chapel. The ballerina-length gowns were alike, with form-fitting sleeveless tops, tight waists, and full skirts. The silk of the skirts was overlaid with tulle of a matching color. The only ornament was the little silver belt at the waist.

Outside, the small building was packed with people and the two bridesmaids were waiting to be given the word to go in. Alix was secreted away with Jilly in another tent.

Last night the three young women had gone out for a bachelorette party at the island's liveliest nightspot. But they hadn't stayed long because the whole place seemed to have been taken over by one man.

As soon as Lexie saw him, she said, "He's a Kingsley."

"I think in this case he's a Montgomery," Alix said. "Jilly told me a man was flying in for Toby."

Lexie looked surprised.

"To walk me down the aisle," Toby said. "Roger is for you, but I need someone."

"Plymouth?!" Lexie exclaimed. "You got my boss to fly in just to walk me down the aisle?"

"Yes," Toby said, "I did."

"Why didn't you ask me?" Lexie said.

"Because you would have said no."

"Yes, I would have. That man —"

"Come on, guys," Alix said. "This is my night. No fighting."

Reluctantly, Lexie had stopped arguing, but she didn't smile.

The three of them had ordered drinks, but the place was so loud that they couldn't talk. The Kingsley-Montgomery man and the people around him were causing too much commotion. Great howls of laughter, both male and female, filled the place.

"He certainly does love to party," Lexie said. "I got the impression from Jared that the Montgomerys were paragons of virtue."

"There's always a black sheep."

"Uh-oh, he's spotted us," Lexie said and looked away.

The man removed the young woman from his lap and sauntered over to their table. He did look like Jared, but he was younger and there was a devil-may-care look in his eyes that Jared had never worn.

"And what are you lovely ladies doing here all alone?"

Lexie started to speak. After all, he was probably a distant relative, but without a word, Toby got up, left the table, and went outside.

"Looks like we're leaving," Alix said as she finished her drink in one gulp, got her purse, and left.

"See you tomorrow," Lexie said and followed the other two outside.

Now they were at the chapel and there he was, dressed in a tux, standing at the door and ushering people in.

"That's not him," Toby said.

"Are you kidding?" Lexie said. "That's the man we saw last night. He's doing well at covering up his hangover."

Toby didn't say anything more as she

stepped back inside the tent.

Lexie had never been one to let a challenge go by. "Pssst," she said to the man. When he looked, she motioned for him to come to the tent, then held back the flap for him to enter. Toby had stepped away, but was watching them. "How do you feel today?" Lexie asked.

"Well enough," the man said. "And you?"

"Great. I'm Lexie and this is Toby. I take it that you're Jilly's relative who will be walking Toby down the aisle?"

The man looked at Toby in her pretty blue dress, thought how perfectly it matched her eyes, and smiled. "Graydon Montgomery," he said and bent his head forward in a sort of bow.

Toby didn't move, nor did she say anything to the man.

Lexie was a bit annoyed at her rudeness, especially since she'd never before seen Toby even be unpleasant to anyone. "I think you and I are cousins of some sort — I'm a Kingsley through my mother."

"Ah, yes. I got in late yesterday and have yet to meet any of my new family."

"Not too late," Lexie said. "You don't remember seeing us last night?"

"I'm not sure."

Smiling, Lexie looked at Toby, whose face was immobile. What was wrong with her? "I can see why you don't remember us — or anyone else. You were really plastered."

"Oh," he said and there was a bit of color rising in his face. "I see. Singing? Dancing? Champagne?"

"So now you're remembering?"

"Yes, I do remember evenings like that." He looked at Toby. "Perhaps you and I should rehearse before the ceremony?"

Lexie looked from one to the other. Toby might not like him, but he certainly seemed attracted to her. "I think that's a great idea," Lexie said. "Start at that end of the tent and walk slowly to the other end and back."

He held out his arm to Toby and she took it, but she kept her body as far from his as possible.

When a waiter came into the tent and took Lexie's attention, Graydon said to Toby, "Did I offend you last night?"

"The man who came to our table was quite unpleasant," Toby said. "He seemed to think that we had gone there for him."

"I do apologize," he said. "I didn't mean to give offense. Perhaps tomorrow I could have the pleasure of your company at dinner. I don't know anyone here and —"

"You hate to eat alone?" Toby said, her tone disdainful of the unspoken cliché. She stopped walking and pulled her arm from his. "Look, I don't know what your game is, but that wasn't you last night and I have no idea why you're trying to make us think it was. I don't like liars, so the answer is no, I won't go out with you. Now, please leave until they call for us."

He looked shocked, as though no one had ever said such a thing to him before. Without a word, he turned and left the tent.

Just outside, he saw his aunt Jilly standing beside the bride's father and talking quietly. Ken looked quite glum.

Graydon would never tell his aunt, but a family meeting had been called to discuss their beloved Jilly's sudden involvement with a man they didn't know. After what had happened with her late husband, they were quite worried about this new man. All that they'd found via the Internet was good, but they'd wanted to learn about him on a more personal level. When Jilly called with her request for a groomsman, everyone had looked at Graydon.

"I don't think that would be appropriate," he'd said at first, but then the idea had begun to appeal to him. Why not? Three hours later he was packed and on a plane to Nantucket.

He'd started asking questions about Ken as soon as he got into the ratty old pickup some man named Wes had met him at the airport in. As far as Graydon could tell, no one on the island had the least bad thing to say about Kenneth Madsen. And when they were introduced, Graydon had liked him.

"There you are," Jilly said when she saw Graydon coming out of the tent, and Ken stepped away. "Everything settled?" she asked. "Did you get to rehearse walking down the aisle?"

"I did, but . . ." He glanced at Ken, who was standing close by, but he didn't seem to be listening to them.

"Is something wrong?" Jilly asked.

"No, nothing," Graydon said. "It's just that . . ." He smiled a bit. "Something rather odd happened. The young woman I'm to escort down the aisle . . . Toby, is that her name?"

"I believe it's a nickname, but what about her?"

"She and her friends saw Rory last night — I didn't even know he was here — and the other woman . . ."

"Lexie?"

"Yes. Lexie said they saw *me.*"

"That's understandable given that you and Rory are identical."

"Yes," Graydon said. "We are, except that Toby got rather angry because she said I was lying, that it was *not* me they saw."

"Oh, my goodness!" Jilly said, her hand to her mouth.

The alarm in her voice made Ken come out of his reverie. "Is something wrong?"

"No," Jilly said, but her eyes were wide and fastened on Graydon's. "But surely this has happened to you before."

"Never. Not even once."

"Oh," Jilly said. "What are you going to do?"

"I think I might arrange to stay here on this island for a while. Lexie and Toby are roommates, are they not?"

"Yes," Jilly said, caution in her voice. "What are you thinking of doing?"

Graydon smiled in a way that let her know he wasn't going to reveal what was in his mind. "I think I should find out about this, don't you?" He picked up his aunt's hand and kissed the back of it. "I think I'll be seeing more of you in the coming weeks." He looked at Ken, nodded, then walked away.

Ken looked after the young man. "I don't mean to be nosy, but what was that all about?"

"It seems that our dear Toby can tell the twins apart."

"You have to give me a clue as to what that means," Ken said.

"It's just that identical twins run in our extended family, and there's a silly — ridiculous, really — saying that whoever can tell the twins apart is a person's True Love."

"And Toby can do this with this young man? Graydon, is it?"

"Yes, it seems that she can," Jilly said.

"Does this mean our Toby has met her True Love?" Ken was smiling at the idea.

"I don't know, but Graydon is certainly curious."

"Why do you look so apprehensive?" Ken asked. "Is there something wrong with this young man?"

"With him personally, no. It's just that the circumstances of his birth are rather extraordinary."

"What does that mean?"

"Graydon is the crown prince of Lanconia."

Ken's eyes widened. " 'Crown' prince? Doesn't that mean he will be . . . ?"

"That someday he'll be king? Yes, it does."

Ken thought about that for a moment. "The first time I held Toby she was about four hours old, and I've watched her grow up since then. In my opinion, if your prince can win her, he's the one who'll get the prize."

"I'm not sure, but I think Graydon may feel the same way."

Smiling, Ken kissed her cheek. "Queen Toby. Sounds good to me." He took a deep breath, looked at his watch, and the smile left him.

"Is it time to go?"

"Yes," he said, "it is." Together, they walked toward the chapel.

Feeling as though he was going to the gallows, Ken walked to the front of the chapel and looked out at the many guests. The little building was packed with chairs full of people and there were more guests standing around the perimeter. They'd brought in generators so the building was lit with soft lights, and the walls were hung with ribbons and what looked to be bouquets of wildflowers. And candles were everywhere.

Standing beside him were three women wearing dresses the color of spilled grape juice. They were to have been Izzy's bridesmaids and he'd heard that she hadn't chosen them. The women weren't pretty to begin with, but their sour expressions made them worse. They'd been loudly complaining because no one had given them bouquets to carry. No wonder Izzy ran away! Ken thought.

Since he taught at a major university, Ken knew he should be used to speaking before a crowd, but as he looked at the many men and women, he felt nothing but fear. The people in the little wooden chairs were mostly Izzy's and Glenn's relatives.

On the front row, separated only by a narrow aisle, were Glenn's and Izzy's mothers. Both women were wearing silk suits and they looked like they had tried to outdo each other with the amount of jewelry they had on. In a dark room they'd still sparkle.

Both women were frowning, glaring really, at each other, and when Ken stepped to the front, they turned their glowers on him. The wedding was already late and there was still no sign of the bride or groom, but Ken knew that Jared was just outside the side door.

"I have an announcement to make," Ken said loudly, but no one paid any attention to him — which made him look at his ex-wife. She sat at the end of the front row, beside Dr. Huntley, and every once in a while she'd look at the man with a dreamy expression on her face.

What is wrong with her? Ken wondered. She hadn't taken one potshot at him all day. Usually she couldn't go fifteen minutes without making a crack about whatever Ken said or did. But not today. He wondered what she was up to.

Louder, Ken called the room to attention and a few people in front stopped grumbling and looked up at him.

"There has been a change in the plans for this lovely evening," Ken said and he couldn't help glancing at Victoria. He knew she hadn't been told of the bride switch and that when she heard, she was going to be furious — and there was no doubt in Ken's mind that *he* would be her target.

He looked back at the crowd. "Everything is the same," he said, "except that there will be a different bride and groom. And attendants," he added with a glance at the unlovely bridesmaids near him.

That shut everyone up. In an instant, every person in the chapel, even the ones standing in the back — who were mostly Nantucketers — quit talking and looked at Ken.

For a moment, he tightened his shoulders as he awaited the onslaught, but it didn't happen. Everyone, even Victoria, was staring at him in silence.

Ken took a breath and continued. "Glenn and Izzy decided that they wanted a more private wedding, so they and their siblings and a couple of friends flew to, uh . . . Lanconia to get married there."

"Instead," he said as he looked directly at Victoria, "Jared Kingsley and my daughter, Alix, are going to get married today." In a reflex motion, Ken prepared to duck, for surely Victoria would start throwing things. When all she did was smile in the most self-satisfied way he'd ever seen, his jaw dropped.

When he'd recovered himself, he realized that the rest of the guests had risen from their seats and were coming for him. Only Victoria and Dr. Huntley stayed seated.

"This is *our* wedding!" one of the mothers was shouting. "I came here to see *my* daughter get married. It was bad enough that we had to fly to this place and now to —"

"Where is my son!?" the other one demanded. "We were told by that Kingsley man that Glenn and Izzy were already here. If he doesn't —"

"Was this a plan for those two to get a free wedding?" one of the fathers said. "If you think I'm going to pay for this, you have —"

"Glenn's mother said I could be a bridesmaid and I'm going to be one even if I have to —"

"Alix has always tried to upstage my daughter. I think Izzy was run off from her own wedding by her. It's always been —"

At that comment, Victoria got up and confronted the woman. Victoria was taller and a great deal more majestic than she was. "How dare you say that about my daughter! She has always helped Izzy! Alix has —"

Ken looked over the audience. Everything was in chaos. The front door had opened and as many Nantucketers who could fit into the chapel were lined up along the walls and enjoying it all immensely. All the bride's and groom's relatives were out of their seats and shouting — at Ken, at each other, and at Victoria, who was holding her own in the yelling. She was defending Alix, Jared, the island, and the institution of marriage. Overall, the tone of anger was rising by the second.

The only person still seated was Dr. Huntley. In fact, he was calmly reading the menu for the coming meal. To look at him one would have thought there was nothing going on around him, that everything was peaceful.

It was only when one mother shoved the other that Dr. Huntley looked up. He didn't seem concerned, just mildly interested.

Ken sidestepped the two angry fathers, who were arguing over money, to get to the shoving mother just as the other one raised her hand to administer a slap. Ken grabbed the slapping woman's wrist and held it firmly. Holy mackerel, but the woman was strong! She pulled against him so hard he didn't know if he was going to be able to hold her.

Meanwhile the other mother — the shoving one — turned to Victoria. "Is all this *your* doing? Is it some kind of stunt to help sell those books of yours?" She was practically spitting in Victoria's face, which was now as red as her hair.

A movement caught Ken's eye and he saw Dr. Huntley put his hands on his knees and slowly stand up. As Ken struggled with the woman — they were now almost wrestling — the man made his way through the screaming crowd to the front of the chapel to stand before the big stained-glass window.

He stood there for a moment, shaking his head as though he couldn't believe what he was seeing, then he took a breath and bellowed the word, "QUIET!"

To say it was loud was an understatement. The windows seemed to draw inward, the stained glass quaked, and a number of chairs fell onto the tile floor.

Everyone froze. Hands on other people's hair, arms in midair, sentences being shouted all came to a halt.

"Sit!" Dr. Huntley ordered and, meekly, everyone began to go back to their seats. He waited but not for long. Ken stepped back against the wall; Victoria took her seat. All eyes were on Dr. Huntley. He clasped his hands behind his back as he walked and began talking.

It was his stance, his hands, and especially his voice, that made Ken feel he was seeing a ship's captain from long ago. A man who had to be heard over a raging sea. A man who could take charge over an entire crew.

"You will get your money back," Dr. Huntley said in a voice that didn't allow any interruptions. "That you should consider coins over integrity, over kindness, is despicable. The lot of you harassed young Isabella until she ran off from *her own wedding.* All of you should be ashamed!" Turning, he glared at each one of them, his eyes lingering on the two mothers.

"That you should do something like that to your own kin is without honor. It is the lowest form of inhumanity. And especially when that lovely girl is carrying a child!" He stopped to scowl at them.

"I didn't mean —" Izzy's mother began.

"Quiet, woman!" Dr. Huntley shouted so loudly that the windows rattled.

He waited in silence for a moment, then lowered his voice. "Outside of this room is a bride. Whether you believe her to be the right one or not, she is due the respect that all brides deserve. *And you will show it!* Do I make myself clear?"

He waited until he'd seen every guest nod his or her head. As for the Nantucketers in the back, they were smiling as though they were at last seeing the world set in its proper order.

"Let me assure you that if any of you don't behave yourselves, if you don't *sincerely* wish the bride and her fortunate groom the best life has to offer, I will personally pick you up and throw you out of here — and that goes for the women too." Again, Dr. Huntley looked at every set of eyes.

In the back, a woman's voice said, "Me first," and there were a few female snickers, but Huntley's steely gaze stopped that. He turned to Ken. "Take your place, now. You are the father of the bride." Victoria came to her feet and looked as though she was about to say something. "And you sit down," Dr. Huntley said and she obeyed instantly.

With one more stern look at them, he walked toward the side door, where Jared stood staring. Dr. Huntley strode toward him, shutting the chapel door hard behind him.

"Landlubbers! If I had them on a ship I'd keelhaul the lot of them."

Jared was still staring at the man, unable to make words come out of his mouth. A few minutes earlier, the voice that had come through the door was one that he'd heard all his life. It certainly wasn't Dr. Huntley's soft, placid tone. And when Jared opened the door he'd seen a man whose every movement, every gesture, was that of his grandfather. Dr. Huntley, who usually walked with his shoulders bent, was standing so straight that steel poles would envy him. And there was nothing meek or mild about him. He was angry and he let the crowd know it. It was nearly impossible for Jared to comprehend, but he was seeing his grandfather alive and in the body of someone else.

Now, staring at him in disbelief, Jared reached out his hand to touch the man's shoulder.

"It is a weak body. I must strengthen it."

"How? When?" Jared whispered, not believing what he was thinking. Was this actually his grandfather, Caleb?

"It is I," he said. "You look at me as though you're seeing a ghost." This jest seemed to amuse Caleb a great deal, but when Jared kept staring in silence, he relented. "Last night, my father left Huntley's body."

"You mean he died?" Jared asked.

"Yes," Caleb answered. "I was not expecting that." For a moment he looked away and there were tears in his eyes. "When my father was no longer in a body, he could see me and he remembered all the times we've been together. He offered me this body if I wanted it." Caleb took a breath. "Then my mother came to get him. For one brief moment, the three of us were together again. They kissed me and left. They were so happy to be with each other. And I found myself back in a human body."

Jared was still staring. "What did you do then?"

"What do you think I did?" Caleb asked, looking at his grandson as if he weren't very bright. "I went upstairs and climbed into bed with Valentina. Two hundred years of celibacy makes a man eager."

Jared blinked a few times, then burst out laughing before grabbing his grandfather and hugging him.

Caleb embraced him back, but in the next second he stepped away. "I am not of your century. Control yourself!" His words were chastising, but his eyes were glowing.

Jared couldn't help again putting his hand on his grandfather's shoulder. It was so odd to feel him as a solid form. His face was different now, older, not quite as handsome, but good. But the eyes were the same ones Jared had been seeing all his life. "How does this body feel?"

"Heavy!" Caleb said. "This morning I ran into a wall."

Jared laughed.

"And it feels very strange that people can see me. I think —" He stopped because behind them the music had begun. "You must go to claim your bride."

Jared started toward the chapel but he paused at the door. "What are you going to do now that you have a body?"

"I have a job. I am going to marry Valentina and —"

"Victoria."

"Whichever. She is the same. And you are going to produce half a dozen grandchildren for me to spoil. What more is there to life?"

"Right. What more is there?"

Smiling, feeling that a thousand pounds of worry had been lifted from his soul, Jared went into the chapel and took his place beside Tim.

The audience was very quiet, subdued, and one of the mothers gave Jared a tentative smile. As they waited for the procession to begin, Jared said to Tim out of the side of his mouth, "When you looked in on Victoria this morning, was she alone in bed?"

"No. The man sitting beside her was there this morning too. That guy has a voice on him, doesn't he?"

"You didn't think to tell me that someone else was in bed with her?"

Tim gave his partner a look as though he were crazy. "If a woman who looks like her had been alone, I would have remarked on it. As it was, it seemed perfectly natural. What's up with you that you need to know what your mother-in-law does in bed?"

"It's not her, it's him," Jared said. He

started to say more, but the pastor cleared his throat. It was time for them to stop talking.

Lexie was coming up the aisle, her arm hooked through that of some man Jared had never seen before, but it didn't take much for him to figure out this was her boss. Too pretty, was Jared's first thought, but Plymouth did have a look about him that he might enjoy a Nantucket sleigh ride.

Next came pretty Toby. She held the arm of a tall man who looked like the Montgomerys Jared had met in Maine, but he didn't remember this specific one. Whereas Lexie's boss was holding her so close it's a wonder he wasn't tripping on her skirt, Toby was walking rather far away from her escort. A porpoise could have been passed between them.

In the next minute, the attendants broke apart and went to stand at the front of the chapel. Behind them was Alix. Never in his life had Jared seen anything as beautiful as she was in her white dress. A light veil covered her face, but he could see her smiling at him.

He watched her, never taking his eyes off her, as she came toward him, her arm hooked with Ken's. When they reached him, he stepped forward and Ken put his daughter's hand in Jared's.

As Ken raised his daughter's veil, he said,

"I'm entrusting you with my most precious possession." It was what Victoria had said, and only Jared heard him and saw the tears in his eyes.

Jared nodded in agreement, a sacred vow between the two men, and Ken stepped away to go sit by Jilly.

They had decided not to write their own vows, as the words in the traditional ceremony said everything. "Through sickness and health." "Till death do us part."

At the mention of death, Jared thought of his grandfather and what he had endured to be with the woman he loved. Jared smiled at Alix, who smiled back. As always, they seemed to have the same thoughts at the same time.

Alix repeated her vows to him and Jared thought how they were all about sharing. Sharing all that you had, all that you were, with another human being. He remembered her telling Victoria that she thought Jared's life had been lonely until now. He'd never thought it was but he knew she was right. One by one, he'd lost the family he'd been born into, but gradually Alix's family had replaced them. And now the circle was complete.

"I do," Alix said, and in the next moment the pastor said, "I now pronounce you man and wife. You may kiss the bride."

Jared took Alix in his arms and kissed her

sweetly, a kiss of promise. For a second he held her, and their eyes seemed to say it all. Turning, they looked at the many people inside the chapel.

It was as though all the anger and hostility had been erased by the magic of the wedding, and the crowd began to applaud joyously.

Jared took Alix's hand and started to run back down the aisle. But when Alix stumbled over her long skirt, he picked her up in his arms and carried her. The audience loved the gesture and broke into spontaneous laughter and even more applause.

Outside the chapel, Jared set Alix down. For just a second they were alone. "To forever," he said.

"Yes," she answered. "Forever."

# Epilogue

Jared leaned back in the chair and looked at his grandfather. It had been three weeks since the wedding and as he'd predicted, Alix had wanted to go to New York right away to see his offices.

All the way there she'd been nervous that once they left Nantucket things would change. Specifically, she was worried that her new husband would turn into a different person, that he'd become the Great Jared Montgomery.

Of course it hadn't happened. While it was true that most of the employees were in awe of him, Alix wasn't. No matter how other people saw him, she saw the man — and let him know it. The first day they had a rather loud argument about a house remodel that was to go out with his company's name on it.

"I hate this thing! And you cannot possibly allow anyone to see this. It's so far beneath your usual work that you should be embarrassed by it," Alix said with passion.

"There's nothing wrong with this plan," Jared answered just as vehemently.

Alix proceeded to tell him in detail what was wrong with every window, door, and wall. One by one, the other employees tiptoed down the corridor to listen and watch. They were shocked that anyone would talk to Jared Montgomery like that.

But Tim, also watching, was grinning.

It was only after Alix had gone over every detail of the twelve pages of drawings that she realized that actually, Jared agreed with her. She looked around, saw the office watching, and knew what he was doing. He was showing everyone where Alix belonged, that she had veto power over *all* plans, his included.

Suddenly, she realized that the design wasn't Jared's. It was the product of someone in the office — who was now going to hate her. Her face turned red, she rolled up the set, and held it up. "Who did this?"

A young man with dark hair timidly raised his hand.

Alix tossed him the plan, then, too embarrassed to speak, she left the room.

It took Jared some coaxing to get her to forgive him, not for what he'd done but how he'd done it. It was only when she saw that instead of being hated by the people in the office, she was very much liked, that she forgave him.

The employees saw Alix as the perfect step between Tim's anything-goes attitude and Jared's "No" that rarely came with an explanation. By the end of the first week, Alix was indispensable to all of them. Tim asked her about everything from making the employees stop using so much copier paper to presenting Jared with a bill for new computers. The other architects asked her to look at their plans before Jared saw them.

As for Jared, he was so happy to turn things over to her so he could create that he could hardly stop smiling — something few in the office had seen.

Last night they'd returned to Nantucket for the first time since the wedding, and this morning Alix had run off to see her mother and Toby. As soon as she left, Jared went to see his grandfather at Dr. Huntley's house in town.

Since Victoria was living in the little house with him, and because Jared knew she wouldn't like the modest place, right away he'd offered them Kingsley House.

"I never want to enter that house again," Caleb said with so much venom that Jared laughed. They had a lot of catching up to do. It was too soon for him to have mastered a keyboard or even a cell phone, so they'd left everything to when they saw each other in person.

"Did you find out from the journal what

happened to Valentina?" Jared asked.

"Yes," Caleb said. He was sitting by a window and lifting his face up to the sun, loving its warmth. He knew Jared had waited a long time to hear the story, so he didn't postpone it. "Even when I was here on the island, my odious cousin Obed used to follow Valentina around. He would skulk and hide behind trees to watch her. I threatened him more than once."

Caleb took a breath. All this was hard for him even after so many years. "Valentina begged me not to go on what was to be my last voyage, but I wouldn't listen. I was so full of myself! Anyway, after I left, Obed must have seen the symptoms in Valentina and known she was in the family way. He didn't wait long before he told her a lie. He said that he'd had news that my ship had gone down with me on it. This was years before it actually happened."

He paused, remembering the story. "Valentina wrote in her journal how gentle Obed was when he told her about my death, and how kindly he offered her marriage. He said he'd give my child the Kingsley name, and he swore to love them both and to build them a fine house on Main Street. Valentina wrote that she was so miserable at hearing of my death that she couldn't think clearly. She married him."

"But it was all a lie, wasn't it?" Jared said.

"The only truth was that my son got the Kingsley name. Obed always was a skinflint and he kept Valentina in what was little more than a shack on the North Shore. I'd given him that place but I'd meant for him to build there," Caleb said. "What Obed *really* wanted was her recipe for soap. It seems that when he'd been stalking her he'd been trying to see how she made it." Caleb shook his head. "I was so in love with her that I thought everyone looked at her as I did." He grimaced. "Yes, it was all a lie. After they were married, Obed treated my son like a servant, and he kept Valentina making that damned soap fourteen hours a day."

Caleb took a breath. "On the day she disappeared she wrote that she'd paid an off-islander to take her and our son to the mainland. She was going to make her way home to Maine. She felt she could tell no one she was leaving, not even Parthenia, because she feared what Obed might do to them when he found Valentina gone. She also knew that his rage wouldn't be because she and the child had left, but would be due to the fact that she was taking her soap recipe with her. But then she saw that as her son's future."

"He did get the recipe," Jared said, and he knew the next part of the story. After Valentina disappeared, Obed had continued to make and market Kingsley Soap. It made

Obed rich. Besides that, when Caleb exchanged ships with his brother and wrote a will leaving everything to Valentina and their son, that money went to Obed. For a while he had been a very rich man.

But it hadn't lasted long. A few years after his ship went down, Caleb had shown up as a ghost. He'd been confused and dazed, not understanding what had happened to him, and the *only* person who could see him was his young son, Jared.

When Obed saw the boy talking to what looked to be nothing, the man reacted out of fear. Obed beat the child. That night Caleb's anger made him so strong that even Obed could see him. The man screamed in terror and died instantly — before Caleb could get an answer from him about Valentina.

"He must have found out about her plan to escape," Jared said.

"Yes. She said she thought he'd always paid people to spy on her. He was the lowest of the low and always loved sneaking about."

"What did the journal say happened?" Jared asked.

Caleb got up from the chair, went to a cabinet in the wall, and withdrew Valentina's journal. He sat back down, opened it to the last page, and began to read.

I have killed my wife. I did not mean to. May God forgive me but what the woman said

> put the devil into me. She said she would rather be with Caleb in death than with me in life. At her words, my soul was taken from me. For a while I could not see and when I was myself again she was dead on the floor, her neck twisted half around. I go now to give myself over to the authorities and take mortal man's idea of justice, although I swear I am not guilty. As she always did, Valentina forced me to do what I did not want to. She deserved her ill fate, but I do not. May the Lord and my fellow man have mercy on my innocent soul.

When Caleb finished reading, he looked up at Jared. The pain in his eyes was breathtaking.

"But he didn't turn himself in," Jared said.

"No. I figure he took her . . . her body to sea, then he blackened her name forever. He must have paid those men who told her relatives that they'd taken her to the mainland."

Jared was thinking about what people did for money. Obed's treachery, his greed, caused the deaths of many people. Caleb, in his urgency to get home, had taken an entire shipload of men down with him.

But Obed hadn't lived long enough to receive the full benefit of the soap company he'd killed to get. Caleb's son and Susan, the woman Obed had married soon after Valentina's disappearance, had run the company.

For a long time the Kingsley family had been very wealthy, but many years later, Five wasn't good at business so he'd sold the company and squandered the proceeds. By the time Jared was growing up, nothing but some old houses that needed constant repair were left. And it was only through Caleb, with Addy's help, that they were saved from being sold.

"Why didn't he destroy the journal?" Jared asked. "You'd think that with his confession written in it, he'd be frantic to find it."

Caleb smiled. "He probably was, but young Alix found the book and hid it."

"*My* Alix? Oh. You're talking about reincarnation again."

"I am. She was Alisa back then, the daughter of John Kendricks and his first wife. Parthenia —"

"Who is now Jilly."

Caleb smiled. "You are right. Parthenia is Jilly. Does this mean I have taught you something?"

"Don't get your hopes up," Jared said, grinning. His grandfather may look different but he was certainly the same man.

Caleb chuckled. "Parthenia was John Kendricks's second wife, and she was a very good mother. But in between, young Alisa loved Valentina, just as she does now. When she heard that Valentina was missing, she stole the journal and hid it where only Valentina would look for it."

"Why didn't she tell people what was written in the back of the journal?" Jared asked.

"My guess is that she didn't have time to read it. The old place burned down — probably set fire to by Obed — just days after Valentina disappeared. Besides, Ali was just a child. Maybe she forgot. Forgot for a couple of hundred years, that is."

"If you knew where the journal was, why didn't you have someone dig it up a hundred years ago?"

"I didn't know there even was a journal until your Alix came here in this life when she was four. Sometimes young children remember things from before they were born, but they forget them when they're an adult. Alix and I were playing checkers and she told me that she had a very big secret. When I encouraged her to tell it, she said that she'd sneaked into the bad man's house, found her mother's favorite book, and put it in the oven. Of course I thought she was talking about Victoria, and it wasn't until years later that I figured out what she meant. Mother in this life; friend long ago."

Caleb smiled in memory. "But even though I knew where the journal was, it wasn't the right time to dig it up. Ken had to get over his anger, and Parthenia had to come home to us. Everyone had to be in place, starting with your young Alix, but she had no reason at all to return to Nantucket for any length of time. Addy had always felt bad for not searching more for Valentina, so she and I concocted the will that made you so angry."

Jared smiled. "Sometimes we don't know what's good for us."

"In your case, that happens often."

Jared groaned. "I can see that having a human body hasn't softened you."

It was Caleb's turn to groan. "I had forgotten what human pain feels like. This body creaks and aches. And Victoria's demands . . ." He gave a little grin.

"Speaking of which, does Victoria know the truth about you?" Jared asked. For all of his grandfather's complaints, Dr. Huntley's body was looking a great deal healthier than it had a few weeks ago.

"She pretends to know nothing, but she's always been one to keep secrets to herself."

"Like how she knew about the wedding?" Jared's head came up. "Did you know she knew about that? Or did you tell her?"

"I may have helped, but it wasn't difficult to guess what she was up to."

"I certainly didn't see it!"

"You weren't meant to, but that doesn't make you less of a man. Valentina has often put me in places I didn't want to be." He smiled. "Now it's time for you to go to your wife. And need I tell you that I want grandbabies right away?"

"I'll give it my best effort," Jared said as he got up to leave. He started to say more, but didn't. He wanted to know how his grandfather was doing at his job, and more about how he was adjusting to being alive again. He had thousands of questions and he planned to get to them all, but not now. "I'm glad you came home," Jared said.

"So am I," Caleb answered.

Jared paused at the door. "Tell me, now that you have Valentina back, was she worth a wait of two hundred and two years?"

Caleb smiled. "You waited thirty-six years for Alix. How much longer would you have gone?"

He didn't hesitate. "Forever."

"Yes," Caleb said. "You will wait for True Love forever."

# ACKNOWLEDGMENTS

Spending time on the island of Nantucket has been an experience like none other, and I'd like to thank a lot of people.

Betsey Tyler has written books on the individual histories of houses on Nantucket, books I greatly admire. As fellow historians, she and I hit it off at our first meeting and she lent me a book that was very helpful.

Nat Philbrick answered my questions about research and inspired me with his great books. I am in awe of his research! His wife, Melissa, talked to me about weddings and what's happening on Nantucket. They are both delightful company!

Nancy, a.k.a. Nancy Thayer, and Charley Walters. They drove me around the island, took me to Daffy Day, and put on the most wonderful dinner parties at their beautiful old house so I could meet people. It was kind and generous of them.

Twig Perkins and all his gorgeous, intelligent, funny (GIF) men. Twig answered all my many questions about the HDC and building permits, and gave me some insider hints. Plus he and his GIF men did a fabulous job of remodeling for me — even though each man made me prove myself to him. Twig stood back and laughed at it all. Oh, the joy of hearing, "She's right."

Twig's wife, Jude, and I met while I was on a garden tour. She has chickens and a fabulous house. Our names being the same has caused great hilarity.

Julie Hensler for architecture. Julie was in her glorious garden digging up flowers and I interrogated her about becoming an architect. I thought I knew everything, but I asked her just to be sure. After I found out that I knew nothing about the schooling needed, she took me on a tour of a Harvard classroom.

Dave Hitchcock (one of Twig's GIF men) for helping me with the fishing and showing me his beehives. And for shortening all the furniture in my office so it fit a normal-size person.

Jimmy Jaksic let me tag along to one of the weddings he was putting on. I kept asking everyone if they knew of a wedding planner I could interview, but no one did. Then one day I was in my side yard and said hello to my neighbor. We started chatting and I found out Jimmy was a wedding planner. I almost jumped over the fence to start asking him questions.

Tricia Patterson takes care of my hair and entertains me with stories of what's going on around the island. So far, I haven't found a book she hasn't read.

Jose Partida and his men (also GIF) of Clean Cut Landscaping took on the horrendous job of bulldozing my little half acre and putting in a beautiful garden. They helped me fight the War of the Deer (we lost) and Jose was always dragging me away from my pages and telling me I work too much.

Georgen Charnes for supplying me with lots of books for the research of the glorious island of Nantucket, and for sending me maps and journals. Scott Charnes for taking me out on his boat. Cassie for being her perfect self.

Zero Main is real and the clothes are wonderful! Noël lets me stand in a dressing room, brings me lots of clothes to try on, and tells me what looks good.

Downyflake. I don't know what I'd do without Downyflake. I sit there and write while they serve me and it's wonderful! Some of my best ideas have come to me while eating my eggs and cranberry muffin. And the excellent staff entertains me with stories of what's happening on the island.

John Ekizian, my publicist. John runs the Facebook pages, but more than that, he makes me laugh. He is the absolute king of one-liners. He's made me laugh so hard my stomach muscles get sore.

Linda Marrow, my dear, beloved editor who has the magic ability to instantly see what's wrong with something and how to fix it. Her comments are short and to the point and exactly on the spot. She has a true talent!

By the way, the real name of the historical society in Nantucket is NHA, Nantucket Historical Association. I changed it to NHS because I didn't want to offend anyone by putting a former ghost in as the director.

I would especially like to thank my Facebook buddies. I was dragged into the social media world kicking and screaming. I did *not* want to do it! I only agreed when I was told that I could tell about my daily experiences in trying to write a novel. I wouldn't have to just post that everything was happy and easy, but could say when my fictional characters and circumstances in the publishing world were driving me crazy. I wanted to be *real,* not what people seem to think of writers, that we sit around and wait for ideas to come to us, then casually write them down. Even with that in mind, I still worried about what seems to be the new American pastime of anonymously slaughtering people on the Internet. What a shock I was in for! The people — mostly women — on my site have been truly wonderful! They have been so supportive that it has given me new vigor in my writing. They often make me laugh and have sympathized with my complaining when I had some obstacle put in my way. They answer my daily questions with such insight that all day I think about what they've said. Since they have been with me through every step on this book — even to knowing its true title — I have set up a file on my website that contains a lot of the documents that I created so I could write this book. There's a map of Kingsley Lane, a genealogy chart, before and after rewrites, and even scenes that didn't get into the book. I just want to say thank you to all of them. You are great!

# ABOUT THE AUTHOR

**Jude Deveraux** is the author of forty-one *New York Times* best-sellers to date, including *Moonlight in the Morning* and *A Knight in Shining Armor.* There are more than sixty million copies of her work in print worldwide.

CPSIA information can be obtained
at www.ICGtesting.com
Printed in the USA
FFOW02n1402221114
8990FF